An Honorable War

The Honor Series
By Robert N. Macomber

At the Edge of Honor
Point of Honor
Honorable Mention
A Dishonorable Few
An Affair of Honor
A Different Kind of Honor
The Honored Dead
The Darkest Shade of Honor
Honor Bound
Honorable Lies
Honors Rendered
The Assassin's Honor
An Honorable War

An Honorable War

A Novel of
Captain Peter Wake, Office of Naval Intelligence, USN

13th in the Honor Series

Robert N. Macomber

Pineapple Press, Inc.
Sarasota, Florida

Inquiries should be addressed to:

Pineapple Press, Inc.
P.O. Box 3889
Sarasota, Florida 34230

www.pineapplepress.com

Library of Congress Cataloging-in-Publication Data

Names: Macomber, Robert N., 1953- author.
Title: An honorable war : the Spanish-American War begins : a novel of Cmdr. Peter Wake, Office of Naval Intelligence, USN / Robert N. Macomber.
Description: Sarasota, Florida : Pineapple Press, Inc., [2017] | Series: Honor series ; 13
Identifiers: LCCN 2016034078| ISBN 9781561649723 (hardback) | ISBN 9781561649730 (pbk.)
Subjects: LCSH: Wake, Peter (Fictitious character)--Fiction. | United States. Navy--Officers--Fiction. | United States--History, Naval--19th century--Fiction. | GSAFD: Historical fiction.
Classification: LCC PS3613.A28 H662 2017 | DDC 813/.6--dc23
LC record available at https://lccn.loc.gov/2016034078

First Edition
10 9 8 7 6 5 4 3 2 1

Design by Demi Brown
Printed in the United States

This novel is respectfully dedicated
to two masters of the historical novel genre.

C. S. Forester (1899–1966)
and
George MacDonald Fraser (1927–2008)

Who understood the nineteenth century so well,
and led the way back for the rest of us.

Robert N. Macomber

An Introductory Word with My Readers

When writing this thirteenth novel in the Honor Series about Peter Wake, it occurred to me both new and longtime readers might appreciate a simple timeline of our fictional hero's life until this point. It is thus appended below. I also suggest reading each chapter's endnotes for more information on the places and people in the story.

Timeline of Peter Wake's life from 1839 to early 1898:

1839—June 26—born into seafaring family on coast of Massachusetts

1852—goes to sea to learn the trade in his father's schooner

1855—promoted to schooner mate

1857—promoted to command of a schooner

1861—Civil War begins

1863—loses merchant marine draft exemption and volunteers for the navy—stationed at Key West—"Acting Lieutenant" Wake commands sailing gunboat *Rosalie* on SW Florida coast and the Bahamas—Irish boatswain's mate (bosun) Sean Rork joins *Rosalie*'s crew—Wake and Rork become lifelong best friends
(as depicted in *At the Edge of Honor*)

1864—chases Union deserters to French-occupied Mexico—marries Linda Donahue at Key West, with Rork as best man—engaged in shore operation against Confederates in Florida
(as depicted in *Point of Honor*)

1865—daughter Useppa born at Useppa Island—tumultuous end of Civil War in Florida and Cuba—post-war mission to find ex-Confederates in Puerto Rico
(as depicted in *Honorable Mention*)

1867—gains regular commission as lieutenant—son Sean born at Pensacola Naval Station

1869—court-martialed for mutiny after relieving his captain of duty at sea on coast of Panama while on mission against renegade American former naval officer—acquitted of charges but reputation tarnished
(as depicted in *A Dishonorable Few*)

1874—involved in sordid incidents in Spain and Italy—saved by Jesuits—a French woman enters his life—rescues French civilians in Africa and awarded Legion of Honor by France—promoted to lieutenant commander
(as depicted in *An Affair of Honor*)

1880—embarks on first espionage mission during South American War of the Pacific—cements his lifelong relationship with the Jesuits—awarded the Order of the Sun by Peru—his wife Linda dies of cancer—sinks into depression—helps form the Office of Naval Intelligence
(as depicted in *A Different Kind of Honor*)

1883—espionage mission to French Indo-China—becomes lifelong friends with King Norodom of Cambodia—promoted to commander—awarded the Royal Order of Cambodia—Wake and Rork buy Patricio Island in SW Florida and build bungalows there
(as depicted in *The Honored Dead*)

1886—meets Theodore Roosevelt in NYC—meets José Martí in NYC—espionage mission against the Spanish in Havana, Tampa, and Key West—deadly struggle against Spanish secret police begins—lifelong friendship with Martí and Roosevelt starts
(as depicted in *The Darkest Shade of Honor*)

1888—a search for lady friend's missing son in the Bahamas and Haiti becomes a love affair and espionage mission—begins relationship with Russian secret service—his marriage proposal rejected by his lover after which he falls back into depression
(as depicted in *Honor Bound*)

1888—mission to rescue Cuban spies from the Spanish in Havana—through Martí's introduction, a lifelong friendship with Free Masons begins—barely escapes Spanish secret police in Cuba
(as depicted in *Honorable Lies*)
1890—learns the love affair in 1888 produced a daughter, Patricia, who is growing up in Illinois
1889—espionage mission against the Germans in the South Pacific—awarded Royal Order of Kalakaua by the Kingdom of Hawaii—gains gratitude of President Cleveland—shame at his actions in Samoa
(as depicted in *Honors Rendered*)
1890—leaves espionage work and returns to sea in command of cruiser—his son Sean graduates from the U.S. Naval Academy and becomes a commissioned officer
1892—has love affair with Maria Ana Maura of Spain—brought back into espionage work on counter-assassination mission in Mexico and Florida—saves Martí's life—returns to sea command
(as depicted in *The Assassin's Honor*)
1893—marries Maria at Key West in double ceremony with daughter Useppa and her Cuban fiancé Mario Cano—promoted to rank of captain—Rork promoted to the newly established rank of Chief Boatswain Mate
1895—May 19—dear friend José Martí killed in action fighting the Spanish in Cuba
1897—ends seven years of sea duty with special assignment at Navy Department
1898—Spanish-American war begins

In *An Honorable War*, we find Wake in the thick of events leading to the Spanish-American War, the pivotal event which changed America's role in the world. It is a war Wake predicted for a decade and tried to avert for years. Now, he must fight it. Three novels in the Honor Series will cover the Spanish-American War in Cuba and Puerto Rico.

Wake's active duty naval career will continue beyond this war, not ending until 1908. This means many more novels in the Honor Series, for the turn of the century was full of momentous events, the consequences of which dictated world history for the next ninety years. And what, you may fairly ask, will happen with our man after 1908?

With a fellow like Peter Wake, anything is possible.

Robert N. Macomber
The Boat House
St. James, Pine Island
Florida

Preface by Peter Wake

For twelve years, I'd predicted war with Spain was coming and that we in the navy had to be ready. For many national leaders, my message was not only uncomfortable, it was inconvenient.

Then USS *Maine* exploded in Havana's harbor. Instantly, everything changed. Several officials, who for years had studiously ignored the horrific situation in Cuba, did an abrupt about-face. In their fevered ignorance of modern combat, these politicians righteously shouted this would be *an honorable war* against a despicable and cowardly foe.

Such naïveté was soon echoed among people across the land. Hundreds of thousands of men flocked to the bright colors and stirring sounds of parades. Signing on the dotted line, they enlisted with a grin, as if joining a sports team. Within months, ill-equipped and untrained, they endured experiences in the jungles of Cuba far more terrible than most could have ever imagined. They learned war is not a game. In the brutality of combat, the luxury of honor is one of the first things lost.

I was in the middle of it all, from the beginning to the end. This memoir reveals what happened to me at the beginning of the war. Some of my decisions were subsequently deemed controversial by those august personages who sit in the plush halls of power. I will let the reader decide whether I was right or wrong.

RADM Peter Wake, USN (Ret.)
12 June 1909

1

A Muffled Thud

Havana, Cuba
Tuesday evening
15 February 1898

Though it was the middle of February, the Cuban night was unseasonably warm and quiet. As if the island were exhausted from the tragedies endured by its inhabitants, only the tiniest breath of humid air ruffled the water from the far side of the harbor. Above me, a fleeting glimpse of constellation Leo could be seen between scattered clouds, but the Southern Cross was still hiding below the horizon. Exotic blends of African-Latin music drifted over from the dimly lit taverns along the shoreline. The faint slow rhythm carried with it a whiff of charcoal and stale fried fish.

The whole place was asleep or drunk or, in the case of sailors aboard the scattered ships at anchor, dreaming of getting drunk if they ever got ashore. Life was slow. Its energy was sapped by the indolent atmosphere, as it has been for the past four hundred years in the latitudes of *mañana*. So listless was the scene on the shoreline that, except for the guard boats traversing the harbor, you would never imagine there was a bloody, no-quarter-given, thirty-year civil war going on outside the city and across the island. Tens of thousands had already died, and no end was in sight.

After thirty-five years in the navy, none of this was new or exciting to me anymore. I felt tired, wanting to go home to Maria. Finally, my orders from Roosevelt had arrived and I was heading home at last. But there were things to do first, professional responsibilities which also weren't new or exciting anymore.

The tiny bumboat had just shoved off from the anchored American warship. She was illuminated with lines of electric light bulbs suspended from the rigging, an outward show of friendly intent on her "routine goodwill visit." If you looked closer, though, you could see she was anything but peaceful. On the main deck patrolled an armed double watch of wary sailors and nervous officers. Colt machine guns in the upper works were manned and loaded. The massive ten-inch guns loomed over everything. The pretty lighting fooled few. The huge ship was designed to kill people, ships, and cities, quickly and efficiently. She was ready for action, should her captain order it.

The bumboat headed for the Regla docks, half a mile away. I judged there was a fifty-fifty chance it would sink before reaching our goal, due to a leak in the transom which was filling the bilge. With me in the stern and two ancient boatmen amidships, both of them reeking of rum and cheap cigars, the freeboard was a perilous eight inches at most. Drunk they most certainly were, but I had to admit each of them pulled his oar with a steady stroke and our voyage across the dark harbor was arrow straight. I upped the odds of making it to the dock to sixty percent.

Of course, a proper naval officer wouldn't dress in my present attire or step foot into such a craft. But at this moment in time, I wasn't a proper naval officer. The boat and clothes fit my façade as a down-and-out Canadian tobacco broker. The faded blue cotton suit, half-tied old brogans, battered valise, and floppy straw hat seemed to work. The American sailors and officers on the ship initially believed my ruse as much as the street idlers did on land. The only men in Havana who knew my identity were the captain of the ship and Rork at Regla. No, there was one other—Colonel Isidro Marrón, of the dreaded Spanish secret police.

Two hundred feet from the ship, I heard a muffled thud from behind, seemingly from below the water. I started to turn around to see what had happened.

In that instant, everything erupted into a blur of light and deafening noise.

2

Dead Man Floating

Havana, Cuba
Tuesday evening
15 February 1898

My next impression was of being under water. I was suspended in a curiously blissful state, in a black world. My mouth and stomach filled, but there was no panic, no fear, only stunned resignation at the hand fate had dealt me—*so this was the end?*

Without any effort on my part, my body rose to the surface. The bliss ended.

Fear gripped me. I couldn't see. No stars, shore lights, ships. Everything was still black. I reached for my eyes to make sure they were open. They were, but I still couldn't see. No sounds came to me beyond a loud high-pitched buzzing.

My hands searched for the bumboat. It and the old men were gone. Hunks of metal and wood rained down on my head and shoulders, pummeling me painfully. Blind and deaf and bleeding from a dozen places, I floated, unable to do anything else, utterly disoriented as to where I was and what had happened.

Moments later, I felt waves push over me. Guessing small boats were moving nearby, I tried to call out for help, but couldn't. The most I could do was gag on the filthy water choking up from my stomach.

How long I floated there I cannot say—at least ten minutes, or perhaps thirty. Time had no measure. My mind began to process the scene. In my career, I had been near enough to explosions to recognize the sensations taking over my body, the loss of sight and hearing and mental perception. And I knew those senses might return in minutes, or hours, or maybe never.

Primal instinct took over. This must be an act of violence, of war. Enemies were all around. The slimy water was safer than being taken by the enemy. I would stay hidden in the water.

I had to *think*, to assess. Flexing my hands and feet, I found them sore, but still working. Legs and arms hurt even more, as if forced into unnatural attitudes, but seemed able to function. The back of my head and neck produced a sharp pain when turning my head to the left, the position I was in when everything happened. I deduced the lacerations on my shoulders and arms, already inflamed by the salt water, weren't too deep or the muscles wouldn't have performed. Fear was replaced by reason. Breathing became more regular. I willed myself to remain calm.

Sight was the first sense to gradually return. Darkness evolved into shades, from pitch black to gray. Points of light came into focus, faint colors became discernable, then shapes and movements. My ability to understand what I was seeing came next, and it was frightening.

The warship I'd just been aboard was a huge mass of twisted metal sitting low in the water, enveloped by flaming eruptions and churning banks of red tinged smoke. It all seemed unreal, some sort of grotesque hallucination from Dante's lower levels. My hearing returned, then smell. The shrieking men and the putrid-sweet odor of burning flesh proved this nightmarish tableau wasn't a delusion. It was only too real.

The U.S.S. *Maine*, which I had just departed, was no more. My guess was by a torpedo launched from the nearby Spanish cruiser *Alfonso*. The war my friend Roosevelt had predicted eleven months earlier, and which I had feared for over a decade, had finally begun. Floating there, surrounded by the dead and the dying, another fact progressively became obvious. Officially, to both my enemies and my compatriots, my status had drastically changed.

I was now a dead man.

The logical part of my mind deemed this as a good thing. It provided me with unbounded freedom of action. Spurred by this analysis, I began to use my arms to propel me toward the Regla docks. Rork would be there—if he was still alive.

But the passionate side of me soon intruded into my calculations, bringing visions of my darling Maria. Our last time together had been a stressful confrontation. Emotions rose in my throat when I thought of her pain when she would learn of my apparent death, the details of which would not, could not, be revealed to her by the naval authorities.

I had to banish her from my mind—the memory made me weaker, not stronger. I must think clearly, for many lives, perhaps thousands, might depend on what I did next. I dogpaddled onward, analyzing what the enemy's other moves would be, and what Rork and I could do against them.

Halfway to shore, my psyche and body weakened. Unable to swim any farther, I drifted amidst the debris. Other memories began parading through my mind. They were from eleven months earlier, at a far different place, where my strange journey leading to Havana had begun.

3

Eleven Months Earlier

U.S.S. Newark
Brooklyn Navy Yard
4:45 a.m., Monday
1 March 1897

The high shrill of the bosun's pipe cruelly pierced my slumber like a dagger. It was followed by the ominous bellow of the duty petty officer up on the main deck. "Anchor watch, trice up hammock cloths!"

From up forward, I heard another petty officer rousing his detail. "Hammock stowers and musicians, up and out! Shake a leg, you misbegotten idlers and rascals!"

Hearing all this, I knew precisely what time it was, a quarter to five. I'd overslept—a disagreeable start to the morning. Every moment of every hour of every day on a man-o-war is regulated, only varying in storm or battle. From apprentice seaman to captain, duty never disappears and must *always* be attended closely, on time, every time. There may be reasons for failure to do so, but there are no excuses. Adding to my irritation, my steward Slattery was considerably late with breakfast.

"Nigh onto second bell of the morning watch, and a nasty morning it is, sir," intoned a refined British voice as Slattery padded into my stateroom seconds later, lighting the desk lantern. "But at least we're nice and snug on the dock."

"You're late, Slattery."

"Aye, sir. A full fourteen and one half minutes, to be exact. I sincerely apologize, sir, but the wardroom cook had trouble with the stove coal. Seems it was smoking but not burning. It was the new stuff we got in Martinique, of course."

He wagged his head and frowned as he laid the tray of food down on my chart table. "But then, really, what do you expect of the French? Even their coal won't burn! You can't trust those frog-eaters to do anything right. It really is a wonder Napoleon ever conquered anybody."

"You're late, Slattery."

The refined inflection quickly slid into working class lingo. "Right, sir. I was just explaining why, but hadn't gotten to the most important part. Well, since the bloody wardroom galley was out of action, I went forward and found the chief petty officers' cook up there in the Goat Locker. Oh, blimey, but wasn't *that* old worthy in a damned foul mood this morning, until the bugger realized I was there for the breakfast of hizzoner the captain himself! Then, of course, he hopped to with a proper will. And that, sir, is why I was fourteen and a half minutes late this morning."

Slattery claimed to have been a gentleman's gentleman somewhere in England, and occasionally displayed the manners and skills to prove it, when it suited him. Returning to his show of class, he half-bowed and elegantly raised an index finger, along with his crimson nose, in the air.

"I must add the wardroom cook presents his deepest apologies and regrets, sir. The chief petty officers' cook presents his respects and hopes you enjoy the fruit of his efforts. He was greatly honored we came to him in our hour of need."

We? I thought. At the end of his recitation, he flaunted a rather self-satisfied look. Clearly, he expected me to compliment his efforts. I, however, wasn't game.

There were several bizarre rumors about how exactly Slattery ended up in the United States Navy, most of which centered around escaping a criminal past involving fraud, but I never did learn the real story. Whatever the cause, Slattery was the type who always bore careful watching.

"You're quite the con man, Slattery."

"Aye, sir, that I am," he admitted cheerfully. "And may I say I am profoundly honored to be *your* con man."

He bowed again, this time with the ghost of a sly smile, then laid out my breakfast on the chart table and announced, "Two hard-boiled Bahamian eggs, diced and mixed with the last of our Jamaican pickapeppa sauce; toast, with the last smidgen of the Barbados butter; black coffee from Colombia; and our last Martinique orange from the wardroom pantry, sir. A veritable West Indian feast, as is only right."

I climbed out of the warm bunk. It was damned cold in the stateroom, especially to someone who had just returned from five months in the Caribbean. "What's the weather out on deck?"

"Even nastier than when we arrived, sir. Thermometer says thirty-three degrees and is dropping fast. Wind is still northerly, right down the East River, and has piped up to a near gale. Feels even colder. Gale warnings on the navy yard mast. Constant squall lines and sleet turning to snow. Quartermaster predicts it'll get into the bleedin' teens by noon and below zero by sunset. Good day to be down in the black gang, sir. Pity the lads out on deck in the thick of it."

The ship's bell struck twice—five a.m.—and the bugler sounded reveille. It seemed a bit more plaintive this morning, and I guessed his lips were numb. Within seconds, the ship came to life, for even if a man weren't on a duty watch, the day was beginning and the time for rest had ended. There was work to be done, on watch or off watch. Work never ended on a ship.

Petty officers began rousing the crew up forward in the division berthing areas, faint insistent voices. The one nearest to my stateroom was the gunnery division, located forward of the wardroom and the officers' cabins. This morning the men were being greeted by Chief Gunner's Mate Doyle O'Conner. Behind his back, O'Conner was commonly called Foghorn, for the incredible volume of his voice, a compensation for the gradual loss of hearing over the years from the concussive effect of his beloved guns. O'Conner didn't let it slow him down. He always operated at full speed. This morning he wasn't waking the men gently, but he did add a touch of sailor's mocking humor.

"All hands! Up and out! All hands! Up and out! Shake a leg, you lazy bastards. Trice and stow hammocks! Smoking lamp is lit for them what have it and rate it. Smile, me hearties, it's another *beautiful* morning in Uncle Sam's blessed Navy. There's nary an enemy in sight but our dear Mother Nature—*and I have work for you to be done!"*

The ending part elicited groans and curses by the men in the hammocks, which only made Foghorn laugh and roar, "Tardiness is next to cowardice, you skulking lubbers! Now move quickly my little darlings, or I'll think you don't love me anymore!"

Finishing breakfast a few minutes later, I heard Foghorn make his next announcement, telling the men in the time-honored phrases to start their morning duties of cleaning the ship.

"Sweepers, sweepers, man your brooms! Give the ship a good clean sweep down, both fore and aft! Sweep down all weather decks, all lower decks, all ladder backs and passageways! Chippers and scrapers, Mother Nature is awaiting topside and I know who you are, so lay forward to the foc's'l to get your weapons and do battle with the evil ice and snow!"

My first official visitor of the day arrived right about then. Commander James Southby was *Newark*'s executive officer and number two in command. He already looked weary—executive officers are the hardest working officers on a warship—as he sat in the chair near my desk.

He laughed quietly and said, "Morning, sir. I hear Foghorn thinks it's another beautiful day in the navy. The old boy's in rare form this morning."

"That's because he won't be out on the weather decks chipping and scraping. Inside of ten minutes, he'll be drinking coffee with the other salts up in the Goat Locker."

"True. I've got him scheduled for main gun maintenance later, though. Muzzle tampions and locking gear need to be greased."

"Good. Say, did they ever get the wardroom stove working?"

"No, sir, not yet. Lots of grumbling about it, too. Heard the petty officers' cook did your breakfast. How was it?"

"Pretty good, actually." A whimsical thought entered my head. "Maybe we should steal him from them?"

Southby got into the spirit. "It would be fun, though I worry about what they'd do in return."

"Something Machiavellian to ruin our careers when we least expect it, no doubt. Maybe we'd better not."

"Yeah, you're right, sir. I suppose we shouldn't. Never mess with the CPOs. Evil-hearted bastards."

I liked and respected my number two. A soft-spoken but iron-willed descendant of Indiana farmers, James went through the naval academy in the late 1860s and stayed in the navy to escape rural life, see the world, and experience adventure. For thirty years he'd sailed the world and trained for a war which never came. A member of the Naval Institute since it started in `74, graduate of the Naval War College in `88, former commanding officer of a gunboat on China Station in `93, observer at the Sino-Japanese War in `95, fluent in Spanish and well-versed in the Caribbean, he was exactly the kind of intelligent, decisive officer who would be needed when the horrors of modern warfare were eventually unleashed on our navy.

But James was thinking of leaving the navy, fed up with the sycophantic toadying at headquarters, the fiefdoms and petty personalities of the senior officers, the bureaucratic inertia of the navy's support functions, and the faked reports of readiness some ships and bureaus presented so their officers could look good. He, and I, and several other officers in the navy, knew we weren't ready for a war with a European power, even a weaker one like

Spain. And the army was in far worse condition than the navy. The jingoists, press moguls, and politicians who called for war had no clue what they were talking about, as ignorant as they were arrogant.

Putting a pile of reports and mail on my desk, Southby said, "We got in last night just in time, sir. According to the duty officer in the yard this morning, they're getting reports coming from up and down the coast of ships in distress. Had a barge sink in the Hudson. Hell of a trip up the East River, wasn't it? You impressed all hands with that maneuver. Talk of the ship this morning. Spinning her from the stern in a confined area with a foul wind and tide, on a lee shore. I've never seen anything like it done. Didn't even know it *could be* done!"

I hadn't known it could be done either. "We were damned lucky. Now, let's go over the paperwork this morning. What's the schedule for us from the yard?"

The ensuing discussion centered on the long list of overhaul and refit from the yard workers. Southby had it all well in hand and I had only to periodically provide official approval, but my mind wasn't in it. I kept thinking about what he'd said earlier about the night before.

Our voyage from Martinique ended when we finally moored at Brooklyn Navy Yard at midnight, after a harrowing transit up through the Narrows dodging fishing smacks in a nasty nor'easter. Entering the East River, a deluge of rain from a squall line hit us. But the very worst part of the entire two thousand-mile voyage came in the last mile before our destination.

A chill went through me as I remembered how close I'd come to killing hundreds of my men, and probably a fair number of civilians, only five and a half hours earlier.

4

The Last Mile

U.S.S. Newark
East River, New York
11:30 p.m., Sunday
28 February 1897

It happened right after we steamed northbound at five knots under the Brooklyn Bridge. A small ferry suddenly dashed out of the gloom from the Catherine Street dock in Manhattan, bound right across our course for the Main Street dock in Brooklyn. I immediately backed both engines full emergency astern, something which always incurs the barely submerged wrath of the senior engineering officer since he knows he'll need to repair the inevitable gear damage. As she began to slow and go astern, I ordered *Newark* into a turn to port.

It worked. We missed the small craft's stern by less than ten feet, our deck crew giving the ferry passengers a spontaneous education in nautical terminology not found in any book. Reducing the engines to slow astern, I then stopped them and glanced at the ferry as she plowed across the river. The stupid ferry captain was blissfully waving at me from his wheelhouse. As angry as I was at the idiot, there was no time to vent my indignation. Our emergency maneuver had saved the ferry, but put *us* in grave peril.

The ebb was flowing rapidly, increased by the north wind funneling down the river, and *Newark* had ended up broadside to current and wind, with the Brooklyn Bridge a scant five hundred feet to leeward. All eyes in the wheelhouse locked onto mine as the bow continued to swing west, then southwest, with the ship inexorably sliding sideways toward the massive bridge piers on the Manhattan side. It was too late to turn back to the starboard. We were about to hit the docks and there was no room.

I saw only one option in the three seconds I had to make a decision.

Keeping my voice steady, I risked the command: "Full right rudder. Full astern on port engine. Half ahead starboard engine. Sound the collision alarm."

By rote instinct, the officer of the watch dispassionately echoed my orders and the petty officers acknowledged carrying them out. Luckily, the lee helmsman was a quick thinker and signaled the engine room on the annunciator the instant I gave the order. Several excruciatingly long seconds passed before the shafts were engaged and the propellers bit the water.

The bow spun around fast, and quickly pointed directly at the bridge pier, suddenly only fifty feet away. The steam horn blared out the seven long blasts of the collision signal, echoing off the surrounding buildings and the bridge's deck high above. A crowd of dockworkers from the Manhattan side railroad ferry docks rushed to line the shore and watch the disaster.

"Midship the rudder. Emergency full astern both engines."

The officers and men gripping the rails, tables, and bulkheads around me were no longer watching my face. They were looking up at the bridge pier looming above our bow. It was a frightening, mesmerizing sight. The bridge pier, which held up the suspension towers and bridge itself, had a low seawall jutting out around it. We would hit that first, ripping our hull open, then ride up and smash into the giant pier, possibly bringing down the entire bridge. Without orders, everyone instinctively knelt down and braced for the impact. Only the quartermaster at the wheel, myself, and Commander Southby remained standing.

Newark's decks and bulkheads rumbled and shook from the immense strain on the shafts and propellers as they dug into the water. Pencils and dividers rattled off the chart table. It felt like *Newark* was going to shake apart. We were stern-first into the wind and current by then, with seas washing over the transom.

It took forever for the full 8,900 horsepower of her engines to take hold, but at last she checked her forward motion toward the seawall and bridge. The bow was so close I couldn't see the seawall below it, and the bridge pier looked as if the bow lookout could reach out and touch the damned thing. But the old girl did it.

Then, ever so slowly, as if she were teasing us, *Newark* began to move astern against wind and tide. When I reduced the shaft revolutions to half speed she still made sternway, and we continued in this undignified fashion all the way up the river past the navy yard to Corlear's Hook on the Manhattan side, where the East River bends.

Only then, when I had the relatively larger area of Wallabout Bay to leeward, did I dare to turn the ship around and steam ahead into the docks at the yard. The entire agonizing time I waited for an engine or gear failure, with the anchor detail standing by to let the main hook go, but *Newark*, and her engineers, did their work well.

At midnight we moored with our bow fifty feet behind the ancient supply and barracks ship *Vermont*, on the west wall of the Cob Dock, at the Brooklyn Navy Yard. As soon as the lines were doubled, everyone's nerves visibly calmed. When all was secure, I descended to the engine room and had the entire watch assemble to witness my compliments to the chief engineering officer on the outstanding work of his men. To say my accolade to them was profoundly heartfelt, is an understatement. They were the heroes of the ship.

Thirty minutes later, I lay completely fatigued in my bunk, but keyed up and drenched in sweat despite the bitter cold. Only the dreamy image of my dear wife Maria, and the knowledge I would soon be with her on a two-month leave after a fourteen-month absence, eased me into blessed oblivion.

Maria and I, both previously widowed, had been married only forty-three months by then. Our marriage was unusual in the hidebound aristocracy of the navy's officer corps, for Maria was Spanish and Catholic. This, of course, made for some wildly creative gossip during the years of increasing tension with Spain over Cuba. It didn't bother me a bit. I had never been part of the naval social strata, not having graduated from the academy and never having been accepted as an equal. Let the old fools gossip. Maria was beautiful and smart and loving. And all mine.

I had been at sea for a total of thirty-two months since our wedding, but my time in *Newark* was ending soon. I knew my next assignment would be duty at a shore station somewhere, for regulations required it. A shore job would allow us to be together at last. What I didn't know was where and what my assignment would be. Maybe it would be some soft billet commanding a naval station in a warm clime, or heading an advisory board. I'd more than earned one of the navy's easy jobs for a couple of years. I fell asleep among fantasies of enjoying a comfortable life at some pleasant place, living well in spite of all we'd been through.

5

The Pleasure of Your Company

U.S.S. Newark
Brooklyn Navy Yard
Monday morning
1 March 1897

Southby and I completed our administrative business by the time "Colors" was sounded at eight bells for the hoisting of the national ensign at the stern staff. Once he departed for other duties, I made my daily morning tour of the ship. This time it included the Goat Locker, where I found Foghorn telling the others a sea story. Judging by their expressions, it was of dubious veracity. He stopped in mid-sentence when he saw me in the passageway looking in. They all rose to attention.

"Beautiful morning, isn't it, Gunner?"

"Aye, sir. A fine navy day!" he said with a grin.

"Yes, well, I've just been out on deck, Gunner. Your men are working hard on that ice, but I think they could use some additional command presence. Good for them to see they are led from the front. What do you think?"

His reply wasn't nearly as enthusiastic this time. "Aye, sir."

"Excellent! Then I'll see you out there when I take my next turn on the weather decks," I said, showing my own grin, adding, "And by the way, thanks for the breakfast this morning. Your cook did a fine job of it. He has talents I didn't know about."

Worried looks came my way, until I said, "Don't worry, men. I won't steal him from you. We need the real backbone of the navy to be well fed."

When I reappeared a few minutes later on the foredeck, there was Foghorn, bundled up like the rest. Walking up and down the line of sailors scraping ice from the ground tackle and railings, he was entertaining them with outrageous stories of prostitutes in various ports of the world who had colder hearts than the ice the men were attacking. The sailors were having a tough time of it keeping the decks and rigging free of a buildup of ice, but it had to be done, and not for appearance sake. Too much ice added too much weight too high on the ship.

My stateroom seemed positively warm when I returned to go through my correspondence. *Newark*'s accumulated mail had been brought aboard and I was hoping for a definitive word from Washington on my next orders. In one week, the ship was to be decommissioned and placed in ordinary—standby condition — for a year. That meant only a skeleton crew to maintain her, under the command of a lieutenant at most. Hundreds of *Newark*'s men would head off to their next ship or station within two weeks, and I was one of them. But, unlike the others, I hadn't received any official word on my future. It was quite unusual, and more than a bit worrisome.

The pile of personal letters and naval correspondence was fully a foot high. I separated them into stacks: one for official things, the next for personal, with a third one for Maria's scented letters, which I always kept until after I'd handled everything else. I tore open each blue Navy Department envelope, looking for the one with orders. There weren't any. My concern mounted.

On the second pile were letters from friends and acquaintances around the world—Pierre Loti in the Med, my daughter

Useppa in Tampa, my son Sean aboard the U.S.S. *Olympia* in China, my dear friend Sean Rork at the Washington Navy Yard, and Cardinal Mario Mocenni in Rome. Then I saw one from my young friend Theodore Roosevelt, New York's energetic commissioner of police, who lived not far from Brooklyn.

For some reason, I opened it first. The letter was on his personal stationery and typical of Roosevelt—dramatic with a hint of intrigue, with no indication the recipient would do anything other than comply.

Captain Peter Wake, U.S.N.
U.S.S. Newark
Brooklyn Navy Yard
28 Feb 1897

My dear Peter,

Welcome home from the sea! I have been informed you and your magnificent ship will be in our city tomorrow, and she is to be decommissioned for overhaul. The commandant of the Brooklyn Navy Yard assures me you will be free to leave the ship.

Therefore, I must absolutely insist you give Edith and me the great pleasure of your company in our home at Sagamore Hill on your first night ashore. A carriage will be at your dock at five o'clock, to take you to the Brooklyn train station, where you have a reservation for passage to Oyster Bay on the Long Island Railroad. My man will pick you up there. The telephone number here at Sagamore Hill is Liberty 555, should your ship need to contact you during your overnight stay.

I am delighted you are here. However, I will fully admit there is more than our long friendship as the cause for this urgent invitation. There are crucial naval matters afoot which will directly impact our mutual professional futures quite soon.

We need to talk.

Theodore

I had no idea what exactly he meant, but I did know Roosevelt was connected to the political powers in charge of the incoming national administration of William McKinley. The presidential inauguration was on the fourth, just a few days away.

I hadn't planned on leaving the ship until the seventh, when she was officially decommissioned for her refit and overhaul. Then I would head south to Washington, report to headquarters for my orders, and start my leave. First, I'd cross the Potomac and meet Maria at our small home off Fort Hunt Road just south of Alexandria. The plan was to spend three days there, then take the train to Florida where we'd spend six glorious weeks at our cottage on Patricio Island—away from everything and everyone.

Roosevelt's letter stopped me cold, though. He knew something he couldn't convey in the letter. Something important, which involved me.

I uncapped one of the brass speaking tubes lined up on the bulkhead near my desk. "This is the captain. Please pass the word for Commander Southby to come to my stateroom."

He looked like an Arctic explorer when he arrived, undoing four layers of coats and foul weather gear when I bid him to sit and have a cup of coffee.

"How're they doing on the ice?" I asked.

"Making some headway, sir, but they're freezing. I'm having them work half an hour on deck, then come in for half an hour and get some hot coffee before they go back out. Rigging some steam hoses too. Saw Foghorn out there. Even had a scraper in his hand, though I think it was for my benefit."

"Good idea on the half-hour breaks. I don't want anybody getting frostbite."

"At least we're not out at sea with solid water breaking over the deck."

I'd grown up at sea on the North Atlantic, and nodded my agreement. "Everything else all right?"

"Aye, sir, no major problems. Taking on provisions enough to last the week. Got the last of the personnel orders from headquarters. Everyone's spreading out, but about fifty men will have to wait a couple days in *Vermont* until their new ships come in. Bet she's still drafty as a barn. Boston won't be pleasant either."

Southby was heading for a shore assignment at Boston Navy Yard, if he stayed in the navy.

"*Vermont* is a floating wreck and a disgrace. I visited her a couple years ago for ten minutes and was appalled at her condition then. Now, as to *Newark*, since things are under control, I'll be leaving the ship at five o'clock this evening and staying at the home of Theodore Roosevelt near Oyster Bay for the night. It's about twenty-five miles from here. Should be back in the ship by ten tomorrow morning."

I handed him the address and telephone number. "There are trains running until late at night and starting early in the morning. Or I can get a carriage ride back, if necessary. If there is any problem, do not hesitate to immediately contact me. Understood?"

"Aye, sir. Understood fully."

He paused, then asked, "Did your orders ever come through, sir?"

"No, they haven't yet. But I have an uncomfortable feeling they will tonight."

Southby looked at me quizzically but said nothing.

6

Survival of the Fittest

Sagamore Hill
Oyster Bay, Long Island, New York
Monday evening
1 March 1897

Roosevelt was as restless as his letter indicated. Tapping his water glass the entire time at dinner, he could hardly wait until dessert was over. Soon afterward, his rambunctious but lovable clan retired for the night and he quietly invited me into his library, repeating the phrase used in the letter—we needed to talk about "crucial naval matters which are afoot."

In a position of honor off the front hall and across from the parlor, Theodore Roosevelt's library is quite a place, more of a museum than anything else. I'd been there on several occasions over the years, and loved it every time. It is large and imposing, yet comfortable and intimate. The many book shelves are full, intriguing mementos beckon from every table, and solemn pictures hang along each wall, the largest being a magnificent portrait of his venerated father, which commands the room. It is the den of an upper-class patrician, oozing power and confidence, demanding respect from all who enter.

There is an eerie, quite uncivilized, side to the scene as well, for one is never alone in the library, even when no other human is present. Gazing at you from the floor, tables, walls—all around, below, and above you—are wild animals of every type and size. All are dead from Theodore's own hand. Many are preserved by him as well, for more than anything else, the man is an accomplished naturalist and taxidermist. Various predators are shown in full rage, while numerous prey seem apathetic about their impending doom. It is a stunning display of Roosevelt's dictum of life—survival of the fittest rules both nature and man.

My young friend has only to look in the mirror to confirm his hypothesis, for he is living proof. Theodore is physically fit and martially adept, in the extreme. But it wasn't always so. In his childhood, he overcame crippling asthma which doctors promised would kill him by age thirty. In his young manhood, he battled the ruthless jungle of New York politics while effectively working for the betterment of the people, emerging with reputation not only intact, but enhanced.

He endured the death of his adored father and mentor, while finishing intense studies at Harvard. Several years later, he endured the tragic deaths of his beloved mother and wife on the very same day—Saint Valentine's Day—only a few days after his daughter Alice was born. He survived brutal weather and rough men in the Bad Lands of Dakota and finally returned to an active life in New York when a record-breaking blizzard destroyed everything he'd built out West.

In addition, he's read more books than anyone else I've ever met, can converse in four languages, is a respected expert in several sciences, and has maintained a prodigious work schedule of writing articles, essays, and books on everything from naval history to politics to social reform to several natural sciences.

In recent years, Roosevelt applied his energy toward tackling federal civil service reform under two presidents, and police reform in the notoriously corrupt New York Police Department, his current work when I visited him that night. In spite of daunting odds and enemies, he was successful in both governmental missions and became renowned for his honesty and courage.

The enemies he had accumulated for years were starting to take their toll, however, and at present he was faced with a scandal involving the police commission and the upper ranks, with which the press was having a field day. I had no doubt Roosevelt, who possessed an uncanny ability to utilize the press to his advantage and rally public opinion over political pressure, would emerge victorious. The only question was when.

But his note to me hadn't mentioned his work as police commissioner, and the subject hadn't been brought up so far in the evening. During dinner, in addition to the nervous tapping, I'd noticed something else about him. The deviously complex thirty-eight-year-old mind was clearly preoccupied and not at all genuinely involved in the light banter around the table, as usual. His face was tense, the spectacled eyes fixed not on the antics of his children, but on something far beyond the confines of the dining room, and those famous teeth were set in a positively predacious grimace.

Oh yes, Theodore definitely had something big up his sleeve. And it wasn't in reaction to any problems aimed at him in the police profession. He was *creating* problems for someone else, far bigger and more dangerous game than the local city politicos. The disturbing thought occurred to me that Theodore wanted me right in the middle of whatever he was planning.

He motioned for me to come over closer to the roaring log fire and have the sole cushioned rocker. I felt the shrewd scrutiny of his father peering down from above, reinforced by two stag antelopes on either flank. At my feet, any attempt to escape would be deterred by an angry black bear, spread out across the burgundy and tan Persian carpet. Thus surrounded, I waited for the answer to the riddle of his summons.

Theodore took the other rocker, a plain unadorned chair, and started pitching fore and aft. No after-dinner drink was offered me other than tea. Theodore wasn't much of a drinker, and then it was only one gin and tonic on the verandah or one glass of white wine with dinner. I could've used something stronger than tea, but didn't ask. Not that night. I was on high alert and wanted to be completely prepared for anything he might say.

He began with the unique style of conversational cadence he subconsciously employed and became famous for. "At *last* we have privacy! *Peter*, I am so *dee*lighted you could make it. And *very* glad *Newark* had no deaths in the absolutely *abysmal* weather this winter, unlike poor *Maine* last month. The sea can be *so* cruel and *un*forgiving, like life itself."

He referred to the *Maine*, which had men go overboard, lost forever, in another terrible winter storm off the Carolinas three weeks earlier. Other ships in her squadron, including *Newark*, had several men badly injured. Fortunately, none of ours died. We'd been lucky.

"Yes, we try to mitigate it, but the danger is always there," I said. "Part of going to sea."

The patented full dental smile spread across Theodore's face. Whether it is involuntary or calculated I've never deduced, but it always disarms the most prepared opponent or jaded friend.

"*Well!* You and your men are *safe* and sound *now*. I think you know, Peter, how *much* Edith *loves* having you visit Sagamore Hill. And the *children* are absolutely *enthralled* by your sea stories. I am *too!* How is your *dearest* Maria? And how are those *accomplished* children of yours?"

It is impossible to remain depressed around a fellow like this, and I heard myself responding in a similar upbeat attitude. "Maria's letters say she's quite well, Theodore. Thank you for asking. Of course she'll want to hear all about how you and your family are doing, and I'll be pleased to give her a positively glowing report. That'll be in a week or so, when I go on leave. My children are well. Useppa is thirty-two now. She and her husband Mario are still living in Tampa, where he practices law. He gets his American citizenship pretty soon. Sean is twenty-nine and a lieutenant in *Olympia* out on the China Station. By all accounts, he has a good reputation, though I fear his sense of humor may sometimes get the best of him."

To change the topic, I asked, "So, enough about me and mine, Theodore. How's police work these days?"

His brow furrowed and the rocking stopped. "Not very good, Peter. Oh, the policemen are doing *their* work much more efficiently and honestly. We've added sixteen hundred fine young fellows, chosen by merit instead of money. They are armed better now with standardized pistols, and their operations much more efficient . . ."

He turned in the chair to face me squarely and leaned forward. The right Rooseveltian index finger, known to so many campaign audiences, shot upward to accentuate his next words.

"But, the *sinister* dark *shadow* of political machine *chicanery* has descended once *again* over the department. This fellow *Parker* is the *obstructor* in chief and my main *foe*, backed by the *criminal* class, and his *intransigence* on the board of commissioners has *stymied* all my good efforts. He should *immediately* be *dismissed* in *disgrace!* But *I* am *backed*, to misuse the word, by city *leaders*, to misuse another word, who have the spines of *jellyfish*, so the miscreant *remains* in his seat on the commission. I can't move *forward!* This is extremely *frustrating*, Peter, to say the very *least*. Why, in *Heaven*'s name, can't these people *demonstrate* some *backbone* and do the *right* thing? If not as a *rule*, then for *one* day? Get *out* the *deadwood*, I say to men who haven't got the *gumption* to do anything but sit and *talk* and go to parties. *Frustrating!*"

Roosevelt could rant forever, so I asked directly, "Theodore, it's getting rather late. What did you want to talk to me about? You said crucial naval matters were afoot."

The furrow evaporated and the grin returned. "Pre*cisely!* I'll get right to the point. Times are a-*changing* and we are moving *forward* for a *modern* navy. Which is *exactly* why you and I needed to talk tonight. You *need* to know *I* am going to be *running* the navy soon."

That's not what I'd read in the morning papers. "Now Theodore . . . the president-elect has already designated his secretary of the navy, and it isn't you."

He dismissively waved a hand and harrumphed. He began rocking again. "Yes, yes, of course. And former Governor John D. Long of Massachusetts is a fine *old* gentleman of impeccable *political* pedigree who will *sit* in that cabinet seat. But as fine an *old* fellow as he is, Governor Long has no *understanding* of the navy, no *interest* in it, and no *vision* for what it can and should be. Plus, he has no *familiarity* with current *world* affairs."

I agreed entirely, though I wasn't about to say it. Long was about to be my superior and I was not going to be dragged into a disparaging conversation about the man. So I interrupted Roosevelt before things got worse.

"Theodore, first off, we need to set the record straight. Governor Long isn't *that* old—he's only half a year older than *me*. It's you who is young—twenty years younger than me. And Long is an intelligent and accomplished man. Phi Beta Kappa at Harvard, like you, and former governor of a major state, Massachusetts. It was your close friend, Senator Lodge of Massachusetts, who helped get McKinley to give him the position. And as for being a politician, you sound like the pot calling the kettle black, my friend."

"Peter Wake, that sort of *blunt* talk is why I have always *listened* to you! But those *valid* points aside, we both *know* he will be an *absentee* overlord for the navy. And we both know the *real* power will reside in his *assistant* secretary—don't we? Now, my older and wiser friend, *who* do you suppose *that* will be?"

I was stunned. The political bosses despised Roosevelt. They would never let him have such a powerful post. The naval shipbuilding contracts alone were worth millions of dollars, and Theodore would insist on them actually going to the best companies. He had alienated damned near all of Washington when he was Civil Service Commissioner under Republican President Harrison, and subsequently under Democratic President Cleveland. It was completely impossible any of them would allow him back. Ludicrous to even entertain the notion.

But then I looked at his beaming face and reconsidered. Theodore Roosevelt frequently pulled off the impossible.

7

L'Avenir Déjà Vu

Sagamore Hill
Oyster Bay, Long Island, New York
Late Monday evening
1 March 1897

I forced myself to say it. "You?"

For the first time in our eleven-year friendship, I saw a hurt look flash across Theodore Roosevelt's face. The rocking stopped. The rapid-fire cadence slowed. "Of course, and why not? I *am* the best man for the job. No one knows yet, so you *must* please keep this quiet."

"Theodore . . . does *McKinley* know he's giving the position to you? He hasn't been a supporter of the navy and knows nothing about it himself."

"No, he hasn't yet made the decision. The man is quite busy right now and these things take time, Peter. But Bill McKinley is a *very* smart fellow, and I am *certain* he will come to the obviously *logical* conclusion quite soon."

Unlike my young friend, the president-elect had been in the carnage of Antietam, and other scenes of horror thirty-four years earlier. He had repeatedly said he never wanted to see Americans go through such agony again.

"McKinley campaigned on peace and neutrality. Your views on both probably scare him, Theodore."

"True, but I have *assured* the proper people I will be a *loyal* servant within the administration. My job will be to make the navy *ready* for war, should it ever come, not to make the *decision* to go to war. Going to war is the sole prerogative of the *president*—and the Congress, of course."

I couldn't imagine Theodore keeping his mouth shut and following the new administration's official policy on Cuba, which was to ignore the war dragging on there. Roosevelt never ignored anything, once he learned about it.

"You've obviously got your pal Henry Cabot Lodge lobbying for you, but what about Boss Platt in New York and Boss Hanna in Washington? They aren't enamored of you at all and will never go along with it. Hell, Hanna *runs* McKinley and he's going to be president in three days! And what about Long? Does he know yet?"

"Hanna will come around, and so will Platt. No, Long hasn't been informed, but he will soon, once the president makes the decision."

"Theodore, this whole idea is absurd. Please do *not* speak about this with anyone else."

He leaned back in the chair, looked over at me with incongruous paternal affection, and said, "Oh *ye* of little faith. Peter, you are a *master* seaman and *spy*, and I have always looked *up* to you on naval and international matters, but your knowledge of the interior *machinations* of the American political class is simply *not* up to snuff."

Then he winked at me and said, "And I've saved the very *best* news for last."

"There's more?"

"Indeed there is, my friend. You're *curious* about your new orders, aren't you?"

The roaring fire had dwindled to half of a log over a bed of glowing amber coals. I had dwindled, too. After conversing with Theodore for an hour, and with little sleep the previous two nights, my endurance was waning. I wasn't in the mood for word games, and it reflected in my tone.

"So what the hell will it be?"

He ignored my attitude, his eyebrows raising in pure boyish joy. "You will be the *personal* aide to *me*, the incoming Assistant Secretary of the Navy! And that *dee*-lightfully *incorrigible* friend of yours, Chief Bosun Mate Rork, will be your assistant. I happen to *know* you are up for a two-year shore assignment. This is the *perfect* one for you! The happy couple will be able to be *together* at last. Your leave is up on May *eighth*, and on May ninth, you report in to the office. Springtime is *wonderful* in Washington. You and Maria will *never* have to *leave* your honeymoon home in Alexandria. A *bully* idea, even if I do say so myself."

"I was hoping for Key West or Pensacola. Some place calm and warm."

"Nonsense. Those *backwater* billets are for semi-retired *old* men. Peter, you would go *crazy* down there, and you *know* I'm right."

As young and active as he was, Theodore had no ability to understand I *wanted* to be semi-retired for two years. My body ached and my mind was tired. I wanted to be with Maria, far away from the sadly insane world of Washington.

I sighed, thinking about it. "What are the duties of this personal aide position?"

He stood and walked around the room, rattling off his statements like an admiral giving orders in battle. "Simple but *challenging*. Help me *modernize* the navy. *Prepare* it materially and organizationally for the *war* which we both *know* is coming, probably with *Spain*, or perhaps with Germany. Get continuing *accurate* assessments of our *foes*. This is *critical* work, and I need *you* to do it."

He unconsciously looked around the room as if it was full of people, his voice rising to stentorian level. "Think of it! *You* and *me*, Peter, taking on the encrusted *barnacles* at the navy department and *cleaning* ship! By *our* actions and *accomplishments*, we will *make* the *malevolent* men of Europe realize it would be sheer *suicide* on their part to ever try to *hurt* or obstruct *this* nation *anywhere*, in any way. Some of them may still try, but such a war will be short and decisive. *America* will be *safer* because of *our* work!"

If a crowd had been there, he would've received a standing ovation. He didn't get one from the animals, or from me. "Yes, it's a commendable vision, Theodore. But let's get back to my assignment. I presume it includes intelligence work, of a clandestine nature, no doubt . . ."

"Periodically, *yes!* Something *interesting* to get the old blood *pumping* is good for every *man.* Besides, you are *extraordinarily* good at it. *L'avenir, déjà vu*, as our friends the French say—the future, already seen!"

This was infuriating. My old blood was pumping just fine, without returning to the sordid world of espionage. I didn't want to return to that world and I sure as hell didn't want to work for Theodore. He'd planned it all out, obviously, with help from inside the navy.

"You had my orders changed, didn't you? Somebody in the Bureau of Navigation put them on hold, until you could get in there and issue new orders. It had to be a captain or above. Who was it?"

The grand oration was over, so he sat down again. "Why do you want to know such *trivial* things, Peter?"

"Because whoever it was, I want to hurt him, Theodore. And I'm thinking about hurting you right about now."

"Ah, *ha!* Now *there's* the Peter Wake I know and *love!* A man of *decision*, of *action!* Been practicing your *martial* arts, eh? Tomorrow morning, we'll have a proper *match* and see how you've progressed. Boxing? Or perhaps *fencing*, with *sabers?* I designed the front piazza to be *big* enough for that, you know."

I couldn't take any more. "I'm tired, Theodore. I'm going to bed. Notify me immediately if my ship contacts the house."

With that said, I trudged up to my guest room. Behind me, Theodore kept talking, wishing me a pleasant sleep and informing me the match would start at eight, right after a *bully* good breakfast.

I didn't have the strength, patience, or courage, to reply.

8

The Island

Patricio Island
Pine Island Sound
Florida Lower Gulf Coast
Easter Sunday evening
18 April 1897

The full moon shown through the high gumbo limbo trees and coconut palms, bathing the bungalows and citrus grove in a breathtakingly mystical light, making you want to stay awake all night to see what apparitions might appear. The evening land breeze from Pine Island to the east teased the trees to wave and dance, the broad-leafed bananas most of all, casting whimsical shadows across the shell mound ridge, and long ruffled silver lines across the bay.

Maria and I sat, entwined as only lovers can be, in the wicker sofa on the east side verandah, watching the moon rise through the sky. At first a pink tinge on the horizon, then a pale golden disc emerging from the mangroves, minutes later it was a magnificent silver orb, like some royal symbol of power. In a way, it was, for the moon performed its monthly duty for tides and lovers, just the same as it had for millions of years.

My bungalow is named "Serenity." Sean Rork's bungalow is eighty feet to the north of ours on the ridge. Its name is "Fiddler's Green," the traditional Irish sailors' term for Heaven, where all good seafarers go to rest in peace. He and I, with an old Florida Cracker named Whidden and a motley group of troubadour friends, built the two bungalows, along with a smaller one for Whidden, back in '84.

We had no house building abilities, so we used skills from our profession. The homes were clinker-built, like ships, and just as water-tight and stout. Each one had a parlor, a galley, a bedroom, a storeroom, and a wraparound verandah deck with wide roof overhangs. Every window had a hatch cover for foul weather, cheese cloth for fair weather. On sunny days and moonlight nights, they were open and well ventilated. In storms, they could be battened down to make the inhabitants snug and safe.

I noticed Sean and his fiancé, Minnie, curled up in the sofa on their east verandah too. Minnie was a fifty-year-old widow of an ancient French sea captain up at Sarasota Bay, thirty miles to the north. Though she was nice enough, Maria and I doubted her long term compatibility with Sean's somewhat whimsical sailor personality.

Like many women I've known, Maria is a shrewd judge of character. She was convinced Minnie wanted Rork because he had an income, and real love had little, if anything, to do with it. Nonetheless, we supported the idea when the two became engaged two weeks earlier, mainly because of Rork's enthusiasm when he announced their decision. The Baptist wedding, a major concession for the born and raised Irish Catholic Sean Aloysius Rork, was planned for August, when the circuit preacher would come back through the islands.

A slightly slurred Gaelic lilt came across the shadows to us from Fiddler's Green.

"Ooohee, Peter, me boyo. God's a happy one in Heaven tonight, an' puttin' on a grand show for us mere mortals, now ain't he though?"

I snuggled closer to Maria and called back, "That he is, Sean. That he is."

"Aye, an' here's a wee toast to the likes o' us, all me friends, for in the morn we must face them that have no love in their souls, no music in their heads, an' no humor in their hearts."

It was an old Irish lament, usually uttered when intoxicated, and directed toward the English overlords in Sean's homeland of County Wexford, Ireland, from which he escaped to sea as a ship's boy. Rork was directing it then toward the leadership in Washington, a cold Calvinistic New England and Ohio bunch who lacked the essential qualities he thought necessary for a fulfilling life. I completely agreed with him.

Maria and I had left our place in Alexandria two days after I got to Washington. My orders from the Chief of the Bureau of Navigation were simple: effective immediately I was on annual leave. But it wasn't the eight weeks I was due by the department, ending on May eighth. Instead, it was ending in six weeks, on April twenty-first, when I reported to my new office in Room 209 of the State, War, and Navy Building, right next to the presidential mansion. The bureau chief was conveniently absent the day I received my orders, but the personnel officers promised me the two other weeks of leave could be used "sometime during the year," depending on the new assistant secretary of the navy's authorization.

With that bit of bad news, Maria and I rode the train for two days, to the end of the line at Punta Gorda, Florida. Along the way, she informed me of other news which distressed her. Her twenty-two-year-old son, Juanito, a minor functionary inside the ministry of the overseas colonies at Madrid, had written her yet another letter which included anti-American rhetoric. He and his older brother Francisco, a Franciscan priest stationed in Havana, had vehemently opposed our marriage, the youngest for nationalistic reasons and the oldest for religious reasons. It was a constant source of anguish for Maria. There was nothing I could do about it but listen sympathetically to her fears of never seeing them again and never knowing her grandchildren.

From Punta Gorda, we took passage in the little fish company steamer which dropped us off at Patricio Island on its way to Punta Rassa. Sean Rork arrived on the island a week later, a breath of irrepressible gaiety which always cheered Maria up.

When old man Whidden had died years earlier, Black Tom Moore had taken over as caretaker for the island. Black Tom was a former slave from up the coast at Gamble Plantation. His own best guess as to his age was somewhere in his seventies, but he had the constitution of a forty-year-old. With his mahogany skin, iron strong muscles, incredible skill at fishing, and an infectious laugh, he was a natural foil for Rork's mischievous mind. Though a devoted Methodist Episcopalian who became literate by learning the Bible, Tom is good-natured toward our drinking, finding our path to perdition somewhat amusing. It wasn't always that way, but over the previous four years, Rork had eventually worn down Tom's initial disdain.

Spring is a wonderful time of year in our islands, and the stay at Patricio was therapeutic for both mind and body. The main occupations of the day were farming the island's many fruits and vegetables, a pastime Maria loved; fishing the abundant waters around us, Tom's specialty; and repairing the island's boat, the job of Rork and me. On this visit, our thirty-foot sloop, *Nancy Ann*, needed recaulking in her hull, and restitching on her mainsail—chores second nature for navy men.

Evenings always begin on the west verandah of Serenity Bungalow. Everyone gathers for sunset and the traditional sounding of the conch shell, accompanied by a toss of Matusalem rum, as a salute to God's incredible array of bay and islands below a pastel painted sky. Responding conchs from other islands report "All's well here," and while the sunset's afterglow dims, we sit down to dinner. Though Tom guards his rights as chief cook, Maria is always allowed to use the galley to prepare special

Andalusian dinners, a cuisine I'd fallen in love with twenty-five years earlier when on a mission in Spain.

But now, the inevitable final night on the island had arrived with a gloriously jasmine-scented breeze under the benevolent moon. I held Maria tighter, memorizing everything about the scene: the faint lavender smell of her hair, her captivating eyes, the smooth feel of her skin, the swish of the trees, the lingering taste of mango and paella, and our tranquil mood.

Rork's lament was only too right. He, Maria, and I were returning to a place and people far different from our island refuge.

9

Back into the Fray

Navy Library & Reception Room
Room 474—State, War, & Navy Building
Washington D.C.
Friday evening
23 April 1897

Maria had never seen the Navy Library and Reception Room—officially designated by the government as "Room 474." It is a beautiful place, as it should be, for it is the most expensively appointed room in the entire building.

The library is a two-story-high room, open aired and surrounded by a mezzanine deck, the walls of which are lined with bookcases. Large chart tables usually arranged in rows on the lower floor were removed for the reception to officially greet the new cabinet appointees, Secretary Long and Assistant Secretary Roosevelt, and their staffs.

The effect of the room is palatial, grandly decorated from floor to walls to ceiling in the ornate French style of moldings and buttresses. Nautical imagery is embedded everywhere. Sea shells lie over the Italian and French marble wall panels. Seahorses and dolphins play in the cast-iron railing of the mezzanine balcony. Neptune's trident helps hold up each pillar capital. Stars for navigation are sprinkled across the ceiling, and there is a compass rose in the center of the azure blue English Minton tiled floor, just in case anyone needs to know what direction is east.

The Washington Navy Yard provided a small band, which played in the background. The Marine Barracks marched over a guard of honor to stand watch and look magnificent for the ladies. Someone had arranged a delectable display of hors d'oeuvres. It was all rather well done, as only official Washington can.

The affair wasn't exclusively for the navy. The president lived two hundred feet to the east, so he and his wife came plus other cabinet officers, their wives, and their staffs. Along with everyone else, the senior generals of the army trooped in from the War Department in the north wing of the building. For some reason, even foreign ambassadors with their military and naval attachés showed up. Naturally, the leadership of Congress couldn't be ignored, since budget hearings were about to begin, thus they arrived to add their contribution to the already heated air. And, of course, the senior officers of the navy made a point of being noted in attendance. All in all, it was an amazing collection of pompous, shallow-minded, and thoroughly boring men, accompanied by their equally dreary wives.

The line to pay respects to the three honorees, President McKinley, Secretary Long, and Assistant Secretary Roosevelt, was very long. Fortunately, as a relatively senior officer in a truly senior post, I no longer was at the tail end of the line, which was somewhere out on 17th Street. After thirty-four years' service to the navy, eleven separate wounds from enemies around the world, and elevation to the rank of full captain, I had finally made it to the *middle* of the damned line.

There was one bright spot in all of this, however—my wife was beside me. While I chafed miserably inside the stifling high collar of a full mess dress uniform, complete with a row of bangles and baubles dangling from my chest, Maria was stunningly beautiful and serene.

She favors a muted, comfortable appearance, but for this occasion she was decked out in a green satin dress with black lace trim. Her raven black hair was done up in a loose wavy sort of twist. Her hypnotic eyes were accented by unique jewelry: a carnelian onyx and emerald necklace, with matching earrings and bracelet, all filigreed in an ornate Moorish-motif. At least four hundred years old, these family heirlooms were from the Muslim-Jewish era of the Iberian Peninsula. The entire effect garnered admiring glances from men and women alike.

Eventually, we made it to the president and his wife.

I half bowed, shook his proffered hand, and introduced myself. "Good evening, Mr. President, Mrs. McKinley. Captain Peter Wake, special personal aide to Assistant Secretary of the Navy Roosevelt, sir." Gesturing toward Maria, I continued, "Mr. President, may I present my wife, Maria Maura Wake."

She half-curtseyed as only Continental ladies can, her accent making a simple greeting sound exotic. "Good evening, Mr. President and Mrs. McKinley."

McKinley's wife Ida was next to him, seated due to a chronic nervous illness afflicting her since her two young daughters had tragically died over twenty years earlier. She smiled shyly at us, looking as distinctly uncomfortable and worn as I felt.

The president turned his attention to Maria. "Mrs. Wake, this is indeed an honor and a pleasure. Your husband is known for his skill and bravery. Now I see why he is so inspired. This is my dear wife Ida."

The ladies exchanged pleasantries and we moved away from the receiving line, but not before McKinley whispered to me, "I would like a word with you and Roosevelt later. This line won't take much longer than a few minutes."

I'd planned on our leaving right after being "seen" by the president and my superiors, but alas, now I had to stay. At my urging, Maria went home to Alexandria. As I knew would happen, McKinley was wrong on the timing. "A few minutes" turned out to be two hours, my mood deteriorating by the minute as

I waited in the corner with a few other bored officers. I tried to deduce the reason for the order to remain. Theodore said he had no idea. Whatever the president wanted, it couldn't be good.

At ten o'clock, I was summoned by a harried aide to meet the president and Roosevelt in Secretary Long's office. The secretary wasn't present, having excused himself earlier in the evening, shortly after Theodore suggested he looked unwell and should spend the weekend resting. Such advice would be repeated several times over the next year, to Theodore's benefit.

A quick description of Long's current office is in order, for over the years I have spent many an hour briefing presidents, secretaries of state, and navy secretaries on foreign affairs there. It is as impressive as the Library and Reception Room and is a place where I've witnessed major foreign policy decisions being made.

The walls and ceiling are decorated with hand-painted symbolic naval stencils. The floor is cherry, mahogany, and white maple, covered with small Persian rugs. The two fireplaces are Belgian black marble with large gilded mirrors over stout mantles and Minton tile hearths. Both had fires crackling away to take the spring chill out of the room. Two chandeliers dominate the space above, each equipped for gas and electricity, with gas globes on top and the electric light bulbs below. Ship models, books, and maps are everywhere. There are no frivolous decorations or displays. It is a serious room, evoking American power and its relationship to the world.

Secretary Long's desk had its accoutrements carefully organized around the periphery. Unlike Theodore's desk in nearby 278 and mine in Room 279, there were no piles of documents, no paperwork of any kind, in sight. It was a telling sign about the secretary, for although decisions are expected to be made inside the office, the work of preparing and executing them goes on elsewhere. Mr. Long had no interest in either. His preferred topic of conversation was the garden of his home in Buckfield, Maine. To Theodore's joy, the garden was blooming quite nicely right about then, and demanding more of the kind old gentleman's attention.

The president plopped down in the secretary's chair with a sigh and turned his large unblinking eyes to Roosevelt, who was seated bolt upright in a guest chair, like a pupil summoned before the headmaster. I was seated to Theodore's right and slightly behind him, sitting at attention as well.

McKinley got right to the point. "Gentlemen, I've seen war close up, and never want to see it again. I will *not* have us in a war or confrontation over Cuba, or anywhere else beyond our borders. This country will remain at *peace* with everybody. Is that abundantly clear to both of you?"

My reply was an automatic and quick, "Aye, sir."

Theodore paused and leaned forward, his eyes focused on the president's while he formulated an answer.

Outwardly, I remained impassive at McKinley's statement. Inwardly, I was a bit disconcerted at having the president of the United States lump me in with Theodore's well-known penchant for bellicosity. *Why was the president including me in his lecture?*

I was the one who frequently counseled my superiors over the past seventeen years to be cautious of involvement in various foreign crises, particularly in Cuba. I had also given this president my opinion that our army and navy weren't yet ready for war with Spain, no matter what the situation in Cuba. I was known for my opinions—strongly pro-Cuban independence, and against any American colonial acquisitions. McKinley had already sought my advice on Hawaii, which was simple—reverse the U.S. moves toward annexation—and he seemed to agree. *The president wants me as a witness to his statement to Roosevelt,* I decided.

Theodore's response emerged in an uncharacteristically subservient tone, without his usual fervent accentuations.

"Mr. President, I am a loyal American and entirely at your command, both personally and professionally. My only goal is to keep the United States Navy ready at all times to do precisely your bidding, whatever and whenever you decide. As for Captain Wake here, he knows the situation and personalities in Cuba better than anyone else in our national government. He will provide factual information about the evolving state of affairs inside Cuba so reasoned executive decisions can be made with a high degree of confidence. And I guarantee Captain Wake will promptly and efficiently follow his orders without personal prejudice or delay."

McKinley seemed satisfied, nodding his approval. Either he did not understand, or chose to ignore, a salient but subtle point around which Theodore had deftly detoured—that I would promptly and efficiently follow orders *from whom?*

10

Cuba's Pain

Secretary of the Navy's Office
Room 274—State, War, & Navy Building
Washington D.C.
Friday evening
23 April 1897

Having delivered his policy statement to Roosevelt and me, the president swung around in the secretary's chair to face me. "Please read this, Captain Wake."

He took some folded pages from his coat pocket and presented me with a five-page letter from General Máximo Gómez, the senior military commander of the free Cuban forces inside Cuba. It was dated the ninth of February and asked McKinley to condemn the widely known Spanish atrocities on the island. I noted it specifically emphasized the Cubans were not asking for any United States intervention in the war. I handed the letter to Roosevelt to peruse.

The president asked of me, "I want your opinion of this man, Gomez."

The moment I saw the letter, I knew I would be called upon to educate the president on the Cuban situation. Typical of our presidents, McKinley had never been outside the country, knew nothing of foreign languages or cultures, and been a Congressional politician for much of his career. When international incidents demanded presidential attention, they always summoned the Navy for answers, for we were the only ones in the government who understood the world.

"Aye, sir," I replied. "I met General Gómez once, in 1886. He is a serious man of impressive demeanor and gravitas, educated and compassionate, and very professional in military matters. Born in the Dominican Republic, he fought as an officer in the Spanish army there in the 1860s and grew disillusioned. He then left that army in 1868 and went to fight with the Cubans for their freedom. Gómez has never wavered from his duty or his sense of honor, and has paid a heavy price—his son was killed in action with Maceo. The general is universally revered among the Cubans."

McKinley, the former combat soldier, grunted in appreciation. His next question was one many in Washington had inquired of me.

"With all this leadership and motivation, why haven't the Cubans beaten the Spanish yet? It's been almost thirty years since they declared they wanted independence."

"Supplies, transport, and communications, sir. The Cubans have little of those three necessities for modern military operations. Due to the neutrality embargo our country has placed against Cuba, few of the necessary munitions, supplies, and equipment are getting to the freedom forces on the island. This is critical, and is what General Jomini called *logistics* in his seminal work on military science sixty years ago, titled *Summary of the Art of War*. Inefficient Confederate logistics helped defeat them three decades ago. Lack of crucial supplies is the main reason for the lack of a Cuban victory to date—not Spanish military skill or élan."

He huffed and shook his head. "Hmm, well, the embargo will have to stay right in place, Captain Wake, otherwise it will mean a general war with Spain for *us*. Our army's logistics are completely unready for anything like that. What about the Spanish army in Cuba?"

"The Spanish army, unlike the Cuban army, is a well-equipped and supplied modern army. Their officers are professional. The troops are reasonably well trained. The Spanish forces outnumber the Cubans about ten to one, if you include the pro-Spanish militia units on the island. A significant point to remember, though, is that even with their advantages the Spanish are primarily on the defensive. Other than the occasional foray, they stay mostly within the major towns and cities, and inside the three fortification lines built across the north-south width of the island, which are known as *trochas*. Plus, many of their troops brought from Spain are conscripts, who are far more sickly in the tropical jungle and much less motivated than the Cubans."

"The Cuban army officers, what are they like?"

"Gómez has weeded out most of dilettantes and fools, so they are generally very good, with intimate knowledge of their operational areas. They have excellent intelligence about the Spanish strengths, weaknesses, and forays; which is important. They also have a penchant for action, when it will be successful."

I added something I thought might be important to McKinley, well-known to be a Freemason. "Many of the Cuban officers, as well as the political leadership, are Freemasons, sir. It is a commitment taken very seriously in Cuba."

As I expected, he didn't visibly react. Freemasons seldom do in front of non-Masons such as me. I continued, "The Cuban forces have general control of most of the countryside and, combined with their intelligence advantage, they therefore have the military initiative over place and time of contact. Their main problem is exploitation of their successes. For that they need logistical support immediately available to them."

Leaning forward with his elbows on his knees and hands clasped, the president asked another question I'd heard many times. "What about the average Cuban soldiers?"

"Most of the rank and file in their army are farm peasants who know the lay of the land quite well. These *mambis,* as they are called, have incredible endurance. Most important, they've perfected a chilling tactic taught to them by General Antonio Maceo before he was killed in battle. It is a machete cavalry charge, and it terrifies the Spanish soldiers."

McKinley looked out the window and grew pensive. I wondered if my explanation had kindled old memories of battlefield terrors. At last, he said, "I see. What is happening there right now?"

"Pretty much a stalemate, sir. For the last six months, the war has begun to bog down for both sides into a war of attrition, with no knockout battles. Morale among the Spanish soldiers is worsening and desertion is increasing. I would say that attrition favors the Cubans, but very slowly."

And what of my new boss Roosevelt during this discussion? Apparently content to stay out of the conversation, he'd been sitting impressively mute—the first time I'd ever seen *that* happen.

"How long will it take for the Cubans to win this thing?" McKinley asked.

"Without our help? At least another five long bloody years, sir."

Never taking his eyes off me, the president sat back and pondered for a moment, then said, "And what about this General Weyler? The press calls him 'The Butcher.'"

"A shrewd, tough character, sir. Career soldier since the age of sixteen who has fought in several wars. Been the governor of Cuba and several other colonies. His methods are brutally efficient, especially the concentration camps he has forced the rural poor into, but very short-sighted. The press accounts of thousands starving in those camps have horrified many of the moderates in Cuba who supported autonomy within the Spanish Empire, instead of outright independence. Weyler doesn't care. He says many of his tactics simply echo Sherman's policy in Georgia and South Carolina during our rebellion—scorched-earth, total war."

Another presidential sigh. "Cuba's a disaster, no matter which way you look at it."

"Yes, sir. The island is in pain."

McKinley stood, as did we. "Thank you, Captain Wake. You've been refreshingly informative and concise."

He turned toward Theodore. His voice was hoarse from the reception line, but I detected an ominous edge. "Hopefully, Mr. *Assistant* Secretary, we won't have to use your navy for *anything* regarding Cuba or Spain."

"I *agree*, Mr. President," replied Roosevelt, with a remarkably straight face.

11

El Consorcio de Azúcar

Sagamore Hill
Oyster Bay, Long Island
New York
Late Sunday evening
4 July 1897

Ten hectic weeks later, Theodore Roosevelt was in fine fettle. He had kept unaccustomedly muted for three months. That ended with a fiery speech at the Naval War College at Newport, Rhode Island in early June, espousing the virtues of war, mentioning the word no less than sixty-two times. His speech received compliments from the attendees, but the president and navy secretary were not amused, for they were on the receiving end of the great consternation engendered amongst the "chattering class" in Washington and Europe.

Theodore, naturally, was completely oblivious to the critics, telling me a week later, "I simply told the *truth*, Peter. And as is *well* known, the *truth* is *always* an abso*lute* defense!"

It was now Independence Day weekend at Sagamore Hill. The veritable squire in his manor, Theodore was surrounded by adoring family, as well as Maria and me, his guests for the weekend.

A festive dinner was followed by an impromptu football game in the yard and fireworks on the nearby beach. It was all led with unbounded boyish enthusiasm by "Papa," as his children called him, after which the utterly exhausted family and guests retired to their beds. Having celebrated my fifty-eighth birthday a week earlier, I was utterly exhausted too, and headed to join Maria upstairs in the guest bedroom. My host had other plans, and intercepted me in the hall. It seemed Theodore wasn't tired in the least. He wanted to discuss the "Sugar Consortium."

I knew the drill and headed for the library, the sanctum sanctorum for confidential conversations in the house. Sitting in a leather chair, probably furnished from some exotic victim of his, I waited to be interrogated thoroughly, for Roosevelt is the most informed man in government I've ever known. He actually reads the volumes of reports which pass through his office, a rarity in Washington, and thereafter makes inquiries which get straight to the core of the matter, another rarity. His ability for rapid consumption of printed material, and the memorization and recitation of its contents, is well known—and dreaded by subordinates.

"Peter, I want an overall situation report on our Sugar Consortium," he said while sitting down in a rocker, all business now. "Start with the *administrative* details: finances, communications, staff personnel, and subject matter areas. Then we'll cover the two main *operational* goals."

He was speaking of a clandestine web of agents I'd been putting in place inside Cuba since late April. It was my initial assignment from him, an hour after I had arrived in my office. Though other projects regarding Germany, Venezuela, and Chile came my way, the Cuban espionage operation was to be my number one priority. There were no reports yet for him to read, however, for this was highly secret work and completely segregated from regular ONI intelligence efforts.

My previous network of spies in Cuba—code named *Los Aficionados de Ron*, or "The Rum Enthusiasts" in English—from ten years earlier had dissolved. When he initially chose me for the position, Roosevelt knew I still had contacts among people on the island and surmised they could be productive in obtaining a true picture of the Spanish presence and plans. This was part and parcel of his "getting the navy ready" goal, and one with which I agreed. The president would need *facts* to make valid decisions regarding Cuba. I was to furnish them.

Thus, "The Sugar Consortium," or *El Consorcio de Azúcar*, was born. A week after Rork and I moved into Room 279, I had the general framework of the operation worked out. A month into it, we had half the agents set up. Now, after two months, the entire network was in operation.

The reader might wonder about the chosen moniker. In sugar-dominated Cuba, the name was sufficiently ubiquitous as to not generate undue alarm should it come to anyone's attention. It would be used only among those in the know at naval headquarters in Washington, no more than seven men at most, none of whom would be *officially* part of ONI. Should the term be overheard, its true nature would not be apparent.

I launched into my briefing. "Finances first, sir. Payment to agents inside Cuba is done as we originally planned, through accounts at a French bank with branches in Quebec and Martinique, the *Banque de Crédit Commercial*. Each Cuban agent receives fifty dollars a month. Each of the other agents inside the Bahamas receives twenty a month, on accounts at the Bank of England sub-branch in Nassau. The naval officer agents receive nothing but their pay. Payment is approved by me, and subsequently by you, before coded fund transfer messages are cabled to the banks. Payments began June first and we just made another this last Friday, July second."

He gazed up at his father's picture. "*Excellent.* How much is left in the fund?"

"After expenses for the agent payments, safe house rentals, and retainers for transport and supplies in Nassau, the fund has twelve hundred dollars left in it."

"And these *foreign* banks, what do *they* know of the transactions?"

"These are routine transactions, and no one knows the incoming money is from an American connection. The funds being deposited into the agent accounts are sent from a false company which I run, Benkelsky Soap and Perfumery of Amsterdam."

Theodore beamed and thumped the arm of the chair. "*Bully* good, Peter! What about *communications* to and from the agents?"

"All communications are in substitution code, which is known only to the agent and my three men in Washington. Each agent gets a different substitution code, so they can't be cross-compromised in the event of capture. We are not using the standard ONI or diplomatic codes."

"*Good.* And cable traffic?"

"Telegraph cables from and to agents inside Cuba connect initially with Mr. Helmut Koch, an alias I set up in Montreal. The Koch cables are separately sent to Daisy Cake Company in Baltimore, an alias I set up in Baltimore. The secondary route for communications, should the first be unavailable for whatever reason, is to cable Jean Lafluer in Cap Haitien, Haiti, another alias which is run by me and is likewise separately connected to the Daisy Cake Company. Regular mail from any agent in Cuba goes to Johan Fisk at Sint Maarten in the Dutch West Indies, which is another of my fronts. There will be no mail going *to* any agent inside Cuba."

"Ah, a double layer of *conundrums*, and also an emergency contact should all else fail."

"Yes, sir. Also, our agents within the Bahamas cable directly to the Daisy connection, with any mail from them going there as well."

"What are the *subject* matters assigned to the agents?"

"Information categories needed to comprehend the total picture in Cuba—of both the Spanish and the Cuban rebels. This includes the Spanish military and naval order of battle, along with the police and militia order of battle. Fuel, supply, repair, and training status of warships. Commercial and industrial status, and activity in the major ports. And, of course, Spanish secret police personnel and procedures, particularly the Orden Publico's counter-intelligence operations."

That got a sly grin from him. "Ah, *yes*, the covert branch of which is run by *your* old *nemesis*, if I recall correctly."

Roosevelt didn't know the details of exactly how Marrón had become my nemesis over the years, or how I'd tried my best to kill him in a Havana cathedral, of all places, nine years earlier. Hopefully, Theodore never would. I didn't want him talking about it.

"Aye, sir. Colonel Isidro Marrón is still around."

"*Frequency* of reports?"

"We will get monthly reports. They can send one anytime in the event of urgency."

"*Who* will be responsible for *receiving* the incoming intelligence and *organizing* it into briefings for me?"

"I will do the brief, sir. Two officers on temporary duty assignment to me will receive and organize the intelligence, Lieutenant Brecount and Ensign Connally. Both served under me at sea. They are sharp minded and quiet tongued. Invoking your name got them loaned to me for six months by the commandant of the Washington Navy Yard. They report in at my office tomorrow morning, but have no prior idea of their duties. They, or Rork, will check the Daisy connection in Baltimore each day, travelling out of uniform by the fast train."

"Hmm, your office *will* be a bit *crowded*, won't it? You've *already* got Rork in there."

"Aye, sir. Crowded, but secure. I've had the locks changed."

"Are you still going to be the sole connection to the chief Cuban rebel and his headquarters in New York?"

"Only myself, or Rork, will be in contact with President Tómas Estrada Palma, sir."

Adjusting his spectacles, he asked, "Señor Estrada Palma was a *colleague* of your *friend* Martí, wasn't he? Does *he* know your *profession?*"

"Aye, sir, on both questions. He took the presidency-in-exile after Martí was killed in action in Cuba two years ago. Very smart man, who has many friends in the New York press."

"Very *good*. Exactly *who* knows about this operation?"

"Right now, the only people who know about any of this are you, me, and Rork. Brecount and Connally will know tomorrow when they report in. That will be all, unless you decide otherwise, and I hope you don't. The cover story for other staff at headquarters is suitably boring—we are comparing U.S. and British naval equipment inventory procedures for a report expected by you at the end of the year. And yes, sir, we will be actually doing one up for you, on the side."

"*Bully* fine work, Peter! Are we sure *all* of the agents in Cuba are still *unknown* to *Marrón* and his henchmen, and *ready* to start *communicating* their intelligence?"

"Yes, sir, as far as I know. The fifth of this month they are to send their first reports. By Tuesday we'll have a clearer view of what is going on inside Cuba, or we'll know who has been compromised by the Orden Publico."

"We have two main goals—obtaining *Spanish* defensive plans and setting up American *offensive* plans. When can we start getting results on the Spanish defenses at Havana?"

"It will take about six months to get the Spanish defense plans for Havana, so figure next January. That will also be a good time for me to reconnoiter inside Cuba for our offensive contingency plans. All of this depends on our agents remaining uncompromised."

"Yes, but how will *we* know they are *compromised* if they still *send* a cable, but under *duress?*"

Good question. "If they are communicating under duress, there is a code word. Only Rork and I know it, sir."

The reader will have noticed Roosevelt didn't ask me the names or particulars of the agents, and perhaps wonders why. When we began in April, I explained to him I would never divulge such information and not to even ask. To his credit, he never has.

I waited for the next question, but Theodore grew pensive, and focused on a mutely snarling bear head and skin on the floor. Then he curtly nodded.

"Let it *begin*, Peter, and let *us* understand more than *they* know we do, so when the time comes we'll know *when* and *where* to *strike*."

With that said, I went upstairs to Maria. As tired as I was, sleep didn't come quickly. My mind was on six men inside Cuba, whether I could trust them, and the consequences of failure.

The next day, I was in the office by nine in the morning to meet my new staff members. They were enthusiastic about the mission. Equally important, they understood Rork, though only a petty officer, would be senior to them in the decision-making. Even Brecount readily agreed, which surprised me since he had ten years of service.

By nine o'clock that night I was still there when Rork, Brecount, and Connally returned from Baltimore. Rork reported, "Happy to say all the agents' cables arrived from Cuba, sir."

Everyone waited while Rork deciphered the cables. More good news. None of the agents were under duress. The information sent was basic and contained nothing previously unknown, as I had fully expected. It was a solid start.

I telephoned Theodore at his sister's place in Washington and filled him in, still using a code to thwart any listeners. "The transactions came through, sir. We have strong prices and production is expected to be high."

"*Bully* fine work, Peter! See you in the morning."

The Sugar Consortium was in business, and my life was about to get very busy.

12

Quo Vadis?

The Celestial Club
Lafayette Square
Washington D.C.
24 December 1897

Busy is an understatement. I made monthly journeys to the Bahamas to meet agents, arrange payments, and solve problems. The cable reports provided so much information, and events were unfolding so rapidly, that we had to increase the frequency to weekly reports. This necessitated four different code changes over the next five months, because the Spanish were past masters at secret communications and penetrating layers upon layers of cypher protection.

By December, I was nervously optimistic. The network was producing solid intelligence, and no penetrations were apparent. Brecount and Connally were naturals at espionage, comfortable with the trade craft but not cocky or complacent—Rork saw to that.

But the situation in Cuba was reaching a climax, for the various factions exerting pressure were aware the turning point was approaching. It was an unsavory stew of personalities, politics, and policies, kept stirred up by uncompromising old men in each group on the island. The die-hard Spanish loyalists and their dangerous *Voluntarios* militia favored continuing the current colonial occupation; the Autonomists favored a home-ruled island, kept within the Spanish Empire; and the rebel *Insurgentes* demanded the full independence they had been fighting for thirty years to achieve.

Added to the mix was the colossus of the north, the United States. We had our own adamant factions who were no less inflexible. It was a motley collection: the industrial giants had considerable commercial interests in Cuba, wanting stability on the island and low U.S. sugar tariffs in order to maximize profits; the New York press wanted instability in order to sell copies and make money; the exiled Cuban independence movement in New York and Florida supported the rebel insurgents and fed the press propaganda; President McKinley wanted to avoid war with anyone; and our Congress, some of whom wanted freedom for all in Cuba while others feared a Spanish withdrawal would create a race war against whites, inspiring blacks in the American South.

In the middle was the U.S. Navy. Nowhere in the debate was the U.S. Army, which clung to their antiquated coastal forts, bloated seniority system, and quaint memories of fighting small bands of Indians out West.

I looked forward to a quiet weekend, including a nice Christmas dinner with Maria and Rork. Cuba, Spain, the U.S. Navy, and Theodore Roosevelt would not be topics of conversation.

Rork had already headed over to his quarters at the Navy Yard. As I was preparing to leave the office, Roosevelt stopped in. He invited me to meet him at his club, the Celestial, a convivial gathering place for intellectual types in the capital, for a cup of tea. It was a favorite location for him to hold confidential conversations when in Washington, away from the eavesdropping common among bureaucrats. This would be a brief stop for him, he said, before getting the long train ride north to Sagamore Hill for the Christmas weekend.

Only "Yes" would do. As I made the short walk across Lafayette Square from the State, War, and Navy Building, I hoped the talk with Theodore would be brief, for I had to catch the short train south to Alexandria, where Maria was expecting me.

I got there first. He joined me in the club's lobby a moment later, then led the way to the enclosed loggia where we sat at a table by the window overlooking the square. The club was quiet, with only an elderly servant in sight. Outside, the square was also deserted in the fading light of an overcast sky, for those in government service, meaning everyone in the area, had gone home hours earlier.

Not so for Theodore, and therefore me. The servant arrived with our tea and disappeared. A bright crimson bird flitted in for a landing on the outer window sill, where he squatted and studied us. My friend's stern demeanor changed instantly.

"Why, hello there, my little feathered friend. Don't be envious of our warmth in here, for you, sir, are nothing less than the noble *Cardinalis virginianus.* You have true *freedom* out there."

He leaned forward, swiveling his head to see to the left and right out the window. "Now, *where* is your less magnificently feathered *missus?* She should be close by . . ."

Only two things could divert Theodore from a naval topic: his family and wildlife. My train left the station south of Capitol Hill in thirty minutes. I cleared my throat. "Sir, we don't have much time before your train."

Roosevelt's head swiveled back and I was rewarded with a sheepish smirk. "Well, she *is* close by. They mate for *life*, you know. And when courting, he feeds her. Quite *romantic*. But, duty calls, and I *must* have an update on *Cuba* and our Sugar Consortium. So first provide me an update on the situation in *Spain*, then Cuba."

"Aye, sir. Regarding Spain, you may recall that two months after the Italian terrorist assassinated the Spanish PM in August, Sagasta and his liberals returned to run the government. Three weeks after that, Weyler was recalled and far saner policies were initiated with regard to Cuba. In early November, Spain granted amnesty to all political prisoners in Cuba and Puerto Rico. In late November, the Spanish granted Puerto Rico political autonomy within the empire. Sagasta wants to do the same in Cuba. I believe it will be formalized on January first."

"A *fortuitous* turn of events, indeed. Any bad news?"

"The bad news is Sagasta is seventy-two and worn down by the political battles he's fought for the last forty years. He is the glue holding the liberals together, but I don't think he can physically last much longer. The die-hard conservatives are still powerful. We dare not underestimate them. The Spanish businessmen in Cuba were irate when General Weyler was removed, and the general was greeted by cheering crowds on his return to Spain. This outpouring of opinion is not only anti-Cuban insurgent, but also anti-American.

"Hearst's constant drumming for war in his newspapers is not taken lightly in Madrid. The Spanish conservatives were also incensed by our new ambassador's October ultimatum to the government to end the war in Cuba. They declared they would defend the honor of the Spanish Empire and monarchy and not yield an inch on anything about Cuba. It was noted one of your naval confidents, George Dewey, was just sent to take over the Asiatic Squadron, close by their Spanish Philippines."

"*Good!* By gad, they *should* take note. I *want* them to take note. With Dewey out there they won't catch us unprepared for *action*. It's the *best* deterrence against war."

"Yes, sir. But logic may not be a dominant factor in Madrid's decision-making, or with the colonial authorities in Havana. The conservatives still control a large percentage of the army and naval officers. The army is confident of a fight with us in Cuba, the navy less so. The rhetoric is getting hotter."

Roosevelt huffed. "President McKinley's annual address from two weeks ago *praised* Sagasta's peaceful policies. I thought it a very *restrained* speech, and devoid of *any* warmongering."

"The Spanish hard-liners completely distrust our president and anything he says, sir. Almost as much as they distrust you, in fact."

He laughed and slapped his knee. "Really? I rather *like* that."

I continued. "Now, as to the situation inside Cuba. It is unchanged as far as the internal military conflict is concerned. The Cuban and Spanish armies are still stalemated. But there is a new aspect. The lack of military progress has frustrated and angered the Spanish loyalists in Cuba. They despise the new home rule authorities in Havana and loath Sagasta in Madrid for compromising far too much, both with the Cuban insurgents and with the United States. They fear losing everything they have in property and rights, and the black Cubans. As a result, there is growing animosity toward American citizens, whom they view as spies and provocateurs."

Roosevelt wasn't laughing now. "I am *not* cowed by those Spanish *thugs!* Those *hotheads* are *exactly* why I have sent *Maine* to Key West. She should arrive tonight, and can be at Havana within *nine* hours once Consul General Fitzhugh Lee sends word for help. Let us go on, Peter. What are the latest reports from the Sugar Consortium?"

"Agents R7 and R33 independently report the anti-American riots in Havana and Matanzas are being instigated by certain army and secret police officers, Colonel Marrón being one of them. The number of refugees from the fighting in Matanzas has increased to about a quarter of the population—about sixteen thousand people. The food riots there in October were in reaction to the utter inability of the government to protect or provide for the inhabitants. Tension is increasing in various cities. Americans are being warned to stay off the streets, even in the daytime."

"The rebels—what of them?"

"They are resisting Madrid's amnesty offer for rebels, sir. General Gómez issued an order that any Cuban officer who tries to take advantage of Spanish amnesty will be executed for cowardice—and everybody knows he means it. So far, very few have surrendered, and their rebel army fights on.

"Their supply lines from outside the island are still tenuous, and many of their men who actually do have rifles are down to five rounds each. Agent R94 reports the Cuban Army in the central region has enough men now to go on a large-scale offensive, if only they had the munitions. He thinks they could take Matanzas in a week."

Theodore thought about that for a moment. "I heartily wish I could find a way to help those *brave* people, but that would be a violation of U.S. neutrality. Ha! As if anyone with a *heart* could possibly be *neutral* in the face of the Spanish *oppression* in Cuba." He raised a finger, and his voice. "Hearst and his *minions* may well be jingo-spewing *opportunists*, but they *do* make a good point. *Innocent* people are *starving* in those concentration camps in Cuba!"

I waited without comment. Theodore's face calmed. "What about the European powers?"

"Brits are with us, sir. French and Dutch are neutral. Germans are officially neutral, but quietly pro-Spanish. They now have three warships in the area, with another heading there. They would be an added problem in the event of war."

"That would be to their regret. Is this the end of your report?"

"Yes, sir. "

Nodding his acknowledgment, he said, "Very good, Captain Wake."

Whenever Theodore called me by my rank in a private conversation, I knew something unpleasant was coming. He sprung it on me in typical Rooseveltian style—in Latin.

"It appears all the foregoing leads to a *significant* question. *Quo vadis, Pretus?* Has the time come to shift from *reporting* actions to *making* them?"

Quo vadis, Pretus? I dredged the recesses of my educational memory to come up with the definition. Ah, yes, it came back to me. Conjugating verbs in Mr. Stonehead's Latin class, when I was fifteen. I hated Latin class, but did recall the meaning. *Where are you going, Peter?*

Two could play this silly game, so I answered in my bad French, which I knew was far better than Roosevelt's atrocious French. "*Pour trouver la victorie, sans effusion de sang.*"

To find victory, without the spilling of blood.

"Ah! A *dreamer* to the end!" he exclaimed. "May it be *so* on this Christmas Eve."

He whispered his next words in a grimly determined tone. "*Still*, Peter, if and when war is imminent, I'll need a level headed *American* naval man, or two, already *inside* Cuba. Men I can trust completely. So be ready, for soon you and Rork will have to go there."

Rork and I had discussed this very thing, appreciating the smoldering situation in Cuba even better than Theodore Roosevelt and guessing at our mission when the inevitable happened.

The thought greatly saddened me—I would be returning to the brutal insanity of war, against my dearly beloved wife's own people. What would she think of me?

Quo vadis, indeed.

13

Two Dollars

1819 N Street
Washington D.C.
6 p.m., Wednesday
12 January 1898

Nineteen days later, Rork and I were in the study of Roosevelt's new home in Washington, a mile north of his office. Normally we, like Theodore, walked the route. However, due to the urgency of our task, and the Arctic blizzard raging outside, I had Rork dragoon an army carriage from the secretary of war's staff livery. Some general would not be amused and complain, but in the meantime we arrived warm, dry, and in great style. The driver thought it a delicious joke.

We weren't the only ones thus transported. Across the street from Theodore's place, at the famed British Legation, elegant carriages carrying the highborn were lined up by the curb, waiting to disembark their passengers for a posh dinner party.

Roosevelt had gone home early to be with his wife Edith, who had been very ill lately. His young sons Ted and Kermit were sick also. The seriousness of Edith's condition was indicated by Theodore's cancelling his attendance at the annual dinner of his beloved Boone and Crockett Club, which he founded a decade earlier, up in New York City.

The cook answered the door and solemnly bid us to enter, the nanny and maid being upstairs nursing the various invalids, and the butler off seeking medicines at the pharmacy. The place was unnaturally quiet, apart from a cough or moan, and the constant bawling of two-month old Quentin. It was quite a different scene than the usual Roosevelt domestic ambience of laughter, running footsteps, and strident proclamations.

"How is she?" I asked when we walked into his study. It was smaller than his office at Sagamore Hill, but just as crammed with books, charts, and dead animals. Waning flames crackled in the fireplace at one end and the gasoliers were turned low. He was seated at his desk, hands resting on an open astronomy book.

There had been a five-hour-long partial lunar eclipse several nights earlier. The day after the eclipse, Roosevelt had taken great glee in describing the earth's umbral shadow covering part of the moon. The most exuberant part of his tale was showing us, by word and gesture, an image he understood well: "It was as if a *chunk* of the moon had been *bitten out* by a giant *predator!*"

But now the exuberance was gone, and Theodore looked more depressed than I'd ever seen him. He gestured to some chairs and we sat. His reply was subdued, almost tearful. "Edith is in a bad condition, Peter. Fever won't go down. Might be typhoid, they've told me, but they can't be sure."

My heart went out to him. Theodore's mother had died of typhoid thirteen years earlier, on the very same day, and in the same house which his first wife Alice had died of Bright's Disease. It was on February fourteenth, and he never celebrated Valentine's Day again. My first wife Linda had died of cancer that same day, four years before Roosevelt's tragedy. It was a sad bond between us.

"How are the children?" I asked.

"The girls seem to be fine. Ted's condition is mostly nervous exhaustion, they think. Kermit is simply sick with a child's cold. Quentin is upset over his mother not being with him."

He paused, glanced down at the pile of papers beside the book and shook his head. "And here is yet another challenge for me—one arranged by the bureaucrats of the state of New York, who insinuate I have been less than accurate in documenting my place of residence and paying my taxes. These parasitic, pencil-necked, paper-pushers in Albany seem to specialize in the Chinese *lingchi* method of death by a thousand little cuts. Oh, give me a charging cougar and I know precisely what to do. But these . . . mindless fools, devoid of logic. How do I deal with them?"

I interrupted him. "We have a message, sir."

"Yes, you said as much on the telephone, and that it was confidential. Our Sugar Consortium, I presume? More about the Spanish mine which exploded in Havana harbor last week?"

"Concerning the mine, I got a cable this afternoon from agent R94, who heard from his source it was an accidental power surge to an electrical mine near the Spanish naval station's floating dock. But that's not why we are here, sir. It's because of a message from Consul-General Lee in Havana. He sent the special coded phrase requesting help in a cable to Key West. The anti-American riots are spreading and expected to get worse."

Roosevelt wasn't subdued anymore. He nearly sprang from his chair. "*What!* He sent the '*two dollars*' phrase? Lee's requesting a *warship?* Finally, by Jove, we have something *decisive* by somebody! Bully for *him!* Hmm, this means things are getting *desperate*, indeed. When *exactly* did this cable come in?"

"We received it from Captain Sigsbee in Key West an hour ago. Secretary Long has seen it and walked over to the mansion to tell the president. He's still there now. They are evaluating the options available to the president."

Invigorated by events in Cuba evolving as he had predicted, Roosevelt pounded the desk and began rattling off commands.

"Options? *What* options? We *know* what to do! We've already *planned out* what to do! The *first* thing we *must* do is *immediately* gather all of our ships and *configure* their squadrons into *fighting* formations. They are *far* too scattered hither and *yon* by themselves, and thus are incapable of *decisive* action. Concentrate the North Atlantic Squadron at *Key West.* Concentrate the European Squadron at *Cherbourg.* Concentrate the Asiatic Squadron at *Hong Kong.* There is no time to waste, gentlemen."

He leaped up and headed for the fireplace, where he started pacing, his orders increasing in velocity and volume. Rork and I remained seated, neither of us taking notes. They weren't needed. We'd heard it all before, *ad nauseam*, during his discussions of various war plans which had long been on the books. I agreed with his views, but the problem with setting the plans into motion was two-fold. First, we weren't at the confrontational stage requiring a war order yet. Second, the civilian leadership of the country didn't understand what was needed for modern naval warfare, especially the required logistics. Even worse, they didn't want to know.

With only the briefest pause for breath, Theodore resumed his oration. "Each captain *must* immediately *fill* their ship's bunkers with the *highest* grade coal, and their magazines with *all* the *ammunition* and powder charges they will hold. Provisions and medicines *must* be brought aboard, and *all* woodwork and *extraneous* flammable materials *must* be discarded forthwith. *Every* ship in the navy must go on *war* alert from this instant, *everywhere* in the world. *Stop* all enlisted discharges, commissioned officer retirements, and *activate* the state naval militias."

He suddenly stopped pacing, his jaw clenched. Cleaning his spectacles, he asked, "Well, what do *you two* think of this development?"

"It's a riot, not an act of war, sir," I said, trying to lower the temperature in the room. "The request was for the *Maine* to visit Havana as a stabilizing force, not attack the city. And Secretary Long is waiting for the president's decision. I do agree the navy needs to be alerted and readied for action, but concentrating the squadrons would take Secretary Long's approval and send the kind of signal the president has repudiated repeatedly to date. Remember, no Americans have been hurt in this rioting, and the whole thing may subside in a few days."

My opinion was not what he wanted to hear. "Humph. Duly noted. Now, what about the Havana *defense* plans we're working on? We *need* those."

"Thought we'd have them by now, but staff changes at Spanish army headquarters have delayed us."

Roosevelt swung his gaze to Rork, who had assumed the stoic pose of a veteran petty officer in the midst of senior officers. "Well, what exactly do *you* think we should do in Cuba?"

"Oooh, methinks `tis not for the simple likes o' me to venture into that sort o' nasty political mess, sir—too bloody many snakes in striped pants. Me superiors know far more than an old bluejacket about such things."

"That sounds like *obfuscation*, Rork," said Roosevelt sternly. "I expect *plain* talk from officers *and* enlisted. *Especially* from the *both* of *you*, of all people. I asked for your *opinion*, so give it to me."

"Aye, aye, sir," Rork replied, unfazed by the admonishment. "Me opinion is the same as the Captain's. Never go to war `till you're sure you're in the right, an' there's no other way to get what needs to be gotten. Then, if war be the call, kill every one o' the bastards as fast as you can, an' get the damned thing over with. Methinks we're in the right an' those Spaniardo buggers're in the wrong, but we've not yet made certain there's no other way to get what needs to be gotten."

"Which is?"

"Cuba free of Spain, sir."

"We've tried to *buy* the blasted place from them several times, Rork, but Madrid refuses to even *discuss* the offer."

"Not us buyin' the island, sir, but let the Cubans be free o' everybody, includin' us."

"No matter—Madrid won't *let go*. We've called *attention* to their *atrocities* and *warned* them time and *again!* But they *ignore* us. Cuba is our *neighbor*, and we *cannot* ignore the *suffering* there! And *I*, for one, will *not* ignore it, or *permit* it any *longer*. I will *resign* tomorrow morning and *volunteer* to lead *American* men to *liberate* that island from the yoke of *bondage!* I have military *skills* useful in the *cavalry*, and should find *no* problem in getting a posting. Maybe I should form my own outfit. I could do so *quite* easily from the *tough men* I know out West. Oh, the Spanish will *rue* this day!"

Theodore has military skills? I thought that statement a bit too much. Rork glanced at me with a look which conveyed, "Help me with him."

I stood up and said, "Theodore, you want candor? Then here it is. Yes, a terrible war is coming, but please don't succumb to using jingoism to speed it up. Keep in mind the reality of the situation in Latin America. Atrocities? We ignore them all the time, particularly when U.S. business money is involved, even inside our closest neighbor, Mexico."

Losing the wind from his sails, Roosevelt was mute with shock. Next, I addressed his most egregious error in professional judgment. "And what the hell is this about *resigning your office?* You have the skills and insight and energy we'll sorely need when we do go to war—don't waste them playing soldier and wandering around in the Cuban jungle. I want and need you *here*, in control of our navy. Secretary Long has no clue what to do—but you do."

And now to the most intimate point. "There is a personal side to this as well. Honor has many depths, but the deepest is to one's family. You have a wife and several small children now. Your wife is upstairs and seriously ill. She needs you right here, now. How *dare* you abandon them for personal glory?"

I sat down again. "There, I've had my say . . . sir."

He sat down too, staring at me. The bravado had evaporated from him when he finally spoke. "Well, I did ask and thank you for your advice. Rork, it is true we are not yet at the point demanding naval action, and other ways can be used at this stage. Peter, yes, my wife does need me right now, as does Secretary Long. Any decision regarding my role in this war will take them into account. But there are things we in the navy can, and must, now set into motion. We *must* be prepared when the worst happens—as we know it will. The two of you are crucial to our success."

Here it comes, I thought, knowing what his next words would be. We'd already worked out the scheme of what to do when the international situation reached this point.

Theodore's right fist impacted the left hand. "It is *time* to implement our plan! I am sending you both into Cuba, effective *immediately*. We've not much time. I need those Havana *defense* plans, your study of the potential *offensive* operations area, and your general *assessment* of the situation on the island. Tomorrow morning at eight o'clock, I will write out your orders and have a *final* meeting with you. I expect you *inside* Cuba within a week. Understood?"

Rork and I echoed our acknowledgment. I stood to go, telling my young boss, "We'll get you the information, sir. Please make sure it's used wisely."

Rork and I parted ways outside the home. He flagged down a cabriolet, bound for the Navy Yard. I headed for the train station and the short trip home to Maria, who knew nothing of what was about to happen, but was fully aware of the tension in Cuba. I dreaded telling her I was leaving for an anonymous place and undetermined duration.

As he climbed aboard, Rork, who somehow knows my thoughts, quietly said, "Courage, me friend. Just remember this, she's got a heart o' oak, an' fully knew what she was gettin' into when she married the likes o' you, even though she mayn't show it tonight."

14

Mending a Broken Heart

Woodgerd Cottage
Admiral's Road
Arlington, Virginia
10 p.m., Wednesday
12 January 1898

I should have known. The signs were there, right in front of me, but my mind was in Cuba. A rudimentary marital error.

Maria had one of my favorite dinners waiting for when I walked through the door. The sweet earthy aroma of a paella Valenciana greeted me inside the cozy cottage. At the table was a bottle of Duero red wine from central Spain, with a complex and heady scent. It all transformed my attitude by the time I sat down.

So did the lady's appearance. Maria's classic beauty was set off by a simple but very flattering yellow cotton dress, her long dark hair cascading down around her shoulders in the Spanish style. I lingered over dinner, savoring the paella, the wine, the after-dinner Spanish brandy from Jérez, and the exotic lady who looked at me with such admiration. Cherishing each and every moment, I knew there would be times in the near future when these memories would be my sole connection to sanity and peace.

Finally, I summoned my courage and gave the speech I'd practiced on the train ride home. "I have news, dear. Just got orders tonight from Roosevelt, which is why I was running late. Rork and I leave tomorrow for Norfolk and out to sea. Not sure for how long, but probably not more than four months. An assessment job, like I've done a hundred times before."

Her face lost its softness. "The means you will be spying inside Cuba, does it not?"

When I first met Maria in 1892 while commanding *Bennington*, then staff duty in the mid-90s in Washington, and likewise when commanding *Newark* in recent years, I would frequently tell her humorous anecdotes from my work. Those pleasant days were a stark contrast to the current state of affairs, however.

For the past year, I'd worked on clandestine projects for Roosevelt. I didn't have many funny stories about the office, and never spoke in any detail of what I actually did. I kept my work segregated from our married life.

Maria never asked particulars. I never volunteered them. It was our *modus vivendi*, which I now attempted to maintain through ambiguity. The moment it came out, I knew I'd made a mistake.

"Not absolutely sure of what and where my duties will be, dear, except an assessment of the situation in the North Atlantic Squadron's area of responsibility. I never discuss specific duties anyway, as you are well aware."

She looked down at the dish before her. It was from her mother's set of formal china, hand painted in a classical Moorish gold leaf design. With the slightest sniffle, she traced the design with a finger, touching her family's past.

Her voice began to tremble. "You spoke to me, Peter, but you never answered my question. And did it not cross your mind to ask how I am? Or how I've been feeling lately?"

It hit me then. The entire ambience of the evening, from her attire to the china to the dinner, was classical Spanish. Maria read the newspapers, kept up with developments in Europe, Cuba, and Latin America. She corresponded with friends and family in Havana, Madrid, and Seville. She knew exactly what was going on. But it was more than a frigid January in North America, more than her missing her native culture or worrying over Spanish-Cuban politics.

She was about to cry. This was a deep personal hurt. She must have gotten more letters from her sons. They resented her decision to marry me.

"Letter from Francisco or Juanito?"

"Yes."

"With the same message? Get your marriage annulled and come home to Spain and the Church?"

She shook her head slowly, trying to stay calm. "No, Peter. They are well beyond that point. It is a letter from them both, for Juanito was transferred to Havana last month. A letter of final goodbye. They called me one of Spain's enemies, and one of the Church's enemies, and therefore, an enemy of the Maura family."

I tried to keep the anger from my voice. "May I see the letter?"

She took it from her skirt pocket. I examined the envelope and letter for forgery, but I recognized her sons' handwriting. The note was only a few blunt lines, the meaning of which could not be misinterpreted: by voluntarily joining the barbaric *norteamericano* culture, marrying into the military of Spain's foe, deciding to become a heretic from the True Faith, and after ignoring repeated pleas from her sons to return to her senses, they had come to the realization their mother had intentionally turned her back on their family, faith, and country. Above their signatures were none of the usual words of affection and hope. They had simply written "*adios*." Goodbye.

It was appallingly cruel, especially for educated modern Christian men: a Franciscan priest and a foreign ministry official.

My instinctive reaction was to hurt them for causing my wife this incredible pain.

Maria knew me well. She murmured, "Please do not do anything about this, Peter. I know you love me and want to protect me, but you cannot mend this wound. I cannot either. My sons are surrounded by political men with souls of stone. Only God has the power to change Francisco and Juanito's hearts. I will ask Him every day to bring compassion to them, and to us. They are my babies, not the enemy. Right now I need to know you love me, because you are all I have left in my life."

I calmed down. She was right. "Maria, I do love you. You saved my life when you married me, and you are everything to me. I will leave the navy tomorrow to bring you happiness and repair your broken heart, if that is what you need. Tell me."

Her tone grew determined, a certain sign her spirit was returning. "No. I do not want you to quit your work. It would bring you despair, and thus me also. This is not about you and me, Peter. It is about my sons and me."

"Your sons love you. They do, despite what you read. Their emotions overcame their wisdom and even their compassion. I am sure they are probably filled with regret."

Those indigo eyes penetrated my core as she asked, "Will they be safe when the war comes? They are good men of peace, not warriors. Peter, I will not be able to live sanely if they are harmed or killed."

I wasn't so sure about their safety. Many of the Spanish army's chaplains were Franciscan, and many of the younger government officials held reserve commissions in the army. Given the fervor common at the outbreak of war and their obvious loyalty to the Spanish cause, both sons might well volunteer their services and end up in harm's way.

But this wasn't the time for equivocation. I pulled her chair close to mine and put my arms around her. "They will be safe, Maria. You raised decent men. I am convinced someday we will all be reconciled and sitting at the same table, enjoying a meal such as this, as a family."

"I've lost my sons for now, and I am afraid I am losing my husband."

"You'll never lose me, my love." I kissed her lips softly and assured her, "I'll be back, Maria. This assignment will be over soon."

She didn't reply, but clung to me tightly. We sat there silently, until I suggested, "Come on Maria, let's get some rest."

Taking my face in her hands, she kissed me tenderly and sighed. "We have each other here tonight, Peter. We can face the world tomorrow."

15

A Man Named Rooster

Canasí, Cuba
Tuesday morning
18 January 1898

By way of a Cuban fishing smack skippered by a nasty-tempered little runt called Gallo, Rork and I sailed from Key West to Cojimar, just east of Havana. Gallo is the Spanish for "rooster," and I've known many men in Latin America who preferred it for their moniker—most of them had been criminals. Thus forewarned, I kept a close eye on Capitano Gallo and his crew. I ended up thankful I did.

Close-reaching fast with a southeast wind, we arrived a little before one in the morning on the eighteenth of January. A waning crescent moon was still large enough to highlight the lines of gentle surf rumbling along the coast. The coconut palm-shrouded village along the western side of the small cove was asleep. No sound was heard or light seen. The ancient Spanish fort on the point seemed deserted. You would never know the island was at war. Indeed, it was an idyllic vista—in any other endeavor it would be romantic. Rork, whose Gaelic background includes many superstitions, opined it a positive omen for our entry into the land of the Spanish foe.

Cojimar was not where I wanted to enter the island, for it was too close to Havana. Rork and I were remembered, and not fondly, by the authorities there, chief among them Colonel Marrón and his henchmen. But Gallo insisted, saying he had friends in the village, knew the reef well, and would go nowhere else with a load of illegal *yanquis*. Since time was of the essence and Gallo was the only Cuban fisherman at the dock in Key West, I agreed. Two hours later, we departed.

Approaching the coast, Rork did what he is uniquely equipped by size and strength to do. He scowled at the skipper and his gang, making a point of standing close beside Gallo at the roughhewn tiller. This was to let them know we weren't without the ability for revenge, should things go wrong for us.

All went well, though, and we sailed without incident into the gap in the surf line. As we prepared to climb down into the dinghy from the starboard shrouds, wearing nondescript clothing and burdened by a sea bag of our weaponry, a pouch of gold coins, a valise filled with fake business documents, and two small ditty bags of extra clothing, I spied a movement on the western horizon.

It was a low, wispy dark cloud blocking the stars. It hadn't been there seconds earlier. Soon I could see a more tangible form beneath it, and a second later, a speck of white at the bottom of the form. I knew immediately it was the bow wave of a Guardia Costa cutter, heading right for us.

I turned toward Gallo at the stern. He was watching it too, but instead of alarm, he was faintly smiling. *Not a good reaction on his part*, I realized, then wondered what or who was hidden in the shadows ashore. Before our departure, Gallo'd had more than enough time to use the Key West-Havana telegraph cable to alert the Spanish coast guard.

Rork, busy with our heaviest gear, hadn't seen any of this, so I quietly called his attention to the new developments. He had one foot lowering to the dinghy, the weapons bag already having descended.

"It's a trap, Rork. Look west about four miles. There's Guardia Costa cutter headed full speed for us. We need to take over and get out to sea."

There was no time for further discussion. I pulled my .44 caliber Merwin-Hulbert revolver with the "skull-crusher" frame, strode aft, and put the muzzle right into Gallo's sneering mouth. No longer sure of himself, his hands went straight up as I guided him down to the deck with the revolver.

Meanwhile, Rork pulled his Navy Colt and had only to growl something Irish at the three-man crew for them to get the message. They all went up and sat at the bow as he prepared the sheet lines to tack the sloop. I turned my attention to the course and helm. She went around on the tack, and I settled her on a course out to sea.

Once we were moving well, I leaned over and suggested to Gallo in Spanish that he return our money. He did so without protest, but with a quick glance to the west. I knew he was mentally gauging the interception probabilities. Normally, they would be in his favor. But one factor which he hadn't considered was our faded sails were no longer perpendicular to the cutter and easily seen. They were eased out on a broad-reach, and therefore edge-on to the cutter, making them much harder for the Spanish to see us in the night.

It's an old blockade-runner trick I learned the hard way, during the war in Florida thirty-five years earlier. Back then, I was the one on the cutter, so I knew exactly what they were now seeing, or not seeing. I imagined they thought the fishing smack had continued into the cove and would be docilely awaiting their triumphant arrival, which wouldn't be long at their speed. With the prize a pair of *yanqui* spy-filibusterers, there would be a medal in it for them, and a promotion for the commanding officer. My assessment was validated by the cutter's course, still straight for the cove.

Gallo's obvious fright deepened with his next glance westward. The cutter was approaching the cove, not heading out after us. I could well imagine his deductive processes: Gallo knew what *he* would do with useless prisoners when running for his life.

To pre-empt any desperate action on his part, I explained we would let him go—if he remained calm and did not make me nervous. Then I told Rork in English to kill them all if he even thought they were about to try something. Gallo and his crew got the gist of the order loud and clear.

The Gulf Stream flows from west to east at about three knots in that vicinity. My plan was to head north until the mountains of the coast were below the horizon and I could feel the Stream through the different wave pattern. Then we'd alter course to ride the current for thirty miles before turning south again. We'd find some small place, get ashore, make our way to the railroad line, and get out of the area by sunrise.

Behind us, the cutter entered Cojimar cove, her searchlight reflecting among the few stone buildings. A few minutes later she reappeared, stabbed her light in an arc across the sea, then headed to the west, toward Havana. Gallo looked almost grief stricken.

Several hours later we sailed into a dimple in the coast which I recognized. The tiny Canasí River runs out between two rocky headlands, and inside the shoal mouth, there is no harbor or village, only a couple of fishermen's huts with small boats on the beach. Two miles inland is the town of Canasí, a village of seven hundred farmers and a few shops, perched along the railroad line, just south of the coastal wagon road.

I woke Gallo rudely and told him we were near Escondido, which in actuality is another tiny village four miles east. Then, using a crude version of Spanish, I carefully informed him of two things he should bear in mind for a long time: Rork and I were dear friends of the famous General Gómez of the Cuban Liberation Army, who would have anyone hurting or harassing us shot immediately. But infinitely far worse, we were also brotherly friends with a unit of Gómez's black *mambi* warriors, and Gallo and his men would be dead by a thousand machete cuts, the first of which would be to his most valued parts, should anything *ever* happen to us.

Gallo understood completely, and assured me in impressive detail that the entire evening's adventure was no longer in his memory and, but of course, he had always been a supporter of freedom for Cuba, the famous Gómez, and equality for his black Cuban compatriots. Having concluded that unreliable arrangement, Rork and I got the fishing smack hove-to, commandeered her dinghy, and set off into the inky darkness.

We ran the dinghy into the rocks on the east side of the inlet, out of sight from the huts. Scrambling ashore, we were confronted by a densely wooded steep hill behind and it took a while to make the top. As the first light showed on the eastern horizon, we followed a trail along the east bank of the river, which was really little more than a shallow winding creek. Trudging at least three miles, we finally reached the railroad where it makes a sharp bend outside of the village. There, we hid in a weedy bush and supplied blood to a swarm of voracious insects. Luckily, the wait for a train was only fifteen minutes.

Our transport was a ramshackle sugar hauler of ten cars pulled westbound by an ancient locomotive puffing a prodigious trail of thick smoke. Slowed down by the curve and a wooden bridge across the creek, we had an easy time clambering aboard the next to last car and hiding ourselves inside the stack of sugar stalks. Within minutes we had succumbed to exhaustion.

So far, our plan had unraveled. That was to be expected, however. They always do.

16

The Ditch

Near Jibacoa, Cuba
Tuesday
18 January 1898

Because events were changing more rapidly than anticipated, the plan to secretly enter Cuba and make contact with our network had been formulated in *ad hoc* fashion. Secrecy was paramount. Besides Rork and me, only one other man knew the details. Agent R7 had been in my employ since 1884 and was my most trusted operative inside Cuba. The reason for my unqualified confidence in the man, a rarity in the world of spies, shall soon be apparent to the reader.

We were to meet R7 at five o'clock in the morning of January eighteenth under the railroad bridge where it crosses the third culvert east of Jibacoa, a peasant village of thatched huts, which turned out to be about six miles west of where we had gotten aboard the train. It would have been relatively easy if we'd been ashore earlier, but as things turned out, we weren't.

Having missed the initial rendezvous time, we resolved to hide out until the secondary meeting time, eleven o'clock that very evening, in the palm grove on the northwest side of the intersection where the Aguacate-Santa Cruz Road crosses the tracks just west of Jibacoa. This required disembarking the train before it arrived in the village, where I assumed the train cars would be unloaded at the regional sugar mill.

We rolled off the cane car as it slowed on a bend east of Jibacoa, and struck out across the farm country for a two-mile hike around the town, keeping to the hedge rows of bamboo and areca palms which divided up the muddy fields. It was slow going in the soft ooze. We reached the place I had in mind near noon, a woefully bedraggled pair of sailors. Once there, we collapsed under palmetto bushes along a drainage ditch at a spot a quarter mile from the rendezvous location, yet close enough to observe any troops arriving prior to the meeting. Fully expecting a crocodile to protest our incursion into its swampy domain, I took the first watch as Rork, who has the enviable ability to nod off anywhere, anytime, snored softly.

When nightfall arrived, we set out from our lair and crept around the perimeter of the area, trying to ascertain the lay of the land and where any possible foes might conceal themselves. There were three threats which could prove fatal to us.

The first was the pro-Spanish local Volunteers (*Los Voluntarios*, sometimes known as *Los Guerrillas*), a militia which roamed the night looking for anyone out of place, the penalty being non-judicial execution, as they say in an American court of law, otherwise known as lynching. Frequently, their morale is fortified by copious amounts of rum before heading out for evening patrol, thus lowering their reasoning or common decency. You could not talk your way out of a confrontation with these fellows.

The second hazard, equally perilous, was encountering grim-faced pro-independence Cuban insurgents (*Los Insurrectos*), peasants who could only dream of getting enough money for a proper drunk like their enemies did—*insurrectos* were paid haphazardly, if at all. These fellows waited in the night for Spanish army or pro-Spanish volunteer columns to walk into an ambuscade. They didn't lynch, they decapitated with a machete.

Our final worry was the regular Spanish Army. They were well armed and led by gentlemen, mostly. But many of their rank and file were reluctant conscripts from Spain, and they seldom left the barracks at night. The nearest one of those was five miles away at Santa Cruz on the coast.

Based upon what I'd seen of the area so far, I assumed there probably would not be much traffic on the road that night. I was wrong.

No fewer than three noisy *voluntario* units, two far more stealthy *insurrecto* groups, along with various farmers with cane knives stuck in their rope belts, ended up stimulating us seven times into hiding further inside the bug-infested jungle. The seemingly desolate countryside was teeming with armed men!

I am embarrassed to report they were not the only impediment to our progress. We also got slightly lost, for the map I carried didn't have a lot of detail. In addition, recognizable landmarks were few and hard to discern in the starlight before moonrise, and our impromptu detours avoiding detection only complicated my task. Eleven o'clock arrived, but our precise location was still undefined, a failure which lay squarely upon me. Although, in fairness, I did have it narrowed down to somewhere within a mile. Or so I thought.

Since both of us were getting a bit cranky, I ventured a whispered morale-building comment for the benefit of the sole member of my crew. "Well, we're late, but don't worry. Our man will wait for an hour. Now that we've thoroughly confused the enemy as to our position, it's time to find R7."

Such quips had worked in Africa, Indochina, and South America, when we found ourselves in the heart of enemy territory and surrounded by people determined to kill us. But this time Rork was not at all amused and let me know it.

"Methinks we're well an' truly buggered in this friggin' hellhole o' an island! We should've killed them piratical scum in that boat before leaving it. Now this mess. Not lookin' good at all. Maybe we're just too damned old for this stuff anymore. Me own solution is to call a spade a spade, steal some rum an' a boat, an' head back to Key West afore the next disaster hits."

Loath to give up the humorous high ground, I quietly countered with a quaint old Cuban saying that usually got a laugh out of him. "Ah, but Rork, remember, in Cuba, for every solution, including yours, there are a hundred problems. Maybe a thousand, these days. No, it's too early to quit now. We'll keep looking for our man for another hour. If by then it's no go, we'll head southerly, away from the coast, until dawn. Then we'll head east toward our other contact at Sagua."

"Bloody friggin' hell," was his reply.

Sometimes, insubordination is a matter of viewpoint. I decided to ignore his comment. After another ten minutes of walking along a dirt trail, we found the railroad track and turned east, searching for the main road crossing. Just as I vaguely saw it ahead, we heard the crack of a twig snapping ahead of us and to the left of the track bed.

It was loud, as in a man's boot breaking a thick twig. Not good. *Insurrectos*, our ostensible allies if we were given enough time to prove our identity, were too poor to have boots. They also were masters of silent stalking and walked carefully. My guess was unsettling: *voluntarios*.

We both instinctually dove into the ditch on the right, where some tall weeds gave some concealment. Normally, our movement would be a good idea. Most men are right-handed and their shots frequently wander to the right of their target. Thus we would be to the left of where their rounds would impact.

A solid volley of gunshots roared out, but not from the other side of the track, where the twig cracked. The blaze of gunfire came from our side, right down the line of the ditch ahead of us. I registered it wasn't the deep booms of the older rifles and shotguns carried by the *voluntarios*. No, they were the high-pitched cracks of Mauser rifles.

That meant our opponents were regular Spanish army troops. This wasn't some unmotivated draftee outfit either. They were out patrolling at night, responding to quiet commands, and aggressively filling the dead ground with bullets. The twig had been a decoy, and their rounds were most definitely *not* wandering to the right—they were incredibly accurate, scything the air within inches above us. We pawed down into the slimy mud.

"Where's the Extra?" I yelled to Rork, referring to a special dynamite explosive I'd insisted on bringing with us.

"In the bloody sea bag right next to you."

I frantically searched our sea bag. After what seemed an eternity, I found what I wanted at the very bottom.

Another volley blasted down the ditch toward us, the bullets zipping like bees. One thudded into the sea bag. Another severed a cane stalk next to my face. The flashes were at ground level and I realized how they had targeted us so effectively—the Spanish had lain low as we approached them, silhouetted nicely against the moonlit horizon. "Damn it all to hell, those bloody bastards've nicked me arse!" I heard beside me.

We hadn't returned fire yet and the Spanish would rush us any second. We had to get out of the ditch.

"Dammit Rork, can't you be a little quieter when you're shot? And I need a match for the Extra. I seem to be out."

"Cor blimey, how in hell can you be without a bleedin' match to light the dynamite? Here." There was the sound of a scratch but no flame. "Friggin' thing's wet as a diaper." Another scratch, and a whoosh. "Here, this one's workin' fine. Hand me the damned stick."

I heard an officer calmly order some soldiers to circle our right flank. We were getting boxed in against the railroad bed. Handing the stick of dynamite to Rork, I soon heard a sizzling fuse.

"Hand it back. I'm a better pitcher," I said, which he did.

"Run to the right when it goes off," I added, closing my eyes at the final moment to preserve my night vision. "And keep running!"

The explosion went off above the ground where the Spanish officer's voice had been, about sixty feet away from us. A solid mass of searing hot air slammed into me. I jumped up, put the sea bag to my shoulder, and ran out of the ditch and away from the tracks, Rork loping along next to me. No reaction came from the Spanish at first, then stray shots began to ring out.

We ran until we could run no more and dropped gasping into another drainage ditch. I was now hopelessly lost—somewhere north or east of the main tracks was all I knew. Neither of us spoke for some time. We couldn't get enough air to form words.

"Welcome back to hell, me boyo," croaked Rork after a while. "Cuba's just too bloody much fun, ain't it?" Another gasp. "Oh Lord, me bones're far too old for this sort o' thing anymore. An' me arse is still bleedin'—there's no artery there, right?"

"Not an important one. It'll stop when we rest. By next week your arse'll be fine."

We were looking for a place to stretch out when I heard the baying of a hound from behind us. Two more dogs joined in.

"This isn't getting any easier. Those're bloodhounds, Rork. Let's go."

Rork groaned again. "Ah, hell. Let's just sit here an' shoot the whole damned lot o' `em, an' then ourselves."

I was about to explain the folly of that idea when the bushes rustled to our left and a voice called out in French-accented English. "Good morning, my sons. May I offer you a ride?"

I spun around with my revolver leveled, but didn't fire.

It was R7.

17

Too Much Fun

Near Jibacoa, Cuba
Tuesday evening
18 January 1898

In my shock, I blurted out, "Jacques Lizambard, you beautiful old son of a bitch!"

"Now Peter," he answered with mock severity. "Is that any way to address a well-respected septuagenarian Jesuit priest? Especially from an officer and gentleman such as you, named after one of our most beloved saints."

Rork leaned over and shook the priest's hand. "Aye, Father Jacques, we shan't expect much at all from me boyo here. He's a heathen heretic o' the worst sort—a Methodist, o' all things. Will ye please pardon a good Catholic lad such as meself, the sin o' associatin' with the likes o' `im?"

"Asked and done, Sean. But you really should get Peter on our team. I think he'd be happier."

The hounds bayed again, this time far more excitedly, and much closer. I estimated a hundred yards, at the most.

"Can we postpone this religious discussion to another time, gentlemen. Jacques, you said something about a ride?"

"Of course, Peter. My carriage is right over there." He pointed fifty feet away, where a landau with two horses waited in the moon shadows cast by some trees. We ran to it.

I couldn't believe what I saw when we got close. The landau was parked in a palm grove, adjacent to the main Aguacate-Santa Cruz road where it crossed the tracks. There was even a large sign post for the locomotive driver. I must have led Rork within a hundred feet of it and still missed the rendezvous point.

Someone shouted an order and the dogs were released, the baying mixed with growling. A gunshot cracked toward us. Then another.

"He was here the whole time? Bloody damned friggin' hell . . ." grumbled Rork as we climbed aboard and got under way. "You're gettin' daft as a donkey, Peter."

"Sorry, Rork," was all I could think to say as the carriage accelerated away from the scene. Jacques seemed amused by the entire experience. Ignoring the mortal chaos behind us, he quipped, "We all make mistakes, Peter. Did I ever tell you about the time I accidently shot the bishop of Santa Fe during a bird hunt? I think we have time, because we've a long way to go."

As we hurdled down the faintly moonlit road, Jacques proceeded to regale us with his self-deprecating tale of peppering a bishop with birdshot, and the ensuing transfer to a small church in the jungles of the Philippines. As we held on during the bumpy ride, I thought about our remarkable rescuer, a very unlikely spy.

Father Jacques Lizambard, originally of Bordeaux in France, had been a priest of the Society of Jesus, the Jesuits, for a long time. He was a tall thin man, still in good physique at seventy-one years of age. The lined face was ruggedly handsome, framed by thick snow-white hair and a thin goatee and mustache, with eyes tinged by a latent sadness. A life in the more perilous parts of the Catholic world had produced a sense of perspective about danger, and calm in the face of death. Extracting us from the clutches of the Spanish Army did not even rise to the level of worry for Lizambard. He'd been through far closer calls.

With a suave Continental charm to match his looks, Father Jacques was a frequent dinner guest among the Cuban, Spanish, and foreign elite in Matanzas. Fluent in Italian, Spanish, English, and French, not to mention classical Latin, Greek, and Hebrew, like all Jesuits he was highly educated and could hold his own in conversation with any academic, theologian, politician, or mogul.

After a lifetime of dedicated service around the globe, he'd found a final home in Cuba, the climate of which was beneficial for his increasing rheumatism. The culture was agreeable to his tastes and his devotion to the people of the island and their eventual freedom was genuine. That was why he agreed to help me and became Agent R7 fifteen years earlier. His role in my Cuban network was facilitator of transport and information, never anything lethal.

Naturally, women inwardly lamented Lizambard's life choice, but clearly loved to be around him. So would Theodore Roosevelt, I estimated. The two of them could have long discussions on flora and fauna, for Jacques was a teacher of biology at the university, and specialized in tropical birdlife. The priest would be utterly fascinated by Theodore's dead animal zoo at Sagamore Hill. They would have, as Theodore likes to say, a *bully* of a good time together.

Jacque and I first met when he worked for Father Benito Viñes, a mutual friend who taught astronomy and meteorology at the Belem University in Havana. Two years later, Rork and I were on the run from Colonel Marrón, following a quite chancy operation which had completely fallen apart. Benito helped us escape the island. Jacques had assisted.

Since then, Jacques and I corresponded regularly. From the beginning, it was more than an acquaintanceship. Occasionally, we shared information pertinent to our interests and needs, which every now and then converged. The information he gained went to Rome. Mine went to Washington. It was "an unlikely symbiotic relationship," to use his scientific description.

Sometimes this was accomplished via coded messages in cables or letters, sometimes in person at the bar of the Victoria Hotel in Nassau. He preferred the latter, it being far more enjoyable, and the evening would go late indeed. Meeting Jacques in Nassau was always a considerable burden on my expense account, but it frequently yielded substantial intelligence of Spanish and Cuban activities. One of his gems was that he knew the names of all the disgruntled girlfriends of the married Spanish authorities in Havana and Matanzas.

There was yet another aspect to Father Lizambard. Though he was outwardly obedient to the official political position of the Church that Cuba should stay in the Spanish Empire, I knew his personal leanings. Jacques was quietly in favor of the Cuban rebels' cause of freedom.

Unlike most of my other agents, money never changed hands between Jacques and me. Our exchange of information and assistance was a matter of mutual professional courtesy. Among spies, it is the best kind of bond.

18

Blue Mold and Black Shank

Sagua Grande, Cuba
Wednesday
19 January 1898

It was very a long ride, done mainly on the coastal road, sometimes known as the King's Highway. Several civil guard or *voluntario* roadblocks were encountered en route, but Father Jacques was always waved through when they saw his collar and cross, for the Church and the Crown were intertwined. Senior Jesuits were almost untouchable and Jacques was the well-known rector of Jesuits in Matanzas. Exchanging horses at several churches and small liveries along the way, we arrived the next morning, Wednesday, at a rural monastery.

Once there, we were cared for by the resident Franciscans who, after a closed-door conference with Father Jacques, never asked our names, nationalities, or the reason for our odd accoutrements. I expected sullen hostility, but was wrong. Quite the contrary, they were quite pleasant. Rork's embarrassing flesh wound was treated. Our bodies and attitudes were rejuvenated by decent food and wine, served by smiling monks who quietly padded around the place. Only the head fellow actually spoke to us. The others were observing a period of contemplative silence.

Most importantly of all, Rork and I got total rest in real beds. It was nothing short of heaven on earth.

The monastery was in the province of Santa Clara and located near Sagua Grande, over 150 miles east of where Jacques had rescued us. This was fortunate for our mission, because Sagua Grande was where I was to meet my next agent, R94, who held an important nexus in the espionage network. It was Jacques, in fact, who had brought R94 into the fold, back in November, recognizing the potential benefit of the man's occupation and political leanings.

At eight o'clock the next morning, our recuperation ended and Jacques, Rork, and I were back in his landau, heading for a tavern in the center of town. There we would meet R94.

Rork and I were clad in middle-class attire appropriate to our new roles. I was a Canadian tobacco broker of Danish heritage named Peder Fisker, and he was an Irish shipping broker named Patrick Clooney. We had the identity documents, business papers, and belongings to prove ourselves to any inquiring policeman. Our sea bag of weapons, both long and short, was padlocked and labeled "hockey sticks—McGill University—Montreal." The label was my idea, which I thought rather inspired. Our revolvers were under our coats and ready for use. Our excuse for possessing them was "to ward off the notorious rebel bandits of Cuba."

During our ride into Sagua Grande, a town of fourteen thousand, I asked Jacques for a briefing on how the war had affected the local area. He reported most of the sugar plantations, and nearly all the sugar grinding mills, had been destroyed by General Gómez's forces. The tobacco plantations had fared slightly better, some being owned by Americans and Germans who paid "taxes" to the Cuban army. Much of the livestock everywhere was dead, taken for food or transport by both armies. Many of the countryside peasants had gone over to the Free Cuban side—that way they could find something to eat. In summary, the area was devastated financially and commercially.

A major military factor in the area was the *trocha*, or north-south barrier line of Spanish fortifications extending from the Caribbean southern coast to the Straits of Florida on the northern coast. There were several *trochas* across Cuba, each one a theoretical wall beyond which the Cuban rebels could not pass. In reality, they were traversed by small Cuban units frequently. Still, I recognized them as a military obstacle to be reckoned with in any war.

We entered the town, which immediately impressed me by its layout, much more orderly and city-like than most towns in Cuba. The streets were wide, with modern sidewalks and solid-looking buildings. But you could tell it had seen better times, for the avenues and buildings were mostly deserted. Paint was peeling. Trash lay in piles. Vehicular traffic was sparse, with few carriages in the class of ours.

The tavern, which lacked a name on the front, was emblematic of the forlorn atmosphere. The place was falling apart, with wide gaps in the boards of the walls and a front door barely attached by one hinge. It was located on a side street down by a railroad bridge across the eighty-foot-wide Sagua Grande River, a grandiose title for the sluggish stream I saw. I asked Jacques for details about the river, couching my inquiry in a bored tone to hide the fact it might be of vital importance.

He said it made its way ten miles north to the coast, where there was a little village called Isabela on the west side of the mouth. Jacques shook his head when explaining the village, saying it was a nondescript collection of structures on pilings along the edge of a swamp, populated by mostly rough lower-class types who were known for their "aversion to societal norms." I asked for clarification.

"They are mostly drunks, prostitutes, and thieves. A modern day Sodom and Gomorrah in Cuba. Very bad place."

But, he announced, Isabela did have a significant attribute. There was a wharf, used by medium-sized cargo ships of less than a thousand tons. A twenty-foot-deep ship channel meandered south from the Straits of Florida, through the coastal mangrove islands, across a bay to the Isabela docks. Sugar and tobacco were the main cargos out, coal and manufactured goods were the primary import. Alongside the well-used road between Isabela and Sagua Grande was a parallel railway line. Just south of Sagua Grande, it connected to the main railway and thus cargo could go to and from the interior. In the last three years of war, however, the docks and railway had been little used.

The tavern was empty of patrons when we walked in. A woman of indeterminate age, and in serious need of a shave, was desultorily cleaning bar glasses. We waited for her welcome, but none came. She did pause to swat some large purple flies on the wall, after which she wiped her nose on the cleaning rag, which then was used for more glasses.

I had been a bit thirsty until I saw that. Rork, who is not known for being picky on the subject of female company, looked at her and winced, suggesting breakfast at an abattoir might be more appealing.

"Please remember we are all God's children, Sean," admonished Father Jacques, who then nodded ruefully and quietly added, "I do see your point, though."

The woman grunted something unintelligible and gestured to a table near the back corner. When we sat down, Father Jacques tried to take the social high road, flashing his best smile at her, but it didn't work. She glowered at him and grunted another phrase, which I believe was something about breakfast. Irked by his rare failure at charming one of God's children, Jacques curtly acknowledged her and held up four fingers. She grunted something else, sounding none too pleased.

"Obviously not a good Catholic," he muttered to the floor. Rork soberly nodded his concurrence. I tried not to laugh, more than a little afraid of her.

Agent R94 arrived a few minutes later. From Jacques's cables, I knew the basics about him. Raul Gonzart was the twenty-five-year-old son of a Cuban widow who recently married the elderly German owner of a small tobacco farm. Gonzart had been to school and spoke English fairly well. He was a quiet supporter of the *insurrectos* and had the important post of senior telegraphist at the post office in Sagua Grande. Even more important for my purposes, he sometimes worked at, and always had access to, the telegraph station at nearby Santo Domingo, which was where the cable lines from both north and south coasts intersected the main line from Santa Clara to Havana.

What I did *not* know prior to seeing him in the doorway was his appearance. Six-foot-five, as big as Rork, he had the face of a boy years younger than his true age. Misgivings began to percolate in my mind, for Roosevelt and I had made big plans for Agent R94.

In Cuba, the Spanish post office administered the mail, the telephone system, and the telegraph system. Thus, they were in a perfect position to monitor all forms of communication to and from everyone on the island—a very effective tool for the secret police.

And therein lay an opportunity. If I could get a man on the inside of their post office telegraph system, as I knew the Cuban rebels already had done all over the island, I could read the Spanish government and military messages. Jacques understood that as well and had cultivated Gonzart carefully before recommending him for our organization. R94 became our man inside the Spanish communications system of Cuba.

Gonzart smiled shyly and sat down. His manner did not inspire confidence. Then, in a pleasant but slightly squeaky voice loud enough for the barkeeper and anyone else nearby to hear, he said, "Welcome to Sagua, Mr. Fisker. Father Lizambard here told me he heard you were looking for quality wrapper leaf for cigars. Our farm has an excellent crop of *corojo* leaf growing this year, twenty hectares worth. I am glad you came all the way from Santa Clara to see them. My stepfather does not speak English so he sent me. I can answer any questions you have."

"Any sign of blue mold or black shank disease in your fields?" I asked in an equally loud tone, trying to sound knowledgeable while hoping no detailed debate would ensue. I am not a smoker and knew only some rudimentary information hurriedly gleaned from an encyclopedia in the Navy Library. I had not a notion as to what those diseases looked like or did to a plant, or what the hell a *corojo* leaf was.

"Absolutely none!" the young man proclaimed. "We protect our plants very carefully at Stahl farm. After our meal, I can show you."

He was equally pleasant during the rest of the conversation, which was on tobacco prices, as we forced down a truly wretched breakfast of unrecognizable ingredients, purported to be rice, beans, and some part of a chicken. When we finished as much as we could, I reluctantly paid the woman good money for the mess, only because it was in keeping with my façade as a commercialist.

Once back in the landau, we headed north out of town, ostensibly to inspect tobacco plants at Stahl farm, but actually to inspect the docks at Isabela. It began as a quiet drive with polite discussion about the farm and Mr. Stahl, but once past the outer perimeter of the town, our young man changed his character.

That was when the real Raul Gonzart appeared.

19

A Little Complication

Isabela, Cuba
Thursday morning
20 January 1898

Gonzart's eyes shed the youthful innocence of the past hour and narrowed in on me. His tone was now clipped and pure business, like a Boston shipping baron. The change was disconcerting, and I studied him carefully as he spoke.

"Enough of stupid tobacco talk, Mr. Fisker. You obviously know nothing about the subject. My advice is to not to speak about it with any Cuban in the future. I have also heard that a suspected *yanqui* gunrunner was cornered in a cane field by a Spanish patrol west of here a couple nights ago, but somehow got away. I presume that was your bungled entry into the island. Not an impressive performance so far. I further presume you asked for this rendezvous, which might imperil all of us, for a serious reason. What is it?"

Father Jacques grinned at me. Rork glared at Gonzart.

"I appreciate the candor, Mr. Gonzart," I countered, with new respect. He was smarter than he allowed others to perceive, a valuable attribute in a spy. Ignoring his negative assessment of my efforts so far, I said, "Yes, there is a serious reason for this personal meeting, but you don't get to know it. I am in charge, not you. Instead, you will give me the information I pay you to provide. Now, what is the disposition of the Spanish forces, army and navy, in this specific coastal area? Start with the navy."

My rebuke didn't startle him at all. He thought for a moment, before reciting a detailed report. "The Spanish Navy has the following ships at Isabela. The *Lealtad* is a newly built 30-ton patrol boat with a machine gun, under command of Lt. Chereguini. It can go ten knots, has eight crewmen, and needs just under two meters of water to float. The *Mayari* is a 40-ton, 20-meter-long, 12-knot gunboat built two years ago. It needs over two meters to float, carries thirteen men, and has one 42-millimeter gun in the bow and a 37-millimeter Maxim gun in the stern. Lt. Lisarregui is in command. He is senior to Chereguini. The two boats patrol the coast for ten leagues both east and west of here. Their dock is the small one south of the ship docks. Usually, one of the boats is at the dock when the other is on patrol."

"What about those two officers? Have you met them? Age, experience, temperament?"

Gonzart didn't hesitate. Either he was a very good liar—entirely possible in wartime Cuba—or he knew his subject extremely well.

"I have met and conversed with them, when they were at social events in Sagua. They are both from Spain, have about ten years of service, and are professional in their deportment. Chereguini is slightly younger than Lisarregui. Both would like to be assigned on a more prestigious ship in the oceangoing fleet."

"Any other naval vessels on this coast?"

"Yes. At Cárdenas, there are three gunboats and a tugboat. The three gunboats are the same design, 43 tons and 23 meters long, and built three years ago in Britain for the Spanish. They are named *Alerta*, under Lt. Pasquin; *Ligera*, under Lt. Perez; and *Ardilla*, under Lt. Bauza. Each needs two meters to float, can go eleven knots, and has thirteen men. The guns are the same as for *Mayari*. The lieutenants and their gunboats have been in Cuba for two years. I have not met them and do not know of their personalities or experience."

"And the tug?"

"It is 68 tons, about thirty meters long, named the *Antonio Lopez* and was originally built in . . ." Gonzart paused in his recitation, then proceeded slowly, "Phi-la-del-phi-a, in Penn-syl-va-ni-a, in 1883. I do not know how much water it needs to float or how many men it carries. I do know it can go ten knots and has bigger guns than the other boats—one 57-millimeter Hotchkiss rapid-firing gun on the bow and a 37-millimeter Nordenfelt gun on the stern. It is commanded by Lt. Montes, who is senior to other naval officers on this part of the coast. I do not know him."

"Are you certain of everything you just told me? There are no other Spanish patrol or gunboats between Cárdenas to the west and the Cayos Romanos to the east?"

"Yes, I am certain of the facts I have stated. For two months I have been asking quietly about the navy boats at Cárdenas, and I have personally seen the ones at Isabela. There are no more gunboats stationed on this section of the coast."

I was impressed by his phenomenal memorization, but wasn't going to say so yet. I pressed him further. "Where are the coal supplies for the navy boats? What is the condition of the ship channel, from the open sea through the islands and into Isabela?"

"A small amount of coal is kept here. A bigger amount is kept at Cárdenas and also at Nuevitas, much farther to the east. As for the channel, I have heard it has markers along the way and is six meters deep. I have never been on a boat in that channel."

This entire time we'd seen no vehicles on the road and no train on the tracks beside it. One little Negro boy was the sole pedestrian. Ahead of us, I could see the tops of some buildings begin to show through the mangrove trees. We were nearing Isabela. I needed to conclude the interview soon.

"What about the Spanish Army in this area? Tell me about their units and commanders. Start with the senior commander."

Gonzart's reply was matter of fact, but hatred began showing in his eyes. "Colonel Arce commands the area around Sagua Grande. At Olayita Plantation two years ago, the men of his *voluntario* battalion murdered the plantation manager, Braulio Duarte, a respected Frenchman, by hacking him to death as he stood wrapped in the French flag. Then they burned all the buildings and slaughtered twenty-three innocent women and children who were staying there under Duarte's protection. The bodies, some still alive, were thrown into the flames. A Chinese laborer was the only survivor. He escaped with six Mauser holes in him and told me what happened."

"God bless their souls," intoned Jacques. "And bring justice to their tormentors."

"Arce was there?" I asked.

"He was in personal command at the scene."

That explained a lot. I guessed at the rest. "One of those victims was your friend?"

"My fiancé." He said it without tears. He was past them. That was good, because he would need to be rational and calculating when the war came. Or to be more accurate, I should say when the U.S. got into the war which had long been raging. My demands on him would be increased.

My daughter Useppa had lost her Cuban fiancé, ironically also named Raul, to a Spanish agent's bullet at Key West. I could well imagine Gonzart's pain. "I am very sorry for your loss, Raul, but we must continue with the briefing. What of the other senior Spanish Army officers in the area?"

"Colonel Carrem also commands a *voluntario* battalion. He is similar to Arce in personality and works with him. Colonel Carrera is in the area from time to time. I do not know him. Colonel Velasco is well respected, a man of honor. He commands a regular infantry regiment near Santa Clara which comes this way now and then, but does not kill innocent civilians. We call the innocents *pacificos*. Those are the colonels. There are no Spanish generals here."

"What about Spanish Army units defending Isabela?"

"None are assigned to Isabela permanently. They are fighting the Cubans in the interior, not defending small villages on the coast."

We were approaching the outer shacks of Isabela village. No one greeted us. Most stared with open mistrust at the three men in the expensive landau. Some had more devious gazes, as if estimating their chances of stealing the vehicle and robbing the occupants.

"You can now see what I mean about this place," said Jacques. "Evil is here."

"And what about the Cuban forces and leaders?" I asked Gonzart.

"Brigadier General José Francisco Lacret is senior commander. He reports to General Gómez, the supreme commander. Lacret is about forty-nine, esteemed by his men and the civilians. He was wounded in the foot back in `76 during the early years of our struggle for independence. It never healed well, so he walks with a bad limp. He speaks English. Oh, yes . . . I remember hearing that he married a Cuban lady in Key West fifteen years ago. I do not know where she lives at this time, maybe back there."

"The other Cuban officers?"

"Major Borde is chief of staff and very smart, also fluent in English. I think he was a lawyer and lived in the United States for a couple of years. Major Quentino Bandera is a black man in his sixties, and commands a battalion of four hundred men. He was born a slave and is famous among the Cuban people, especially the *mambises*, the peasant warriors, for being very fearless. He is the most successful commander against the Spanish in this area and the enemy soldiers fear him. He makes the Spaniard, Colonel Arce, look like a fool, which is not difficult. Arce hates Bandera and was looking for him when he went to Olayita and committed the massacre. Recently, I heard Bandera is being promoted to lieutenant colonel by General Gómez."

"Sounds like me own sort o' lad," opined Rork. "Bet he fancies a tot o' rum every once in a while, too. I could surely use one right about now."

"I believe he was a disciple of the great 'Bronze Titan,' General Antonio Maceo," said Jacques. Gonzart made no comment.

Guessing what his answer would be, I asked, "How long have you been a member of the Cuban Liberation Army, Raul? You are a lieutenant on the staff, probably under Major Borde, correct?"

I checked Jacques' reaction to my question, which also was what I expected—bland. He'd never told me R94 was in the rebel army, but it was now obvious. Gonzart knew too much about too many senior officers. Equally clear was that he was the Cuban agent inside American intelligence. It bothered me Jacques had left out a lot when briefing me about his protégé. What else was there about the young Cuban I should know? And correspondingly salient, what had Gonzart learned from *me* which he could pass along to Borde and Lacret?

He made no attempt to deny or disguise his affiliation. "Yes. I have been a staff lieutenant under Major Borde for two years."

Since the massacre at Olayita, I noted inwardly before asking another question. "And therefore, all of the communications between us in the past, and those we may have in the future, will be repeated to the Cuban Liberation Army?"

Gonzart's eyes showed no emotion. "Of course. You need us as allies, no?"

I cast an accusatory glance at Father Jacques, who adopted a kindly pastoral manner. "Now do not be angry, Peter. After all, we are all on the same side—peace and freedom for the Cuban people. This is only a little complication, my son. In God's greater plan of things, it is a minor detail."

20

Reconnaissance Among Pirates

Isabela, Cuba
Thursday
20 January 1898

The village of Isabela was even tinier than I imagined from the reports and charts I'd perused in my office at headquarters. The community is perched along a 250-foot-wide mangrove peninsula which juts out of the coastline northward for a quarter mile into a large bay. The eastern side of this peninsula is bordered by the mouth of the Sagua River, and the western side faces the open water of the bay. The northern perimeter of the bay is composed of more mangrove and scrub-covered islands forming a barrier to the open ocean beyond. In no more than one minute, we travelled the entire length of the village and stopped at the docks on the western side.

Gonzart switched back to his public persona and smiled broadly as he swept his hand over the view. "And this is where your ships can load our tobacco, Mr. Fisker. This place is much easier and faster than Matanzas or Havana. Combined with our good prices and quality leaf, it makes a powerful argument for you to buy from us for your Canadian customers."

Following Gonzart's gesture, I saw before us two wooden wharves in need of serious repair. The railroad tracks from Sagua split into two sidings which led onto each wharf. One of the wharves was large enough to berth a moderate-sized ship. I saw no large coal pile or loading derricks. Clearly, Isabela was seldom used by steamers.

On both sides of the only road were crudely thatched shacks on stilts, many out over the shallows with long planks connecting them to shore. To the north, across the vast bay surrounded by mangrove islands, I saw a ragged line of confusing marker posts delineating a channel. It headed for a gap between two dark green islands in the distance.

"That is the Maravillas Channel, Mr. Fisker," my Cuban companion explained. "The island it passes in the bay is Cayo Paloma, and those two out there are De La Cruz and Maravillas islands. Beyond them is the ocean. And thirty miles out in the ocean are the Anguila Keys of the Bahama Islands, your fellow subjects of the beautiful Queen Victoria!"

I dutifully nodded at his reference to the 79-year-old monarch, who was anything but beautiful, but my eyes and mind were on that channel, which was bottle-necked between the two islands. When I'd examined the chart in Washington, it appeared there'd be more room to maneuver. But seeing it in person, I realized it would be damn near impossible to get through that channel in the dark under enemy fire.

Even a light field-gun set up in the village, if skillfully employed, could delay an invasion force long enough for Spanish reinforcements to arrive. Surprise and speed would be crucial in my plan. Anything that hindered them had to be eliminated.

The tactical subject reminded me of another factor and I surveyed the shoreline to the left of the docks. Just like Gonzart had explained, the *Mayari*, the larger of the two small Spanish gunboats stationed at Isabela, was moored to a dilapidated jetty alone. Evidently, *Lealtad* was out on patrol. There was no naval depot, only a small office shack.

No officer or petty officer was in sight. Two young sailors were lounging on deck, pretending to do rope work. We were too far away to gauge the state of readiness of her guns, but the general appearance of the vessel was good. In these waters, where a shallow draft gunboat could dart among the islands, she was a very dangerous foe.

"You are a convincing salesman, Mr. Gonzart," I said to my companion and the audience of piratical-looking ne'er-do-wells who had gathered around us. "I will be in contact with you, but now I must return to Sagua Grande so I can make the train for Caibarién. I'm expected there for a business dinner later tonight."

Needless to say, I had no intention of going on a sixty-mile rail journey to the east for dinner. It was just another false trail laid for the confusion of the enemy, who surely had informants among our spectators. Under my breath, I added, "I will need to meet with General Lacret, in about four days' time, if possible. Can it be arranged?"

"No problem, Mr. Fisker," Gonzart announced in his stage voice. "My stepfather will be pleased to meet you when you return from Caibarién."

The ten-mile trip back to Sagua Grande was done in contemplative silence, each man having a lot to think about. We stopped down by the river, a block from the post office. Gonzart wandered off to his desk to check for telegraph messages.

He returned with a telegraph message form. As I expected, it was a short message in a simple two-time substitution code from Roosevelt personally, sent that very morning. Rork and I walked over to the river bank with the telegram. Theodore used the alias CAGED. It was addressed to an alias he'd chosen for me, BLUEBIRD—ornithological humor of the Rooseveltian kind. It read:

XXX—BOARD SAYS NO TO BANK—XX—YES TO MINER AS SOON AS THEO SAYS YEA—XX—IF DEAL

LOOKS GOOD STAY AND WORK ON CUSTOMERS—XX—NO OFFER FROM WILSON—XX—CHECK ON WHY—XX—MINER HAS YOUR FUNDS—XXX

This was nothing unforeseen by me: the president (BOARD) was continuing to resist calls for war (BANK), but he was finally sending the *Maine* (MINER) to Havana, once he got permission of the Spanish government (THEO). Rork and I were to reconnoiter the potential invasion site at Isabela (DEAL) and continue preparing our espionage network (CUSTOMERS). Our agent in Havana (WILSON), whom we had taken great pains to cultivate and keep safe, hadn't sent the defense plans (OFFER) which were expected by then, and we were to go and find out why. The final line said Captain Sigsbee of the *Maine* would have Roosevelt's next message (FUNDS) for me, so I was to meet with him, too.

I uttered an elongated and vivid curse, something I try not to do often in my older years, which caused Rork to glance worriedly at me. I handed him the message. Seconds later, he echoed my reaction.

We had to get to Havana, find our wayward agent, get the Spanish plans, and meet with Sigsbee—all of which I had previously told Roosevelt was far too dangerous. The city was crawling with informers, counterintelligence agents, vigilante militias, policemen, soldiers, and revolutionaries. Rork and I were known by the Spanish, in particular, Marrón.

But Theodore, for some reason unknown to us, was clearly desperate and had ordered it done, so that was that.

"Any reply?" asked Gonzart when we returned to the landau.

"Yes. Please send this today." I wrote it out on a piece of scrap paper.

XXX—DEAL LOOKS GOOD—XX—WILL SEE MINER—XXX

Before we went to Havana, our work at Sagua had to be completed. Rork and I checked into the Grand Hotel at Sagua, using our aliases of Fisker and Clooney. For the next four days, Rork stayed mainly in the room, guarding our equipment while pretending to do accounting work on tobacco offers. I roamed the countryside with Lizambard and Gonzart, visiting tobacco and sugar plantations, carefully examining leaves and getting prices. In actuality, I was evaluating the terrain, railways, roads, telegraph cables, telephone lines, Spanish army garrisons, bridges, the militia units we encountered, and most important of all, the attitude of the inhabitants.

My conclusion was the area was not optimal for a largescale invasion force from a logistical point of view, but few places in Cuba were. It was certainly doable, though, with decisive commanders and the aforementioned surprise and speed at the outset.

A brigade-sized force—four infantry regiments, one cavalry, and one of artillery—could be landed at Isabela within the first forty-eight hours, if the ships were properly loaded and organized beforehand. By the next evening, it would be in possession of the Sagua Grande area. Another full division could be landed at Isabela in the ensuing week and strike across the island the seventy miles to Cienfuegos within eight days of the initial assault. Taking the city from the rear, they would thereby have gained a port on both the north and south coasts for further reinforcements.

Joining forces with General Gómez, the American army regiments could then move west along the island and take Matanzas, then Havana. If begun by the beginning of March and prosecuted vigorously, the campaign could be concluded before summer rains slowed military movement in June. The campaign had to conclude successsfully before July and the advent of the deadly fever season, when yellow fever and malaria would begin to decimate foreigners in Cuba.

The U.S. Navy and Marines would have the responsibility for the initial assault on Isabela. They would secure the port and its environs, and handle harassment of the enemy along the adjacent northern coast, the landings of men and materiel, and transport and communications inland to Sagua Grande.

The U.S. Army would have to take it from there. I felt confident of the naval services' ability to handle their tasks. Our land-based colleagues were another matter. They weren't prepared for anything like a modern war with a European enemy. The Spanish, in spite of the New York jingoists' opinions, were well armed and well led in Cuba. They would fight.

This was the report I would give to Sigsbee. I hoped to be out of Cuba and back in Washington shortly thereafter, where Rork and I could construct a far more detailed war plan.

But, as has happened so often in my career, a whim of fate intervened to subvert my design. This time, it arrived in the form of a distraught mother.

21

Searching for Goatsuckers

Sagua Grande, Cuba
Monday
24 January 1898

The next cable came in on our last day in Sagua, the day I was to meet General Lacret. Rork and I were with Lizambard in his landau and had just picked up Gonzart for a trip to see the countryside west of Sagua Grande. I wanted to evaluate the terrain for the right flank of an invading army.

Gonzart handed me the cable message when he climbed in. The sender was Mario Cano, my Cuban attorney son-in-law in Tampa, who was deeply connected with the Cuban exile government in New York and the rebel fighters on the island. He sometimes forwarded confidential information he thought I might be interested in.

The unexpected telegram was in plain English and addressed to one of my clandestine names in Baltimore which were regularly checked by my staff in Washington. Connally, bright soul that he is, had guessed at the importance, and forwarded it onward to Sagua.

This communication was different, though. It was a purely personal matter.

XXX—MOTHER LEFT HERE TODAY—XX—
ENROUTE TO SONS—XXX

I asked the priest to stop the vehicle. Rork and I walked to the riverbank and I told him the news. "Maria just took the Plant Line steamer from Tampa to see Francisco and Juanito in Havana."

He read the message. "Ooh, 'tis Maria's heart she's listenin' to, but this is dangerous as hell. What do we do now?"

"No choice, Sean. We'll have to find Maria in Havana, and get her the hell out of Cuba before Marrón gets her. Then we can get back to the job we're here for."

Rork's jaw tightened. "Methinks after Maria's safely out o' Cuba, we should find Colonel Isidro Marrón again an' *this time* we can kill that slimy bastard once an' for all, in *proper* naval fashion, with a marline spike into his demented brain."

Rork referred to employing his false left hand. It was a work of art made out of India rubber by a French navy carpenter's mate in Indochina fifteen years before. A sniper's bullet had mangled the arm and gangrene forced the surgeons to amputate it at the forearm. So perfectly painted that most people never guess it is a replica, the hand was posed in a permanent gripping position. This enables Rork to hold an oar, a belaying pin, or a bottle of rum. He has it lovingly repainted each year by a lady friend of his who nocturnally worked the street beside the Washington Navy Yard. It's her annual Christmas present to him.

The fake hand served another role. It was the outer concealment for a silent and deadly weapon within. The hand could be easily unscrewed and removed from its base plate, where a five-inch-long steel marline spike waited for either benign or malevolent use. Rork is inordinately proud of his unique "appliance," as he sometimes refers to it, keeping the thing polished and extremely sharp. The threat against Marrón was not rhetorical.

We walked back to the landau and climbed in. Gonzart asked about sending a reply.

"No reply to this cable is necessary," I told Raul. "Unfortunately, gentlemen, our plans have changed. We won't be able to meet General Lacret tonight. Please pass along my sincere regrets and my respects to him."

Gonzart was visibly surprised. It hadn't been easy to set up the meeting. "When will you be able to meet with the general?"

"Not sure. We have to go to the south to see about some things which just came up, so this is where we must leave you. I'll be back in touch soon. You've done very good work, Raul. Thank you."

"Where exactly are you headed, Mr. Fisker?" he asked too nonchalantly. "Perhaps I can help."

Nice try, I thought. "Thank you for the offer, Raul, but Father Jacques will take us. Rork and I are headed down to Santo Domingo, where we'll catch the train for Cienfuegos on the south coast. We should reach there by tonight."

We left Gonzart pondering our explanation and headed the carriage south. Half an hour later, as a hot sun baked the land around us, we reached the junction with the east-west coastal road.

Jacques stopped the landau. What little wind we'd felt from our forward movement ended. The heat settled over us in an oven-like weight of air.

With his usual bemused expression, he asked, "Peter, I am certain we are not continuing south to Santo Domingo so you can catch the train to Cienfuegos. I understand it was a *ruse de guerre* because you do not fully trust Raul Gonzart. So, which way do you want me to turn? East to Santa Clara, or west to Colon? I know of a very nice place to lodge for the night and dine in Santa Clara, by the way. No bed bugs. Decent food. Good rum."

I decided that at this moment in time, Jacques did not need to know about our plans. So, ignoring the bit about mistrusting Gonzart, I half bowed in mock formality. "Sounds delightful, my friend. Another time, though. Right now, Rork and I are going to take some time off and go camping. We've accomplished what we need to do, and now we'll take a few days to see the flora and fauna of this beautiful island. A rare bird or two would be nice. One must always take time out to commune with nature, don't you think? It enhances our appreciation for the wonders of God's magnificent work."

Lizambard paused with a momentary doubtful expression, then said, "Ah, a secret naturalist. I am seeing a completely new side of you. I had no idea. How romantically Thoreauvian, Peter."

I knew that Jacques knew I was lying. But he was a humorous soul and enjoyed repartee, so I continued the vein of dry wit. "Yes, well, I don't like to show it often. Looks bad for someone in my profession."

"Oh, I understand completely. I have to maintain my gravitas also for, alas, it is expected of me. Goes with the collar," he said ruefully. "Any specific birds you are searching for?"

"Why yes, indeed, Jacques. Rork has long wanted to see the Antillean goatsucker in the wild," I said with a straight face.

Rork nodded enthusiastically. "Ooh, right he is. The goatsucker's a hellova bird!"

"Well, well . . ." said the clergyman-scientist. "The famed *Antrostomus cubanensis*, commonly known as the Cuban nightjar, or, among the less enlightened, the goatsucker. I would suggest the best time to see one will be at dusk tonight, when they come out to eat mosquitos and gnats. You two can be the bait for their prey."

Rork held up his false hand and retorted, "Aye, but pity the poor mosquitos. For we all know you can't get blood from rubber."

"*Touché*, my son," said Lizambard. "You win this round!"

Rork and I got out and shouldered our gear. The priest grew solemn. "I will not warn you to be careful, for that is not your mission or style. But please know you are in my prayers. God be with you."

Rork made the sign of the cross. I replied, "Thank you, Jacques. Expect a cable soon."

And with that, my ecclesiastical friend turned the landau west, toward his comfortable university life. The two of us waited until he was out of sight, then hoisted our gear onto our backs and started walking back to the railroad tracks. An hour later, we were hiding in a precariously overloaded cane car, heading west ourselves. It took four horrendous days, stowing away aboard five trains while hiding from guards, before we finally arrived at the one place in Cuba I dreaded most.

Havana.

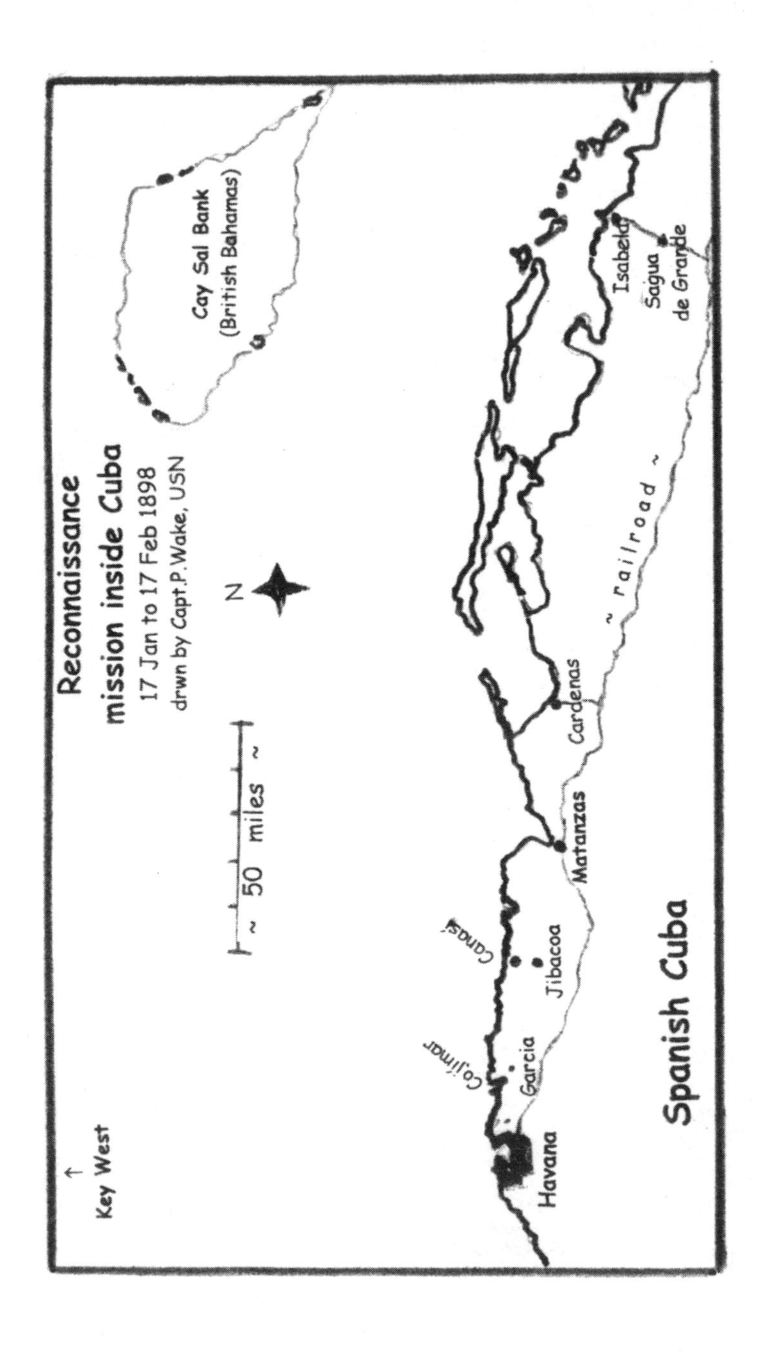
Reconnaissance
mission inside Cuba
17 Jan to 17 Feb 1898
drwn by Capt.P.Wake, USN
N
~ 50 miles ~
Key West
Cay Sal Bank
(British Bahamas)
Havana
Cojimar
Garcia
Canasi
Jibacoa
Matanzas
Cardenas
~ railroad ~
Isabela
Sagua
de Grande
Spanish Cuba

22

City of Shadows

Havana, Cuba
Friday
28 January 1898

It had been several years since I'd been inside Havana. They hadn't been kind to the city. Away from the waterfront restaurants and taverns, where rich Spaniards and foreigners congregated, the ambiance was sadder, without the laughter and music of the old days. Fear was palpable in the common peoples' furtive glances and cautious words, never knowing when a comment or gesture would be construed as disloyalty by the police or militia.

Havana was a city under siege in an ugly civil war.

Detachments of *voluntarios* were everywhere, searching everyone and everything with self-important zeal. The Spanish garrison's troops paraded each day, but more as a show of force than the traditional show of pride and heritage. The police were nervous, and never went about unless in groups of three or more.

I'd always thought of Havana as a city of shadows, even in the daytime, because of the narrow streets between the two- and three-story buildings. For years I had been comfortable within those streets. The shadows were still there, but now all was changed. Even the shadows weren't safe. Our ostensible identities might stand up to a police encounter out in the hinterlands, but not in Havana, where the authorities were far tougher to fool, and more desperate to protect the capital of the colony.

The time spent hiding during our journey had given me enough time to come up with a plan to accomplish my priority—finding my wife. Much of the search would be by proxy, utilizing old contacts. This, as the reader can discern, was a leap of faith, for in wartime the concept of loyalty, even among those you have previously trusted, often adjusts to prevailing factors, which may be unknown to you.

We laid low in the poor quarter, west of the Antares fortress. Rork and I used this *barrio* on operations back in the `80s, and it was well suited for our current needs. A Spanish five-*peseta* silver coin, accompanied by the story we were Bahamian rum smugglers, and backed up with an evil grimace from Rork, ensured a remote corner in a lean-to at the back of an alley. It also gained us the daily delivery of a plate of *lechon asado*, the roasted pork of Cuba. It is my favorite when done correctly. Stale and greasy, this stuff was not done correctly.

Maria's oldest son, Father Francisco lived and worked at the Saint Francis of Assisi monastery and church. It is a massive place on Oficios Street, initially built in 1608 and expanded continuously since then. Most inconveniently for us, the Spanish custom house and naval commandant's headquarters are right across from it. Armed men in uniform are always circulating in the area. Particularly vexing was that police, including Marrón's special section of the Orden Publico, would be there too. Some would remember Rork's and my face.

Maria's youngest son Juanito worked in the Spanish government's colonial offices, which were a short distance north of Francisco's church, and adjacent to the palace of the captain-general, the royal governor of Cuba. I knew not where Juanito resided, but guessed it would be nearby.

Agent R4, with the street name of Flaco Pájaro, was a disreputable man I had paid well for information in the 1880s. He was an emaciated old man, with teak-colored skin, yellowed eyes, and rasping voice, and thus usually underestimated at first glance. That would be a mistake. Flaco was a *bozal*, a former slave who was born and raised in Africa, and deceptively strong and fast. He had been the victim of great violence in his life, with scars on his back to prove it. Flaco only fought to kill.

I can't think of anything Flaco wouldn't do, or arrange, for money, including murder. He was just the man I needed right then, for he knew the city by heart, and at night moved through it at will along the rooftops, as if a ghost. A shrewd judge of character, he knew everyone's vulnerabilities. Flaco Pájaro was a man who could get things done.

I put Rork on the mission to find Flaco. In the meantime, another complication was added to the list. On the twenty-fifth of January, three days before Rork and I arrived in the city, the U.S.S. *Maine* had steamed into the harbor and anchored right off the Spanish admiral's office. The German cruiser *Gneisenau* and the Spanish cruiser *Alfonso XII* were anchored two hundred yards away. Crowds still gathered along the harbor's shore, silently looking at the American warship in her gleaming white hull and buff-colored funnels. There was no joy in their eyes.

Maine's commanding officer, Charles Sigsbee, was an oceanography expert and one of the smartest officers in the navy. I'd met him occasionally while on duty at headquarters. In the days after arriving, I was glad to see Sigsbee wisely kept his men, and most of the officers, from going ashore on anything other than absolutely necessary supply or pro-forma diplomatic runs.

The pro-Spanish Havana press had a field day nonetheless. The always present anti-American emotions of the Spanish-born classes in the city, which had been ebbing since the riots ended, were stoked once again. Protesters returned to the streets, fiery speeches were made at social clubs, and epithets flew in the direction of the U.S. cruiser from passing boats and the shore.

The newspapers ignored a lot of the mob's bad behavior, but reported in great detail that the Spanish admiral of Havana, Vicente Manterola, was scrupulously gallant in rendering all expected international naval courtesies to *Maine*'s captain and officers, including invitations to bullfights, receptions, and professional demonstrations of naval skill. His efforts were described as proof of Spanish civility and patience, in contrast to the uncivilized behavior of the New York newspapers and Washington politicians calling for Spain's ouster from Cuba. Spain's newest and most powerful battleship, *Vizcaya*, was steaming across the Atlantic for a reciprocal visit to frigid New York, and Havana's press predicted American hospitality would pale in comparison to that of the Spanish Navy in Cuba.

Let us now return to the desperate effort at hand—finding and extricating my wife from Cuba. Leaving several messages at taverns for him within hours of our arrival in Havana, Rork got word Flaco was still alive and would meet me that very night. The rendezvous was held in an alley off Desamparados Street, in the seedier part of the waterfront. Rork stood a few feet away, guarding against interruptions, his shotgun casually pointed toward Flaco.

I kept my request simple and vague. "An elegant Spanish woman named Maria Maura is visiting the city. Find out where she is staying and let me know. Tell her name to no one, and do no harm to her. Understand?"

Flaco studied me a moment, then Rork. He nodded. "Yes, yes, I no tell name to nobody. Woman no hurt." He gestured at me with a filthy hand. "When you need?"

"Tomorrow night."

He spit, as if the time period was impossible. Then, his ghoulish eyes never leaving mine, he rubbed his forefinger and thumb. "How much you pay?"

"Twenty Morgan dollars."

His head shook dismissively. "Forty."

"Flaco, they're pure silver. You'll get twenty."

"I must pay other man. Need thirty."

"Twenty-two. I have no more."

"Need twenty-four. No less."

"Too much, Flaco, but I will agree, this one time. Half now, half *after*."

He shrugged. "Yes."

Rork sauntered over and laid his left arm on Flaco's shoulder, the uncovered spike inches from his face, the shotgun's muzzle near his groin. "An' no talkin' to police, Flaco. *Comprende, muy bien?*"

The old man was used to worse threats and didn't even flinch. In fact, he seemed unimpressed. "I understand you words. No meet here *manana*. Danger here—Spanish *policía*. Meet . . . *mediodía* . . . at Figueras. At . . . *extremo del canal*."

The time would be at noon. I knew the location. It was an alley in the slum quarters which led to the end of a drainage canal, near the gas works. The area was full of derelicts and criminals of all descriptions. Flaco's peers. A dangerous place for even the police.

I had no choice and agreed. I gave him twelve silver dollars, half of which disappeared into his left shoe and the other half into a trouser pocket. The three of us walked out to the street. Flaco turned left and headed for the nice part of the waterfront. We went to the right, back to our lair in the slums.

23

Big Trouble for Woman

Havana, Cuba
Saturday
29 January 1898

The next day Rork and I set up a watch over the alley an hour ahead of time. We paid a ragged little boy twenty *centimos* to warn us with a whistle if he saw any official-looking strangers from outside the neighborhood coming near. Flaco arrived early, stumbling his way down to the end of the canal and along the steep bank. He sat down on a crate in the shade of a bush and within seconds he was apparently asleep, just another drunk passed out. After fifteen minutes of observing him, we entered the alley, which stank from the contents of the canal.

Flaco's performance ended as we approached. He stirred, one hand sliding into his pocket, and looked coldly up at us. Rork seized the wrist of Flaco's hand, then swung his false left forearm around and put that wicked spike right between Flaco's eyes. I studied the periphery for signs of a trap. None were visible.

"Slowly, Flaco. Pull your hand out o' that pocket. Very slowly," Rork demanded.

"No danger. No problem," Flaco said with an evil smirk, as if he got pleasure from making Rork tense. To show his disdain, he calmly pulled out a cigar and stuck it unlit in his mouth. Rork backed the spike away, but kept it within striking distance.

"What do you have for me, Flaco?" I asked.

"Friend tell me woman lives at *convento de monjas*—no understand English word for this. *Convento* near church of San Francisco. *Manana*, she go with priest son to *desayuno* with *norteamericano* sailor mans at Havana boat club at Marianao." He held up nine fingers. "*Nueve* morning time. Big show for *norteamericano* sailor chief. Spanish, Cubanos, *norteamericanos*—all friends at *desayuno*. Talk about peace. *Yanqui* sailor chief go in little boat to club."

From Flaco's fractured English-Spanish, I deduced Maria was staying at the nunnery near Francisco's church, and would go with him to a special breakfast the next morning for Sigsbee and his officers at the Havana Yacht Club. Evidently, Sigsbee and his officers were headed there by ship's launch and it was a goodwill event. Why Maria? Why her son, Father Francisco?

Flaco wasn't done, though. "Day before I ask about woman, other man ask friend about same woman."

"Who?" I asked quickly, worried about the answer.

He didn't tell me. Instead, sensing my anxiety, the scoundrel said, "Money no for that. Money for find woman. Ten *mas* Morgans for this."

Rork hissed an oath, ready to impale the man, but I stopped him with a glance.

"No, Flaco. Five more Morgans—*after* I meet the woman."

Flaco nodded his agreement. "You pay after. I trust you. My friend say Orden Publico man ask about woman." He shook a finger for emphasis. "Orden Publico man no have uniform. *Investigador especial* man. Big trouble for woman."

It was the worst news possible. Colonel Marrón was targeting my wife.

24

Love in a Linen Closet

Havana Yacht Club
Marianao suburb
West of Havana, Cuba
Sunday morning
30 January 1898

To enter the Havana Yacht Club through the front doors, one had to be a member or an invitation-bearing guest. I was neither. Courtesy of sordid information gained from Flaco—for another five Morgans—I was a successful trespasser through the back door. Such a feat came by way of extortion, which was exacted by me upon the club gardener, who had a long-term secret love life with the assistant *sous-chef de cuisine* in the kitchen. Both men desired to keep their affections private and their jobs secure. Havana, after all, is not Paris.

Doors were left unlocked and the word spread among the butler staff that I was a guest who had lost his invitation. A moment later I was portraying myself as a Canadian journalist named Melville Brinson, who had fled a Toronto blizzard two weeks earlier for sunnier climes and a story on Cuban-American friendship in the midst of the Island's vicious civil war.

None of the staff stopped me or even cast a wondering look. Once inside, I was above their strata and beyond their reproach. Rork remained outside, keeping watch on the gardener to ensure devotion to our bargain.

At nine o'clock the naval party arrived. Its conveyance had not been the *Maine*'s steam launch, but rather a small private steam yacht owned by a successful Cuban businessman. The group was led by none other than the chief U.S. diplomatic representative to Spanish Cuba, Consul-General Fitzhugh Lee.

Sixty-three-year-old Lee was quite well-known due to a busy life and legendary name. A graduate of West Point in 1856, he was wounded badly while fighting the Comanche under his uncle, Robert E. Lee, then served as cavalry instructor at the academy. He resigned to become a Confederate cavalry officer and rose to the rare rank of major general. Postbellum, Lee echoed his famous uncle in calling for reconciliation. He became a successful Democratic politician, governor of Virginia, confidant of President Cleveland and, in 1896, was appointed by the president to his present post. Fitzhugh Lee was a unique man and a force to be reckoned with.

The naval officers and diplomats were met by various liberal members of the Cuban elite, six American reporters from New York and Chicago, the Chinese consul, a London *Times* correspondent, and me. Maria, her son, and any Spanish authorities, were conspicuously absent. My worry mounted.

In Washington, I had met Sigsbee several times and Lee twice. But with my two-week shaggy goatee, unkempt long hair, and clear-glass spectacles, as well as my comparatively shabby suit, hastily unpacked from the sea bag, I presented a far different persona and thus passed unrecognized by them. As added insurance, I stayed at the rear of the crowd and sprinkled my sentences with Canadian-sounding dialect.

As the others fawned over Sigsbee, I asked the Brit correspondent, "Where are the Spanish government people?"

"They've already had their grand affair for the captain at the palace in Havana. I thought they did it up rather nicely. Lee set this one up for Captain Sigsbee to meet the other side of the equation: influential Cuban businessmen, along with some pro-independence Spaniards. I do believe there will be a priest and a lady, who are both Spanish as well."

Maria was pro-independence, but was her son? Not from what I knew of him. The Church supported the Spanish government's policy of denying independence. That was either a mistaken impression on the Brit's part, or a duplicitous ploy on Father Francisco's part.

"Really?" I replied. "They must be running late. We're about to sit down."

"Ah, well, it is Cuba, after all . . ." said the correspondent, with a shrug.

I heard a commotion at the foyer. The Brit looked at the doorway and sighed. "My goodness, what a lovely lady . . ."

There she was, elegant in a yellow silk dress trimmed in white. All eyes turned her way. Maria's son was taller than I had thought. He had a gentle smile, and began shaking hands, introducing his mother in English—by her previous married name of Maura.

They entered the dining salon and made their way down the line of gentlemen toward me, stopping at each one for polite conversation. I ducked out the side door and waited until Maria was separated from her son, then asked a waiter to deliver a one-line note to her.

Meet me in the side hallway—the man from Patricio

Her face was clouded by confusion and anger when she rounded the corner into the hallway. As she walked by, I leaned out from a storage closet and pulled her inside, closing the door. A small window provided barely enough light to see as I led her to the back, behind some linen shelves.

Maria still wore the same expression as I kissed her and said, "Shssssh . . . Darling, please don't say a word. Listen to me first, please."

Her face hardened and I thought for a moment she was about to slap me, but instead, she waited for me to speak.

"Thank you, my love. I am working inside Cuba, obviously, and people here think I'm a Canadian reporter. It won't be much longer and then I can come home. I have learned Marrón's men know you are here and have been targeting you for two days. They probably followed you here and are watching this place now. You must trust *no one*, not even your sons. I beg you to leave Havana immediately, on the next steamer to Key West. *Get out of Cuba*, Maria. This isn't a game. You know what Marrón can and will do, especially here where he has no restraints. I will meet you at home soon. Do you understand?"

"May I have permission to speak now? Or am I a prisoner of the U.S. Navy, or whomever you work for right now?"

"Maria, you are not a prisoner. I had to get you alone."

She interrupted. "You lied to me about your work, Peter. This is no evaluation of the situation. You are spying inside Cuba, using deceit to fool the one person who loves you dearly. And now, just look at you. I thought you were some sort of sleazy salesman, or worse. Somebody told me the disheveled man was a Canadian journalist. How ridiculous."

"Maria."

"I have not finished! Unlike you, I am here openly, with my son, who is a respected and honorable man of God. We came here because I have convinced him freedom for Cuba is both a decent Christian, and a decent Spanish, duty. We are here to show not all Spaniards are the monsters depicted in the Hearst and Pulitzer newspapers."

"Have you spoken with Juanito, also?"

"Yes, and both my sons have pledged their love for me. They appreciate their mother making the journey to see them, and we have enjoyed our reunion. I will go back to North America when I want to, Peter."

I didn't like the sound of that. "Have Juanito and Francisco changed their minds about our marriage?"

"No, they have not, at all. In fact, Francisco said he could arrange an annulment, so I could return to the Church." She paused and my heart stopped. "But I promised my love to you and reminded them I would stay true to my husband. However, I *have* gotten Francisco to see my view on Cuban freedom. Juanito is still against independence."

Honorable man of God he might be, but I completely distrusted Francisco's abrupt political conversion. Given the circumstances, I kept my opinion to myself.

"Maria, I'm overjoyed you have had such a wonderful reunion with your sons. But Marrón *is* a monster. He knows we are married. You will disappear off the street when it suits him. Remember our wedding night in Key West, when they tried to kidnap Mario?"

"Yes, certainly."

"You will be used for his purposes, most likely blackmail or ransom. Your family's old connections in Madrid, your son's church, and the United States of America won't be able to prevent him. Marrón has the senior government authorities in Cuba under his thumb, and his cronies in Madrid who run the army do what they want. For the five years we've been married, we've discussed this. And now, the situation in Cuba is worse than ever and damned explosive. Marrón will stop at nothing to keep his position of power. He is fighting for his demented life."

She stepped back, tilting her head back defiantly. "Yes, Marrón is a monster and capable of anything. But he would not dare to hurt me or my sons. My affiliations in Spain are strong enough to prevent that."

"Your family and friends won't even *know* he has you, Maria. You will disappear, your body dumped in a hole. There is no good ending to this. That's how he works."

I was angry now and could no longer keep it out of my tone. "Look, there is no time to waste with pointless discussions—this is life and death. You won't help your sons or me by getting killed. Listen carefully . . . when you return to the convent after this event, get to the passenger office at the Plant Line steamer dock and get a ticket for tomorrow's passage to Key West and Tampa. Do *not* tell anyone what you're doing. Your life and our future depends on it."

Maria's defiance was visibly wilting. She knew I was right, but she still shook her head angrily. "I will not lie to my son, Peter."

"There's no need to lie to anyone, just don't tell them. Write them a letter from Key West. Your sons would never hurt or betray you—intentionally. Unintentionally, however, by conversation or behavior, they will allow others to surmise your departure. Then Marrón will strike. You must tell *no* one."

She closed her eyes and took a breath, a sad surrender of a proud lady. "Very well, Peter. I will do as you say. Is Sean here also?"

"Yes, Rork's outside right now. When you return to the gathering, treat me like a stranger. I am a Canadian reporter, Melville Brinson, from Toronto. No prolonged eye contact, no touching, no whispers."

"How long will you stay like this inside Cuba?"

"Maybe another week. I want us both to get home, dear, where we will be safe." I held her tightly. "I love you, Maria."

"You are making me cry, Peter. I know you love me. I have always known, even before you did. Now I must go to the ladies' necessary room, to repair my appearance. I must not look tearful at such a happy event."

Maria straightened her dress and ran a hand through her hair. When she next spoke, it was with confidence, spiced with a dash of dry wit. "Now, Mr. Brinson, is it not? Please be kind enough to tell your acquaintance Peter Wake his wife loves and misses him intensely. She will arrange quite a romantic reunion when he returns home from his journey in the tropics."

I opened the door and made sure no one was in the hallway. As we emerged, I told her, "I will make sure he understands your sentiments and invitation, ma'am. I can assure you he's dreaming of nothing but that moment. I regret to say I must part company now. I am here to interview this American naval captain named Sigsbee for my Canadian readers, eh?"

Maria headed for the ladies' room. I went back to the breakfast. Sigsbee glanced up at my entry and smiled politely at me, clearly oblivious that in a few minutes he would be giving a Canadian in Cuba a confidential coded message from the Assistant Secretary of the U.S. Navy.

25

Rooseveltian Humor

Havana Yacht Club
Marianao suburb
West of Havana, Cuba
Sunday morning
30 January 1898

After toasts and speeches, the affair ended with applause. It was time to make my move. Sigsbee headed to the door, surrounded by his Cuban admirers, politely trying to disengage from them so he could board the carriage for the train taking the naval officers back to Havana.

According to the contingency plan Roosevelt and I had hatched in my office in Washington, if things got bad and I had to make contact with an American warship commander visiting Havana, I was to utter a phrase to him which would signify I was not whom I appeared to be but, in fact, a brother officer. Likewise, ship captains likely to be sent to Havana were alerted to recognize the phrase's speaker was in actuality Captain Peter Wake, U.S.N. They were then to give me Roosevelt's message and to receive my own, to be sent onward to Roosevelt.

I came alongside Sigsbee as we headed for the door, nudging him with my shoulder.

"Say, have you had an opportunity to see the famous Cuban boa constrictor on your visit, Captain Sigsbee?" I asked, using the phrase which was yet another example of Rooseveltian humor. When telling me the phrase, Theodore also asked me to get him a specimen for his collection, "preferably embalmed in an *action* pose," as long as I "happened to be down there in Cuba."

Sigsbee stood still, his face blank. "What? Oh! . . . well, yes, I mean no, I haven't." Then he stopped, clearly forgetting the counter phrase. The poor fellow wasn't used to the clandestine life. He peered at me intently, starting to see a resemblance to a naval officer he'd met before.

"Would you like to?" I prompted, wishing Sigsbee would just hand me the damn message. Neither of us needed to go any further through all Theodore's ridiculous cloak and dagger stuff. After all, I knew who Sigsbee was, and I had given him the proper code to show him who I was.

"Yes, I would like to see one of those boa constrictors," he said.

"Snakes?" interrupted Fitzhugh Lee, hovering nearby. "Stay away from them, myself. Adam learned that the hard way a long time ago! However did we get onto snakes?" He swung his bulk toward me. "You're the Canadian journalist, aren't you?"

I stuck out a hand. "Melville Brinson, of the Toronto *Express*, sir. We met at the French consul's soirée here in Havana six months ago."

"Oh, yes, quite right, of course, Mr. Brinson. I do recall our delightful conversation."

I smiled at them both, then suddenly looked out the window, as if peering at something important. To his credit, Sigsbee took the hint and smoothly guided Lee to the window with his left hand, while retrieving something from a pocket with his right.

"Look at the grand view of the ocean, General Lee. Magnificent, isn't it?" Sigsbee suggested.

Then, as everyone around him turned their faces toward the expanse of sea, Sigsbee edged close to me, sliding several small-sized papers into my coat pocket. He walked away with my report on the feasibility of using Isabela—Sagua Grande for an invasion target in his hand, quickly stuffing it into his trouser pocket. The entourage, including Maria and son, followed him out the door into the foyer with none the wiser.

At the portico, I said goodbye to some of the guests, but kept my distance from Maria. For an instant our eyes met and she gave the slightest of nods. Feeling considerably better about her safety, I wandered off to examine a huge yellow hibiscus flower, thence sauntered to a hedge of brilliantly purple bougainvillea.

Rork materialized from behind the bougainvillea. "How'd it go?"

"Maria was angry, but listened. She's leaving tomorrow. Her priest son is evidently pro-Cuban independence now. Nothing else new from the meeting. It was all the standard diplo drivel."

Upon returning to our slum lair, Rork went out to retrieve an important item. Kept heavily wrapped in oilcloth, it was hidden in a crevice inside the end of a sewage drain pipe, on the bank of a nearby gulley. This was a regrettable but necessary sacrilege, for it was an 1863 New Testament Bible in Danish—a gift from an Episcopal priest in Mississippi, of all places—and the code book for secret messages from Roosevelt. Specifically, it was the rare eighth edition of that particular Bible, which had been translated from the original Greek. Other editions, before and after 1863, had variations in the text, a seemingly minor but actually important factor. Theodore had an exact copy of it in his desk at Washington.

Thus, we could use our two copies to form and decipher coded messages.

I spread out the other items required for the translation: the three pages given me by Sigsbee, a tiny English-Danish pocket dictionary, and a scrap of paper for figuring. It would take concentration and time to decipher Roosevelt's message, so I turned to it with a will, anxious to discover when and how I was returning home to my wife.

26

Numbers

Havana, Cuba
Sunday afternoon
30 January 1898

The method of decipherment might be of interest to the reader of this memoir, so I will explain the process, the basics of which are commonly used by many of the world's secret services.

The three sheets given me were each a different color, and each contained lines of numbers. They were intentionally disarrayed to render the numbers out of the proper sequence, the first layer of security. I put them in the right order, from lightest color to darkest color, with the three sheets not side by side, but columned. This provided a total of thirteen lines of numbers. Each line had thirteen numbers written boldly, appearing thus:

0169840132008
0246331028505
0521070491001
3747731762908
5122340837602
6323673234104

0617152778801
1820201099805
0093844531306
6201961712801
6252120389801
1792393556403
2128981821204

The numbers were without discernible patterns and designed to appear as standard European commercial telegraph code at initial glance, the second layer of security.

Then came the third layer of security: false numbers imbedded within each line—the fourth through sixth, and the ninth through eleventh digits. Eliminating the false numbers gave me this:

0160108
0241005
0520401
3741708
5120802
6323204
0612701
1821005
0094506
6201701
6250301
1793503
2121804

The fourth layer of security was the rare Bible in our possession. The first three digits of each line of numbers were page numbers of the Bible. The second two numbers represented which line of text down from the top of the page. The final two numbers were the ordinal of the word on the specific line.

Thus, the mathematical geography of the Bible verses produced a list like this:

Page 16, line 1, word 8—Matthew 5:43
Page 24, line 10, word 5—Matthew 9:1
Page 52, line 4, word 1—Matthew 18:5
Page 374, line 17, word 8—Acts 23:27
Page 512, line 8, word 2—Colossians 1:10
Page 632, line 32, word 4—Revelations 11:7
Page 61, line 27, word 1—Matthew 21:20
Page 182, line 10, word 5—Luke 10:7
Page 9, line 45, word 6—Matthew 3:9
Page 620, line 17, word 1—Revelations 3:12
Page 625, line 3, word 1—Revelations 6:11
Page 179, line 35, word 3—Luke 9:37
Page 212, line 18, word 4—Luke 19:14

The Bible was small, the type font was neo-Gothic. Therefore, the words were difficult to see with my aging eyesight, especially in the less than optimal light conditions of our hideout. Danish has a different alphabet than English, adding one more factor in the equation.

What finally emerged from my analysis was this list of words, arranged in horizontal text in the English version of Danish lower case letters:

fjende skib og haer stigende krig snart forbliver indenfor stad indtil naeste besked

Using the Danish-English pocket dictionary was my final task. The translated message was not what I expected, so I calculated and read everything three more times, sure I had made a mistake. I hadn't. Rork looked over my work, but he found it accurate. Then he swore a distinctly un-Biblical blue streak in Gaelic.

The message read:

Enemy ships and army increasing. War soon. Stay within city until next message.

The next morning, I sent a street boy to the telegraph office with a cable request to "Mr. Roald Fuglmand" in Montreal, from "Mr. Hopf." It had the following numbers as the message: "4592732499845." Page 459, line 24, word 5, which was in 2nd Corinthians 1:14, and meant: "Acknowledged."

I dared not add my personal opinion.

27

The Invisible Functionary

Hotel Mascotte
Oficios and Luz streets
Havana, Cuba
Early February 1898

We still had to obtain the Havana defense plans and get them to Sigsbee, and receive the funding from him, but first we had to take care of a more immediate problem. Our rum smuggler charade was losing validity among our fellow denizens of the slum, and I judged it necessary to make a change in our base of operations. I chose a middle-class hotel in the nice area of the harbor front, Mascotte Hotel, named for the Plant Line passenger steamer which docked right in front of it. It was an ideal location: full of *norteamericano* tourists and businessmen, so Rork and I wouldn't stand out. Facing the harbor from the corner of Luz and Oficios streets, it was close to the steamers to Key West, and the ferry which crossed the harbor to the town of Regla.

The reader may well question my decision, but the yacht club breakfast affair had given me new confidence in our aliases and changed outward appearances. Rork and I were much thinner, our faces were completely changed by spectacles, long hair, and beards, and we'd grown used to our new names and occupations. Maria and Sigsbee were the test. If my wife couldn't recognize me at first look, I guessed most of Orden Publico wouldn't either. In hindsight, I will admit my reasoning was influenced by the dismal food, lack of sleep, and aches and pains incurred from living in a crude hovel. That we were constantly surrounded by a menagerie of truly dangerous neighbors, any of whom would cut our throats for a dollar, was the tipping point. One can only fool them for so long.

When I suggested the change, Rork agreed. "Ooh, me weary ol' bones're mutinyin' this sort o' life, boyo. They're hopin' for somethin' a bit more posh. If we're goin' to die in this hellhole, let's die clean, well-rested, an' damn well fed, with a wee touch o' somethin' decent to drink."

And so Mr. Melville Brinson and Mr. Angus McGregor, Her Britannic Majesty's loyal Canadian subjects, were installed in a comfortable corner suite on the hotel's second floor. Our view was panoramic and perfect for our purposes, spanning from the Spanish admiral's office two blocks north, the *Maine* at anchor in front of us, and the Spanish cruiser and German warship anchored to the south.

For the next week and a half we lived very well, with my intention being to spend all of our remaining original funds in maintaining an impressively lavish lifestyle. Rork said we more than deserved it. I countered it was operationally necessary to support our deception.

During this time, I would dutifully make the rounds of administrative Havana, seeking official information about the rebel war for my fictitious newspaper in Toronto. This was a predictably unsuccessful enterprise, since the Spanish authorities were well known for obfuscation and disinformation with members of the press, but it did provide cover for my real work, which was to find agent R8 and get the Havana defense plan from him.

Due to ongoing security concerns, because his enemies are still out there, I shall give R8 the *nom de guerre* of Vinatero, for his family had been vintners in Spain before relocating to Havana in 1762. The timing of their arrival was unfortunate, a month prior to the British occupation. He'd initially come into my employ in 1887 and was extremely valuable for me, for he was a senior copy clerk in the secretarial office of the captain-general's staff.

Vinatero was a plodding bureaucrat, a droopy-eyed widower without family or friends. Like many of his peers, he was a forgotten functionary no one above his status would suspect had the gumption to do much of anything. But I recognized his potential. Vinatero had a servant's unnoticed proximity to high level people in the army's headquarters, with daily access to documents in the filing cabinets. And I knew sooner or later I would need one of those documents.

His motive was unknown to his superiors, and it furnished him with impressive gumption. A Freemason, he had an affinity to American-style liberal democracy and the rights of man. He also had brother Masonic friends among the Cuban rebels. Best of all, Vinatero had a long-standing but unexplained grudge against the Catholic Church, which was so closely allied with the Spanish government as to be almost synonymous.

Over the years he had supplied me with routine information, easily verifiable, and we continued our distant relationship, the payments to him being in the nature of a retainer for when I really needed him. Then, in August 1897, he sent word he could obtain a copy of the defense plans of Havana, if we wanted them. I didn't hesitate in agreeing.

Because of the value of his position and the efficiency of the Spanish security apparatus, any communication with Vinatero was very circumspect and rare. In fact, there had been no communication from him, either by telegram or letter or courier, since his last to me in November, when he predicted he would have the plans in December or January. Vinatero was to send word they were ready to be handed over, but no word came.

Vinatero might assume that I or one of my men might be aboard *Maine* and that the three drop sites which we'd used many years earlier could still be used. With that optimistic thought in mind, every other day I did my rounds of them, varying my times and routes. A week went by, but no envelope was found. I feared the worst and told Rork the issue was probably moot.

The next day, on the tenth of February, I tried one last time. Nothing was found at the first two places, but the third yielded results. Behind loose bricks in the north wall of the alley behind Castillo de Farnes, a tavern and boarding house on the eastern side of the theater district, I found a battered old valise.

Inside the valise was a blue pouch. I smiled when I saw it, for though Vinatero worked for the army, he'd put the plans inside a small Spanish naval courier pouch. It was a clever red herring should the drop site be discovered by the authorities.

Leaving the valise *in situ* so anyone else checking the location would assume it had not been found, I put the pouch inside my coat and strolled off toward the west, the direction away from my hotel, after scanning for anyone watching. Two streets over, I discarded my recently obtained coat and put the pouch inside my shirt, then began a broad circumnavigation of the area to get to the hotel. Within a couple blocks of my destination, I ducked down an alley and into an alcove, and there I paused to look at what was in the pouch.

It was a map. But not just any map.

It was the latest update in the defense plans of Havana—an incredible coup. Noted as the ninth copy of a total of twelve, it was dated the first of February and signed by the chief of engineers. All Spanish installations and fortresses, their armament, and their units' barracks and encampments were shown in detail.

I removed my undershirt, wrapped it around the map, and quickly reached up to cram it into a crevice of the ancient alley's wall, about seven feet off the ground. I then stuffed the crevice with dirt to make it flush with the wall and hurried back to our room at the hotel to share the good news.

Rork asked, "Any mail?"

"Mail" was our euphemism for the plans. I replied with similar language, "Yes, some extraordinary mail, as a matter of fact. Now that we've delivered the Sagua tobacco assessment, the distraught lady departed, and this mail has arrived, I think our work here is nearly done. We just have to deliver the mail and we'll be going home soon. I'm thinking first-class cabins on a Plant steamer."

"Homeward bound . . . now me ears're happy. This calls for a proper celebration!"

We celebrated very properly, enjoying a nice dinner of real *lechon asado*, a decent Tempranillo wine, and for a digestif, our favorite sipping rum, Matusalem. The conversation was suitably non-naval, centering on women we'd known, loves we'd lost, and dreams yet unfulfilled. I had the best sleep since I'd arrived in Cuba.

The next day, everything changed.

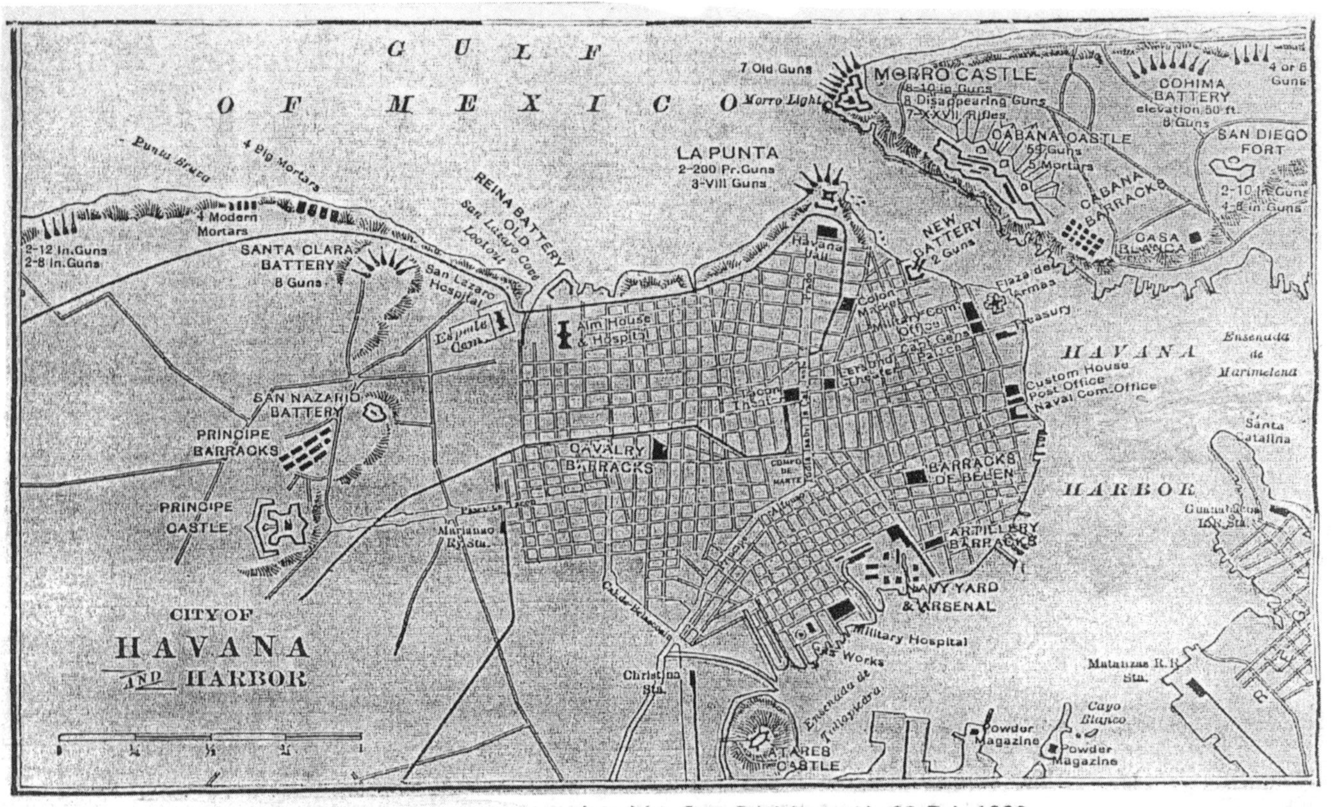

Spanish defense plan for Havana, translated by Capt. P. Wake, USN, 28 Feb 1898

28

A Diplomatic Bombshell

Havana, Cuba
Friday
11 February 1898

The first salient event of the day was the delivery of a hundred copies of William Randolph Hearst's February ninth issue of the *New York Journal.* They'd been rushed to Havana by a Plant Line steamer from Tampa, where they had been sent by special overnight express train from New York. This was the fastest delivery of a newspaper from New York in Havana's history. I got a copy five minutes after it was ashore, spending three times the cover price, and shook my head in disbelief at what it contained. Bad news does travel fast.

The *Journal* was dramatically headlined, "Worst Insult to the United States in Its History." The article detailed a letter which had come into the paper's possession the day before. The article stated Enrique Dupuy de Lome, the Spanish ambassador to Washington, had written a private letter to a Spanish government friend who was visiting Havana. The letter was intercepted by the Cuban underground in Cuba and sent north, where it was passed by the Cuban junta to their friends in the New York press.

The ambassador's letter—printed in its entirety for the entire world to see—was a bombshell and unintentional gift for the Cuban rebel cause. In just a few pages, de Lome managed to insult an incredibly wide variety of people.

De Lome's letter said the Cuban insurgents fighting for independence would leave the field of battle, come over to the Spanish, and give up their fight: "Neither one nor the other class had the courage to leave in a body and they will not be brave enough to return in a body." He angered the pacifists in Cuba, America, and Spain: "Without a military end of the matter nothing will be accomplished in Cuba. . . ." He castigated the press: "Nearly all the newspaper rabble that swarms in your hotels are Englishmen, and while writing for the *Journal* they are also correspondents of the most influential journals and reviews of London." The British government was also a target of his wrath: "England's only object is that the Americans should amuse themselves with us and leave her alone, and if there should be war, that it would stave off a conflict which she dreads. . . ." He also didn't think much of the United States Congress: "Have a man of prominence sent hither, in order that I may use him here to carry on propaganda among the senators and others. . . ."

Last, but most certainly not least, the ambassador vented his opinion of William McKinley, the president of the United States: "McKinley is weak, and a bidder for the admiration of the crowd beside being a would-be politician who tries to leave a door open behind himself while keeping on good terms with the jingoes of his party."

The newspaper reported de Lome, confronted by his gross error in diplomatic judgment, had resigned his position. The American reaction to the exposé was predictable and fast. The press and jingo crowd wanted blood in the name of national honor. De Lome's letter became a rally cry for war.

I could just imagine Theodore Roosevelt's reaction—jumping with glee in his office and shouting to the world map on his wall, "*Bully* for de Lome! He accomplished in one letter what *I've* been trying to do for a *year*. Now maybe they'll wake *up* around here and take *action!*"

In Havana, the article caused universal gasps among all parties who read it, and within an hour everyone wanted to read it. Copies sold at five times the regular price. The population, from the Spanish governor to Cuban *insurrectos*, waited for the American response.

The second event on the morning of the eleventh was the arrival of the American Navy torpedo boat *Cushing*, which steamed into Havana with black mourning bunting and moored alongside *Maine*. Soon word of a tragedy aboard her was spreading in the city. The nor-wester which had been pounding Havana for two days, also swept Ensign Joseph Breckinridge, grandson of John C. Breckinridge, former U.S. vice-president and Confederate secretary of war, overboard. Despite the efforts of two petty officers who heroically tried to save the young man, he was lost.

"Pity about the young officer, but that's the way o' the sea. Just hope *Cushing*'ll have new orders for us," said Rork, watching the two warships from our balcony. "Got a bad feelin' about stayin' here. Odds o' Marrón's thugs findin' us're gettin' bigger the longer we stay."

"I agree, Rork. We'll have to bribe a bumboat to get us past the Spanish harbor patrol to the ship to find out, but only after we enjoy a final dinner ashore. Can you arrange a boat for later tonight? Once aboard *Maine,* we can stay on her until they return to Key West."

With more enthusiasm than I'd seen from him in days, Rork nodded his assent. "Aye, sir. I'll attend to it straight away. There's a couple o' likely fellows down by the gas factory docks."

"Good. Later, I'll head over to pick up the mail where I left it."

That was the plan. It didn't work out that way, however, for that afternoon the third significant event of the day greeted me at the door.

29

Bad-Mannered Behavior

Her Britannic Majesty's Consulate
Havana, Cuba
Friday afternoon
11 February 1898

Rork had been gone for some time when I was about to head out and retrieve the defense plans from their hiding place. I was stopped by a knock at the door just as I was reaching for it. Assuming it was the maid, I opened the door without thinking.

It wasn't the maid. A captain in the uniform of the Orden Publico regiment stood there, and he had two of his men with him. They stayed directly behind him, blocking the hallway. All three had holstered pistols.

The captain's English was excellent, his tone dictatorial, and his eyes dead cold. With no preamble, he declared, "Mr. Melville Brinson, you and Mr. Angus McGregor are British citizens and required at the British Consulate immediately. I will escort you there now."

Over the years of portraying myself as a Canadian at risky locales, I've had several confrontations with local authorities, but have never been summoned by the British consulate. None of this seemed legitimate in the least. Would I ever see the British consulate if I went with them? I played for time to deduce how much the captain knew about me and what his real orders were.

"I'm afraid you are mistaken, Captain. Mr. McGregor and I are not British citizens. We are *Canadian* citizens and loyal subjects of Her Britannic Majesty, our most gracious Queen Victoria, may God grant her many years more. Evidently you don't know we Canadians became an independent dominion back in sixty-seven. Not to worry though, son, many Europeans make the same mistake. Completely understandable. So have a nice day, eh?"

The captain ignored my inane banter. "You both will go now to the British Consulate."

"No can do right now, Captain, but we'll be delighted to stop by later. It's probably about them wanting to invite us to the Valentine's Day dance. They like to invite everyone in town. Maybe I can get you and your wife an invitation too. It's always great fun, eh? I'll let you know."

I started closing the door. He blocked it with a boot and stared at me. Obviously, being the nice Canadian wasn't working. It was time for taking the other tack. How exactly does an irate Canadian sound, I wondered? I wasn't sure, but gave it my best try.

"My friend isn't here right now, Captain, and I am quite indisposed myself. And I must say I find your behavior to be distinctly bad-mannered, even for a Spaniard. Kindly tell the British Consulate that I do not appreciate their rude interruption of my siesta. Mr. McGregor and I are professional journalists, and we will be pleased to stop by and say hello in the morning. Say about ten, eh? If this sort of thing keeps up, we most certainly will *not* attend the Valentine's Dance and *will* notify the foreign ministry in London of the uncivilized behavior of their representatives in Havana. *Canadians* do not put up with this, sir, from anybody!"

My bombast fell flat. The Spaniard's stone face never reacted. "You are under arrest. Where is McGregor?"

Devoid of other ideas, I continued posturing. "I don't have a clue as to the location of *Mister* McGregor. Last saw him this morning with a very pretty girl at breakfast and imagine he's doing what one does with a pretty girl, eh? What's this, did you say *arrest?* That is utterly ridiculous. One word from me and Queen Victoria will demand her friend, the Spanish king, order you shot for such impudence!"

Damn all, in my haste I'd forgotten an important fact. Spain's king was only twelve years old. His Austrian mother was the real royal power, and not a close friend of Victoria. The captain sneered at my comment and produced a set of handcuffs from the gun belt around his waist.

"You are under arrest and will go with me."

All three of them stepped forward into the room. Faced with such a development, I had two choices left. Stun him, steal his pistol and shoot all three of them. Or go along with him quietly. The reader may think less of me, but the latter option seemed a bit easier and far less messy.

"No need for those, old chap. I am a gentlemen journalist. We view fisticuffs as a barbaric lack of manners. So I will accompany you, but the British consul-general better have a damned bloody good explanation for all this nonsense."

I went peaceably, *sans* shackles. The captain ran his hands over the outside of my clothing in a token check for weapons. As his hand went down my right side, near where my Merwin-Hulbert revolver is stowed, I turned slightly so the hand descended over a less ominous portion of my torso. At the same time, I extended my left hand toward the parlor table and picked a flower from the vase there. I put the flower in my lapel. The gesture occupied the captain's attention for a moment, so he didn't understand what I was really doing.

"One *must* look his best when visiting Her Majesty's consulate. I'm sure you understand, Captain," I said with imperious gravity.

The real reason for the flower was to allow me to rearrange the flower vase's position on the table. It was only moved six inches but that was enough. Its new location was the signal between Rork and me that something amiss had occurred while the other was out of the suite. Upon returning to the room and seeing the signal, we would instantly, but carefully, flee the hotel. The emergency rendezvous was across the harbor in Regla. Each midnight for an hour, during the ensuing seven nights, we would watch for the other at the corner of Barrero and Soledad streets.

The ride in the captain's wagon only took a few minutes, during which no one spoke to me. To my surprise, we actually drove to the consulate. Once there, my escorts marched me into the musty anteroom. In front of an indifferent clerk, the captain clicked his heels with parade-ground precision, ordering him to announce to Mr. Harpford, deputy third secretary of the legation, that we had arrived. After a yawn to show the captain he wasn't impressed, the clerk disappeared to find Harpford.

The clerk reappeared several minutes later. He bid me to follow him, and for the captain, *et al*, to seat themselves in the anteroom. The captain, clearly upset by this assertion of British authority inside their own consulate, declined to repose in a chair. Instead, he shifted to a position of parade rest, which his minions tardily assumed a second later.

I followed Harpford to his tiny windowless office in the back of the building. On the way, we passed an open window in the hallway. Since it was on the first floor, the drop wouldn't be that bad, I reasoned, and noted it for emergency egress should things prove difficult.

Once the door to his office was closed, Harpford installed a monocle and sat down ceremoniously at his paper-bestrewn desk. Straightening his wrinkled vest and coat, and seemingly oblivious to the draconian manner of my coming, he thanked me for coming so promptly. Harpford then waved me to a cane-back chair and gestured to a gray-suited young man seated three feet away.

"Mr. Brinson, this is Mr. Juan Maura, assistant to the deputy chief of the foreign affairs section at the colonial ministry here in Havana. Mr. Maura is the Spanish governmental liaison with foreign journalists. He has come to us with a matter regarding you and Mr. McGregor, since we at the consulate represent all Her Majesty's imperial subjects in Cuba."

Juan Maura—Maria's Juanito? One look at him told me I was in serious trouble.

30

Claudine

Her Britannic Majesty's Consulate
Havana, Cuba
Friday afternoon
11 February 1898

Juan Maura was quite different from his older brother—shorter, stockier, with a darker complexion and attitude. Sitting ramrod straight with a briefcase on his lap and sheaf of papers in his hand, he cast me a stern look, but said nothing. In the dim light of a lone electric light bulb in the ceiling, I couldn't tell if he shared his mother's indigo blue eyes, but I could tell they weren't friendly.

Trying not to react to his name or scrutiny, I did a little half bow. "Melville Brinson, Toronto *Express*, at your service, sir. Nice to meet you."

I extended my hand, which he took with a surprisingly strong grip. If he knew who I really was, he didn't show it. I smiled at him and turned to Harpford.

"I say, my good man, if this is about an invitation to the Valentine's dance, I'll be delighted to come. A nice little bit of home tradition, way down here in the tropics, eh?"

"There is no Valentine's dance, Mr. Brinson," said Harpford humorlessly. "This is a bureaucratic issue, which needs to be resolved today, for our dear friends in the Spanish government are quite troubled about it."

Harpford was clearly bored with the meeting, and wanted this intrusion into his siesta hour over as soon as possible. I viewed his attitude and the topic as a positive sign—the entire thing was apparently some minor routine problem, easily explained away.

The Brit droned on. "Having said that, it seems there are some irregularities as to the position of you and Mr. McGregor in Cuba. Mr. Maura, would you care to state your concerns?"

Maura wasn't bored at all and, unlike Harpford, didn't mince any words.

"We have no record of your passport, no record of your entry into Cuba, and no record of your registration with us as required for foreign journalists in a war zone. There is no record of a newspaper called the *Express* in Toronto, Canada, having asked our government for permission to have one of their reporters work here."

"My goodness gracious!" I replied, thinking about how long it would take me to get to that open hallway window. "Well, somebody back at the editorial office in Toronto has buggered this up in monumental fashion, eh? Thank you for letting me know, and I sincerely apologize for their mistake. Gentlemen, I will get right over to the cable office and send them a telegram, post haste. We'll find out who fell asleep on that job, eh? I bet it was old Pinky—nice enough chap, but not really sharp with the paperwork, you know. The old boy is simply overwhelmed by too much to do."

I wagged my head in solemn empathy, then resumed. "They will send a cable back tomorrow, and mail all the paperwork you require for your records. And let me add this about that: my article about the efficiency and hospitality of the Spanish government in Havana will be centered on the man who truly knows what he's doing. That will be you, Mr. Maura. A real credit to your profession. With any luck, there'll be a promotion in it for you. Oh, and I won't forget you, Mr. Harpford. You have been a fine representative of Her Majesty. Again, gentlemen, thanks for informing me of this silly oversight. Damned embarrassing, eh?"

Harpford, who'd been leaning back in his swivel chair and daydreaming, gazed feebly at Maura and me. He'd done his duty, the matter was closed amiably, and he could go back to whatever he wasn't doing. The monocle was returned to his vest pocket.

Maura wasn't impressed by my explanation. "Present your identity papers now, Mr. Brinson. I will examine them."

Presenting a sincere look of confusion, I began fishing through my pockets for those papers, while estimating it would be twenty to thirty seconds to reach the hallway window. More if Maura tried to stop me. Shooting him wasn't an option—too loud.

"Let me see, where did I put those damned papers?"

Maura drummed his fingers on the chair arm and looked at the door, as if ready to call for the captain to come in and help me find them. I got the hint and brought out my personal documents.

"Right, here they are."

They consisted of an Ontario provincial press pass, a letter from my editor on the newspaper's stationery, an Imperial passport, and a Toronto bank statement—all reasonably well forged by a criminal acquaintance of mine in Washington. The point of having them was to bamboozle some street policeman, not a trained expert, which my stepson increasingly seemed to be.

He silently took them and slowly analyzed each one, writing notes about them in a ledger. That task took at least ten disquieting minutes. I glanced over at Harpford, who shrugged vacantly, for all this fuss wasn't his predicament. It would, though, make an interesting anecdote at the staff dining room later.

Finally, Maura finished with a disapproving harrumph. Without returning the papers, he announced, "These do not appear to be correct, Mr. Brinson. There is no entry stamp into

Cuba on your passport, no Spanish government endorsement on your company stationery, no Spanish government press pass, and no mailing address for the Toronto newspaper on this stationery."

"Oh, you need the address, eh?" I said. "No worries, old boy. They've just moved and I can have that sent down straight away. As for the passport, the fellow at—"

Maura interrupted by slashing his hand up through the air. He was done with small talk.

"Enough! I have already tried to contact the Toronto *Express* by telegraph and was told there is no address in Toronto for such an organization. I then had the Spanish consulate in Ottawa investigate and they reported your newspaper does not exist and has never existed. What do you say to *that,* Mr. Brinson? Now, state precisely how and when you entered Cuba. Tell me all of your locations while you have been here. And then include why you were at a private reception for the American naval captain, where treasonous anti-Spanish sentiments were expressed."

For the first time, his face showed emotion, and not the kind I wanted to see. It was a vicious little sneer. "Brinson, you are an imposter!"

Harpford was wide awake now. This wasn't a clerical error. His brows lowered ominously as he regarded me with new interest. I could see the machinations of his brain—*this man Brinson could be trouble for my career.* Both men leaned forward, eager to hear how I was going to answer. Maura's right hand was near his coat pocket and I wondered if he had a pistol ready to draw.

Slumping my shoulders, pouting my lips, and holding up my open left hand in the universal indications of submission, I gave Maura what he wanted, a confession. With their concentration centered on my face and words, my audience didn't notice my right foot hooking around the leg of my chair, and right hand slipping under a pile of papers on the corner of Harpford's desk beside me.

With plaintive voice I gave them a salacious reason for my deceit. "You've got me, gents. I lied, and it's all because of my lover, gentlemen. Claudine is a beautiful French girl, a Quebecoise, and I confess I have no power to resist her desires. The winter has been so bloody awful in Canada, you see, and dear Claudine wanted to come to Cuba where it is warm. She said she wanted to lie back on a beach under a coconut palm, without all those winter clothes, and feel the tropical sun's warmth on her lovely smooth skin."

My hand launched the entire pile of papers toward Maura's face as I leaped up and kicked my chair toward his legs. He tried to stand but fell backward in a heap as I jumped up and spun around toward the door. A second later, I was racing down the hallway toward that blessedly open window.

My leap out the window was ungainly, but I landed on both feet. As I ran down the side alley, my mind prioritized the route. First, retrieve the Spanish defenses map. Second, get to the rail yard. Third, hide on an eastbound cargo train to escape the city. Fourth, leave the train as it passed through Guanabacoa. Finally, I'd walk north to Regla and the rendezvous spot.

When two streets away, I heard the Orden Publico captain shouting far behind me. He was too late, for I was blended into the pedestrians by then and halfway to the map.

I figured with any luck I could make Regla by midnight.

31

Jupiter's Thunderbolt

Barrero & Soledad streets
Regla, Cuba
3:30 a.m., Monday morning
14 February 1898

My estimate was far too optimistic. The journey of ten miles took three days, most of which was spent hiding in alleys, bushes, and trees.

It was well over two hours after the agreed nightly meeting time when I hobbled into the rendezvous location. Rork wasn't in sight. Since I had nowhere else to go and my feet were throbbing, I sat down by a derelict coal wagon which had been relieved of its wheels and the brake. Its condition was symbolic of the place.

Regla was a filthy little town, covered by a thin layer of black dust and reeking of kerosene. The leading characteristics were the steamer docks, the attendant mountain of steamship coal, the railroad from the docks to Guanabacoa and Matanzas, several large Standard Oil Company-owned kerosene storage tanks, the rundown bullring, and the Church of Our Lady of Regla which boasted a famous black Madonna. Surrounding all this was a tenement slum.

In the early evening when the taverns were open, the town was a bustling place, for there were many ways to spend your money in Regla. Notwithstanding the church, most of them were associated with forms of vice. Those who furnish it were plentiful. But after midnight, it was quiet, dark, and vacant. Perfect for a clandestine rendezvous.

In pleasant contrast to my dismal environment on terra firma, a dome of clear winter air had arrived from North America, making the night sky a stunning palette. Sailors appreciate and use the heavens every day at sea for navigation, and surveying them is always a welcome respite. I felt the tensions within me easing away as I took it all in.

To the southeast, a half moon was rising over the hills on its timeless orbit to the other side of the world. Fortunately, its illumination wasn't bright enough to diminish the stars overhead. They glittered like diamonds strewn across a lady's black velvet cape, and the image of Maria wearing hers on special occasions came to mind.

Below the moon was the ruby flicker of Antares. In the constellation Scorpius, it's commonly known as the heart of the scorpion, one of the most insidious and dangerous mythological beings in the celestial sky. Childhood memories flashed from when I was a youngster at school and Mr. Stonehead regaled us with the stories from Greek and Roman mythology, connecting them to the stars above. Love, treachery, jealousy, bravery—the scorpion was in the middle of many of them.

To the east of Antares was mighty Saturn, Lord of the Titans. The pale-orange planet shone as a symbol of perennial power which couldn't be ignored. To me, it was a metaphor for many of the foes I'd battled in my life.

But the most impressive beacon in the sky was high overhead—Jupiter. Considered by the Romans to be king of the gods, Jupiter used thunderbolts to destroy his enemies. His likeness was prominently displayed by Rome's legions as a warning to enemies of what to expect if they dared to oppose the empire.

Lying on my back and gazing up at this cosmic history, I felt a sense of awe at the mythological supremacy imperial Rome maintained over its world. For a moment I wasn't in Cuba. I was up there among the planets and stars, sailing through the night. My eyelids grew heavy, and dreams took over.

"Ooh, boyo! The thunder king o' the gods `tis a bright little bugger tonight, now ain't he just? Methinks a scholar like our young Theodore could read somethin' into that!"

I nearly jumped out of my skin, instinctively reaching for my revolver.

Rork sat down beside me with a weary groan. He was dressed in dark clothes, blending in with the shadow of the wagon. I, on the other hand, was in stolen white trousers and light blue shirt, now in far more ragged shape than when first purloined two days earlier.

"Dammit all, Rork, don't ever scare me like that again! I almost shot you."

"Well now, that's a fine hello for your dear ol' shipmate. An' by the by, methinks it'd most likely be the other way around, *sir*, for you're the lad who let his guard down an' didn't notice me comin' on you."

Rork studied me closer. "You look like hell. What'd ye do, rob a beggar for his rags?"

There was something odd about his clothing too. "No, he was a farmer. Long, bad, story. What is it you're wearing?"

A touch of pride could be heard in his reply. "Oooh, just a little somethin' what get's me a free pass from the Spaniardos. They dearly love the one and true Church, unlike the likes o' you heathenly heretical Methodists."

He pulled open an overcoat and showed his black shirt. A white collar and gold crucifix gleamed at me.

"Why you old pirate," I said. "You stole it, didn't you?"

"Aye, regrettably, `tis the truth o' the matter. But they'll never miss it, an' Jesus will understand. Maybe."

I slapped him on the shoulder. "Well done! Where's mine?"

"*You?* Nay, nay, me ol' friend." He shook his head in grave disapproval. "There's such a thing as scruples, don't 'cha know. Jesus might be understandin' o' me in this rig, one o' his blessed peoples, but He'll not fancy for a wee second a Protestant such as you wearin' one!"

"Rork, you're sounding a bit over pious to me. You hardly ever go to church," I reminded him.

"Aye, an' mores the pity. Besides your wayward beliefs, there's a practical reason. Could only lay me hands on one o' these, an' it wouldn't do to return for another. Never nick the same place twice, so said me ol' Uncle Conall. An' he was a man who knew well the inside o' the gaol. But no worries, sir, we'll find somethin' for you `round here. So tell me what the hell happened to make us both take French leave o' Havana?"

I filled him in on my interrogation, escape, and the prolonged journey to get to Regla. His trek was simpler. He simply took the sewage barge across the harbor, telling the skipper he was a German seaman trying to get back to his ship. At Regla, he hid out behind the church rectory until I arrived.

"Damn, I wish I'd thought of that route," I muttered.

"Wouldn't work. Those boyos'd see through you in a heartbeat, sir. You're not rough an' tough enough lookin' to be a common sailorman. A gentleman is what you are, through an' through."

Rork laughed, then shook his head. "You gettin' hauled into the Brit consulate was part o' somethin' bigger an' uglier. This very mornin' got bad news from a young priest at the Regla church."

"Wait just a minute. The priest thought you were a brother priest? Isn't that blasphemy?"

He frowned at my interruption. "Well, now, me own tongue never actually *said* to the lad I was a priest. He *assumed* I was. His mistake, not mine.

"Be that as it may, me tale o' the bad news ain't done. The young priest at Regla church told me about his older brother, a sergeant in the uniform regiment of the Orden Publico, seeing Father Francisco Maura's dead body lyin' there in the trench at Cabaña Fortress. That was three mornin's ago, on the eleventh, the same day you were hauled in to face Juanito. The soldier knew Francisco well as a priest over at the Assisi monastery. Francisco's body wasn't in his cassock, though. He was in peasant rags, like he was a common rebel. The priest said his brother is a devout man an' very upset by a priest bein' murdered. Said the brother was even more upset the newspaper yesterday listed an unnamed Franciscan priest as the deceased victim of a bandit gang outside the city."

The trench at Cabaña is notorious for being where Cuban rebels have been executed since 1868. The fortress is one of several located on a bluff across the harbor's entrance channel from Havana city. Marrón moved the location of his special unit's interrogations four years earlier, from the basement of the Carcel, the old criminal court jail, in Havana, across the water to the lower levels of Cabaña. It is far more removed from the public, rebels, senior authorities, and prying eyes. I knew of no prisoner who'd ever come out of Cabaña alive. The mere mention of the place causes many Cubans to shudder.

"Let me get this straight. This soldier is *absolutely sure* it was Father Francisco Maura?"

"Exactly me own question, an' he said yes, his brother was certain o' it. An' there's a wee bit more, sir. An' it's a nasty wee bit."

I steeled myself. "Which is?"

"The sergeant brother o' the priest asked about the dead body. The lad's officer told him the body was a rebel spy workin' for the *norteamericanos*, passin' messages to `em from the rebels."

"At the luncheon with Maria at the yacht club."

"Aye, sir. An' that means they've connected it all—Maria, Francisco, an' you. Thank you Jesus our dear lady's safe at home, an' that you got away from the limey embassy when you did."

The information, if true, was staggering. To arrest a priest was serious, even if only for an interview and involuntary transfer out of Cuba. It could only be undertaken with the highest approval in the colonial government and church. To murder a priest was far beyond anything a senior official would authorize. I'd never heard of anything like it.

I remembered Juanito Maura's question on why I was at the luncheon for Sigsbee where treasonous statements were made. Francisco had been verbally supportive of his mother's comments at the luncheon, but they were more pro-peace than anti-Spain. In the fearful atmosphere of Havana's secret police, however, that was enough. It told me Marrón must be completely panicked and devoid of any last shred of sanity.

"Maria's heart will be broken . . ." I said in despair.

"Aye, a mother's grief has no end."

"We've got to get the defense plans out to *Maine.* I saw she's still at anchor in the same spot."

"Aye, sir, that she is. But me hands've not been idle while waitin' for you. Made arrangements here in Regla to get you out to *Maine*."

"Rork, you continually amaze me."

"Well, don't be congratulatin' me yet, sir. It ain't gonna be a posh ride, but it's the only one available for the likes o' us right about now. An' it'll only be you goin' out to the ship."

"Only me? You're going too."

He shook his head. "Two days ago, before me unofficial joinin' the priesthood, a villainous ol' sort here in Regla told me he'll do it for twenty in gold tomorrow night—but he wants his rummy pal along to help on the long row from here to the ship an' back. The dinghy's pretty small, seen it with me own eyes, so only one o' us at a time can go with `em in the boat. Me an' the bag o' gear'll wait by the docks for your return, or a message to come on out."

"Very well. I'll either come back in person, or send word for you to come out."

Rork laid back and took in the heavenly display above us. "Ooh, now there's the thunderbolt. Bad omen."

I followed his pointing finger, but my mind was on other things. "What?"

"The celestial thunderbolt. `Tis the line o' stars from Jupiter's hand down through the moon to blood-stained Saturn and Antares. Hells bells, Peter, you're the one who taught me about it back in Florida durin' the war. `Tis not a favorin' sign at all. Best be careful on that wee little boat with those two ne'er-do-wells."

I suddenly remembered that night, back in 1864, off the Dry Tortugas. Then I saw what he meant tonight—a jagged line of twinkling fire from the heavens to the earth. To Havana.

"Rork, your Gaelic superstitions are getting the best of you."

I'm a Christian and dismiss such lore, but couldn't ignore the chill that swept through me.

32

Things Are Looking Up

U.S.S. Maine
Havana Harbor
Tuesday night
15 February 1898

After hiding out overnight in an open sugar cane barn, the next morning Rork "found" a suit of clothes for me near the back door of a nearby laundry. I was still sweaty and grimy, but at least my attire was appropriate. Since "Melville Brinson" of Toronto probably had become *persona non grata* in the area around Havana, I returned to my earlier alias used at Sagua, that of "Peder Fisker," the Canadian tobacco broker of Danish heritage.

Rork took me to meet the dinghy man at a half past eight o'clock in the evening. A less inspiring fellow would be hard to find, and that's saying something in Regla. Ancient, arthritic, drunk, with shifty yellow eyes and greasy hands, Perro and his unnamed crewman offered a garbled greeting, then descended unsteadily into a rough-built dinghy of perhaps ten feet. Water slopped aboard in the process, prompting Perro to giggle and cough, spewing phlegm all over his friend. Then he gestured for me to come on down.

Rork looked apologetically at me and said, "He wasn't this drunk when I made the deal, sir. Maybe we should belay this idea? Or, we could just steal the damn boat an' do it ourselves."

I'd been thinking the same thing, but there wasn't time. "No, we'd have to kill them to stop them from howling about it. Then we'd have to hide the bodies. This seems to be the only way, so this it is. I'll swim back if worse comes to worse and we sink on the way out."

To my amazement, it didn't come to worse. The two reprobates were veteran boatmen, and once under way they handled their oars well, rowing without comment through the crowded harbor toward the brightly lit American warship. After evading two Spanish guard boats on the way, they also had to wait until another Spanish guard boat went around to the other side of *Maine*'s bow before making the final approach to the warship's port quarter.

"Boat ahoy!" called a petty officer from the main deck, as a cone of light from aloft swung around to settle on the dinghy.

"I am a Canadian friend of Captain Sigsbee, with a message for him about the boa constrictor he wanted," I shouted to the blinding light. Of course, I didn't *look* like a friend. My companions and I looked like bandits. And the boa constrictor part was absurd.

A new voice, presumably the officer of the deck, boomed out of the light. "*Who* exactly are you?"

I knew there were now half a dozen rifles and a machine gun aimed at me.

"Mr. Peder Fisker, of Ontario, Canada, eh. I am a tobacco broker visiting Havana. Please inform Captain Sigsbee I am arriving. He's expecting me."

I didn't wait for an answer and instead urged my motley crew to action, for the commotion was sure to attract the unwanted attention of the Spanish guard boat on the other side of the warship. Without permission, I leaped onto the boarding ladder and over my shoulder told the Cubans to head back for me in half an hour.

When I reached the main deck, my reception committee was fully armed and ready to repel boarders, not a single one of them recognizing me in my present dishevelment. An angry lieutenant stepped forward.

"Stop right there. I am Lieutenant Randal Briggs, officer of the deck. Do you have any identification?"

I was prepared to explain my real name and profession, but we were interrupted by a man calling from the bridge deck forward. "I know him, Mr. Briggs. Please guide the gentleman to my cabin."

"Turn the searchlight away from the dinghy, Mr. Briggs," I said in a low voice, changing my tone from friendly Canadian trader to one accustomed to command. "It is coming back in thirty minutes for me. Please do not shine a light on it then either. I do not want the Spanish guard boats to be alarmed over it. And you don't have to escort me to the captain's cabin—I know the way quite well."

Briggs instinctively straightened to attention. "Aye, aye, sir," came the automatic but perplexed reply from the young officer, who then escorted me anyway.

Once we got to Sigsbee's cabin and the door was closed behind me, I said, "Forgive my intrusion, Captain Sigsbee, and thank you for seeing me so unexpectedly."

He greeted me with a slap on the shoulder and broad smile. "No intrusion at all, Captain Wake, I was just writing some letters home. I must say, you do lead an unusual life, don't you? So now it's Mr. Peder Fisker, a Canadian tobacco broker? I expected you before this."

"Yes, well, we had some unfortunate difficulties ashore and have been trying to evade the attention of the Spanish authorities. Hence the change in alias and my rather irregular appearance and arrival."

He nodded sympathetically. "You look like you could use a bath, shave, decent meal, and tot of something strong. We can accommodate all of that straight away."

The mention of such luxuries weakened my resolve, but I declined quickly. "Maybe later, Captain, when I have a bit more time. I brought out a secret document which needs to get to Washington immediately—the Spanish defense plans for Havana. Go ahead and take a look at them. You need to know them more than anyone. I thought *Cushing* could get it to Key West, but I see she's gone."

"Left this morning." He took the defense map. "My goodness. They've really reinforced them, haven't they? I won't ask how you got it, but this is an incredible find, Captain Wake."

"Yes, it is. I think you might have our orders from Secretary Roosevelt. Did they arrive?"

He handed me a steaming mug. "Yes, they did. Sit down and drink this while I get the envelope."

As he disappeared into his office, I sat down in one of his navy blue velveteen chairs and lifted the mug from the cherry wood side table. It was black coffee laced with rum and tasted delicious. I leaned back in the chair and admired his plush cabin. It was even better than my captain's sanctum in *Newark*.

"Here it is," Sigsbee said when he returned and handed me the envelope. "Want me to leave you in privacy?"

"No, you don't need to leave, but another mug of this coffee would go down nicely while I do some deciphering. Won't take long from what I see."

It was a short message, using sets of numbers which would be translated into Biblical text, the same as before. From inside my coat, I pulled out the small Danish Bible and Danish-English dictionary which Rork had saved in his sea bag. Unwrapping them from their protective oilskin waterproofing, I laid everything out on the coffee table before me and commenced to deduce the message.

There were only five sets of numbers, spread out on three sheets of different shades of blue paper. Arranging them lighter to darker with the lightest first, they read:

0364921291306
0120341675503
0063003365106
0107244483203
1001484500701

Removing the false numbers inserted into each set, left me with:

0361206
0121603
0063306
0104403
1004501

They pointed toward certain words in Matthew 12:4, Matthew 4:22, Matthew 1:20, Matthew 4:3, and Mark 4:36.

In Danish it said: **Tilbagevenden straks tage bestilling skibe**

The process was the same as earlier, but this time I had a hindrance. The fourth word caused me trouble. I uttered a curse directed toward the assistant secretary of the navy, because it was the Danish word to "order," as in telling someone to do something. Out of the corner of my eye, I saw Sigsbee's eyebrow rise in reaction to my insubordination.

"Trouble?"

"Roosevelt can be difficult at times," I explained. He laughed, for every officer in the navy knew that.

Literally translated, the message was: **Return immediately take order ships**

That didn't make sense. I presumed Biblical Danish was different than conversational Danish, just as it is in English. Theodore had used the closest thing he could find in the copy of the Bible he possessed. I would have to infer what he really meant, by trying several synonyms in the message.

One of them did make sense: **Return immediately—take command ships**

In late December, Roosevelt and I discussed how to quickly increase the size and capabilities of the navy when war came. We came up with a novel way to increase the navy's inshore operational capacity, but I hadn't heard anything more about it. This message indicated he had proceeded with our novel idea, a special squadron of small ships brought into the navy to work the onshore waters of Cuba.

I had no desire to be involved in the project, only suggesting it based on my own experiences against the Confederates three decades earlier. To the contrary, if war came, I wanted command of a cruiser in the battle fleet. Roosevelt was giving me the job no one else wanted.

Sigsbee saw my expression. "Bad news? Can I help?"

"No, not bad news at all—just surprising. I'm ordered to return immediately. When are you scheduled to depart Havana?"

"I'm not, Captain Wake. *Maine* is to remain here until further orders from Washington. The *City of Washington* is departing early tomorrow morning for New York. You could go in her if you get passage and a cabin tonight, if there's one left. Get that bath and shave, too."

"Yeah, I suppose you're right. I'll go aboard her tonight. I think the defense plans should stay here, though. They'll be far more secure in your safe. There *is* something important you can do to help. Can you write me out an endorsement I can show the steamer's captain, so he'll let Rork and me aboard? The dinghy will be coming back alongside any minute now and we've got to get away before the Spanish guard boat comes back around and sees us."

Sigsbee beamed in response. "More skullduggery!"

Sixteen minutes later, as the duty quartermaster's mate struck three bells in the first watch, or nine-thirty p.m., I stepped into the dinghy, my rummy crew being right on time. We shoved off for Regla. My shoes and ankles were soaked due to the water in the bilges being even higher than before, and I felt around in the dark for something to bail with.

Fortunately, our departure was without interruption from the Spanish guard boat, the officer of the deck having conveniently engaged them in conversation on the other side of the ship. The only problem I saw was the dinghy sinking. As we headed across the harbor in the sultry night, I found a small bucket and started emptying the dinghy. Perro saw me and giggled again, never missing a stroke of his oar.

Despite the condition of our craft, I was feeling pretty good. Rork and I were going home, and on a passenger liner, no less. He'd be delighted. After a perilous month in Cuba, things were finally looking up.

33

Just Lollygagging Around

Havana Harbor
Tuesday night
15 February 1898

That was when it happened. Two hundred feet from *Maine*, I heard a muffled thud behind me. It rumbled from below, in the water instead of the air. I turned to see what had happened.

Everything erupted into a mass of light and noise. *Maine* had turned into an inferno. The screams of the wounded filled the air.

As the reader of this memoir has already seen at the beginning of the story, the next hours were agony and terror for me as I tried to swim across the harbor while evaluating what had happened and what I should do. I cannot give precise times for this period, for my pocket watch disappeared. I do know it was several hours later when I reached the Regla side of the harbor.

The place was jammed with people. Emerging from the water in front of the crowd of Spanish military and police at the ship docks was out of the question, so I swam east through the harbor toward the dark shoreline of Ensenada Marimelena. Much later, my feet touched bottom in front of a beach. I saw a small group of people, the distant firelight from *Maine* reflecting in the faces. I was about to try to wade ashore and take my chances with them when I heard an Irish brogue behind me.

"There's one, over there. *Por ahí! Remar el friggin' barco* like *men*, ye damned sons o' bitches! Them Spaniardo bastards behind us're headin' our way!"

Relief filled me as I watched a boat get closer. Rork was standing in the stern sheets of a six-oared launch, silhouetted by the shore and ship lights behind him. His false hand steered the tiller, and in the other I saw his Navy Colt at the ready, quite an incongruous sight in his priest's rig. Farther astern, another launch was heading toward us.

I tried yelling to him, but it came out as a croaking sound. My arms were too useless to wave above me.

Rork's launch closed to within fifty feet. "Ship yer oars!"

The launch glided up to me and three pairs of arms reached out. They were rough-looking waterfront men, and quickly pulled me up and over the gunwale. I was passed aft like a bag of potatoes, collapsing in the bilge at the stern.

Rork and I hugged. I tried to say thank you, but ended up rasping out something unintelligible instead.

"Were you on her when she blew up?" he exclaimed, as he gave me a swig of grog from a flask. I took three more, washing the salt out of my mouth, enabling me to speak more normally.

"No, no . . . I was in the dinghy, heading back to you."

"Bloody friggin' damnation, Peter Wake, then just what the hell're you doin' *lollygaggin'* around over here in the middle o' nowhere? Jaysus, Mary, and Joseph, I've been worried sick while you were takin' a leisurely swim around the damned harbor. Hell, I had to pressgang this bunch o' evil-eyed buggers at *gunpoint* an' steal a boat, an' we've been searchin' all over this friggin' harbor to find your carcass for over two bloody hours!"

Over two hours? I wracked my mind for the time I'd left *Maine*—about nine-thirty. *That made it almost midnight now.*

I took another drink. Rork stopped for a moment and looked back at the Spanish boat, gauging their course, speed, and intent. To the "evil-eyed buggers" in his crew, he barked, "Row, damn you!"

Rork steered a course further east, heading for a point near the mouth of a creek. Turning his attention back down to me in the bilge, he sighed and, his voice trembling with emotion, whispered, "As the Lord above knows, I thought you were dead an' gone, Peter. Made me ol' heart crazy scared when we couldn't find you. Don't *ever* friggin' do that to me again."

"Wasn't my idea, Sean. I thought they got you too. Decided to swim somewhere else so I wouldn't get captured. Thank you for not giving up."

My aching body gave up at that point, every muscle ceasing to do anything but lay limp. My mind, on the other hand, was charged up with a swirl of questions.

"Did you see how they sank *Maine*?" I asked. "I only heard one blast. My God, we must've lost hundreds of men, she's completely gone."

"Aye, she is. I was keepin' a watch o' the harbor after you shoved off from the dock, an' there twarn't any firing from the shore forts, before or after the explosion. 'Twas only a single huge blast, as you say, sir. Methinks it must'a been a bloody great mine, or maybe a lucky torpedo shot from that old Spaniardo cruiser anchored nearby."

Rork glanced aft. The Spanish boat had veered off toward the docks at Havana. "Good, she's headin' away from us, sir. We'll go ashore at the creek dead ahead an' get out o' sight. These bastards can have the boat an' some coins."

I looked over at the still flaming wreck on the west side of the harbor. The rum helped my voice return. "The cruiser had her torpedo tubes removed last year. *Maine*'s been anchored in the same spot for three weeks, and it's a Spanish naval mooring. So, if it *was* a mine, it must've already been there, as an electrically command-detonated mine. Maybe that's why they directed *Maine* to that mooring. The mines're controlled from the mine room at Cabaña Fortress, remember?"

"Ah, where Colonel Marrón has his office an' dungeon these days. Do you think that slimy bastard could've done it, to start the war he always wanted with us?"

"Not sure, but I don't *think* so. The mine field is controlled by the Spanish Navy, and I don't think Marrón has much sway over them. Most of their senior naval officers don't want a war with us. I know Admiral Manterola doesn't. Of course, I suppose it could've been a disgruntled junior officer on the duty watch, or possibly one of Marrón's men somehow got inside the control room and set it off."

Another possibility came to mind. "Do you suppose it might've been an accidental explosion in the magazine? I did hear an odd little thump a fraction of a second before the explosion. It seemed to come from *Maine*, and I was turning around to see when the blast hit us. Coal bunker, maybe? Spontaneous combustion there, which lit off the magazine next to the bunker? That would be enough to destroy the ship in one blast."

Rork shook his head. "Nay, *Maine*'s a well-run ship. No heat could build in the bunker or the magazine without 'em knowin' o' it on the regular temperature inspections. Me own money's on Marrón somehow settin' off a mine from that control room at Cabaña Fortress."

We were getting close to shore, and I noticed the crew was casting stealthy glances at each other. I felt for my revolver. Somehow, it was still in its holster. I pointed it forward toward the men, propping my hand on my knee. The ones closest to me pulled harder.

Rork asked, "Did you get our orders and money from Washington, sir? Is it homeward bound, or back to Sagua?"

"No money. Roosevelt's ordered us home. Looks like they're forming the new squadron we discussed with him a while back, and I'm supposed to command it. But after tonight, who knows."

Rork didn't like that notion. "That special squadron you an' young Theodore hatched is a commander's billet. You're too senior for the likes o' that. The main battle fleet's where you should be—in command o' a cruiser, with me as your petty officer aide."

I locked eyes with the man pulling the bow oars. He started pulling stronger. Not taking my eyes off him, I replied to Rork. "I don't think so, my friend. Now the war's come, all the senior officers with academy diplomas and Congressional connections will get those commands. You know how the politics works. But it doesn't matter right now. I've got an idea on what we can do while we're still in Havana tonight."

Rork cast me a quick guarded look. "Oh, no, not another o' your wild ideas. Usually it means somebody's gonna be shootin' at us—an' these days me ol' hull is a bigger an' slower target than yours! An' in case you forgot, your ownself's in no shape to be doin' anythin' strenuous tonight."

He swung his gaze forward, snapping, "Row, you *cabrones!* Row your evil hearts out!"

"Rork, it's just a simple matter of deviousness, really," I said calmly. "Nothing too strenuous."

He groaned. "Jaysus, help me. Me boyo Peter's bein' devious again. An' that always gets me shot."

"Just listen to me and stop being so dramatic, Rork. We're still heading back home, but when I was in the water I did some thinking. I was last seen onboard *Maine*, then I disappeared when she exploded. In all the confusion around here, we'll both be included on the official list of missing, presumed dead. The Spanish will see that list. Everybody on both sides'll think we're dead, including Colonel Marrón. Therefore, nobody will be looking for us anymore, right?"

"Aye . . ."

"And that gives us some freedom of action to get something done before we leave Havana. Something that's been needed to be done since I failed back in eighty-eight."

He caught on immediately. "Sendin' Colonel Isidro Marrón back down into hell."

"Precisely, Rork—it's time."

"Hell, why didn't ye say that up front? Count me in, sir," he said as the boat's hull grounded near the mouth of the creek. "There's nary time to dawdle, so let's strike while this bloody iron's hot."

"We will. Tonight we'll get him out of the fortress by laying a trap—with bait he can't resist."

"An' just who or what would that be, sir?"

"Maria."

34

The Trap

Fortaleza de San Carlos de la Cabaña
Havana, Cuba
4 a.m., Wednesday morning
16 February 1898

The plan was simple and the trap was ready, for the bait had been dangled right in front of the predator as he reposed in the heart of his lair.

Marrón, was lying on a cot in his office deep inside Cabaña Fortress, two layers below ground level, when he received the following note at four in the morning from a messenger. Rendered into English for the reader, it said:

Colonel Isidro Marrón
Special Section, Orden Publico
Fortaleza de San Carlos de la Cabaña
Havana, Cuba
2:30 a.m., 16 February 1898

My Dear Colonel Marrón,

It is my honor to report to you the traitorous Spanish woman Maria Maura Wake, wife of the nefarious American spy, was recognized last night on the docks of Cojímar by myself and Lieutenant

Mateo Rodrigues, both on temporary duty with the Second Battalion of the Cuerpo Militar de Orden Publico. Obviously, previous reports of her leaving Havana were false, and she was in Cojímar trying to escape the island on a fishing boat and get to Key West. This endeavor on her part was unsuccessful, thanks to the patriotism of our islanders, who saw through her many deceits. Having identified her, we immediately captured her and took her away before anyone else knew and could warn her fellow conspirators. We are holding her at a tool shed on the Garcia Plantation, just off the road which runs through the hills from Casablanca to Cojímar.

Due to Maria Maura Wake's influential name and connections in Spain and in the United States, we thought it was more prudent to hold her in the isolated shed, where no one in authority would recognize her, than to bring her to Cabaña Fortress, especially since the explosion of the arrogant yanqui warship. Our interrogation has convinced her to be cooperative, and she has provided us valuable information about the American naval plans for the invasion of Cuba, details about the spy Wake, and a list of her fellow traitors in Havana.

All of this we have kept secret from everyone, for the information is of such importance that few can be trusted with it.

We respectfully request you come here, sir, for we are in need of your skills in these matters. She says she knows no more, but we are convinced she does by her arrogant attitude. Delivering this message is our aide, Sergeant Poyo. He will take you here immediately.

With respect and admiration for your long service and leadership to our beloved Empire, and may God preserve our gracious King and Country, we are . . .

Lieutenant Manuel Bolita
Lieutenant Mateo Rodrigues
Second Battalion, Cuerpo Militar de Orden Publico

Of course, the lieutenants were fictional, but the sergeant wasn't. Poyo was very real, the very same devout and troubled soldier who had recognized Father Francisco's body in peasant rags at the trench of Cabaña Fortress. He was ready to help when approached at his barracks near Casablanca at two in the morning by an Irish priest named Rork. Good man that he was, Poyo naturally assumed the encounter was by Divine instigation. The "priest" did nothing to dissuade his impression.

"Thank you, my son," said Rork. "Your assistance on this mission of justice will be your atonement for being in the regiment which was a part of this tragedy. It is your way of making sure your friend Father Francisco did not die in vain."

Even though the priest spoke terrible Spanish, Sergeant Poyo understood his meaning. The sergeant's duty would be simple, but crucial to justice being served.

"Deliver this note to the colonel. Tell him how beautiful the woman prisoner is, and then lead him to the shed," Rork told him gently in Spanish. "Once he goes inside, return to your barracks. No one will ever know of your involvement, my son."

Half an hour later, Poyo left on his part of the mission.

35

Without Explanation or Dignity

Garcia Plantation
Outside Cojímar, Cuba
5:22 a.m., Wednesday morning
16 February 1898

I knew Maria would be irresistible bait for Isidro Marrón. On the way to the shed, he would be imagining his own vile pleasures with her—after he'd ordered Bolita and his men to give him privacy for a "special interrogation."

I knew his psyche because I'd been his prisoner in 1886. I had vivid memories of the lust in his eyes as he showed me the surgical tools he would use on me to convince me to talk. He slowly turned them over so I could see each probe, blade, and pincer. Marrón's sweaty brow and heavy breathing betrayed his enjoyment of the terror in my eyes.

I escaped his dungeon before he could use his tools on me, but it wasn't long before his tentacles reached into my home and family at Patricio Island. It was personal between us. A team of his henchmen were sent to kill us. They didn't. In 1888 and in

1893, Marrón sent others, but each time they failed, as I did with him in Havana.

Monsters like Marrón never change. Understanding this can be an asset for those among us who must fight them. Once you ignite the lust which dominates them, any shrewdness or caution in their mind evaporates. Their grotesque behavior becomes predictable.

Rork and I were hiding in a banyan tree near the tool shed when Sergeant Poyo and Marrón arrived on horseback. The moon was barely visible in the increasingly cloudy night, and the wind carried smoke from *Maine*, four miles to the west.

Sergeant Poyo did his job well when they dismounted, explaining he wasn't allowed in the shed, per Lieutenant Bolita's orders. The tenor of his words implied the officer didn't want any witness to see the condition of the female prisoner. Poyo gestured for the colonel to enter and then stood at parade rest, as if he would wait outside until he received further orders. Ten seconds after Marrón went inside, Poyo mounted his horse and trotted off toward his barracks.

I could hear Marrón in the shed, asking for the lieutenants. His manner changed quickly from pleasant curiosity to anger. The shed was empty, the few rusty old scythes and cane knives having been removed by Rork and myself. The colonel realized he had been tricked. When he stormed out of the front door with pistol in hand, his solar plexus was crushed by a perfectly placed round house blow with a curved limb from the gumbo limbo tree beside the shed.

Marrón staggered backward before doubling over and falling down, clutching his chest and gasping for air. It wasn't difficult to remove the pistol from his hand as he peered up at his executioners.

He asked me who I was. *"¿Quién es usted?"*

"*Justicia*," I replied.

He knew what was coming. In a strangely detached manner, he asked why. *"¿Por qué?"*

"*Para Cuba . . .*"

Unlike with his victims, the end was quick, by way of Isidro Marrón's own pistol.

His remains were dragged to the bank of a creek close by, where Marrón's kindred reptilians lurked, their red-eyes reflecting in a shaft of moonlight which had beamed down seconds earlier. One by one, the crocodiles responded to their primordial instincts and slithered over to the clump on the bank of the creek. The first of them nudged the body several times, then took a bite. Others followed. The scene soon became an orgy of violence.

It was done in seconds. All traces of the beast who had targeted my family, and thousands of Cubans, literally vanished, without explanation or dignity. I knew then the tide had turned against the henchmen of the Special Section, for the very mystery of Marrón's disappearance would lead to quiet terror among them. Who would be next? When?

For me, the long haunting nightmare of Marrón hurting my family was over. Rork and I were free to return home.

At Cojímar, we found a fisherman willing to sail us to Key West the next night for twenty Morgan dollars. This man was no pirate, offering us rest and food until the journey. After resting in the man's hut during the day, we got under way an hour after sunset, just another fishing boat heading out to work. The Spanish sentries at the ancient fort on the point never even challenged us. Soon we were surging along on a broad reach across the Straits of Florida under all sail and a clearing sky. It felt gloriously refreshing—the very best medicine for our recuperation.

Rork and I stretched out on the foredeck, silently contemplating, each lost in our thoughts. Ahead lay the thin dark line of the Florida Keys and safety. To starboard, Jupiter was rising yet again in the east. Far astern was Cuba.

I knew I'd be back.

36

Mightily Envied

Navy Department
State, War, and Navy Building
Washington D.C.
7 a.m., Monday morning
21 February 1898

Assistant Secretary of the United States Navy Theodore Roosevelt was clearly loving every moment of it, now that his position had transformed from predicting war to running one. Bent over the large globe in his office, he stood muttering to himself as his fisted hand pounded the Philippines. His expression was the most intense I'd ever seen on his face. With eyes narrowed to mere slits, brow wrinkled in decision, jaw clenched in determination, and teeth bared in disgust of the enemy, he was the picture of righteous malevolence.

Then Theodore looked up and saw Rork and me in his doorway. His face went blank. For the first time in the twelve years I'd known him, the man was speechless.

I saved him the effort. "Yes, I know. We're both supposed to be dead. That's what the Marine guard, the receptionist, and your personal secretary all said when we arrived this morning."

Roosevelt is as quick with his mind as he is with his judo, and he recovered swiftly. "You two are—*were*—dead. I saw your names on the list. So much for official reports!"

"Sorry about that, sir. It was a simple *ruse de guerre*, which I judged useful for us. We weren't aboard when *Maine* exploded and we never checked in with the consulate afterward. It helped us get some things done."

I went on to explain that, not knowing if our new orders might require anonymity or a rapid departure again, Rork and I had kept incommunicado during the long journey back to Washington. We never checked in to the naval station at Key West, used a fishing smack to get to Tampa, used aliases for the northbound trains, and upon arrival at the capital went directly to Roosevelt's office. I never even sent a telegram to Maria.

"*Bully* fine *discipline!*" Roosevelt said. "Maria will understand, I'm *sure.*"

"No, sir, she won't. I have no intention of telling her I came to the office first."

He held his belly and laughed. "I understand *that!* To paraphrase Congreve back in 1695, 'Hell hath no *fury* like a woman scorned.' Edith is the same way, Peter. Now, *before* I send you home to a *joyous* reunion, I want to hear *all* about your adventure!"

He shouted to his secretary to clear his appointments, and for the next hour I explained all we had learned and experienced inside Cuba. The sole omission in the recital was my final interaction with Marrón. I simply said we escaped the island through Cojímar.

Roosevelt informed us Captain Sigsbee's cabin safe containing the stolen Havana defense plans had survived the blast and had been delivered two days before our return. He was "*dee*-lighted" the navy now had a clear understanding of what they were up against at Havana. In fact, the plan showed Spanish defenses had been reinforced so much that landings close to Havana were deemed too risky and were cancelled. Hundreds, perhaps thousands, of American lives were saved.

Roosevelt's proposal for an American invasion at Isabela and Sagua Grande, was also cancelled. Instead, the U.S. Army decided to land only in eastern Cuba. The Spanish defenses were thought to be weaker in the east, and their overland communication and supply lines to and from Havana were exposed to depredations from Gómez's Cuban rebel army.

Isabela and Sagua Grande was chosen as the landing place for a battalion of Cuban exile reinforcements bound for General Gómez's western forces. They would be escorted by the American navy, which would also neutralize Spanish defenses in the port. The Cuban exile unit was being assembled throughout the southern states and would embark on a steamer in Florida.

Theodore stood up and marched over to the chart table, beckoning us to follow. "And *that* brings me to *your* next assignment, or should I say *adventure!* I know you'll *both* think it a *capital* idea! I hinted at it in my message to you in Havana."

The two of us joined Roosevelt at the table, where a chart of Cuba's island-studded northern coast was spread out. Part of the central coast was delineated by a red pencil line.

"Did one o' the cruiser commands open up, sir?" asked Rork hopefully. I shot him a disapproving glance.

Roosevelt waved his dismissal of the cruiser idea. "No, not *that*, Rork. Those *boring* commands have all gone to others who don't have the *skills* you and Peter have. No, my dear fellows, this is *tailor* made for the *two* of you."

He straightened up and paused for effect, then proudly announced, "It's nothing less than *command* of the composite *squadron* we envisioned. A *commodore*'s pennant, Peter! Rork, you'll be his senior petty officer aide, *of course*."

When we didn't gush in proper appreciation, he didn't miss a beat and gushed in exclamation.

"*Forget* commanding a *single* ship and steaming around offshore, *tethered* to some hidebound old admiral and *hindered* by the *slowest* ship in the group. *No!* You'll have an *entire squadron* of small, fast, *well-armed*, ships. You'll be *close* to the *enemy* and the *sound* of the guns, with lots of *opportunities* for *innovation* and independent *action!*"

I was about to ask a rather important question, but he started thumping the coast of Cuba with his fist. "It is a *grand* assignment, is it not? Other officers will be *jealous* of you, but *I'll* handle *them*."

No, they won't. They'll pity me, I thought.

He thumped the coast of Cuba again. "Now, to the *meat* of the matter! Your *ships* will be covering the inshore waters along a sixty-mile stretch of the northern coast of Santa Clara Province, from Sierra Morena in the west to Caibarien in the east. You'll *attack* Isabela on the coast, and assist getting the Cuban exile patriots *ashore* and inland to Sagua Grande, afterward establish a *close* blockade. Naturally, you'll be free for anything else you two can cook up in those *fertile* minds to *harass* and *confound* the enemy. Oh, how I *envy* you both *mightily!*"

When he finally took a breath, I seized the opportunity to make an important observation. "But we aren't at war, sir. Rork and I thought we would be when *Maine* blew up, but when we reached Key West, we found out we aren't. According to the newspapers on the trains up to Washington from Tampa, Congress hasn't declared war. The president says he doesn't want war. The Spanish haven't declared war and say it must have been an accidental explosion. Even Captain Sigsbee has counseled everyone not to jump to conclusions about what caused the blast."

Theodore didn't want to hear any of it. With pursed lips he cleared his throat, removed his spectacles, and said, "You are correct, Peter. War has *not* been *declared* by either side *yet*, and the *official* naval inquiry has not been concluded . . . *yet*. I have no doubt, *however*, the inquiry will decide *Maine* was destroyed by a naval *mine*, an act of *war!* We are still burying our *dead*, and you saw the funerals at Key West, right?"

"Yes, sir."

"The *country* saw them too, in the pages of the press, and our *people* are at long last emerging from their slumber and are *angry!* They are *ready* to prepare for *conflict*, even if *some* of the more *jellyfish*-spined politicians in Washington are not. And when it *does* come, *you* and your ships will be in the *thick* of the *fight!*"

"I see, sir. About this composite squadron of . . . special . . . ships, where do I join it?"

His reply began with yet another dismissive wave of the hand. "Well, it's not fully formed *yet*. The funds are pending Congressional action, and I have it on *good* authority Congress will be seeing to that *quite* soon, within two weeks. Once *done*, you will procure, arm, and man the ships in your command and steam thence toward *Cuba*. In the meantime, I want you to set into *action* the clandestine surveillance project on the Spanish Navy we discussed, report to me on that man Holland's *submarine* boat project, and review the list of *yachts* offered to us by owners on the east coast."

With a mock serious look which quickly morphed into a grin, Theodore added a further command. "However, first things *first*. You are both hereby placed on *leave* for one week, effective *immediately*. Come back next Monday morning ready get to *work* and make those reports, then to get your squadron commissioned and ready to *fight* this *war!*"

As Rork and I left the building a few minutes later to head for our respective abodes, I saw he was uncharacteristically pensive. Before parting, we stopped at the bottom of the marble steps and I asked him, "Well, old friend, what do you think?"

He shot me a sarcastic look. "You're wantin' me opinion o' dear Theodore's pipedream about the squadron? Well, methinks this about that: we'll have the element o' surprise, that's for sure, `cause nobody's ever tried turnin' a bunch o' fancy thin-skinned yachts into warships an' sendin' `em into battle. Hell, it was a daft notion when we were talkin' months ago, an' it didn't improve a whisker with age. Only bright side may be those Spaniardo bluejackets laughin' so bloody hard at us, they're not able to shoot straight. `Tis damned embarrassin' for a man in me own position to be associated with such a thing. Not to mention you, a senior officer. You rate better than this foolishness."

I tried to be optimistic. "Hey, at least the accommodations should be nice. After all, she'll be a yacht!"

As usual, Rork got in the last word. "Only for the *officers* . . . sir."

With that depressing note, we parted ways, Rork to the Washington Navy Yard, and myself home to Maria in Alexandria. I couldn't even consider what Roosevelt had told me. My mind was on what I would say to Maria. There was no easy way.

Her heart was about to be broken.

37

Well Done, My Good and Faithful Servant

Woodgerd Cottage
Old Fort Hunt Road
Alexandria, Virginia
Monday evening
21 February 1898

From the moment we first held each other, Maria and I pretended the outside world didn't exist. All bundled up against the cold air and wet ground, and fortified by mugs of hot chocolate, we took a long stroll in the snow-carpeted forest. The trail led over the low ridge to the east, through bare oaks and maples patiently waiting for spring to return them to their splendor. On the nearby Potomac, a lone steamer chugged upriver, not another vessel in sight.

Later, as we lunched on sandwiches in front of the roaring fireplace, we spoke of our children's accomplishments and our hopes for them. She wanted Francisco and Juanito to be happy and productive, the priest to someday be a bishop and the bureaucrat to someday marry and have her grandchildren. I almost told her then, but she was so blissful I couldn't spoil the moment.

After dinner, we drank the last of the Spanish wine in the cellar as I lay back on the sofa and she played her guitar. Maria sang the old Spanish laments of loves dreamed and lost. I can still hear them, floating like wisps of smoke in the night in her hauntingly crystal clear voice. It was an exquisitely intimate time, refilling us with a sense of joy and closeness.

I knew Maria sensed I was there when *Maine* exploded. She could tell I had seen the unimaginable, endured the unrepeatable. But she never asked me and I was grateful. Not only was I incapable of describing what happened, I just didn't have the strength. Instead, we spoke only of the love in our lives. We reveled in silly giggles and affectionate cuddles, letting them linger, savoring them, appreciating how very precious they are.

I waited until quite late, when we'd retired to bed to do what I dreaded, but knew I must. Turning down the bedside oil lamp to a pale dim glow, I held my wife tightly.

Maria suddenly tensed. I knew she had somehow felt the anguish in my heart, before I could even begin to say the words I'd been rehearsing since Havana.

"I have something terrible to tell you, Maria. It's about Francisco."

In an instant, Maria, my feminine tower of strength and accomplishment, became a frightened girl, unable to speak beyond a single word.

"How?"

I respected her too much to prolong the agony with hollow consolations. She needed to know the core truth of what had happened. She would want or tolerate nothing less from me.

"Colonel Marrón had him arrested on the eleventh and interrogated. Rork heard about it afterward from a priest, whose brother is a soldier. He is also a devout Catholic and knew Francisco. The soldier brother saw his remains at Cabaña Fortress and recognized them. He told his brother the priest the next day."

She gasped in horror. The rage would come later. It was an emotion I was well acquainted with. But right then, Maria had only emptiness, and it echoed from her.

"They killed my boy, a man of God. Why?"

"Because he dared to be compassionate to Cuba. Marrón was terrified of what would happen if a priest like Francisco became an example of gentle tolerance and reconciliation between Spain and Cuba."

"My son preached love, as Jesus did. You heard him at the luncheon."

"Yes, I did, Maria. You can be proud Francisco actually *lived* the morals he had learned from you and his teachers at the seminary. He taught by doing, as he lived. He loved you very much. I saw it in his eyes that day."

Maria tightened her grip and blurted out, "Juanito! What of *him?*"

"I've heard nothing. He's likely safe. I doubt Juanito ever learned what happened to Francisco. The newspaper reported a Franciscan priest had been killed by bandits on a road outside the city. It's what most people assume. I also think, at this point, it is better he doesn't know. Juanito's young, and might do something rash."

"But if Marrón went after Francisco, he could go after Juanito. We have to get him out of Cuba! I need to go and talk to him. I can convince him to return to Spain."

I couldn't tell Maria that I'd been interrogated by Juanito the same day Francisco had been seen dead in the ditch at Cabaña. It was obvious to me Marrón, for some reason unknown to me at the time, wasn't after the younger brother, or he would've had him arrested also.

"No, Maria. Juanito is safe and you need not worry about him. Don't concern yourself about Marrón either. He can't hurt anyone, anymore. Marrón died the night before I left the island. Because he either ordered or allowed a priest to be killed, I think his secret unit probably is under intense scrutiny, for I believe the senior Spanish authorities have been told what happened."

She didn't ask how I knew such things. Instead, her voice trailed off. "Then the world will never learn the truth about my poor Francisco. He was such a lovely baby, such a good boy who always wanted to help people. . . ."

"The Spanish authorities will never admit what happened. But God knows. I believe He's already welcomed Francisco home and told him, 'Well done, my good and faithful servant.' "

Through her tears, she murmured, "Book of Matthew. Chapter twenty-five, verse twenty-three."

We spoke no more that night, the pain was beyond the power of words. I held my wife long after the lamp ran out of oil, until we fell asleep in each other's arms.

The Monday I was to return to duty, the last day of February, dawned bitter cold and raining. The front yard was full of slush and mud, adding to the funereal melancholia of the scene. Rork arrived in a coach to fetch me to the station and the short train ride back to Washington. Our reunion was mostly silent, for he saw the sorrow in my home was palpable. This time my absence would have no time limit attached. It was for the duration of the war, which hadn't even officially begun yet.

My wife and I kissed, but it yielded no passion, a pro forma performance done by rote. As Rork and I climbed into the coach and headed off, Maria stood watching from the porch, her anguished expression knifing through me. For a long time, I sat wordless as we clopped down the road past the bleak landscape, feeling a cad for abandoning my beloved Maria. She had sacrificed her comfortable life for one of a naval wife. What had I done for her?

A disturbing debate gripped me. Should I quit the navy and return home to the woman I desperately loved? My pension would be minimal, but her money could carry us through. I knew with every fiber of my being Maria needed me to hold her another week, another month, to get past the torment in her heart. I was partly responsible. My presence in Havana had pushed Marrón to do the unthinkable—kill a priest.

"None o' this is your fault, Peter. Not a wee bit," said Rork, penetrating my despondency as only he can. "Marrón an' his ilk're the villains in this. An' there's no more you can do for her. Your lady's smart an' strong, an' she'll come out o' this. She just needs a bit o' solitude to let out her heartache."

"But I shouldn't leave her alone, Sean. It's a cruel thing to do, leaving her like this."

"Aye, for an average man, there'd be the truth. But you an' me're no average men, Peter. Maria's always understood we've responsibilities others don't. Goes with the profession, lad."

He let that sink in, then switched to his bosun voice. "An' now Captain Wake, we've a hellova lot to do, with damned little time to do it. Concentrate on your orders, `cause this whole bloody war mess'll be out o' control by next week."

"Yeah, you're right on that," I admitted. "And I have a nasty feeling we'll be right in the middle of it."

38

Outwitting the Parasites

Brooklyn Navy Yard
March 1898

A week after the train brought Rork and me back to work with Roosevelt in Washington, we departed yet again, this time for the Brooklyn Navy Yard, our new base of operations. Plunging into our unusual mission, it began to progress as I'd conceived. Traveling around New York and New England, we inspected several yachts offered for sale to the government by Roosevelt's rich friends and found them suitable. This was the easy part.

The hard part, necessitating long hours of paperwork, meetings, and bargaining, was the daunting task of preparing the yachts' conversion to warships. It couldn't actually start yet, but I reserved the necessary armaments from the yard's ordnance officer and lined up the yard facilities to fit them aboard the vessels with the repair officer. I could tell neither of them thought my plan would come to fruition and they'd ever actually have to fulfill their commitments.

Next came officers and men for the ships. Using friendships, animosities, and quid pro quos, enough were found and tentatively allocated. Arrangements for provisions, fuel, medicines, equipment, and a hundred other things, dominated the final phase. All this effort was done without excessive press attention, a key factor I insisted upon, and one of the reasons we were successful to date. The final obstacle was the funding approval from Congress. Once voted, the preparations could be set into motion.

On the seventh of March, Theodore cabled me a dire message. His dear Edith's long illness had turned deadly. He feared cancer. That afternoon the doctors operated on her in an effort to ascertain the cause. Rork and I were anxious, for we knew dynamic Theodore Roosevelt was nothing without Edith. By the grace of God, his next cable relieved our fears. Theodore reported they found a large abscess near her hip and determined it was not cancerous. The surgery was successful. She would recover.

Meanwhile, a State Department friend visiting New York passed along to me the startling news that President McKinley had secretly offered $300 million to buy Cuba from Spain, in an effort to avoid war. The Spanish refusal didn't surprise me. The situation had gone beyond reason. National ego was everything now.

On the eighth of March, Congress unanimously authorized fifty million dollars for emergency acquisition of ships, munitions, provisions, and fuel for the navy, as well as some funding for the army. Roosevelt instantly sent out orders for me to execute the waiting contracts, demanding the squadron to be fully operational within two weeks. We had carefully organized each of the professional components in the project to that very end. But I forgot a salient factor—human nature.

When the news of fifty million dollars being given for war preparations went out by telegraph across the nation, parasitical commercial and naval rats emerged from the shadows to get their nibbles. Within hours, they insinuated themselves into the decision-making at Washington and New York.

At the end of the day, I received an apologetic cable from Roosevelt. From the seven large and fast yachts already chosen, the squadron was reduced to four slow yachts and a freighter. I was ordered to continue to get the vessels converted into warships and operational as quickly as possible.

With a condescending sneer, the commandant of the yard informed me the next morning of what he'd heard from his cronies. Several unassigned high-ranking naval officers at headquarters had learned of my assignment, jealously watching my steady progress. Since they had connections in Congress and wanted command of my fast yachts, they got them. Since none of them wanted to command the slow yachts and the freighter, I was left with those vessels. The arrogant ass further explained this development reflecting the fact that I was the only officer left in the navy who had never graduated from the academy, adding I shouldn't expect to compete equally for decent ship commands.

One can imagine my reaction, but I didn't succumb to temptation and deck the conceited bastard. There wasn't time for that luxury. We were going to war, he wasn't. The next three weeks were a blur of begging, coercion, trickery, and outright larceny on my part, none of it pleasant or worthy of reporting in detail. It matters only that in the end I successfully outwitted the self-righteous snobs in navy blue and the profiteering parasites in three-piece gray. My ships were converted.

By the end of March, the unusual squadron was commissioned, armed, manned, equipped, fueled, and provisioned. Far more importantly, I kept many of the petty officers and junior commissioned officers I'd wanted all along, for when the word went out about my command they volunteered. Unfortunately, the squadron was still scattered between naval stations at New York, Newport, and Boston, and had yet to train together as a fighting unit.

During this time, Theodore Roosevelt, who at forty years of age was far younger than most men he dealt with, came into his own. While others shrank from the building tension, Theodore reveled in it. Freed of fear for Edith, he spent every waking moment asking questions, inspecting ships, issuing orders, promoting scientific innovations, spurring on the clerical staffs—in general, running a *wartime* navy for Secretary Long.

As war loomed closer, the navy secretary grew content with lending absentminded approval to his vigorous assistant's decisions and ideas, some of which were considered bizarre by the establishment. Two of those notions merit mention here, for they are examples of how Theodore was far ahead of his time in the field of naval sciences. One was John Holland's newest submarine, which at Roosevelt's insistence I personally observed in operation off Brooklyn that March. Seeing it in action ended my earlier doubts as to its capabilities, and I became convinced such a unique weapon could be a deciding factor in harbor and coastal defense.

Roosevelt's curiosity extended into the air as well. I found this understandable, given his gifts as a lifelong ornithologist. His old friend Professor Langley's latest aerial machine, of which many in the navy were skeptical, was tested that spring off a specially adapted houseboat on the Potomac. Theodore was a witness, afterward sending me a note enthusiastically reporting the contraption had potential as a fleet gunnery lookout and scout.

On the twentieth, the New York newspapers reported the battleship *Oregon* had gotten under way from San Francisco, bound on a 14,000-mile voyage around the continent of South America for action with the North Atlantic Squadron. My son, Lieutenant Sean Wake, her assistant gunnery officer, was going to war. Pride and worry for my son quietly tore at me as I waited for word from Washington about my own fate.

On the twenty-eighth, the official naval inquiry ruled *Maine*'s destruction was caused by a Spanish mine. I remained uncertain, but it didn't matter anymore. The press and Congress clamored for war.

On the twenty-ninth, the American government demanded Spain leave Cuba, knowing it was a moot point.

On the final day of March, 1898, our waiting ended when orders from Roosevelt arrived. They were simple, and ominous.

XXX—ASSUME WAR STATUS—X—READY ALL SHIPS FOR ACTION—X ASSEMBLE SQUADRON AT CTB—X—SUGAR ORDERS FORTHCOMING—XXX

CTB was the rendezvous point. Plan SUGAR was my squadron's attack on Isabela and the subsequent inshore blockade on the central north coast of Cuba.

I wasted no time in sending off telegrams to the rest of the squadron at Newport and Boston. My captains had been ready and waiting for the word. They would leave port the next dawn, and set a course for CTB, Congo Town, at Andros Island in the Bahamas.

I had arranged the rendezvous location at a cocktail party in Manhattan the week before, while renewing my acquaintance with Admiral Jackie Fisher, commander-in-chief of the Royal Navy's North America and West Indies Station. We'd first met in 1874 off the coast of Morocco, where Rork and I had managed to become prisoners of a local corsair. Fisher, a young ship captain at the time, liberated us in a nasty little fight.

We kept a periodic correspondence during the next twenty-four years and occasionally saw each other in person, the previous time being at Washington six months earlier. Upon seeing me again in New York and hearing my request, he was only too happy to oblige, since it was within his area of responsibility.

The site was perfect for my purpose—remote enough to train our people in secret, yet close enough to the enemy to enable us to strike the instant war was declared. No one, save Fisher, my captains, Roosevelt, and two others at naval headquarters, knew where we were going.

At dawn on April first, my commodore's pennant broke out at the main mast as we steamed out of the Brooklyn Navy Yard basin. Dock workers and sailors cheered us as we slid past my dear old ship, *Newark*. It had been over a year since I'd left her in the care of the yard. Her refit was scheduled to last two years, but with the coming conflict that timetable had been erased. Now she was crawling with workmen hurrying to get her ready as soon as possible.

We turned to port and made our way down the East River, bustling with ships and boats, toward the Brooklyn Bridge, where my career had nearly ended. Pedestrians on the bridge waved and shouted encouragements to our strange-looking warship. A ferry dipped her ensign and sounded a long salute on her steam whistle, the men aboard applauding us. Some of the women were weeping as they waved.

The transit down the upper bay was helped by a strong ebb tide, and before long we were well beyond the city with its smoke and noise, surging past Fort Hamilton and The Narrows. A land breeze piped up from the east, clean and warm. Spring had arrived, and not a cloud cluttered the sky in the lower bay and ocean beyond.

There was a leftover swell rolling up from the south. Our bow knifed through it at eight knots, fans of mist bursting up into the air, creating miniature rainbows. I heard banter from my position on the starboard bridge wing and looked down to the foredeck where two young seamen were securing the ready anchor cable and capstan. Their good humor gave me a smile. I was back at sea, far away from the stifling atmosphere and contemptuous scrutiny of dull-minded naval aristocrats.

Rork was standing alone farther aft on the main deck, swaying easily with the motion of the ship as the wind whipped his gray hair. He was watching the low line of Sandy Hook fade away in the distance, the last land we'd see for a thousand miles.

39

The Squadron

U.S.S. Kestrel *(Flagship)*
Special Service Squadron 2
North Atlantic Ocean

The ships and men under my command were designated Special Service Squadron 2. My flagship was U.S.S. *Kestrel*, formerly the yacht *Gertrude*, of New London, Connecticut. Built in 1894 for a wealthy shipping mogul, her measurements were: length 221 feet, beam 40 feet, draft 16 feet, and her single triple expansion engine drove her at a top speed of 15 knots. Her bunkerage was expanded by sacrificing four of her posh guest cabins, allowing a 1300-mile range at eight knots. Her two masts could set enough sail to provide four knots on a broad reach in moderate winds. *Kestrel*'s armament consisted of two six-pounder rapid fire guns mounted fore and aft, and two Colt machine guns mounted on either side amidships. The additional weight of coal and guns had slowed her a bit from her yacht speed of eighteen knots, but it was a trade-off I judged worth it. She carried five officers and fifty-nine men.

My pen cannot describe my profound gratitude when several of my previous shipmates, upon hearing the gossip about my enterprise, insistently volunteered to serve with me. This came at a time when others were clamoring to get aboard the big ships which were certain to see battle glory.

Senior among these loyal souls was Commander James Southby, who the reader has already met as executive officer of *Newark*. Having decided to remain in the navy for the duration of the pending war, he was still at Boston Navy Yard when he wrote the Navy Department volunteering to join my squadron. I was subsequently asked by Roosevelt my opinion, and enthusiastically requested Southby as *Kestrel*'s commanding officer, and also my squadron chief of staff. In addition, Roosevelt secured his promotion to the rank of captain, even though the secondary nature of the squadron required the chief of staff have only the rank of commander.

My other squadron staff consisted of Lieutenant Grover Yeats, a smart and resourceful young officer I knew from my years as captain of *Bennington*, who would be my flag lieutenant. Chief Boatswain Sean Rork was my petty officer aide, and Boatswain's Mate Willy Mack, from my time aboard *Chicago*, his assistant. Mack was a quiet professional with the distinction of being one of the few black deck petty officers left in the navy.

The rest of my ship commanders were middle-aged gentlemen, completely unknown to me prior to forming the squadron. I was slightly wary of their lack of experience aboard proper naval vessels until Rork reminded me of my own convoluted past.

U.S.S. *Osprey*, the former coastal freighter *Dunwoody*, built in 1888, was commanded by Lieutenant Socrates Bilton, a Massachusetts Naval Militia officer brought into active service by the recommendation of Commander Southby. In his civilian life Bilton was a coastal steamer captain plying the New England coast. *Osprey*'s particulars were: length of 184 feet, beam of 37 feet, draft of 14 feet, speed of 12 knots, carrying four officers and forty-four men. Her armament was the same as *Kestrel*, as was her steaming range.

U.S.S. *Harrier* was the former yacht *Constance Marie*, and commanded by Lieutenant Howard Farmore, also of the

Massachusetts Naval Militia, one of Boston's gilded elite and a yachtsman of some renown. His position had been secured by Senator Henry Cabot Lodge's close friendship with Roosevelt. *Harrier* was the smallest and slowest of my ships, having a length of 164 feet, beam of 34 feet, draft of 13 feet, and speed of only ten knots. She carried one six-pounder gun, two four-pounder guns, two Colt machine guns, three officers, and 43 men, mostly naval militia reservists. Due to her lack of fuel capacity, she would be stopping at Norfolk en route for coal.

U.S.S. *Falcon* was the former West Indies yacht *Paloma Mar*, and commanded by Massachusetts Naval Militia Lieutenant Oscar Brahm of New Bedford, an experienced merchant marine chief mate on coastal passenger liners. Her dimensions were 210 feet long, 42-foot beam, and a 14-foot draft, with a 14-knot speed. She carried four officers, 39 men, two four-pounder guns, and three Colt machine guns.

The day *Kestrel* departed New York, *Falcon* and *Harrier* left Boston, and *Osprey* steamed out of Newport. Each newly created warship steamed southward to meet her squadron mates off the village of Congo Town, on the east coast of Andros Island, in the British colony of the Bahamas.

40

The Hideout

Congo Town, Andros Island
Her Majesty's Colony of the Bahamas
Monday evening
25 April 1898

Kestrel was first ship to arrive at our squadron hideout on the seventh of April. The local natives, most of whom were fishermen, had never seen a U.S. warship. Over the next two weeks, they were delighted with their ringside seats, astonished at how we train for battle. *Osprey* and *Falcon* arrived on the eighth. *Harrier* reached us on the eleventh from Norfolk. The weather was the opposite of New England's—sunny and warm, with a steady trade wind from the southeast.

Notwithstanding the beautiful weather at our picturesque lair in the tropics, I pushed the squadron's officers and men hard with spontaneous drills on gunnery, signaling, formation steaming, damage control, small boat work, landing force tactics, rifle practice, and resupply at sea procedures. This work did not endear the enlisted men, most of whom were soft militia reservists, to me, their squadron commodore, but I wasn't there to be liked. Their petty officers, almost all regular salts, understood my meaning full and well. They roused their men to get things done correctly and quickly with each new exercise.

After my initial inspection of the newly arrived ships, I was appalled to see those from Newport and Boston still contained too many vestiges of their previous lifestyle—a most dangerous factor when ships get impacted by high explosives, as I expected them to be. I had seen the results of such opulence on fire in naval battle at Peru almost twenty years earlier, so *Kestrel* had already been stripped of such useless accoutrements back at Brooklyn.

Instantly, all non-essential flammable materials were ordered to be removed from the other ships, most of it located in the officers' cabins. Now the grousing came from the gold braid club as they watched their plush yacht accommodations being ripped apart by gleeful sailors, who enjoyed their chore immensely.

At first, the results of our incessant drills were sadly ludicrous, but fortunately my captains set a stern tone, for they knew this was their last chance to practice before mistakes would be measured in blood. Training dominated every waking hour of our days and nights, and frequently interrupted those asleep. I kept it up until I was convinced all hands on each ship could perform their duties in an emergency while blinded by smoke and flame, and short-handed by casualties. As we progressed, the men began to show quiet confidence in how to handle the challenges I instigated.

After ten days, Rork, the most cynical of old salts, gave his approval. "Aye, `tis nothin' short o' amazin'. The lads're as ready as they can be, sir."

We continued training, for I worried their hard-won skills might atrophy if not practiced.

At sunset on the twenty-fifth, our time for practicing ended. I gave surprise orders for *Harrier* to immediately establish a tow of *Kestrel*. It was to be accomplished under the assumption we were both under heavy gunfire from a shore battery and *Kestrel* was afire aft. As *Harrier* acknowledged, a small steamer raced into view on the northern horizon. Steamers were rare in that place, and as the vessel neared, a discussion ensued on *Kestrel*'s bridge regarding her identity and intentions.

I knew she was the *Meteor*. While still in New York, I had our agent in Nassau retain her for use as a dispatch boat. The moment new cabled orders for me arrived at Nassau, the nearest telegraph station to us, *Meteor* was to speed the seventy-four miles south to us at Congo Town with the message. She was also to bring our squadron mail, which had been forwarded to her.

Twenty-nine minutes after *Meteor* came into view, Yeats entered my cabin, handing me Roosevelt's message. Remarkably, it had been received at Nassau only five hours earlier, an example of modern communications in warfare. Rendered by the lieutenant into plain language, it read as follows.

XXX—WAR VOTED TODAY—X—ARMY MOBILIZING—X—NAVAL BLOCKADE IN EFFECT—X—MAIN FLEET LEFT KEY WEST FOR NORTH CUBA—X—SPANISH FORCES IN CUBA MOBILIZED—X—SPANISH FLEET STEAMING FROM CADIZ POSITION UNKNOWN—X—EXECUTE PLAN SUGAR—X—RENDEZVOUS WITH BAKER APRIL 27—X—PLAN SUGAR DATE APRIL 28—X—MUST HOLD TARGET FOR 3 DAYS TO ENSURE CUBAN WITHDRAWAL IF SPANISH REPEL THEM—X—MEET COLLIER MAY 1 AT ALFA—X—NO OTHER REINFORCEMENTS AVAILABLE—X—AFTER PLAN SUGAR EXECUTED BEGIN AGGRESSIVE INSHORE BLOCKADE OF ASSIGNED SECTOR—X—YOUR SQUADRON UNDER SAMPSON FLEET COMMAND—X—GOOD LUCK—XXX

I called in Southby and ordered all ships to get under way for the Anguilla Cays, a line of tiny coral islets at the southeast corner of the Cay Sal Bank. There we would meet BAKER, the freighter *Norden*, the master of which was Karl Bendel, a longtime operative of mine. *Norden* carried the battalion of exile Cuban troops who would be landed at the dismal port of Isabela the next day. After holding the port for three days, we would leave and refuel from a collier at ALFA, Salt Cay, at the southwest corner of the Cay Sal Bank.

When he departed I perused the pile of waiting personal mail, opening Roosevelt's first and noting the date.

Washington, D.C. 19 April 1898

My Dear Friend Peter,

The army has finally come to its senses and accepted my offer to form a regiment of horse. I will be the executive officer of the First U.S. Volunteer Cavalry, with the brevet rank of lieutenant colonel. Our friend Leonard Wood will be the commanding officer. It's a wonderful regiment, and is already filling with rugged Western men eager to show their mettle against the Spanish. Onward to Cuba!

My final official day at the Navy Department will be on the last day of April, but actually the twenty-sixth because I must journey out to the regiment in Texas. Henceforth we will revert to our previous correlation, for you will outrank me! I shall be honored and pleased to be able to call you "Sir" once again.

A serious note, my friend: you will no longer have me as your rearguard in Washington, so please beware of the court intrigue which fills the place. Your mission will be difficult to accomplish, but it is nothing a naval mastermind like you can't handle. I look forward to hearing of your success.

I hope to see you again in Florida or Cuba, or perhaps among the vaunted warriors of Valhalla in our afterlife. May we taste victory before death!

Your longtime admirer…
Theodore Roosevelt

He'd finally gotten his wish to test his mettle in battle. Theodore wouldn't be alone in his germinal enthusiasm. Thirty-five years had gone by since our country had tasted the ghastly result of large-scale war, with every family feeling grief. This war wasn't even to defend our land. Once the casualty lists started coming in, patriotic naïveté about a foreign war would turn into revulsion.

I felt the rhythm of the ship's engine quicken beneath me. A shaft of sunlight from the open cabin port crossed my desk as *Kestrel* swung around on her new course toward the north. It settled on the next envelope atop the pile, a letter from Maria.

Her previous five letters had been rambling torrents of anguish and regret about her family, and the situation in Cuba. In her despair, Maria had secluded herself in our home, not wanting to face people or hear any more distressing news.

This letter was different.

17th of April, 1898

Dearest Husband Peter,

I have come to regret the lamentations you received in my earlier letters. They were created by the realization of my uselessness in averting the catastrophe of war. I have lost my oldest son, and my heart will never be the same. But I know now my heartache can and should be replaced by action.

Accordingly, I have decided to volunteer with the Red Cross, as tribute to my Francisco. Having been impressed when meeting Miss Barton years ago, and knowing of the noble work she has done for the concentration camp refugees inside Cuba, I will alleviate the war suffering in any way I can. The Red Cross office in Washington was quite appreciative of my offer and said I would be contacted presently with word of when and where I am to work. They indicated it would be close by, and I would be part of the effort to organize and supply new hospitals. I have full trust you can understand and will support my decision.

I had dinner the other night with Edith, who is thankfully recovering and wanted some company. She told me she heard you will be ordered to sea soon, no doubt for Cuba. She also said Theodore is joining the army so he can fight. She is terrified for him.

Peter, the world is descending into war madness. I can only hope and pray my little Juanito remains untouched by it. I know you will be somewhere in the middle of it all. I beg you to be careful, my darling, for you are not young anymore, though I know you dislike admitting it. Please come home to me. I want us to fulfill our dream of growing old together at Patricio Island, where God's sunsets have magical abilities to salve any wounded heart and any dark memory.

You are constantly in my heart, my dreams, and my thoughts. I live for the day you are back in my arms. May God have mercy upon us and make it soon.

Your loving wife,
Maria

I sat there a long time. My steward came in and quietly closed the ports, saying in an apologetic tone that per the captain's orders no lights could be shown from the ship.

When I reached the bridge deck an hour later, after the last vestige of dusk, we were at war conditions. Guns had minimal crews stationed at them at all times, ready ammunition was distributed, the lookouts were doubled, and interior hatches were dogged down. Everyone was tense. Astern of us, my ships were black forms on the dark sea. It reminded me precisely of a scene from another war, when I was a young officer in command of a small sailing gunboat on another jungle coast.

Even the dread was the same.

41

Blossom Channel

Anguilla Cays
Cay Sal Bank
Her Majesty's Colony of the Bahamas
Tuesday
26 April 1898

Against the wise advice of my staff, I choose the perilous, but expeditious, course to the rendezvous with our new Cuban allies. The usual route to Cay Sal Bank from Congo Town for ships of our size was to first head north and west around the top of Andros Island, the Berry Islands, the Bimini Islands, and Great Bahama Bank, thence south to the Cay Sal Bank, which would require three to four days. That meant our new Cuban allies would have to wait for us, unprotected, at a locale close enough to Cuba to be vulnerable to Spanish naval patrols.

Instead, I led the squadron first south, into the little-known Blossom Channel. This was not a light choice, for it is a thirty-foot-deep snaking course through twenty miles of coral reefs at the bottom of the Bahamas. Few have heard of it, and even fewer have been through it in anything larger than a native schooner. I was met initially with wide-eyed disbelief, but the captains did as commanded and followed the flagship as we steamed the fifty-eight miles from Congo Town south-southeast toward the jagged wall of shallow coral which borders the southern edge of the Tongue of the Ocean.

At mid-morning on the twenty-sixth, when the sun had reached forty-five degrees in elevation and the path ahead lay thus illuminated, we transited from a depth of three-thousand feet to that of a mere twenty-nine in the space of two hundred yards. As we started through the labyrinth, Rork sat in the crosstrees high aloft, calmly calling down course alterations to the officer of the deck for us to avoid the worst of the giant coral heads which haphazardly erupted from the sandy bottom.

Rork and I learned the way through the maze while chasing blockade runners during the Civil War, and yet again in 1888, when we escaped to Nassau from a rather dodgy situation in Haiti.

The southeasterly course lasted for twenty very tense miles. When we reached deeper water it was late afternoon and Rork, relieved at his perch by another petty officer, descended to the accolades of both officer and enlisted. We swung southwest to Copper Rocks and then, as the sun set ahead of us, we steered west along the edge of Hurricane Flats and across the deep Santaren Channel.

The night was rough and dark when we finally arrived at the scrub-covered coral rocks of the Anguilla Cays, on the southeast corner of the triangular Cay Sal Bank, a notorious archipelago of reefs. This was an improbable meeting point, for most ships go out of their way to avoid the area. The strong currents are unpredictable, frequently setting a vessel right into the reefs. Only turtle fishermen who know the reefs go there, and then not for long.

The current was flowing strongly toward the reef, so I kept the squadron three miles to the northeast of the islands, with our noses pointed into the easterly wind. All ships maintained a sharp watch to the north for the Cuban ship, and especially to the south for any Spanish cruiser which might by chance or design come into the area. The night passed in apprehension and sleep eluded me.

At noon the next day, the twenty-seventh of April, I was standing on the starboard bridge deck, staring at the guano-covered islets, when the lookout reported a lone tramp steamer approaching from the north horizon. In ten minutes, I could make out the ship from the bridge. Soon, she was stopped off our starboard, rolling in the swells.

"Is she the one, sir?" Southby asked, rather anxiously giving voice to what everyone else was thinking.

"Yes, James, as a matter of fact that's her, the *Norden*. Right on time."

"Commodore, I'm impressed," he said, shaking his head. "We've gone through a two-hundred-mile navigational nightmare to get to this dismal place, and they've come six-hundred miles against the Gulf Stream, and this meeting is smack dab right on time. Incredible!"

I laughed. "You don't know Captain Karl Bendel. He keeps his word."

Southby's brows arched. "She is a dirty old tub, isn't she? Must be at least thirty, maybe forty years old. Just look at that hull. I'd bet her machinery's in even worse shape."

Naval officers hate to see dirt, rust, or unkempt crew. The steamer before us epitomized all three.

"She's only ten years old," I replied. "Karl intentionally keeps *Norden*'s outward appearance looking that way so port officials don't over-charge him on harbor dues, and customs patrols underestimate her. But down below is another matter. The boiler and engine rooms are very well maintained. Her bottom is kept clean too."

"Sounds like a valuable man to have on our side, sir. But look at *those* wretches."

The steamer's rails were lined with men trying to vomit overboard—the exile Cuban troops. They didn't look in shape for combat the next day.

With my disposition soured, I turned to go below to my cabin. "Please send word for Captain Bendel and the Cuban commanding officer to meet with me as soon as possible. I want you and our ships' captains at the meeting also."

I stopped at the ladder for, as sailors usually do in such situations, our bluejackets began jeering the seasick soldiers.

"And Captain Southby, please stop our men making fun of those soldiers. Many of them will die tomorrow. The least we can do is be decent to them today."

42

Meeting of Minds

Anguilla Cays
Cay Sal Bank
Her Majesty's Colony of the Bahamas
Wednesday
27 April 1898

I was not impressed by His Excellency Colonel Ruben Ramon Armando Zaldivar de Aviles y Vega, commanding officer of the Batallón Nacional Orgullo de Cuba—the National Pride Battalion of Cuba. The high-sounding name and title made the individual who stood before me in a Napoleonic pose even more of a bad joke.

His double chin, fleshy-lipped mouth, enormous black-dyed mustache, and vacant grayish eyes were clearly the product of *bonne cuisine* instead of military discipline. He paused upon entry, waiting to receive my groveling welcome. So did the fawning subaltern who had dashed into my cabin ahead of the colonel and introduced him in hushed reverential tones as the great man himself appeared.

There was a collective gasp behind me from my assembled captains, which I'm sure the colonel perceived as *yanqui* awe of his magnificent uniform. It was one of the best target silhouettes

I have ever seen—a comic opera combination of white trousers and tunic with red piping and belt, accented by brass buttons and colonel epaulettes, and topped with a blue cocked and feathered hat. The chest was adorned with several large antique medals. It was all I could do not to laugh. I made a mental note not to stand anywhere near the fool in a battle.

I did not extend my hand, but directed the colonel to the chair nearest mine at the long table adjacent to my desk. My officers already stood along the outboard side of the table.

"I am Commodore Peter Wake, of the Second Special Service Squadron, Colonel, and the commanding officer of the combined Cuban and American forces on this operation. Welcome aboard *Kestrel*, and please be seated. I presume Captain Bendel has arrived for the meeting, as well as some of your senior staff officers, correct? I understand you speak English, so we will proceed in that language, as it is the most common among those present."

A flurry of Spanish passed between the colonel and the subaltern, who sheepishly reported to me, "His Excellency does not prefer to use English, sir, as his knowledge of the language is not fully developed, so I will interpret all which is said. Both Captain Bendel and our battalion staff are present for the meeting." He gestured to the passageway, where a tightly packed crowd was trying to get into my cabin.

I wondered how Zaldivar could have been a successful businessman in the United States without a good knowledge of English, but didn't ask, deciding it wasn't worth it.

"There's only room for Captain Bendel and a couple of Cuban officers at the table, so pick which ones you want," I said to the subaltern, who suddenly looked uneasy. He translated my statement loud enough for the men in the passageway to hear. A commotion instantly started.

I sat down and waited while the raucous process of determining who was who in the battalion pecking order evolved in the passageway. At long last, one voice emerged louder and angrier than the rest, ending the dispute. To my shock, it was disturbingly familiar.

Three men then entered. The first was Captain Karl Bendel of the *Norden*, an old friend. He was also Agent R33 in my clandestine network of operatives. Next was a solid-built, serious-looking middle-aged Cuban with a badly stitched purple scar across his forehead.

The last man entering was he of the familiar voice, surprising me in the uniform of an infantry captain in the Cuban Liberation Army. He was Mario Cano, a bespectacled Cuban-American lawyer from Tampa and longtime member of the Cuban revolutionary organization, who was also none other than the husband of my daughter, Useppa!

Before I could say a word, Cano gazed straight at me without emotion, clearly not wanting anyone to know our connection, and announced, "Sorry for the confusion, Commodore. I am Captain Mario Cano, battalion adjutant."

He then introduced his companion. "Major Ramon Barida is second in command of the battalion, and a veteran of General Lacret's division in Cuba. Major Barida speaks English well."

Well, that explained that. Zaldivar had given money and political influence to the exile government, getting a commission in return. But the real soldier was Barida, who served under the general in charge of the area we were heading toward.

As they sat down, I said, "Welcome aboard, Major. We are honored to have a combat veteran of Cuba with us. We don't have time to waste, so I will ask some quick questions in order to understand your situation. How many men does the battalion have? Are there veterans among them? Has General Lacret been advised of your coming? Will he provide security forces for your landing at Isabela and subsequent move inland to Sagua Grande?"

The colonel glanced around nervously. Barida ignored him and said, "Sir, I was in New York and received orders to join the unit just before they loaded onto *Norden*. Colonel Zaldivar recruited the men two months ago. It is a small rifle battalion composed of one hundred seventy-eight officers and men in total, sir, including some unimportant staff people.

"There are two privates, three sergeants, and two lieutenants who have had battle experience inside Cuba. The rest are factory workers and tradesmen from around the southern U.S. states. Many are not even Cuban, but they are from Latin America. Their training has been minimal, but they are enthusiastic for the cause. The battalion is organized as two companies of eighty men each. The armament for each soldier is an 1892 Krag-Jorgensen rifle and sixty rounds.

"As for General Lacret, he does not know we are coming and no plans have yet been made to join our forces with his division. That will happen once we arrive at Isabela on the coast tomorrow and move inland to Sagua Grande."

Barida quickly added, "Also, I want to say we appreciate the United States Navy's efforts to help us, sir, and are honored to be allies with you."

None of what he said made me feel any better. "Major, how many people back in Jacksonville knew your plans before *Norden* left port?"

"Six men know we are arriving in Cuba at Isabela, sir. All of them are in the political oversight committee. No one in Jacksonville knows the operational plan of *how* and *when* we are landing at Isabela, because we were never given one. We were only told to go to Isabela with the navy and join General Lacret after we arrived at Sagua Grande."

The cabin grew quiet, except for the colonel, who was wheezing. His subaltern rushed in from the passageway with a water canteen and he gulped it down. I thought I caught a whiff of rum, but wasn't sure.

"Thank you, Major Barida, for the candid assessment. I thought such would be the case. Captain Southby and I have come up with a plan of action for tomorrow. Captain Southby will now brief everyone on it."

43

Briefing "The Liberators"

Anguilla Cays
Cay Sal Bank
Her Majesty's Colony of the Bahamas
Wednesday
27 April 1898

A large chart of the Bahamas and northern coast of Cuba had been spread out on the table, and now it was accompanied by memoranda books of each ship captain and Cano. Every eye went to Southby as he put one hand on the chart at Anguilla Cay and the other at Cayo Cristo, on the Cuban coast.

"Gentlemen, this briefing will cover several factors in the following order: transit from here to Cuba, squadron formation and communication, estimated enemy forces, transit in channel to Isabela, the shore assault, naval gunfire support, the Cuban battalion's landing, the naval landing party defensive perimeter, care of casualties, and the withdrawal of naval forces from Isabela. Please hold your questions until the appropriate phase of the briefing. Understood?"

Everyone had been scribbling notes, but now they looked up and nodded.

"Very well, first the transit to Cuba. Here at the Anguilla Cays, we are approximately forty-six miles northeast of the outer channel approaches of Isabela. In order to conceal our approach to the target area, the squadron's transit will *not* be a direct approach on the rhumb line, but instead will deviate to the west and then south."

He paused for them to write their notes, then continued. "The squadron will get under way at sunset tonight, steam south at eight knots around the shoals below Anguilla Cay, then alter course to the west. This westerly course will be close offshore of Cay Sal Bank, a dangerous route but less traveled. Two hours later, we will execute a line-ahead standard turn to port and steam due south, across the Nicolas Channel toward the Cuban coast. We will be making a perpendicular landfall at Punta Chernas on the west side of Cayo Cristo at eight bells."

Noticing the puzzled look on Barida, he quickly added, "Sorry, Major, that's four a.m."

The Cuban nodded his understanding and Southby went on. "At Punta Chernas, the squadron will follow *Kestrel* in a line-ahead standard turn to port and steam east along the coast of Cayo Cristo. This way we can make the final approach to the outer channel to Isabela from the still-dark western horizon, instead of having any possibility of being silhouetted from the nautical twilight on the eastern horizon, which begins at five-eleven a.m. We will be inside the Isabela channel at five a.m. and hit the town at five-thirty. Actual sunrise is at six-oh-four. Is the transit from here to Cuba understood? Questions?"

There were none. "All right, now as to our formation. Once we are under way from here, the squadron will steam in line-ahead formation, maintaining it all the way to the attack on Isabela. On the transit to Cuba, maintain a quarter-mile separation between ships. Maintain three hundred yards separation between ships once inside the Isabela channel.

"The squadron will be darkened the entire time, with great care by the engineers to prevent embers or illuminated smoke.

Communication between ships will be by narrowly focused signal lamp. All ships' bells will be muffled and all lights will be completely doused, except for one small blue light on the transom, which is shielded to all points but directly astern. A green light above the white light will mean to increase speed slightly. A red light above the blue light will mean to decrease speed slightly. Three red lights mean stop immediately. Three green lights mean to get under way at slow speed. Each ship will be ready to instantly signal these changes to the ship astern of you once you see them from the ship ahead.

"Your helmsmen will have to follow that blue light carefully, because it will be low and possibly obstructed by waves occasionally. Sharp lookouts and signalmen are crucial. Any communication beyond these I mentioned will be for crucial information only and done in Morse by focused signal lamp or, if close enough, by speaking trumpet. Concealment and surprise is everything. Understood?"

They indicated they did. The colonel took another swig and stared at the bulkhead. Cano cast an apologetic look my way.

"Very well," said Southby. "The squadron formation will have *Kestrel* in the lead, then *Osprey*, then *Falcon*, then *Norden*, and *Harrier* as the rearguard."

Flag Lieutenant Yeats placed a detailed chart of the coast around Isabela atop the large one. Each captain already had a copy on his ship and had been told to memorize it, but everyone around the table leaned over to peruse the chart, even the colonel.

Southby pointed to the village of Isabela. "For those who may be unfamiliar with our target, here it is. The enemy forces expected include two Spanish naval vessels stationed at Isabela. *Mayari* is a sixty-five-foot, twelve-knot gunboat mounting a forty-two-millimeter rapid-fire bow gun and a thirty-seven-millimeter Maxim gun aft. *Lealtad* is a fifty-foot boat with bow machine gun and unknown speed.

"Stationed eighty miles west at Cárdenas, are the gunboats *Ardilla*, *Alerta*, and *Ligera*, all of them similar to *Mayari* at Isabela.

There is also a ninety-foot armed tug, *Antonio Lopez*, with a fifty-seven-millimeter Nordenfelt gun and several smaller caliber guns, stationed at Cárdenas. All four vessels at Cárdenas periodically patrol the coast near Isabela and put into that port. We do not know if they are there right now, but must be prepared to face them.

"Spanish Army forces ashore near Isabela consist of one infantry regiment and some pro-Spanish militia. Major Barida, do you have any recent estimate of the Spanish numerical strength in the area of Isabela and Sagua Grande?"

"Yes, sir. As of when I was there one month ago, there were approximately eight hundred Spanish infantry troops operating inland near Sagua under the command of the notorious Colonel Arce, and also an eighty-man company of Spanish volunteer militia which patrols the roads in ten-man groups. In the last several weeks, the enemy has mobilized its inactive reserves and militia across Cuba, so there are probably some reinforcements in the area. We know the Spanish plan is to reinforce all potential invasion areas on the northern coast with reserves, including light field artillery, once war with the United States is declared. Isabela is one of those, but not considered a priority."

He presented the enemy's order of battle dispassionately. I was finding Major Barida an intriguing fellow.

"Thank you, Major," said Southby. "Gentlemen, from Punta Chernas the speed will remain at eight knots, and the course will be to the southeast along the Cayo Cristo coast. We will continue a mile past Punta Practicos to the outer buoy of the five-mile channel into Isabela. The buoy is a white and red striped nun, standing about six feet above the water. Keeping the buoy to starboard, we will execute a hard right turn to lay the course of south-southwest into the channel. There will be two buoys on either side. A mile into the channel, we will pass between the islands of Cayo de la Cruz on the north side, and Cayo Maravillas on the south side."

Barida raised his hand. "Sir, there are fishermen living in huts on the beach of Cayo Maravillas. They will see us enter."

I interjected, "An important point, Major Barida. Thank you. Are they pro-Spanish or pro-independence?"

He shrugged. "They are pro-fishermen, sir, who only want to be left alone to get fish with their sailboats. I do not think they would alert the Spanish in Isabela, but there could be a traitor among them who might light a signal fire."

"Or a Spanish naval lookout newly positioned on that beach," said Cano.

"We could secure the island with a small landing party ahead of the squadron entering the channel, sir," suggested Farmore, Senator Lodge's protégé commanding *Harrier*.

I went over it in my mind, then said, "Thank you, Captain Cano and Lieutenant Farmore. Once we are past those two islands and inside the bay, we have only another four miles to go, which should take thirty minutes at the most. We'll take our chances. Please continue, Captain Southby."

"Yes, sir. As you can see, the channel is pretty straightforward and carries thirty to forty feet of water. Halfway to the docks at Isabela, we will pass Cayo Paloma to our starboard. After that, we will pass Punta Sotavento on our portside, which is the end of a very thin peninsula, on which sits Isabela. The docks are on the northern side of the peninsula. Before we reach the docks, we'll pass Cayo Mendoza to our starboard. This area is the shallowest part of the channel, with shoaling to twenty-two feet at low water.

"Now, as to the assault itself. Listen carefully. It is vital to eliminate confusion once we are in the confined area of the port. At Cayo Mendoza, all ships will reduce shaft revolutions to a speed of dead slow ahead.

"At Cayo Mendoza, *Kestrel* and *Osprey* will turn hard to the southwest and proceed to the large wharf a quarter mile away on the town's harbor front. The other ships of the squadron behind them will stop in the channel and wait. The wharf has thirty feet of water on both sides. *Kestrel* will take the inland or south side, *Osprey* will take the seaward or north side. Shore parties will immediately surge ashore from both ships. *Kestrel*'s sailors head to the right and south, and *Osprey*'s men will head to the left and north. Lieutenant Yeats will be in command of all sailors ashore, assisted by Bosun Mack. As soon as *Osprey*'s shore party has landed, she will back away from the wharf. *Kestrel* will remain on her side of the wharf for the duration of the operation, unless exigent negative circumstances dictate otherwise."

The officers' faces tensed on hearing that. Southby didn't have to elaborate what those circumstances would be.

"We need the shore parties to fan out and take control of the immediate wharf area within the first five minutes. This won't be easy, because you'll only have thirty men ashore initially. Surprise is what we want, so be fast and quiet if at all possible. If the alarm has been given by this point, be loud and lethal to anyone in your way. Are we clear?"

Even grimmer faces nodded and he went on. "The Spanish gunboat docks are about a hundred yards to the south of the wharf, and will be on *Kestrel*'s starboard side. If the gunboats are at the docks when we arrive, our ship's guns will destroy them. We will also cover the only real street in the town with our guns. If there is a field artillery battery or infantry in town, we will take them under fire. I want no confusion on this—*Kestrel* will provide gunfire support to the shore party. Other ships will be responsible for engaging enemy vessels should they appear in the bay to resist our assault."

He paused again until everyone wagged their heads in the affirmative.

"Remember, the wharf is temporary for all ships except *Kestrel*. As *Kestrel* and *Osprey* arrive at the wharf, all of the other ships will stop and loiter by Cayo Mendoza. I want *Osprey* leaving the wharf as fast as possible. When *Osprey* departs the wharf, she will steam around the peninsula to the southeastern side and loiter a mile offshore with sharp lookout seaward and landward. *Falcon* will be next at the pier to quickly discharge her shore party, then she will depart to loiter over near *Osprey*. When *Falcon* departs the wharf, *Norden* will come in and send the Cuban battalion ashore, along with all their supplies. Offloading equipment and supplies will have to be done by hand. There are no derricks. At the same time *Norden* is offloading, *Harrier* will send in her shore party by ship's boat. That will give us a total of forty sailors ashore in the initial assault."

Ignoring the wheezing colonel, who had yet another swig, Southby turned to Major Barida. "Disembarking your men and offloading your field artillery and supplies from *Norden* will be difficult to do quickly, but by that time it'll be daylight and the wharf area will be secured. Your entire battalion should be ashore, equipped and formed up ready for battle, and heading inland by nine o'clock at the very latest, to get inland before the Spanish can react and get large forces to Isabela. Understood, Major Barida?"

Also ignoring his colonel, Barida said, "Yes, sir."

The colonel, to whom the subaltern had been translating all the aforementioned, suddenly spoke up for the first time, giving his minion an earful. The subaltern showed not a hint of embarrassment as he put it into a flat English monotone.

"Colonel Zaldivar says no, not worry, gentlemen. There will be no fighting at Isabela. For two hundred years the peasants of the area belonged to his father when they were slaves, and they are still loyal to his family. They love him and will welcome all of you as their glorious liberators."

Disgust darkened my officers' faces. Barida studiously examined the chart as Cano examined the beams overhead, slowly shaking his head. Bendel slapped his well-provisioned belly and laughed out loud. "Good damn joke, Colonel!"

The subaltern began nervously tapping his knee. The colonel glowered at his unappreciative audience.

"Yes, well, time will tell, Colonel," I said as cheerfully as I could muster. "Let's continue, Captain Southby."

With an audible sigh, he did. "Ah, yes, sir. Well, please remember, gentlemen, our naval vessels have no doctors and only a limited amount of medicines, all of which will be kept either inside the naval perimeter in the town or out aboard *Norden*. Cuban and American casualties incurred at Isabela will be brought by small boat out to *Norden*. Casualties from farther inland from Isabela will have to be taken care of by General Lacret's Free Cuban Army forces.

"The sailors will man defenses at the edge of town for three days, at the most, to ensure a route of withdrawal for the battalion if the Spanish are stronger than anticipated and things go badly. I repeat, gentlemen, The U.S. Navy is leaving Isabela no later than Saturday, the thirtieth, at noon."

I glanced around the table. "Thank you, Captain Southby. Are there any questions, gentlemen? This is your last chance."

Each man, except the colonel and his aide, said no.

"Then you are dismissed. Good luck tonight and tomorrow."

After the others filed out of the cabin, Cano stayed by the table and gave me a plaintive look. "Commodore, please allow me to explain."

"Captain Cano and Captain Southby, please remain for a moment so we can discuss logistical matters," I said, quietly adding. "I want Rork here too."

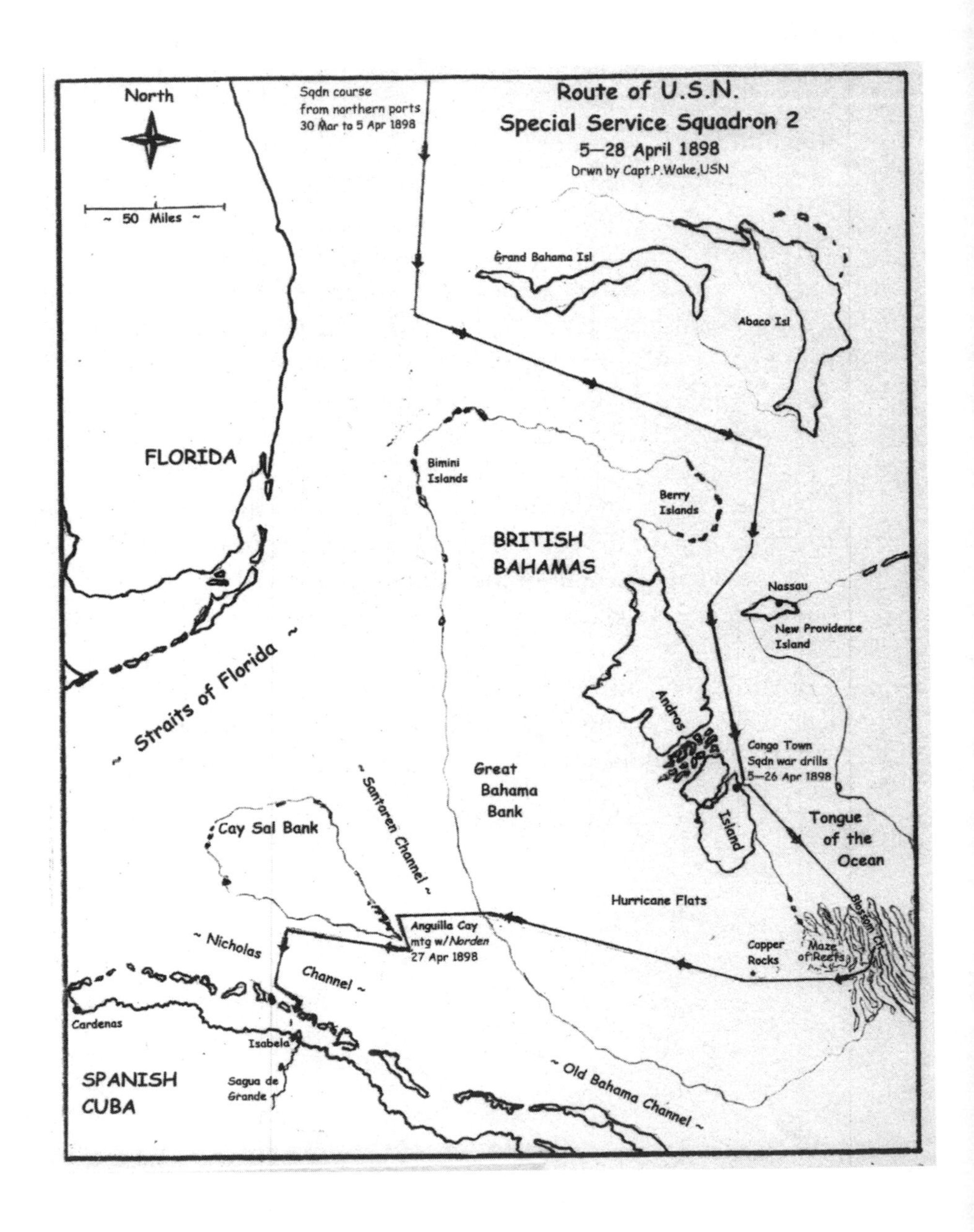

Route of U.S.N.
Special Service Squadron 2
5—28 April 1898
Drwn by Capt.P.Wake,USN
North
~ 50 Miles ~
Sqdn course
from northern ports
30 Mar to 5 Apr 1898
Grand Bahama Isl
Abaco Isl
FLORIDA
Bimini
Islands
Berry
Islands
BRITISH
BAHAMAS
Nassau
New Providence
Island
~ Straits of Florida ~
Andros
Congo Town
Sqdn war drills
5—26 Apr 1898
Great
Bahama
Bank
~ Santaren Channel ~
Cay Sal Bank
Island
Tongue
of the
Ocean
Hurricane Flats
Anguilla Cay
mtg w/Norden
27 Apr 1898
~ Nicholas
Channel ~
Copper
Rocks
Maze
of Reefs
Cardenas
Isabela
SPANISH
CUBA
Sagua de
Grande
~ Old Bahama Channel ~

44

Putting Things in Perspective

Anguilla Cays
Cay Sal Bank
Her Majesty's Colony of the Bahamas
Wednesday
27 April 1898

"All right, Mario, what the hell is really going on here? Start with why you are here, when you're supposed to be in Tampa with my daughter."

Rork, who had been busy with Mack on the boat deck during the briefing, hadn't even known Cano was aboard. His face reflected it when he strode into my cabin.

"Mario, me lad! Why're you here? An' in a Cuban uniform too," Rork exclaimed. "An' how's me dear god-daughter, Useppa?"

"Long story about how I am here, Sean, which I am about to tell. And Useppa is fine."

Southby, who vaguely knew I had a son-in-law in Florida named Cano, fidgeted in his chair and said, "Ah, sir, I've got a lot of things to get done and this looks like a personal issue, so I'll just go attend to my duties."

"Yes, you do have a lot of things to do right now, Captain, but stay. You need to be fully aware of all the factors involved in this operation. This won't take long, for Captain Cano will be concise."

To Cano, I said, "Out with it, Mario."

He adjusted his spectacles, cleared his throat, and began. "Yes, sir. Well, as you know, sir, since our dear friend José Martí asked me back in 1891, I have been a legal counselor with the Cuban Revolutionary Party. After he was killed three years ago, the leaders requested me to remain as their counselor for Tampa and Ocala, and sometimes Key West. Occasionally, I do some work for them up in Washington and New York.

"Five weeks ago, the New York junta leaders sent me to liaise with Colonel Zaldivar as he recruited exile Cubans and other Latin Americans around the Southern states for his newly formed regiment, which he equipped, armed, and provisioned with his own money. Zaldivar left Cuba thirty years ago at the beginning of the fight for independence. His father supported Carlos Manuel Céspedes's original military efforts, but was killed in battle. The family was subsequently forced off the island by the Spanish.

"Once in the United States, Zaldivar used what remained of the family's sugar cane plantation fortune to build up a successful mercantile business in several major Southern cities. He recently began calling for liberation of the area around Sagua Grande, which is where his father's planation was until 1868. Nobody took him seriously until he bought their attention with a sizable donation to the cause. I was assigned to be his liaison with the revolutionary leaders in New York."

"So, to summarize," I said. "You were told to spy on the rich fool who bought his colonelcy and try to keep him from making a total ass of himself, and the revolutionary cause, while recruiting around the United States. Zaldivar seems to have visions of returning to Cuba in grandeur and being the petty dictator of his province once the island becomes independent."

Cano agreed. "Yes, sir. That pretty much sums it up."

"How'd the recruiting go?"

"Sir, you've met the colonel. You can imagine how his exhortations were received by Latin Americans who attended his rallies in various cities. Instead of a regiment of eight or nine hundred men, he got only a hundred sixty-one men to volunteer, barely a battalion. Most of them are idlers or criminals from New Orleans and Charleston. Only a few of them are actually Cuban. He also got a dozen of his own employees to join. They were store managers and all of them are Cuban exiles. Their incentive was that their families will still draw their previous salaries, plus they get bonuses and have been promised land in Cuba when the war is over. They are now the battalion staff and company officers. Only a couple of them have served in the Cuban army."

Rork groaned. Southby's face lost its color. My stomach turned sour. This was worse than I thought.

"And Major Barida?" I asked.

"He is what he appears to be, sir—a veteran combat officer of the Cuban Liberation Army under General Lacret. He is squared-away, as you sailors say. Barida had been up in New York City obtaining a field artillery battery for Lacret and was about to return with it when the revolutionary leaders asked him to join Zaldivar's battalion. His mission is to keep it under control, and get it and the artillery to General Lacret. Major Barida has no artillerymen with him to work the guns. He will use the battalion to get them to Lacret, who does have artillerymen."

"And the relationship between Barida and the colonel?"

"Barida despises the colonel and vice versa, but the colonel knows he needs the major. Zaldivar offered him a bonus if he stays with the battalion once they join Lacret. I was there when Barida hotly refused it, saying his mission with the battalion and the colonel ends when he gets his guns to Lacret. He also told the colonel he considered the offer a bribe and a mark of dishonor. The colonel ignored the insult."

"So what will happen when the battalion goes inland from Isabela?"

"Once we are ashore and away from Isabela, Barida will take his artillery, plus any men who really want to fight for Cuba, and join Lacret as fast as he can. Zaldivar and the others will be left to fend for themselves. The major told me yesterday he thinks quite a few of the battalion's men can improve once he gets them ashore, under proper leadership and professional discipline. On the ship they are seasick, quarrelsome, and useless, and have been since we left Jacksonville last week."

"And what about you, *Captain* Cano?"

He winced. "Commodore, my rank is only temporary. My mission ends when the men join Lacret's division. I have a message for Lacret, and one to pass onward to General Gómez, from the New York staff. Then I am free to return to my life as a lawyer in Tampa. Sir, when they asked, I had no real choice but to do my duty to help the Cuban cause for freedom."

"Does Useppa know what you're doing?"

"In a general way, yes sir. She's not pleased, but understands. I regret not being able to notify you of my assignment, but when I cabled your office at the naval yard in New York, I was told you had already gone to sea. I had no idea our transport would be escorted by your squadron. We were only told some American naval vessels would be helping us."

My mind swirled with unanswerable questions about how this operation would unfold. And on a personal note, I now had the burden of my daughter's husband, who stood a good chance of getting killed while under my command.

My usual self-restraint vanished.

"*Damn it all to hell and back!*" I bellowed while pounding the chart of Isabela. "This convoluted zoo of misfit dregs isn't a battalion—it's a collection of targets for the Spanish! I know Roosevelt didn't authorize this mess, but I *will* find out who did. Lord knows I have seen some colossal errors in judgment and leadership during my thirty-five years in the navy, but I have *never* seen anything like this. And when I do find out which of those pompous bastards up in Washington decided to give me this crap pile of an assignment, I will personally drag his worthless ass out into Seventeenth Street and kick it all the way up to his cronies at Capitol Hill."

I took a breath, and then aimed a salvo of invective at Cano. "And those pencil-pushing politicos in the New York Cuban junta are no damned better! They just wanted Colonel What's-his-name's friggin' money, and in the process have jeopardized you, my ships and men, Barida's artillery, and Lacret's soldiers with this hare-brained scheme. To think our original strategy of landing American troops at Isabela and attacking Havana from the east was thought too ambitious! Yet somebody somewhere approved this . . . this . . . ludicrous notion? Good Lord, how will we ever win this war?"

Southby and Cano lowered their eyes. Rork raised an eyebrow and gave me a conspiratorial wink. I suddenly came to my senses and realized I was looking and sounding like a maniac. I sat down and shut up.

Rork broke the tension. "Aye, sir, this whole shebang was properly bollocks'd up from the start, but really, you an' me've been through far worse. Why, remember the time in the Forbidden Purple City o' Hue? Why we had enemies on top o' enemies, an' they all wanted the likes o' us dead."

"Oh, yeah, I remember every *second* of that mess," I said, as the memories hit me.

Holding up his rubber hand for emphasis, Rork turned to Southby. "Captain, 'twas a dark an' dicey deal, indeed. Why, even our so-called friends turned out to be enemies. Hell, at one time we had the emperor's high mandarins, some shifty-eyed Viet chaps, half the French navy, a couple o' Limey mercenaries, an' a gang o' crazed Chinese pirates, all after us. An' that's not to mention two lovely Oriental lasses who said they loved me but then got a bit disgruntled an' started gunnin' for my Irish arse. Can you believe it, sir? Everywhere we looked, there was somebody tryin' to kill us. Damned disheartenin' it was. In fact, that's where I got me hand shot off an' got me a spike, instead."

Rork regarded his false hand. "Proud as hell o' it, o' course, sir. Best weapon a man could have. But still, `tis a bit awkward durin' romantical moments, if you know me meanin'."

That got Southby and Cano laughing. Having lightened the mood, Rork turned his Gaelic wisdom on me.

"So nary's to worry, Commodore. This little run ashore at Isabela'll be a lot easier than the one fifteen years ago in Vietnam. An' as for the colonel, that ol' windbag'll fold like a cheap brollie at the first shot, an' he'll not be a spot o' bother to anyone after that. Just put 'im to bed on *Norden*.

"Yes, sir, he'll be outta the way then. This Major Barida fellow'll handle those men just fine. This'll be simple, for the only real enemy we've got on this caper is the Spaniardos. An' those poor bastards've never run up against Uncle Sam's blessed blue-jackets. Hell, our lads're so well drilled we could be three sheets to the wind an' still scare the pantaloons off `em!"

Even I was laughing by then. "Rork, after all these years, you are still true to form. Thank you for putting things in perspective."

"Always try me best, sir," Rork replied with faux innocence.

"Gentlemen, I guess now we know who is who and what is what, so let's get on with it. Rork, please get Mario over to *Norden*."

Assuming my most fearsome pose for my my son-in-law's sake, I announced, "By the way, Captain Mario Cano of the Free Cuban Army, it took a long damn time to get my daughter married off. I don't have the patience to start over again. Besides, I want to be a grandfather someday to your children, so listen to this very closely. You do *not* have approval for getting killed—which means you are *not* to do anything stupid. Is that completely understood?"

He straightened to attention and replied, "Aye, aye, sir. And if I may have permission to reciprocate the sentiment, I very much want my children to have a couple of grizzled old salts for their grandfather and uncle, so please be careful yourselves."

45

Luck

Isabela, Cuba
Thursday morning
28 April 1898

The squadron's approach to Cuba was made under a cloudy sky. No moon and only a few stars penetrated the overcast. For the entire transit from Anguilla, not another ship was seen. We reached the outer buoy of the channel and turned south. I hoped our luck would hold.

Steamed south through the channel between the islands of Cayo de la Cruz and Cayo Maravillas, nobody moved or spoke aboard *Kestrel*. Every ear and eye strained to find the enemy. Our guns were trained port and starboard, ready as they could be for a fight. Astern, *Osprey* and rest of the squadron followed. Dark forms on a dark sea, only their bow waves showed some color, a greyish-white line of froth, barely visible. I braced myself for a shout of alarm from the island, or the shot of a field gun.

Nothing happened.

There were small craft drawn up on the beach on Cayo Maravillas in front of a couple of palm-thatched shacks. No lights shown or men were seen. Evidently, they were asleep, unusual for fishermen at this time of the morning. Seconds later we were beyond them, entering the bay and steering straight down the channel. We slowed down to four knots at Cayo Paloma, bare steerageway, so even the bow waves disappeared as the squadron approached the unseen little town ahead.

Southby had bearings on the surrounding headlands double checked, but they proved we were still right in the middle of the channel. The current I feared would veer us off course in the night was slacking and didn't interfere. I checked my pocket watch. We were right on time, and right on course.

The mainland ahead became more defined as we grew closer. Punta Sotavento showed on the port bow, with Cayo Mendoza on the starboard. The clapboard and thatched dwellings of Isabela emerged as pale shapes against the mangrove-jungled coastline. The large commercial wharf took form, looming out of the dusk. I was relieved to see no steamers at it.

"Fishing boat putting off from the beach, close on the port bow!" reported the port lookout as we turned toward the wharf. "There's a crowd of people on the beach. Here comes another fishing boat."

"Hold your course, helmsman," said Southby, standing amidship. "All engines stop. Line handlers, standby with grappling hooks."

"*Qué es eso?*" came a confused shout from the fishermen on the beach—*what is that?*

"*¡Es un buque de guerra norteamericano! ¡La invasión!*" somebody else answered—*It's an American warship! The invasion!*

I was on the starboard side, looking for those two gunboats. I made out *Mayari* an instant later, then saw flashes.

Boom! Boom! Boom!

A staccato series of flames leaped out toward us from a hundred yards away to starboard. It was *Mayari*'s forty-two-millimeter bow gun. The rounds whooshed right over my head. In their haste the Spanish sailors had aimed too high, but I knew their next shots would be corrected lower—right at the bridge deck where I stood.

Behind me, Southby calmly ordered, "All guns that bear—open fire at target to starboard."

Before he finished the command, the Spanish gunboat's stern machine gun quickly opened fire, raking our main deck. I shut my eyes barely in time to not be blinded by what I knew was coming.

With a loud roar, *Kestrel* lit up fore and aft in a blast of fire and smoke as all guns that would bear to starboard—two rapid-fire six-pounders and a Colt machine gun—fired in unison. The simultaneous concussion and recoil pushed the ship to port, crunching her against the wharf.

The impact explosions at that point-blank range were instantaneous, igniting *Mayari*'s ready ammunition, then her magazine. The gunboat disintegrated into a mass of blazing debris hurtling in all directions. The heat wave pushed me backward into a signalman. Seconds later burning embers and pieces of wood and iron rained down.

Mayari didn't exist anymore. Neither did her dock. The small naval depot on shore was burning. I saw no survivors.

"Douse the decks," Southby shouted above the din as *Kestrel*'s foredeck crew reported the bow lines were over and holding. Two young sailors came along and sloshed buckets of water on the scattered embers before they could set off our own ready ammunition.

"Away the landing party to port!" was Southby's next order and a chorus of war hoops told me the sailors were already leaping onto the wharf.

Above it all, I heard Grover Yeats yelling, "Follow me, men!"

"Spanish gunboat closing fast on the starboard quarter!" called the lookout beside me. Machine gun fire sparked at us as *Lealtad* attacked.

"Open fire on target astern!" ordered Southby. The stern gun blasted out three quick rounds. The Spanish never had a chance. Her hull fragmented apart amidship, breaking her in half.

The stern went right down but the bow continued its forward momentum before gradually sinking.

The two most immediate threats having been disposed of, I crossed over to the port side. In the lightening of the dawn I watched as *Osprey* came up the wharf opposite us, her landing party jumping ashore while she was still moving forward. At the head of the wharf, I could see young Yeats rallying his sailors, spreading them out as they went off to the right along the shoreline toward what was left of the gunboat station.

"Situation report?" I asked Southby.

"Phase one is completed, Commodore," reported Southby. "Casualties are Seaman Jackson wounded in the leg and none killed. *Kestrel*'s only damage is superficial to the starboard side, where some debris from *Mayarí*'s explosion hit us."

"Ashore?"

"The wharf is secured. No opposition so far, with no shots fired. Most of the civilians fled inland right away. That crowd of fishermen have taken their boats away too. This end of the town appears empty, but the sailors will search it to make sure."

"The squadron?"

"No enemy ships are in sight. *Osprey* is backing off the wharf and *Falcon* is about to come in and land her sailors. *Harrier*'s launch has already disembarked her contingent, so the naval landing party is almost at full initial strength. *Norden* should be coming in with the Cuban troops in about twenty minutes. We are right on schedule, sir."

"Very well. Anything else?"

My watch showed five-forty-four. Twenty minutes until sunrise. The sky, as is typical in the tropics, was getting lighter fast and a pinkish glow was spreading among the clouds to the east. From the vantage of the bridge deck, I could see out over the village and the lone road leading into it. With every minute more detail could be seen.

The place looked just as dismal as it had been in January. But now the scene was worsened by another sense—the acrid smell of burning ships, and the nauseating odor of scorched flesh. I knew that by noon the stench would be unbearable. By the next day we'd all be used to it.

"Captain, once the town is searched and the perimeter is secured, have a detail of men recover the bodies from the gunboats, along with any personal effects. We will bury the bodies in the middle of the town with full naval honors. I will preside. We will send the personal effects to the Spanish Navy for the families.

"Aye, aye, sir."

"You did very well, Captain. So did every officer and man in the squadron."

"The drills paid off, sir."

"Yes, they did. We also had good luck the Spanish didn't really defend the place. But we've only begun this mission, and the Spanish will come. Chief Rork and I are going ashore for a quick look around at defense possibilities. And don't look so worried, James, we'll be well armed. Make sure the battalion doesn't dawdle in getting ashore."

"Commodore leaving the bridge," announced the petty officer of the watch as Rork and I descended the ladder. Both of us had our pistols, and Rork carried two shotguns with sling straps, his in his hands and mine slung on his left shoulder.

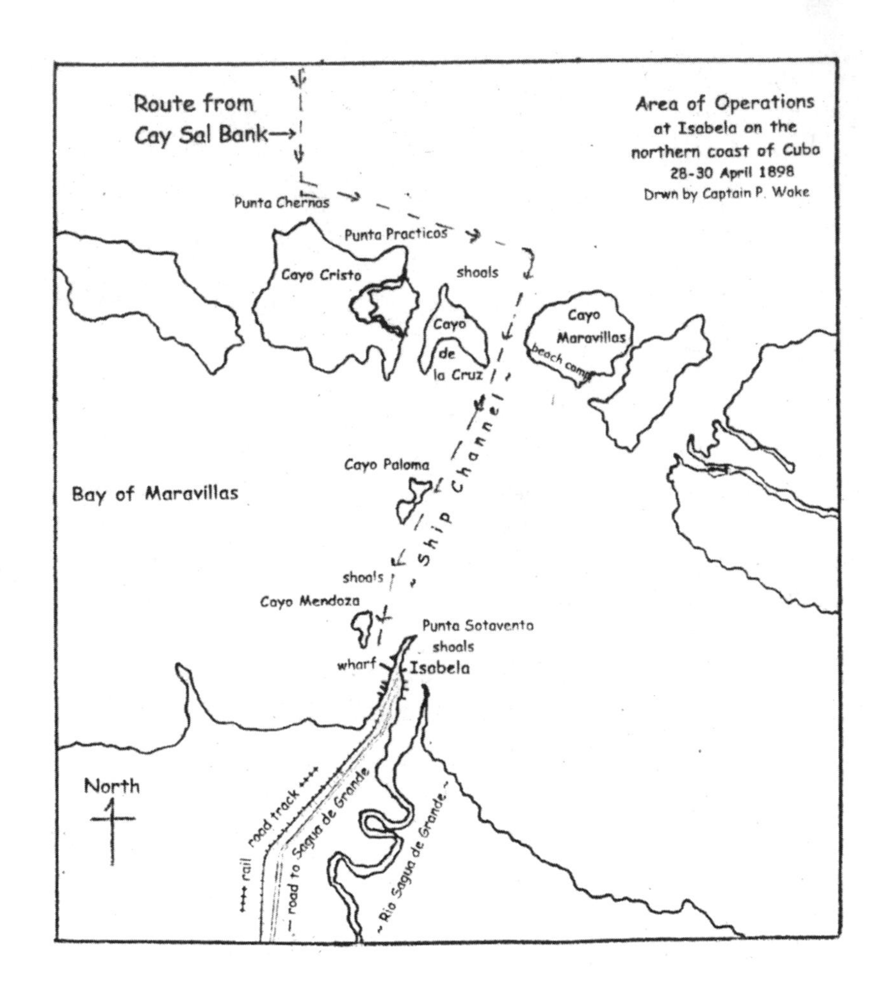
Route from
Cay Sal Bank→
Area of Operations
at Isabela on the
northern coast of Cuba
28-30 April 1898
Drwn by Captain P. Wake
Punta Chernas
Punta Practicos
Cayo Cristo
shoals
Cayo
de
la Cruz
Cayo
Maravillas
beach camp
Ship Channel
Cayo Paloma
Bay of Maravillas
shoals
Cayo Mendoza
Punta Sotavento
shoals
wharf
Isabela
North
rail road track
road to Sagua de Grande
Rio Sagua de Grande

46

Assuming the Worst

Isabela, Cuba
Thursday morning
28 April 1898

The place was empty of people. Walking south along the shoreline past the large cane warehouse, I then headed to the left, through an alleyway between some shacks. Crossing the railroad track, we emerged from the alley at the wide and very dusty main street of the place.

We both carried our shotguns at the ready by this point. Our reconnaissance was done in silence, for Rork and I don't need to speak, just a glance or a gesture to warn of potential dangers.

Returning to the railroad track, we followed it southwest to the very end of the town. Twenty feet beyond was an abrupt wall of mangrove forest, with roots intertwined for a height of two feet above ground and the branches interwoven for another ten feet up. The only opening through this tangle was the straight road, beside its companion railroad track, out of Isabela to Sagua Grande.

We came upon Lieutenant Yeats and Bosun Mack. Their men were searching the shacks to make sure no Spanish forces or Cuban civilians lingered. The lieutenant didn't look pleased to see his commodore show up unannounced, an understandable reaction.

"See any sign of Spanish soldiers having been here, Mr. Yeats?" I asked.

"None, sir. Nobody at all. The civilians must've left in a hurry, because there's still food cooking on their stoves. So much for the locals welcoming us as their liberators."

"They's just poor folks, Mr. Yeats, and don't trust nobody in a uniform, sir," offered Mack. "They'll come back when all the fightin's done."

Mack was too young to have been a slave, but I could imagine his father telling him what the war was like for the South's blacks thirty-three years earlier. I remembered them staying out of sight during those battles too.

"Good," I said. "We don't need them getting in the way when the Spanish army eventually gets here. Carry on with your work, Lieutenant. Chief Rork and I will be looking around the area for a bit."

Yeats detailed two of his men to stay out in front of us as Rork and I walked over to the middle of the road and surveyed the inhospitable landscape.

"So what do you think?" I asked Rork in a hushed tone.

"Nothin' good, sir. Them civilians've already told the enemy at Sagua what happened here. An' after what we did to their gunboats, those Spaniardo navy grandees'll be lookin' for revenge, sure as hell is hot. Navy, army, militia—they'll *all* want a piece o' the *yanqui* barbarians that did that. Methinks we best be settin' up some serious defenses directly, cause me achin' bones're tellin' me it's gonna get damned ugly 'round here real soon."

Bitter experience has taught me to always pay attention when Rork's bones start aching.

"I agree on the Spanish and the defenses," I said. "They'll push hard to get as many men here as fast as they can to try to nip this in the bud. Major Barida will have to get his exile Cubans moving quickly to get down the road and linked up with General Lacret's people before the Spanish block the way out."

"Aye on that, sir. Those exile lads don't stand a chance against regular Spanish troops, especially once they're out o' range o' *Kestrel*'s covering guns."

"Yes, well, that's another thing I just noticed during our little stroll, Rork."

I pointed behind us to the town. "Look over there. *Kestrel*'s guns are masked by the cane warehouse, and they can't elevate enough to lob over them. They can hit the area on the left side of the road, looking south, but not the road itself, the railroad track, or anything to the right of it. And the warehouses are too stout to cut down rapidly with the manpower we have available."

He let out a blue streak of language of the type only a navy chief petty officer can utter. It ended in, "And the squadron's other ships're too bleedin' far from shore to be within effective range to hit the road down here."

"Yes, that's about it. Look, Barida knows the terrain and what he has to do, so he'll push his men hard to get clear of the area today. At the latest, the Spanish will hit us at sunrise tomorrow. They'll come right up this road, in regulation skirmish order out front, and main formations directly behind. We'll be outnumbered at least seven to one in the initial assault, twice that if they can get their entire regiment here by then."

Rork's face tightened. "Aye, sir, an' they'll be proper soldiers that know the area, carryin' them damned smokeless Mauser rifles, an' lots o' ammunition."

"We've got to outsmart them, Rork. They're combat veterans, but they're also conscripts who've never run into well-armed men. Not to mention, you and I know tricks they've never run into before."

"That we do! Something loud an' nasty an' messy—that'll give `em the terrors."

I swept my hand over the landscape outside of the town. "Exactly, Rork. I'm thinking of laying out some surprises for them to funnel their attack toward a killing ground of our choice. Remember back in eighty-one, in Peru? Looked pretty bad for us there at first. The Chileans outnumbered the Peruvians ten to one and thought they were winning, but they ended up in a Peruvian trap. Same concept here."

He nodded pensively. "Do indeed, sir. Those Peruviano blokes prepared the ground well. Let's peruse this piece o' ground an' see what we can conjure up."

The road was sandy, rutted, and about thirty feet wide, with grass extending for another twenty feet on the left, or east, side. On the west side, a fifteen-foot wide, shallow ditch separated the road from the railroad track bed, which rose two feet above the flat surrounding grade. A hundred feet down the track, an empty flatbed train car sat by itself on the track. Thirty feet on the other side of the track bed was the never ending wall of mangrove jungle. The entire width of the attack area was a little over two-hundred-fifty feet.

A quarter mile south, the cleared area was wider. At that point, the road and track passed a stubbled cane field on the left, then curved to the left and proceeded straight south, the cleared area closing back in.

We started heading down the road. I thought aloud as we walked. "The Spanish will have a narrow line of advance with little room to maneuver laterally. It'll be almost impossible for them to flank us in these dense mangroves. A few might get through, but not without making enough noise to alert our flank guards. Therefore, our small defense force will face their whole attack right here, across the road and track. We've got to give them obvious choices to go exactly where we want them."

"False retreat," said Rork cheerfully. "Always fun."

"Yes, a wonderful opportunity for a little theatrics from the boys. Let the Spanish see us retreat from an observation post up there south of the curve. They'll think they're winning. Our sailors will fire some rounds, then shriek and start running like hell back to town, dropping equipment as they go. That'll get the enemy over-confident and sloppy."

As we approached the cane field, I said, "Good, it's just as I remembered from January. Let's look over there."

As is normal in Cuba and Florida, the cane field had been burned after harvesting, to clear it for the next crop. The new crop was starting to peek out of the soot-covered ground. We crossed the field to the far side, where I spied a faint trail from the edge of the field. Rork and I followed it, our sailor guards remaining at the cane field. The trail wound through the mangroves to emerge at the Sagua Grande River, the sluggish stream we'd seen in the middle of that distant town.

I looked up at the sky and said, "Thank you, Lord."

After we returned to the edge of the field, I gestured broadly toward the road a hundred yards away. The pair of sailors wandered closer to hear.

"The Spanish skirmishers will be in good spirits chasing our boys. We'll let them pass by here and will wait until the main formation is just opposite this place. Then we'll engage with sniper fire—I'm thinking four, maybe five, of our best marksmen—against their mounted officers in a long-range ambush. That will start their troops toward the first prepared killing ground on the opposite side of the road, where we'll hit them with overwhelming force of an improvised kind."

Rork held up a hand. "But wait, sir. They're professionals, trained to rush ambushers, while also flankin' them. They'll lay down heavy fire an' start runnin' right across the field at our lads here. It'll get chancy as hell."

"Correct, Rork. That's what they are trained to do. But when they respond to their training and try to rush the ambush, they'll hit trip wires on the road side of the field and see mines in the field."

"We've no mines, sir."

"True. But we can make Quaker mines. The enemy won't know the difference."

"Damned good idea, sir!"

"Thank you. Plus, it's a hundred yards of open ground from the road to the far edge of the field. Any officer in the lead will get hit by our sharpshooters. Right about then, with their officers down and seeing mines all over the field, the ditch on the other side of the road will look like the best place for those leaderless soldiers to take cover temporarily. They'll wait there for orders. Remember, European conscript soldiers aren't trained to think on their own. Once they run into something they're not familiar with, they stop and wait to be told what to do."

"Damned true, sir. Same as we saw in Indochina, Africa, and Samoa. How do we overwhelm `em in the ditch?"

"Fougasse in the ditch. Mechanical tipping device for the accelerant and long fuse for the ignition. Trip wires on either side of our ambushers will slow down the skirmishers that come back down the road, and any Spanish flankers from the main formation. During the ensuing chaos after the fougasse goes off, our snipers will simply disappear, leaving the ambush site by this trail to a boat on the bank. Then they head down the river to the town and rejoin our lines there."

"Bloody friggin' brilliant, Commodore. That'll put a nettle in their nickers."

The two sailors were startled by seeing Rork slap my shoulder in excitement, an open breach of naval discipline. Nearly everyone in the squadron knew of our long friendship, but few actually ever saw signs of it, for Rork and I were careful to maintain decorum when aboard warships.

"Thank you, Rork," I replied. "I consider that a high compliment indeed, coming from such a fertilely demented mind as yours. But we dare not rest on our fougassean laurels, for the Spanish will have lots more men for us to deal with. Their colonel will be doubly incensed by then, which is good, for his judgment will be impaired. His next attack will be a rapid, overwhelming charge, straight up the road at what he thinks is our main defense line, which will appear quite weak. We are, after all, only ignorant sailors. Our earlier success will be put down to mere luck."

"Time for some caltrops, *chevals de frises*, an' *trou de loups*."

"Precisely. Just as they think they're overrunning our final defense line we'll funnel the enemy into another killing ground on their left flank, in front of the flatbed railcar, which is seemingly empty. But under the railcar we'll put that big molasses tank we saw back in town. Packed tight with guncotton and shrapnel, with the seam rivets loosened on the road side, and ignited by mechanical device on a percussion shell, it'll blast out along the road."

"An old-fashioned Rains bomb from the Rebs back in the war. Nasty piece o' work, that was."

"Yes, just like that Confederate general's bomb device, but on a slightly larger scale. One of our Colt machine guns firing from the road in town will complete their panic. The Spanish will withdraw and wait for reinforcements and artillery. I figure that'll take half a day."

"An' when they do come at us again, their men will be scared o' what sort o' infernal hell awaits `em yet again."

I couldn't help a certain smug tone. "But I fear the colonel will be rather disappointed. By then, we won't be here anymore. We'll be on *Kestrel*, steaming away . . ."

Rork let out a whistle and turned to the awestruck sailors.

"Boyos, you've learned a valuable lesson today. Old age an' treachery still work every time—so study your history!"

47

They That Go Down to the Sea in Ships . . .

Isabela, Cuba
Thursday morning
28 April 1898

The exile Cuban battalion was unloading its equipment and forming up on the road when Rork and I returned for the funeral service. Isabela, so quiet before, was now a veritable beehive of activity. Barida came over to me and asked what we had seen in our reconnaissance. I briefed him on my defense plans.

The funeral service for the Spanish sailors was held in the middle of town, just inland from the wharf. All naval activity ended and every American sailor on ship or wharf uncovered his head and stood facing the ceremony. Barida's men lined up in ranks. The ceremony was short, but as dignified as we could make it, given the circumstances.

With Cano translating everything into Spanish, I began.

"We stand before brave Spanish sailors and honor them for their courage. They are no longer our enemies, but our brother seamen, who, like us, have known the perils of storm and battle on the water. We are certain they now rest in eternal peace in Heaven with God, where neither storm nor battle are ever felt."

I then read the 107th Psalm, starting at verse twenty-three, commonly known around the world as the sailor's psalm.

"They that go down to the sea in ships and occupy their business in great waters: these men see the works of the Lord and his wonders in the deep. For at his word the stormy wind ariseth which lifteth up the waves thereof. They are carried up to the heaven, and down again into the deep: their souls melteth away because of the trouble. The reel to and fro, and stagger like a drunken man, and are at their wit's end. So when they cry unto the Lord in their trouble, He delivereth them out of their distress. For He maketh the storm to cease so that the waves thereof are still. Then they are glad because they are at rest; and so He bringeth them unto the haven where they would be."

Captain Cano said a brief prayer in Spanish. Rork called all hands to attention and called the salute. A Cuban drummer beat out the long roll and seven sailors fired three blank volleys. Then a navy bugler sounded taps, and it was over.

Thirty seconds after the end of this sad business, the frenzy of war started up again. It was as if the reality of what they had just witnessed reinforced the will of every man there not be the honorees of the next such ceremony.

The scene became a cacophony of motion and noise, from the soldiers unloading *Norden* and forming up the battalion, to the adjacent sailors manufacturing the weaponry needed for the perimeter defense. Shouted commands in Spanish and English, the hammering of nails, clanging of metal, grunting of men lifting impossible loads, and the ever present curses of petty officers, made Isabela sound alive and industrious. It was already eleven o'clock and the sun was broiling. Even so, a sense of urgent determination bordering on desperation drove everyone to maintain the pace despite the heat.

The squadron's ships had been stripped to the bare number of crew needed for the guns and engines. All others were ashore to assist in the defense at the perimeter and the preparations on the wharf. Thus, we had more than originally planned, but they were still not enough. Every sailor in sight was doing the work of two men.

It was in this moment that I received two reports in my cabin, where I was composing a statement to Admiral Sampson about our progress to date.

The first was from the bridge. *Harrier* had signaled she sighted a Spanish gunboat of the *Mayari* class three miles offshore of Cayo Maravillas, heading east past the entrance to the channel into the bay. *Harrier*'s Lieutenant Farmore further informed the flagship he had established a two-man lookout post at the vacant fisherman camp on Maravillas.

This development was followed by a message from Lieutenant Yeats at our defense perimeter. He had a man there in a wagon by the name of Raul Gonzart who purported to be my acquaintance from a tobacco buying trip years ago. Yeats, thoroughly confused, thought him a Spanish spy and suggested we bring him in for interrogation and execution by hanging from the rigging, not wishing to waste a bullet. Gonzart's identity as one of my agents needed to be protected, so I agreed with Yeats and directed the perfidious suspect be delivered to my cabin for an in-depth examination by myself and Rork.

Gonzart arrived in a state of confusion and indignation. Rork told the petty officer he was free to go and took custody of the prisoner. Once the door was closed and locked, pretenses were suspended. Gonzart and I shook hands. I poured him a chilled orange juice and bid him to relax in a chair. The change on his face from horror to relief was readily apparent.

"Very sorry for the ruse, Raul, but I trust no one with your clandestine identity."

"They thought I was a Spanish spy. That officer told me I was going to be hung by the neck! When I first heard the U.S. Navy was at Isabela, I hoped it was you. Then when I got here,

I thought all had gone terribly wrong and I would killed by our allies!"

"What can you tell me about the reaction to our arrival?"

"The people of Isabela fled to my town this morning and spread the word of your coming, and it is the talk of Sagua Grande. The Spanish are irate and massing their men. The Cuban civilians are cautiously hopeful. General Lacret ordered me to make contact with the Americans and discover their intentions. Is this the invasion?"

"No, it is not. Our intentions are not what they were originally. There is no invasion by American troops coming here. We have secured Isabela only temporarily, for the disembarkation of a few exile Cuban troops, not all of whom are actually Cuban."

This was not what Gonzart was expecting, and his face showed it.

I told him the rest of it. "The unit is designated the Batallón Nacional Orgullo de Cuba, and there is an accompanying battery of purchased artillery. The battalion is now forming up to march inland to Sagua Grande and serve in General Lacret's division. Both are under Major Ramon Barida, whom you may know.

"No, I misstated that. They are officially under the command of Colonel Ruben Ramon Armando Zaldivar de Aviles y Vega, whose family owned a plantation in this area thirty years ago. But believe me, Major Barida is really in command. Zaldivar is a political dilettante who won't last long once the shooting starts."

Gonzart's expression lit up. "Major Barida has come back to Cuba with the artillery! Excellent news. And we have reinforcements? General Lacret will be very happy."

"Tell him not to be. Most aren't from Cuba. Only six have combat experience. They look useless to me, but they do have rifles and ammunition. So tell me, where is the Spanish Army?"

His report on the Spanish Army was succinct and discouraging. Assembling under Colonel Arce at Sagua Grande were eight hundred men, who would be at Isabela the next morning. The only good news was they had no artillery or cavalry. Telegraph intercepts, done by Gonzart at his office job, between the First Corps commander, General Aguirre, at Santa Clara, and Spanish Army headquarters in Havana, provided more ominous intelligence. Elements of the 38th Leon Infantry, veterans of Cuba and North Africa, were en route to Sagua Grande by rail from Havana. They would arrive late the next day. It was unknown if they had artillery or cavalry with them.

"Raul, I need three things from you. One: tell General Lacret I am requesting he send forces here to help get these guns and men out of this area before they are intercepted by Arce's regiment. Two: I am requesting he sabotage the tracks to Havana to slow down the Leon regiment's transit here. Tell the general to hurry, the navy will leave Isabela at noon on Saturday for other missions. Lastly: please take this box of personal effects from the Spanish Navy dead, and get them to their headquarters for their families."

He looked inside the box at the few items which survived destruction. "I will do as you say, sir. I do not know if General Lacret can help, though. Like everyone, the general thought the *norteamericanos* were invading in great strength at Isabela. It will take time to assemble his units and have them travel here to assist Major Barida."

"Anything he can do will be appreciated, Raul. You'd better get going now."

Rork escorted the "prisoner" back to Lieutenant Yeats, with the explanation that Gonzart was a harmless fool I'd met on a previous visit, and to let him go.

Shortly after they left, the resplendent form of the commanding officer of the Batallón Nacional Orgullo de Cuba filled the entrance of my cabin. In an indignant drunken rage, Colonel Zaldivar barged right in and loudly declared in English he wanted vengeance and he wanted it right then. I noted his fluency. Surprising for a fellow who'd needed an interpreter only a day before.

Entering right behind Zaldivar, a short exile sergeant sheepishly escorted a uniformed prisoner whose hands were manacled. The prisoner was twice the size of the sergeant.

Major Ramon Barida sighed and cast the colonel a disgusted look.

48

Time Dwindles

Isabela, Cuba
Thursday morning
28 April 1898

Zaldivar wasted no time. "Commodore Wake, I demand Major Ramon Barida be court-martialed immediately for insubordination and cowardice, the penalty to be death by gunfire!"

The colonel made a shrugging half bow in my direction. "Of course, I would arrange this proceeding myself, but this insidious traitor Barida has exerted undue negative influence over the officers of my battalion and it is impossible for me to assemble the needed court."

"Colonel, I really don't have time for this nonsense. You see, there's the little matter of a war going on, in which your men were supposed to begin taking part *over an hour ago!*"

Zaldivar's nose tilted even higher. "We cannot and will not start the march until this disgraceful matter is resolved to my satisfaction."

That was the final straw for me. "Very well, it will be resolved, right now, right here—to *my* satisfaction. Take the handcuffs off your prisoner and let him get back to work, fighting the Spanish. By the way, congratulations on your rapid mastery of English."

He ignored my sarcasm with an exasperated harrumph. "The key to the handcuffs is in *my* possession, and I will *not* remove the handcuffs until after he has been executed. Discipline must be preserved!"

"I couldn't agree more, Zaldivar," intentionally omitting his rank as I removed my pistol from its holster and leveled it at his right leg. "So, as the senior officer in command of this entire allied operation, I will preserve discipline right now. You have five seconds to get those handcuffs off Major Barida, or you will be shot. One thousand one . . ."

The sergeant didn't understand English, but he understood my pistol, and stood there gape-mouthed. Barida assumed the air of a bemused spectator. Southby, who burst in the cabin at just that point, shook his head in confusion and reached for his own pistol.

Meanwhile, Zaldivar's eyes lost their haughty little sneer when I got to "one thousand four" and cocked the hammer.

"Wait," he sputtered, while digging in his tunic pocket. "I will remove them, but only under protest at your grossly unprofessional and disrespectful behavior. I will complain of your lunacy to your superiors and seek justice."

Barida rubbed his newly freed hands and wrists, and quietly told the sergeant he could leave. That poor soul didn't need any more encouragement and was gone in a flash.

I wasn't done yet. "Major Barida, please handcuff Zaldivar, who is under arrest for whatever charges you prefer. I would suggest drunkenness, incompetence, dereliction of duty, and cowardice. No doubt there has been a misappropriation of funds somewhere along the line also. The court-martial can be at the discretion of General Lacret. I turn custody of the prisoner over to the Free Cuban Army, where I know justice will be served."

"Yes, sir," replied Barida, who then officially arrested Zaldivar in Spanish.

Before Zaldivar's slow mind could form a word of protest, he was spun around with his hands manacled behind his back.

"Major Barida, get your battalion on the move this instant and take the prisoner with you. His perfume is stinking up my ship. I wish you all good fortune in your mission, Ramon. Please present my respects to General Lacret."

Barida saluted me and led a silent Zaldivar from my quarters. Southby cleared the passageway of spectators, closed the door, and sat down by my desk.

"Damn, Commodore. I thought you were really going to shoot him."

I shrugged. "I was."

It was almost noon before the exiles got under way on the road out of town. Barida and my son-in-law corralled the throng into a semblance of a military formation. With skirmishers and scouts out front, they headed off down the road. Zaldivar was in the middle of the column, guarded by four very nasty-looking, dark-skinned fellows with newly pinned chevrons. The guards glared at anyone trying to get close to the prisoner.

All in all, the liberators of Isabela were not an inspiring or imposing sight. In fact, they were damned pitiful. Tellingly, none of our sailors joked with them as the soldiers trudged by with clanking rifles and canteens. The sailors merely nodded and quietly wished them well.

The pit of my stomach churned when I thought of Mario Cano in battle. My daughter couldn't take another heartache in life. Mario was a smart judge of men and situations, understood some of the clandestine arts, but the Cuban lawyer had no military experience at all. He smiled wanly at me before striding up to where Barida marched. I said a little prayer for him, and for them all.

Viewing the defense preparations was decidedly more positive for my morale. It began with Captain Bendel meeting me on the wharf and expressing admiration in his unique way.

"Your people have done wonders, Peter. Even the Imperial German Navy could learn a thing or two. I may try to get some of them to desert to my merchant ship! I will be getting away from the wharf in five minutes and anchoring in the bay, to await the wounded."

I shook his hand. "It's always a pleasure to work with you, Karl. No telling how long this war will go on, so there may be more *quiet work* for you."

"Quiet work" was a euphemism for clandestine endeavors. Bendel had been a valued operative of mine for years. The man was fearless.

Bendel grinned at the idea. "Good! Something more exciting than transporting sheep to the slaughter, like this job. I must be off now. See you later, Peter."

Kestrel's petty officers had clearly gotten into the innovative spirit at the impromptu workshop set up on the wharf. Though they'd never heard of the ancient weaponry and tactics they would create for us, they immediately grasped the concept when Rork or I had explained it to them earlier in the morning. They even made some improvements on the designs.

The machinist mate turned out two dozen caltrops—four or five-armed iron spikes like large children's jacks, with extremely sharp points which stand four inches up in the air no matter how they fall on the ground. Caltrops terrify horses and will stop a cavalry charge.

Assisted by a boilerman, the machinist also worked on the cylindrical molasses tank which was to be placed under the flatbed railcar. Freeing the rivets along one lengthwise seam, they then helped the gunner's mate pack it with all the spare guncotton in the squadron, followed by gunpowder and scrap metal found around the wharf. In a hole at one end of the tank, the gunner's mate placed a standard shell from a six-pounder gun with an impact percussion primer. Then the two of them rigged a mechanical trigger device to set the shell off, activated by a long lanyard.

From lumber scavenged in the town, the carpenter mate and his helpers constructed four *chevals de frise*—twenty-foot-long rails with four rows of three-foot-long wooden spikes radiating from them. Thus, each *cheval de frise* formed a twenty-foot-long by almost six-foot-high barrier, impenetrable by infantry or cavalry charge. Our sailors would be able stand behind the *cheval* and shoot through the small spaces between the spikes.

With compliments given out to all hands on the wharf, Southby and I headed ashore and down the road. Near the end of town was one of *Kestrel's* two Colt machine guns, mounted on a two-wheel push cart in the right side of the road. The cart's mobility enabled the gun to be employed at any needed location, but its main position would be right there, where it could enfilade the enemy on the road, just as the railcar bomb exploded.

A hundred feet beyond the town, across the road in the area to the east, several sailors were laboring to dig three trou de loups—camouflaged trenches filled with spikes in the sides and bottom. When the enemy charged across seemingly benign ground, they would fall through the false roof of kindling and leaves topped with sand, plunging down into the spikes. But there was a problem, the bosun mate in charge informed us. The ground was only sandy for about a foot in depth. Below that it was solid coral and limestone rock. There were test holes all over, but none was more than a foot or so deep.

Southby freed them all from the fruitless task and had them report to the men working on the defenses a quarter mile farther out, to whence we now headed. While we walked in that direction, Rork showed up and reported Gonzart was on his way, and the Cuban battalion was now marching in better order for Sagua Grande.

He then leaned closer to my ear. "Heard a most amazin' rumor from the Cuban lads when they marched past me, sir. They said the crazy *gringo* commodore was goin' to shoot that fool colonel `cause he arrested Barida, an' damned happy they were you stopped that idiocy. Ooh, let me tell you, you're a bloomin' hero to those boyos."

"Did what I had to do, Rork. Come with us to see the fougasse. I want your opinion."

Mr. Yeats was in charge of the outer defense preparations, which was quite a daunting job. Especially the fougasse, for it was a tricky matter. It had to be carefully prepared *en situ* at the ditch across from the field. Any miscalculation, physical or mental, would result in the flaming deaths of our own men.

First, a layer of molasses was poured into the ditch. This ubiquitous Cuban material, part of the rum-making process, would not alarm the Spanish soldiers when they jumped to safety in the ditch. It thickly coated the ditch, preventing the accelerant from dissipating into the sandy soil. The molasses' strong smell would also serve to mask the odor of the accelerant waiting close by. When we arrived, the molasses had already been spread, covering the ditch a foot deep in the sticky stuff, for a length of a hundred-fifty feet.

Next came the truly precarious part—creating and positioning the accelerant. It was a complicated balancing act. The mixture had to be fluid enough to swiftly spread atop the entire length of the molasses. The amount had to be a large enough to provide an overwhelming conflagration. The container had to be small enough to be well concealed and easily employed. And the ignition had to be reliable enough to work via a long lanyard.

Lieutenant Yeats proved equal to the task. The mixture was a combination of coal oil, kerosene, urine ammonia, and the *pièce de résistance*, 180-proof rot-gut aguardiente, liberated from a shack. The concoction was contained in a forty-gallon old oak barrel and concealed with the lush leaves of a small manchineel tree.

This choice of location was a stroke of true genius, for the manchineel is extremely poisonous to touch. No one with any experience in Cuba would get close enough to examine something hidden inside a manchineel's foliage. Yeats explained to me his men used blankets and long shell-handlers' gloves from the ship's gun mounts to hold back the tree's branches so the fougasse barrel could be positioned. Two small braces were underneath the barrel, each with a bight of line around it, so that they could be yanked away, thereby freeing the barrel to fall into the ditch.

With a pleased expression, Yeats explained the barrel would already be flaming when it fell into the ditch, because the first thing that would happen was a flint-lock trigger sparking gunpowder to create a flash, which would ignite the accelerant, which would then race down the ditch. He said the entire chain of events, from trigger to flaming ditch, would take three seconds.

Both the trigger and the brace pulls were operated by separate sixty-foot lanyards led across the adjacent tracks to the edge of the mangroves. There, two volunteers would pull them upon a bugle signal from Yeats in the field to the east. The sailors would then "run like the dickens to the town" while chaos erupted behind them.

"Bloody friggin' marvelous! Well done, sir!" exclaimed Rork. "Bit o' the Irish in your veins, methinks, sir."

"Well done, Mr. Yeats," I said. "This will save our men's lives."

Southby, Rork, and I next crossed the road and visited the cane field opposite the fougasse. Trip wires, staked by cane sticks which blended in nicely, were strung at a height of eight inches all along the roadside edge of the field and off to either flank. Inside the field were several Quaker mines, authentic-looking bombs which were actually wooden replicas. They were scrupulously hard enough to discern in the sooty field to make them seem real and very intimidating.

On the east edge of the field, ten short aiming staffs with notches for the rifle barrels were erected. The sharpshooters would fire from the prone position. We were using only five snipers, and each man would move between two staffs, leading the Spanish to overestimate their number. The accurate gunfire against officers, along with the bugle signal, would make it seem there were regular American soldiers or marines attacking the Spanish, thereby adding to the enemy's inducement to jump in the ditch before the fougasse was ignited.

Yeats ended by telling us *Kestrel's* gig was already waiting on the river bank. The observation post down the road was manned. He and all his men were ready.

I pulled out my watch. It was already three o'clock.

"Time is dwindling, gentlemen. We need to complete our preparations by five this afternoon. I want the men to eat and rest, so they are as ready as they can be for a very crowded day tomorrow. Now, I will take a solitary stroll back to the ship. Thank you all."

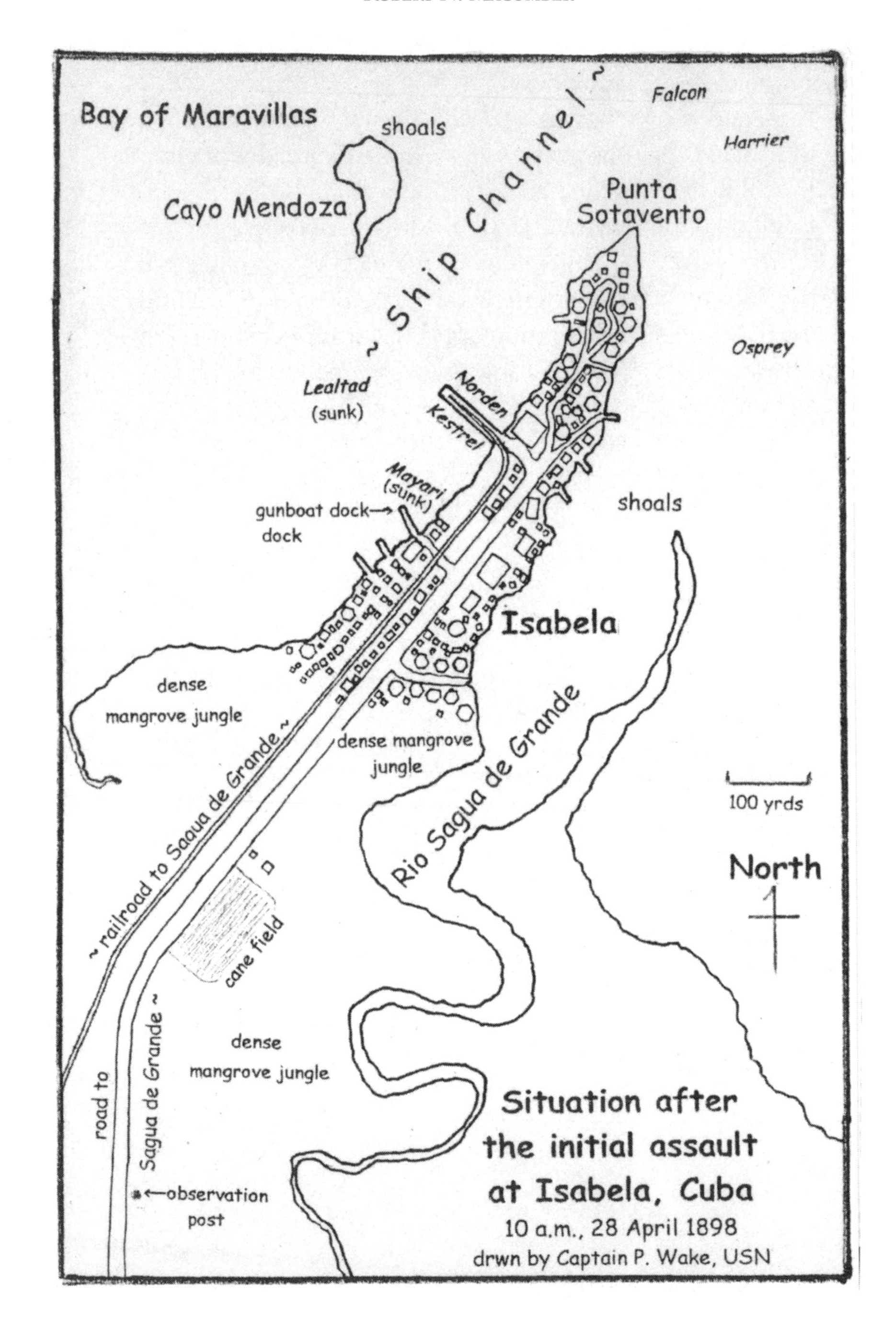
Bay of Maravillas
shoals
~ Ship Channel ~
Falcon
Harrier
Cayo Mendoza
Punta Sotavento
Osprey
Lealtad (sunk)
Norden
Kestrel
Mayari (sunk)
gunboat dock
dock
shoals
Isabela
dense mangrove jungle
~ railroad to Sagua de Grande ~
dense mangrove jungle
Rio Sagua de Grande
100 yrds
North
cane field
road to Sagua de Grande ~
dense mangrove jungle
observation post
Situation after the initial assault at Isabela, Cuba
10 a.m., 28 April 1898
drwn by Captain P. Wake, USN

49

When Minutes Seem Like Hours

Isabela, Cuba
Thursday night
28 April 1898

The worst times for a sailor or soldier facing battle are the moments beforehand. All has been prepared that can be prepared. There is nothing else to do but wait and think.

I needed to be alone, yet I hated being alone, for I knew what it would bring. There is no sleep or true rest for the mind, for it cannot disconnect from the reality all around you. This is magnified when you are in command of others, for they have subordinated their very lives to your judgment. It is the ultimate expression of trust, and burden of command.

Your mind becomes a machine powered by logic, cogitating over and over the probabilities of how things will unfold and how you will adjust to the enemy's actions, to your own men's failures. Then the self-interrogation begins: Did you think of everything which might happen? Have you prepared for unforeseen developments? Have you readied your men for them?

When the probabilities have been thoroughly examined and answered, the mind moves on to more and more improbable potential occurrences, none of which have solutions. Doubts begin to form, sometimes coalescing into more tangible fear, which you dare not show outwardly, lest that precious and precarious bond of trust in your judgment be broken.

Finally, when your psyche is in its weakest state, there are two basic questions which rise inside you. The ones you dread most of all.

Will good men die because you became paralyzed by fear, unable to make a decision?

Every commander faces this question. In my first action, thirty-five years earlier in the Civil War at the ironically named Peace River, I faced that question. I felt the fear, made the decisions, and afterward dealt with my guilt over the consequences. It was a victory, minor and unheralded, but men died because of my decisions. My men. Could I have done better? Would I in the future?

I have been in similar situations many times since then. Each time it is the same. But after a while, you understand you will not panic, not be paralyzed. You will get through the horror. Though some of your men will die and others be maimed, the mission will be accomplished. They will do their job. You will do yours.

But one thing never fades in its intensity or its effect upon you, no matter how many times it is experienced. It is the second question, and it also comes during that quiet time before battle, when minutes seem like hours.

You look at these men who trust you. And you contemplate, which ones will die because of their trust?

So it was for me at Isabela, Cuba, on a calm spring night. I was fifty-eight years old, thirty-five years of which had been consumed with the naval and intelligence service of my country around the world. During those years, I'd faced many enemies, knew the indescribable horrors, had scars all over my body, and survived everything which anyone had ever thrown at me. One would think I would've built some measure of immunity.

Still, I questioned.

Who among these decent men—*my* men—were about to die?

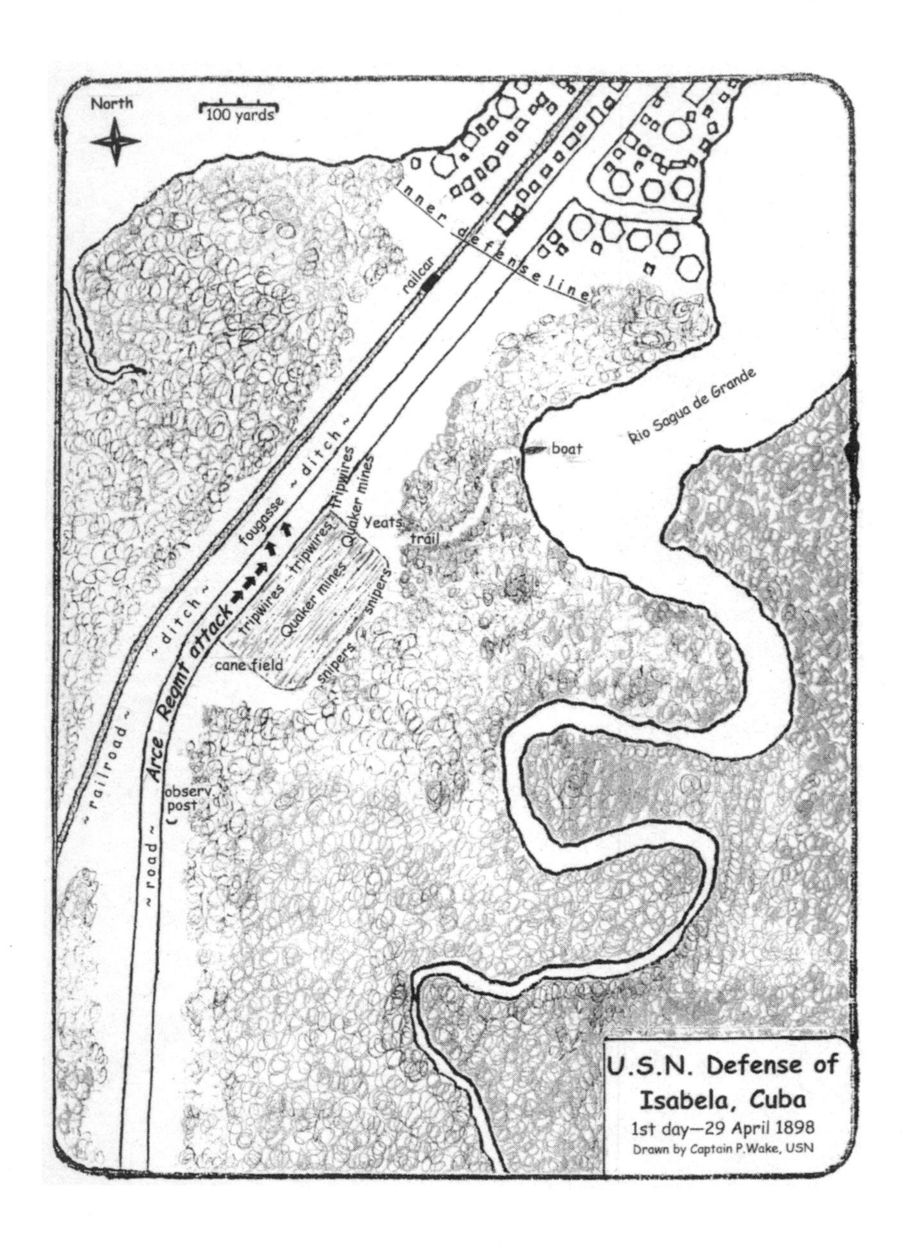
North
100 yards
inner defense line
railcar
Rio Sagua de Grande
boat
~ ditch ~
fougasse
tripwires
Quaker mines
Yeats
trail
snipers
cane field
Arce Regmt attack
~ railroad ~
~ road ~
observ. post
U.S.N. Defense of
Isabela, Cuba
1st day—29 April 1898
Drawn by Captain P.Wake, USN

50

Friend or Foe?

Isabela, Cuba
3:37 a.m., Friday morning
29 April 1898

The triple boom of cannon in the distance brought me out of my semi-consciousness.

"It's four or five miles away," Rork reported as I struggled to stand. We'd been lying on blankets on the side of the road near the Colt machine gun, our ad hoc command post for the land defenses.

I waited for the explosions of rounds impacting nearby. Nothing happened. More booms sounded, which I could register better now I was fully awake. They weren't coming from the road to the south, where I'd been searching for flashes. They were somewhere behind us, near the offshore islands.

"Spanish Navy . . . one of those Hontoria medium-caliber quick-firing guns," decided Rork.

Yeats and Mack were out at the cane field, controlling the sniper positions, the fougasse men, and the forward lookout post. I'd opted to stay the night at the machine gun since it was more central to the expected axis of attack than remaining on *Kestrel* at the wharf. Now I wished I was back on the ship, where I could see the bay.

"Gunboat, offshore of the barrier islands," I suggested as several more shots were heard.

I swung my arm north toward them. "Near the entrance to the channel. Come on, Rork, let's get back to *Kestrel.* Southby may have information."

To Lieutenant Gavin, executive officer of *Falcon*, and in command of the inner defensive line, I said, "Stay here and make sure the lookouts are sharp. This could be a diversion."

On *Kestrel's* bridge we found Southby peering through binoculars. The gunfire had stopped, but he did have information. It was in the form of a signal lamp message from *Harrier's* sailors at the observation post on Cayo Maravillas, which had just been relayed to the flagship.

Enemy gunboat chasing unknown fast small vessel toward channel.

"Except for the coaling rendezvous with our collier later on at Cay Sal Bank, we don't have any other ships planned to be arriving here at Isabela, right, sir?" asked Southby.

"Correct—we're on our own for this entire operation. The vessel they're chasing must be an American, though. Signal *Harrier* to stop her when she gets past the barrier islands and in the bay."

The sounds we heard next were one of *Harrier's* four-pounder guns popping off two blank rounds quickly. From our vantage point up on the bridge deck, we could see over the roofs of the shacks and across the bay to the north. In the dark distance we could see the gun flashes. Lieutenant Farmore was stopping the intruder inside the bay, south of Cayo Maravillas. I surveyed the rest of the squadron to make sure they were in position. *Falcon* was in the channel itself, moving north toward *Harrier* and the suspect vessel while still blocking access to the port. *Osprey* guarded *Norden*, northeast of the town.

A signal lamp flickered in our direction from *Harrier*. The duty signalman called out the message, unable to suppress his surprise at the contents.

Vessel is New York press dispatch boat. Reporters aboard request permission to enter port.

"Well, I admit, that's a new one on me," uttered Southby.

"Me too," I said. Of all the things I'd worried about and planned for, this wasn't one of them. How the hell did they know about our operation? Who else knew? The New York press meant one of the Pulitzer or Hearst jingo-spouting papers. Which in turn, meant trouble of unknown dimensions looming for me, no matter what I decided to do.

I knew many naval officers who would jump at the chance to have their exploits chronicled, and magnified, in such famous newspapers, but not me. Reporters could offer us nothing in tangible assistance, and would in fact end up being a distraction to my men when all hands had to be focused on the impending attack. There was absolutely no logical reason to allow them into Isabela. They needed to leave so we could get our work done.

That choice, though logical, wouldn't work either. I couldn't very well send fellow Americans back out the way they came in. Not with the Spanish Navy waiting to capture them. They'd be treated as spies and executed.

"Send the damned fools here to *Kestrel*," I ordered Southby. "I'll decide what to do with them then. Too bad this yacht doesn't have a brig."

While I was digesting this new development, the starboard lookout called out, "Rifle shots several miles to the south, sir. Sounds like volleys."

Rork rushed across to the other bridge wing, followed by Southby and me. The shots were very distant. No flashes could be seen, being hidden by the jungle. I heard a louder rumble, a volley. It was followed by continuous pops. Then they got more sporadic and ended.

Rork said what I was thinking. "Methinks that's Major Barida's battalion, sir. They're in a fight, at least four miles down the road. The volleys're Spaniardo Mausers. Higher velocity. More o' a ping to the sound. The other shots sound like '92 Springfields and Krags, like the exiles have."

"But the Cuban battalion should be much farther along toward Sagua Grande by now." Southby said. "That's right about where they were last seen yesterday afternoon, marching south."

He was right. I wondered if Barida's battalion was retreating back to Isabela. It was beginning to appear so. This was a scenario I had anticipated. If true, we would have to re-embark the Cubans onto *Norden*, while fighting a rear guard action.

"Captain Southby, please remain here and monitor the seaward defenses. Alert *Norden* to get steam up and weigh anchor. She may be needed to return to the wharf and take the battalion back aboard. Rork and I are going to check on the land defenses. If all is well, I'll return to deal with the reporters. If the Spanish attack, lock them below someplace out of the way."

When Rork and I got to the defense line, Gavin said none of his men had seen anything. Except for the distant shots, which had ended, it was quiet. Then a light winked at us from down the road at the cane field, a message relayed from the observation post farther down the road, out of sight around the curve.

The lieutenant quickly translated it. "OP reports men approaching, range one mile."

Were they Spanish attackers or Cubans in retreat? We would soon learn whether friend or foe was on the road heading toward us.

51

Let the Games Begin

Isabela, Cuba
5:33 a.m., Friday morning
29 April 1898

We waited for an hour, but there was no more word from our forward lookouts. There was also no attack.

No light signal was sent out to Yeats to inquire what was happening, for the approaching men would see it as well, and thereby know our location. Instead, Yeats sent a runner back to us.

I waited for the man to catch his breath, then nodded for him to begin. As a coal stoker, Wax wasn't used to delivering messages to officers, much less a commodore, and he spoke slowly, trying to remember everything.

"Aye, aye, sir. Mr. Yeats presents his respects and . . . he's sorry . . . no, he *regrets* . . . to report the signal lamp dropped. Broke beyond repair, sir. He also says whoever's out there in the dark has stopped coming toward us. They're hiding somewheres down the road, sir. Mr. Yeats went out to the forward lookouts about half an hour ago. He didn't *see* nothing, but he did *hear* wheels squeaking a ways off down the road. He thinks there's Spanish troops hiding out there, not those Cuban fellows. He said to tell you he'll send a wigwag arm signal when it gets light enough in a couple of minutes. Ah, that's all he said to say, sir."

"Well done, Wax. You can return to Mr. Yeats, now. Tell him we are alert and ready. Thank you."

The report of squeaking wheels meant either supply wagons or artillery caissons. Either way, it was bad news.

Rork pointed to the left, or east. "Getting' light fast, sir."

Gavin nodded toward the cane field. "Mr. Yeats signaling us, sir."

Yeats was standing on the near side of a banana tree, so he was concealed from the enemy. I had to use my binoculars to see the exact arm gestures he displayed.

Enemy coming.

A bugle sounded to the south, then a loud cheer. Drums next. They were still south of the curve and out of my sight. It was all I could do to remain still and not dash off to the lookout post to see for myself.

Yeats signaled in a flurry of gestures. I couldn't make them out. My semaphore skills were woefully rusty. I glanced at Rork, but he shook his head.

Gavin tactfully provided the translation. "Sir, the signal reads: Enemy battalion formation in sight. P . . . O . . . X . . . in front."

Gavin canted his head down in concentration, then looked up at me. "Single letters spelling Pox? I'm afraid I don't understand, sir."

"Diseased men?" proposed Rork.

It suddenly struck me. I asked Gavin, "Could that have been a 'W' instead of an 'X'? They're similar at a glance."

"Oh hell, sir, yes, it could've been a 'W.' That makes sense. It's POW—prisoner of war. Sorry, sir. Evidently, the Spanish have prisoners out in front of their attack. Cubans?"

Right at this inopportune moment, two additional factors made their presence apparent to us, diverting our attention. The first was the whine of an artillery shell coming toward us. A split second later, the muffled report of a field gun arrived from somewhere out of sight down the road. The shell blasted a fountain of sand and rock among the shacks behind us, with shrapnel zinging through the air.

Gavin, who had never been under artillery fire before—few were left in the navy who had been—was admirably calm as he called out to the sailors, "Steady on, men! Stay low and keep going about your work. Get that *cheval de frise* a little more to the left."

"That's a bloody Brit army field piece, sir," Rork grumbled quietly. "The 1885 model Ordnance gun, methinks. `Tis a breech-loading twelve-pounder, an' fires an impact percussion fuse shell. Can tell that by the damned annoyin' whine made by the fuze cap. Max range is two and a half miles. Effective directed range is one and a half. It must be `round the bend, out o' sight.

"An' the Spaniardos don't have any o' those, sad to say. Nay, they use Kraut an' Spanish Hontoria guns. But Major Barida had four o' `em when he left here yesterday. Saw `em me own self, so methinks the enemy must o' captured one o' those. An' probably some o' the major's men along with it."

Fear for Mario Cano instantly gripped me, tightening my throat, filling my mind with visions of my son-in-law trying to survive in battle, or in captivity.

As he does with startling regularity, Rork read my thoughts. "Peter . . . Mario's one hellova smart lad, the smartest in that Cuban crew, including Barida, so there's nary a worry about him figurin' how to get out o' any mess he encounters. You know that, so put it out o' your head. We've got our own problems to deal with here."

Rork, suddenly got a strange look on his face, staring at something over my shoulder. It was then the other additional factor arrived, in the form of an Ohio River drawl directed at me from the rear.

"Well, well, I should'a known who'd be the head squid of this newly forsaken cluster of misbegotten fish out of water. What, the senile bastards in charge actually let you out of D.C. to go play war one more time, old man? Looks like your butt's in the boiler now, don't it? Serves you right for volunteering with another hopeless mission."

Several paces away, Gavin was directing sailors moving another *cheval de frise*. His head spun around when he heard the comment. In a rage, he headed for the speaker of such disrespect, but I held up a hand to stop him.

Turning around to face the intruder, I said, "Why I'll be damned to hell and gone. It's none other than Colonel Michael Woodgerd, in the actual sneering flesh and rancid blood. I must say I'm not surprised at all to find you slinking around here. But alas, the virgins have all run off, so you're out of luck again. What, waiting around to rob the dead?"

Two strides got me up to a tall muscular man in a khaki tunic and trousers, the trimmed goatee pointing down from his chin balancing a long gray-haired ponytail trailing down his back. His left hand held a rucksack, and the right a Smith and Wesson revolver. An 1883 Martini-Henri rifle was slung over his left shoulder.

He laughed. "That's your best shot? You're getting elderly, Wake. And your doddering Irish Mick lapdog's looking pretty useless too."

As all around us thought their commodore and the arrogant stranger were about to go to blows, we embraced and I announced, "Michael Woodgerd, you incorrigible mercenary bastard—welcome to Cuba! By the way, whose side are you on in this thing? Should I shoot you, or put you to work?"

Rork came over, punched Woodgerd in the center of his chest, and pulled a flask out of his back pocket. "Dodderin' an' useless? We'll be seein' about that! Bloody damned good to see you, Colonel. Want a wee nip o' Cuban aguardiente?"

Woodgerd took a swig, then answered me. "Neither side offered me enough money, Peter. But some rich kid called Willie Hearst surely did, and I said yes. He owns some newspapers and thinks he's the king rat. Hey, I'm a real live war correspondent now, sent down here to report on what you heroes are doing to bring freedom to the unwashed masses of this cesspit.

"Came in on that speedy little boat this morning, along with some useless precocious brat from London who says he's a writer. The skipper plugged the holes in his boat and got the hell out of here before the real shooting starts. The Limey went with him and I got stuck here. By the way, your man Southby is very inhospitable. Told me not to come ashore to have a look-see and put me in a room on your boat. He didn't know I can pick locks."

Gavin fumed at hearing that, so I explained Woodgerd was a former colonel in the U.S. Army who had become a soldier of fortune, adding we were friends from half a dozen hellholes around the world, and that I rented my cottage in Alexandria from him. I left out the circumstances of exactly how Woodgerd left the army. Gavin wouldn't understand.

"So let me get this straight, *you* are a *reporter?*" I asked my friend. "I didn't know you could even read and write, Michael. How the hell did you pull that off with somebody like Hearst?"

His sniffed with a mock upper-class air. "You may recall I graduated from West Point, Commodore. I can write and occasionally have read a book. And, I might add, they trained me how to act like an officer and a gentleman. Hell, I even know which fork to use for salads. So how did I get the big bucks to come down here and mingle with you poor excuses for cannon fodder? I merely told Hearst over dinner at Delmonico's he needed to send a *real* man to Cuba to get *real* news out of this war. Real men get paid real money."

"How did you end up right here at Isabela, though?"

"Cause it's out of the way and I figured nobody in their right mind would be here. Didn't know you dupes were here, but that just proves my point. There I was, sitting in a bar in Key West with the boat skipper, looking at a map of Cuba. I told him I wanted to sneak ashore here, so I could spy out what's really going on with the Cubans and the Spanish. Had no friggin' idea Uncle

Sam's Navy was playing army soldier here. You can imagine my surprise when we finally get past the Spanish Navy and come smack dab right up against the U.S. Navy."

He cast a doubtful look at the sailors around us, before continuing.

"But please, don't let me interrupt whatever the hell it is you're trying to do here. This little shindig should actually be rather amusing for me to watch unravel. Wish that little writer boy was here to see the show. He could've gotten a story about how *not* to do things."

Another whine split the air, the shell exploding in an airburst a hundred feet short of our inner line. A piece of shrapnel thudded into the ground at my feet.

"Finally!" exclaimed Woodgerd. "A decent bracket shot from someone who knows what he's doing."

Scattered rifle shots came from the south, accompanied by the sound of a military band and boots crunching in unison.

Gavin interrupted. "Commodore, Mr. Yeats is signaling—*Enemy in sight. Full regiment. POWs in front.* OP in retreat."

"Well, here they come now," said Woodgerd as he folded his arms. "Oh, please do go right ahead, gents. Don't let me delay you. The games are about to begin."

52

Them or Us

Isabela, Cuba
Friday morning
29 April 1898

The Spanish formation had reached the bend in the road a quarter mile away and were coming into view. Two hundred feet out in front of the regiment, twenty-one bedraggled prisoners, blindfolded with hands lashed behind their backs, were being pushed forward at bayonet point by a row of skirmishers.

Behind them, the column of Spanish infantry marched eight abreast. Beside the column, several officers pranced about on horses, flourishing their drawn swords as they shouted patriotic Spanish slogans. The regimental music was a funeral dirge, slow and steady and ominous.

The prisoner shield was something I hadn't imagined. It was clearly against the rules of war, but then Colonel Arce's past behavior had been a warning of what he was capable of doing. A warning I'd failed to fully appreciate.

The prisoners precluded the Spanish from following my plan of running after the American sailors fleeing the observation post. Those men were now sprinting up the road toward the cane field, theatrically whooping and hollering, dropping camp articles the whole way.

Obviously, the notorious Colonel Arce was no beginner and had enacted his own plan.

I swung my field glasses up to focus on the miserable hostages in front of the Spanish. They all appeared to be privates in the dark tan uniform of the exile unit, with no officers among them.

Rork offered his opinion. "Methinks the snipers should shoot the skirmishers pushing the prisoners, sir, instead o' hittin' the officers farther back in the formation. That'd give those poor bastards a wee bit o' a chance to flee."

"No," I countered. "Yeats' men will do both. First they'll shoot the skirmishers, then the officers. But we've still got to wait until the main formation is opposite the fougasse."

I summoned Lieutenant Gavin. "Send a runner to Mr. Yeats with this message. Once the main formation has come up to the fougasse, he is to first shoot the soldiers pushing the prisoners, then shoot the officers farther back in the formation."

"Aye, aye, sir."

"I have something else, Mr. Gavin. Once our snipers shoot the enemy guards, I want everybody in your line who speaks Spanish to yell for the Cuban prisoners to come up the road toward us. Everyone else can yell in English. Those prisoners are blindfolded, but they can run toward the sound of our men. Yes, I know some may be killed trying to escape the Spanish, but do *not* send anyone out to bring them in. You must keep your sailors lying on the ground in their prone positions. They must remain down, out of sight from the Spanish. Understand?"

"Yes, sir."

He began a long series of semaphore arm gestures as I turned my gaze back to the spectacle. One of the Cuban prisoners stumbled, then fell on his knees. The Spanish soldier behind him never hesitated, ramming the bayonet through the Cuban's torso, pushing off with his boot to pull it out. The prisoner crumpled in a heap by the side of the road.

The Spanish regiment behind, meanwhile, acted as if on parade in Havana. Every man marched in unison to the incessant beat of the drums. On they came, every synchronized step bringing them closer to the cane field, where Yeats and his men were now fully concealed. Across the road from the cane field, nothing of the camouflaged fougasse preparations or ignition detail could be seen. Yeats had done his job well.

The Cuban prisoners and their tormentors passed the cane field and were approaching the extreme rifle range of our inner defenses. Our sailors on the line, their Model 1895 Lee rifles aimed toward the enemy, buzzed with contempt for the terrible scene before them.

Gavin admonished them in a low snarl. "Silence on deck! Petty officers, control your men."

I expected this bizarre and pitiful sight to instigate some random shots in anger, but discipline held firm. Every sailor had been briefed on the plan. All hands knew it was up to Lieutenant Yeats now.

The leading company of the main Spanish formation passed the cane field behind a younger officer mounted on a black stallion, his epaulettes gleaming in the sunrise. The column behind them stretched back beyond the curve. I estimated the entire eight hundred men of the regiment had been gathered for the assault against my eighty-seven sailors.

Where the hell is Colonel Arce, I wondered. Then I saw a man with more ornate gold tassels and lace on his uniform than those of the accompanying officers. He and his companions on horseback were just behind the regimental color party, a third of the way back from the vanguard. Pointing arms in our direction, I deduced they were discussing the visibly meager defenses of the town ahead of them.

Pulse racing, I willed Yeats to wait until Arce was close enough to the fougasse.

"Nice parade," offered Woodgerd to no one in particular. "Reminds me of the Brits marching through the valleys in Afghanistan—right up until the locals killed them. I take it you have something more to give these fellows than applause, because I'm not seeing much in the way of defenses here."

Rork elbowed him. "Watch an' learn, Michael. An' pipe down while you're at it."

The crack of a rifle sounded, then a ragged volley from the smokeless Lee rifles at the cane field. Five Spanish soldiers dropped near the prisoners. The other skirmishers whirled around in confusion, trying to find the shooters, but the band kept playing and the regiment continued marching.

Within seconds, five more soldiers dropped. The sailors along the inner defenses started yelling in English and crude Spanish for the prisoners to run to them. Several began trying to run up the road. One of the soldiers started shooting prisoners. He was dropped, along with several other comrades, in Yeats' third volley.

At this point, the regimental officers realized what was going on and where the gunfire was coming from. The surviving prisoners were abandoned and ran for our sailors, with the Spanish skirmishers rejoining the main column.

By commands, the band stopped playing, the entire regiment stopped, and every soldier made a right turn. Going exactly by the manual of arms, the three hundred soldiers of the lead companies unshouldered their rifles, came to the ready, then aimed their rifles across the cane field. One of their officers fell off his horse, then another and another, as Yeats gave permission for his five sharpshooters to use independent fire.

Boooooom . . . the Spanish volley rumbled out across the landscape as a hail of lead swept the field. I heard a Spanish officer shout his command—*advance at the run!*

As the second company in the column charged into the cane field with bayonets wickedly glistening, I heard a whine in the air coming at me. It went a few feet over us, the shell exploding behind and to the right. Two sailors yipped when shrapnel nicked them. A red stain spread along Gavin's left sleeve.

The charging Spanish hit the first trip wire at a full run, the entire front rank going down. Another officer was shot as he stood back up and waved his sword. Colonel Arce and the other officers had dismounted and I lost sight of them in the commotion.

Another unit of men charged into the field. They hit the second trip wire line and many fell, but quickly got back up. The lead enemy troops were halfway across the field.

I heard someone yell, *"Minas explosivos!"* and begin pointing at the Quaker mines in the field. Two more soldiers pointed and backed up, then four, then a platoon. A subaltern ran out in front and berated them. His tirade ended in mid-sentence when his head snapped back from the rifle shot.

That did it, and the conscripts began running out of the field and across the road. The rear companies of the column were hurrying at the double quick toward the chaotic scene, where officers pointed at the town, trying to rally their men to assemble and assault the town. One of the reinforcing companies broke away from the column and charged diagonally toward the field, headed for Yeats' left flank.

"Fourteen of the Cuban prisoners made it to our line, sir," reported Gavin.

Amidst the general gunfire, I couldn't make out the sound of Yeats' shots anymore, but their results seemed to have diminished, for fewer Spanish soldiers and officers were falling. There were too many Spanish troops still on the road. They weren't panicking as completely as I had hoped.

We had to adapt in order to exploit our surprise. I looked at my line of sailors.

"Mr. Gavin, please have the *left* half of your line fire three volleys at the main body of enemy troops on the road. Aim higher to handle the trajectory."

It would be at extreme range, but was worth the try. I focused my binoculars at the mass of Spanish troops. They were starting to get more organized. Many were facing the town. Only a few were in the ditch, and they were climbing out. We were losing the opportunity.

The sailors' volley erupted with a roar, and I heard every man pulling his bolt back simultaneously. Seconds later the second volley was sent down the road. The third went out as another artillery round blew up on the left side of our line. Three wounded sailors howled foul curses.

On the road, only a few enemy soldiers were hit, but the rest apparently didn't like the odds and jumped in the ditch. Most began firing at the cane field in confusion, some fired at the town, but the sailors were flat on the ground, out of sight. None were hit.

"Another volley please, Mr. Gavin."

It blasted out, raising a line of dust into the air. More soldiers descended into the ditch, including officers. At least two of the lead companies had gotten down into the ditch. There were still men on the road, but fewer and fewer.

Now was the moment for the bugle signal to set off the fougasse, but it didn't come. My heart pounded, and I focused the glasses to where I'd last seen Yeats. No one was in sight there. Next I checked the railroad embankment by the fougasse, looking for the men hidden in the mangroves beyond, but saw nothing there either. Something was wrong. Had the massive Spanish volley into the field killed Yeats and his men?

I thought of sending the bugle call from our position, then remembered Yeats had *Kestrel*'s one and only bugle.

The Spanish infantry making a flank attack on the southern side of the cane field had slowed down, cautiously moving over the trip wire placed there, heading along the field's edge toward Yeats' position. Farther back, at the curve of the road, the rear Spanish units were spreading out across the road to the mangrove tree lines on both flanks.

Rork shot me a worried glance. I had to buy time for Yeats and his men, wherever they were. "Mr. Gavin, continue with three more volleys, this time from your entire line. Remember to aim high at this range."

The sixty men in the line went through the drill as if they were still on the beach at Congo Town. The ensuing enfilades, loosed at thirty second intervals, ensured the Spanish in the ditch would think twice about emerging for an attack.

After the third volley, gunfire on both sides ended, and the battlefield suddenly went quiet. Only the groans of wounded Spanish soldiers, and the curses of my own wounded men, broke the stark stillness.

It was then I heard Yeats' bugle, a croaking wail fading away in a sour note. It was enough.

A crack resounded near the road, followed by a whoosh. Instantly, a six-foot-high wave of flames raced down the ditch in seconds and engulfed the Spanish. Screams and shouts erupted instantly as dozens, then hundreds, of men leaped out of the ditch. Some of them were on fire, some limping from gunshot wounds. All fled south on the road toward their rear. Officers, soldiers, and horses were seized by utter panic, frantically trying to escape.

The sailors stared in soundless horror at the sight of the enemy roasting alive.

"Them or us, lads," Rork told them. "War is what you signed up for."

"Should we open fire on the enemy soldiers, sir?" Gavin asked quietly.

It had to be done. "Yes, Lieutenant. Open fire, but only with a few of your best shots. I do not want us to waste rounds. We'll need them later for the enemy's second attack. Aim specifically for those enemy soldiers who appear not to be already wounded."

"Aye, aye, sir. Oh, and one of the Cuban prisoners just told our men a pretty bizarre tale about how they got captured. His English is pretty good. Do you want to speak with him?"

No, I didn't, but intelligence about the enemy was of paramount importance. And I wanted to know about Mario. "Yes. Send him to me."

The fougasse fire created its own wind, which blew inland. A thick bank of roiling black smoke and burning embers floated over the fleeing soldiers, as if chasing them. In a few minutes the screaming from the men trapped in the ditch stopped, then even the flames burned out. Only the sickly sweet stench of burned molasses and bodies endured.

Woodgerd walked over to me. "You did good, Peter. But they won't be stupid next time."

"Yeah, I know."

53

The Confession

Isabela, Cuba
Friday
29 April 1898

While gulping down a cup of orange juice and a plantain, Sergeant Julio Rivera, a diminutive mestizo farmhand originally from Matamoros, Mexico, shared with me how he ended up in Cuba. Though I wanted first and foremost to hear about Mario, I let the man tell the story his own way.

Rivera started by explaining how he became a prisoner. Barida's column made it halfway to Sagua Grande when they met a Spanish roadblock. The determined enemy sent fusillades of bullets toward them, several of which found their mark and frightened the raw troops. Barida got most of his men into position and finally got them shooting in the right direction.

At this rather busy moment in time, a small group in the battalion, including Rivera, refused to obey any further orders. They protested they had been lied to about what their military duties would be, and what their remuneration would be, all from Zaldivar's smooth oratory months prior.

Barida, naturally, couldn't have cared less about their complaints right about then. The major's reaction to the mutiny was a very sincere promise to shoot the entire bunch himself. This merely exacerbated the mutineers' fears, which instantly descended into abject terror and panic. In response to my next question, Rivera detailed the beginning of the entire idiotic enterprise. Evidently, in his tour of southern cities in February, right after the *Maine* explosion, when the fever for war was heating up, Zaldivar began on his recruitment tour. Before signing up for Zaldivar's battalion, Rivera never even knew Cuba's location on a map, and still wasn't completely sure.

Rivera and many other ignorant souls based their decision to join on the colonel's rosy promises. Zaldivar said the battalion would be hailed as heroes upon getting off the ship, would only have to hold the town of Isabela, and would not face any major opposition from the Spanish Army. A lovely way to fight a war, if only it was true.

The enlistees were duly impressed and signed up for three months service to end in mid-May, when the war was predicted to be over. After a wondrous celebration of their heroic and bloodless victory, each man would then be given the title to ten hectares of land and citizenship in the new Republic of Cuba. Apparently, the new landowners would henceforth be called by the Spanish honorific of "Don" for the rest of their lives—a powerful inducement for a peasant from the hill country of Mexico.

The reality these naïve dupes found was far different. The men became suspicious when they never got paid their enlistment bonus or monthly stipend. Next, unlike Zaldivar's plush cabin and extravagant cuisine, their crude accommodations in the cargo holds of the freighter were not what they expected. In addition, most of their officers appeared incompetent and disinterested. When the joyous welcome at the miserable hamlet of Isabela didn't happen, the recruits' mistrust turned into outright anger.

The final straw came when they got word Zaldivar was no longer in charge and their lives were forfeited to a real warrior officer like Barida. He actually intended them to fight the enemy for as long as the war would take—forget this ninety-day nonsense. As they marched toward Sagua Grande, the communal complaining in the ranks grew into conspiratorial discussions of how to secure freedom from the predicament they found themselves in.

Then came the Spanish roadblock. With the unforgettable hornet-like buzzing of high-velocity Mauser rounds around their ears, accompanied by the mechanical death chant of a Spanish Maxim machine gun, any hesitation by Rivera and his friends ended. Thirty-four of them simply threw down their weapons and walked away.

Now deprived of his right flank, which was quickly exploited and turned by the Spanish, Major Barida lost one of his cannons and its ammunition and made a hasty exit from the battlefield into the jungle with the loyal majority of his unit. In the chaos of the moment, Zaldivar escaped his Cuban guards, only to be directly captured by Arce's Spaniards.

Captain Mario Cano had been trying to rally the mutineers back to the Cuba Libré cause by appealing to their honor and patriotism, a trait in short supply among the non-Cuban mutineers. His audience, while appreciating his effort, nevertheless made haste in the opposite direction for Isabela. Cano found himself alone and surrounded by foes who knew the value of bringing in such an unusual prisoner. Colonel Arce wanted captured Cuban officers kept alive.

Cano drew his sword and pistol, unwilling to surrender. A Spanish sergeant shot him in the foot, and both his weapons dropped. The soldiers then rushed and subdued him.

The mutineers did not escape Spanish attention, either. When the enemy saw their opponents run, they did what I had wanted and planned for them to do at *my* battlefield—they chased them. This time there was no trap for the Spanish to enter, though, and unfortunately for the mutineers, the soldiers never called for them to surrender as they had the gallant Cano. They simply ran them down as they fled. Only twenty-one of the thirty-four deserters survived; proudly presented to Colonel Arce, who then gave a speech to his own men, saying the deserters were an example of the Cuban rebels' cowardice. It mattered not that none of them were Cuban.

Rivera ended his account with a dejected expression, apparently expecting sympathy for his ordeal. His expectations weren't fulfilled. My sympathy was reserved for Cano, Barida, and those who did not run.

Rork was with me to hear this confession. I didn't have to see his smoldering eyes to know exactly his opinion of Sergeant Rivera and his cronies, or what to do with them. No one is more draconian toward a mutineer than a fellow resident of the gun deck who has not wavered in his duty. Normally I am of like mind, but our circumstances at that precise place and time were anything but normal. In the space of the next twenty hours, I expected hundreds more Spanish soldiers to descend upon us. Moral matters would have to be subordinated to survival.

Sergeant Julio Rivera still sat there expectantly. It was time to burst his bubble of hope.

"Thank you for your confession about being a traitor, Rivera. As senior commanding officer of this allied force, I order that you are hereby demoted to private and placed under arrest. So are all of your fellow traitors. I will hold a court-martial tomorrow at noon. It will end five minutes later, and the entire gang of traitors will be executed five minutes after that, just before we Americans get on our ships and leave Isabela. You disgust me."

He was stunned, for I had been so friendly before. "Uh? What is a traitor? I do not know this word, sir."

"It means coward. *Cobarde, en español.* That is what you are, *un cobarde*. Chief Rork, remove those chevrons from this coward."

He nearly ripped Rivera's arms off in the process, then removed his false hand, allowing his spike to glint in the sunlight.

By now Rivera fully realized his fate and began pleading. "Please, sir. I am not a soldier. I do not want to be a soldier. I am no good for it. *Please*, sir, do not kill me."

My tone was as cold as a corpse. "Rivera, I owe you nothing."

Spittle drooled as he desperately shrieked, "*Please*, sir. Anything, sir, I will do anything you want. I just want to go home to Mexico. I do not want to die here in this terrible place."

I kept him in my gaze. "There is one way for your life to be spared. Be a man. Fight with us and shoot the Spanish when they attack. If you do it well, I will take you away with me from Cuba. If you do not—*we* will kill you."

His relief was pathetic. "We will fight, sir. We will shoot the Spanish. Thank you, sir."

"Chief Rork, take Rivera to the others and make sure he explains the situation to them correctly. Arm them with scavenged Spanish rifles and five rounds each, and put them in the center of the line, in front of the Colt machine gun. Kill them if they fail."

"Aye, aye, sir," replied Rork as he jerked the man up and hauled him away.

54

Trust

Isabela, Cuba
Late Friday night
29 April 1898

I was roused out of a fitful sleep on the ground next to the machine gun by Rork shaking my shoulder. "Gonzart's here, sir. The lad's got news from General Lacret. Came down the river past the Spaniardos in a dinghy tonight, an' methinks you need to hear him out right now."

By the light of a dimmed lantern I saw Gonzart standing in rags, his face haggard, and his arms covered with cuts. He rendered a weary salute.

"General Lacret presents his congratulations on your victory over Arce the butcher, sir. I am very happy to report Major Barida made it to the general's division with his guns and men. Both he and the general thank you for bringing the battalion safely ashore and getting them started inland. General Lacret also sends you a special request, sir."

I gestured for him to sit. "And what is the request?"

"Spanish reinforcements are arriving for Arce by train from Havana. Regular infantry, not like Arce's men. The general views this as a unique opportunity to crush the enemy between our two forces. This would send a strong signal to the people of Cuba, and to the Spanish leaders in Madrid."

My pocket watch indicated the time was a little after eleven p.m. "Really?" I asked. "And how are we to accomplish that? We are not strong on land. I only have a few sailors on shore."

"Yes, sir, but they are well armed and led. If you can hold the Spanish at Isabela until tomorrow afternoon, we can attack their rear and throw them into disarray. Units of the general's division are assembling now, and will be marching toward Isabela tonight. Major Barida will lead the combined units. By the afternoon, they will be in position, ready to attack."

"Raul, my orders were only to seize Isabela, land Barida's battalion, and hold this place for three days so the battalion had a way to withdraw if they were defeated. As I told you before, the three days end tomorrow at noon. At that time, we leave and begin the blockade of the coast. With what you've told me, our mission is now completed and we can get under way right away. There is no reason for us to stay."

"The general understands your naval orders, sir. However, based on my description of you, he expresses the opinion that a man of your experience in war will see this rare situation for what it is, a chance to end the war sooner by vanquishing the enemy here and now. Madrid will realize they must end the war before more American forces come to Cuba. He hopes you will seize the initiative, sir, on behalf of the allied warriors of the United States of America and the Republic of Cuba."

I thought of Yeats and our other wounded sailors. There would be more if we stayed.

"I'm far too old to be swayed by glorious sentiments, Raul."

"Then be swayed by the military logic, sir. This chance will not come again."

"I doubt we could hold out for that long anyway. There will be hundreds of Spanish coming against us tomorrow."

"General Lacret knows, sir. Outnumbered ten to one is the usual equation between the Free Cuban Army and the Spanish.

But with determination and innovation, victory can come to those who are outnumbered. You have enough guns and ammunition to hold them off until Major Barida and the other units attack in the afternoon. This location is a very good one for defense. Together, we will have the enemy in a hopeless trap. They will be forced to surrender."

"What is the earliest time your forces can attack?"

"Early afternoon, sir."

"*Exactly* when will they attack?"

"The general said one o'clock, sir."

"Is that in Cuban time, or is it in real time? I operate on real time. I will not in any way sacrifice my men for vague promises."

"Real time, yes. The general and the major fully understand your concerns about the timing, sir. You have their word of honor."

"How will they know my answer?"

"I will go back up the river tonight in the little boat, sir. If I do not make it and they do not hear from me, they will still attack. Only if I get through to them and report your refusal to help, will they not attack. They trust you, sir."

"I see. Give me a moment, Raul."

He walked off into the dark and I turned to Rork. "Get Captain Southby here immediately."

When Southby arrived, the three of us sat on the ground. I briefed Southby on Lacret's request and asked for his candid opinion. He didn't hold back.

"Don't trust `em a bit, sir. Yes, they're well intentioned and trying hard, but can they really deliver this attack? Is it worth it for us to violate our orders and get stuck here, relying on strangers? Our men's *lives* are at risk. We were lucky today, but tomorrow will be different. When things go bad and our men die for no good reason, *you* will be the one to be blame, Commodore. No one will defend you. Those deaths will be a heavy burden for you to bear."

"Valid points, James. But they are the same valid points in any war, anywhere, with any allies. The underlying question is always the same: is the potential gain *probable* or only possible. Even if it is probable, is it *big enough* to be worth the serious risk?"

Southby disagreed. "I still don't like it, sir. What do you say, Rork?"

Rork glanced at me and I nodded to go ahead. "I need your true opinion, Rork."

"Aye, sir. Well, you know me heart wants to trust `em, sir, but me head can't. Aye, `tis well an' true Major Barida's got the gumption an' brains, but what o' the others in Lacret's division? It'll take far more than just a few Cuban units to turn the tide o' battle if we stay an' fight. It'll take a thousand Cubans. It'll take angry men with military skill, who want that victory more than they want life its ownself."

"I agree, Rork. But what if the Free Cuban Army's attack is substantial and successful, what would be the outcome?" I asked him.

He grudgingly agreed. "Then it'll be the greatest bloody victory in the thirty-year struggle for Cuban independence, an' might end the damned war, sir. An' the Cubans'll love us for what we did."

"So . . . is that potential gain worth the risk?" I asked them both.

"No, sir, because it's not probable," decided Southby. "I still don't trust them to be able to do what they say they'll do."

"The Captain's right, sir," concurred Rork. "Methinks General Lacret can't get enough men here to do the deed by tomorrow, especially by one o'clock."

"Thank you both. I appreciate your opinions. Come back in ten minutes and I'll give you my decision."

One thing was certain. If I did nothing, the war would drag on. How many Americans would die in Cuba? The U.S. Army was completely unprepared, from top to bottom. Used to fighting small bands of Indians on the Western plains, the army was ignorant of operating in the tropics, of landing on beaches from ships, of supplying expeditions, of everything it would be called upon to accomplish. It would be a slaughter to send badly supplied and ill-led troops into a foreign jungle against veteran Spanish soldiers.

And if I tried and failed? Did my professional humiliation even matter, when weighed against the loss of my men's lives?

Probability versus possibility. It seemed to boil down to whether Lacret could get his men massed and ready to attack by one o'clock—twenty-five and a half hours from now.

I knew Lacret had four hundred men under Bandera within fifteen miles. They could make it to the Spanish rear area by sunrise, and therefore were a certain factor. So was Barida and his hundred forty men and three remaining field guns, somewhere near Sagua Grande. They were of minimal ability in a fight. That left Lacret's other four hundred men, scattered in small detachments between Sagua Grande and Santa Clara, a radius of twenty to thirty miles from the battlefield.

Could they be assembled in time? If they all got word by sunrise, then moved at an average of two miles an hour, they could cover fourteen miles. The units farther away would not be at the battlefield until sunset. This meant Lacret would attack with six hundred men for certain, possibly eight hundred, with another hundred or so enroute.

The stars powdering the sky were beautiful, but mute—God wasn't being obvious with his opinion on the matter. I was on my own on this one. I thought of José Martí and our many conversations about Cuba's future, but his ghost didn't help me either.

I called for Southby and Rork to return. I didn't offer explanations. The time for debate was over. "I think it is worth the risk. We'll stay two hours later than planned, until two p.m., then get under way. Call Gonzart over here and I'll give him a message for Lacret. He needs to get back up the river to Lacret and Barida right away."

They both knuckled their brows and said, "Aye, aye, sir."

After Gonzart was briefed and headed back up the river, Woodgerd wandered over to me and sat down on a crate. He sat there, uncharacteristically reserved, looking out at the glow of the Spanish campfires in the distance.

"All right, out with it, Michael," I said.

"Today was just the prelude, Peter. Tomorrow's the grand finale. It's gonna be close. Very close. You need to get some rest." Then he got up and left me alone.

I lay back, but rest didn't come. My mind couldn't shut down.

55

The Cost of War

Isabela, Cuba
Friday night
29 April 1898

Gavin, his bloody arm in a sling, showed up a few minutes later. I nodded for him to sit and start his reports. He collapsed with a moan and began.

"Saw you awake, sir. Thought you'd want an update on the casualty list, sir. Total is still seven men shot and four hit by shrapnel. Three are seriously wounded and have been taken out to *Norden*. The others got patched up and are back in the line."

He paused, then handed me a misshapen bugle with a bullet hole through it. "I'm keeping this for Yeats. The wound in the side of his face is through and through. Captain Bendel says he'll make it, but the jaw is severely mangled. All five of Yeats' men were hit. Two are wounded badly, but the others are able to shoot. Still, Commodore, with three men out of action, and another eight at half capacity, we're stretched really thin, sir."

I tried not to visualize Yeats' face, and all the others' faces. This was the time to sound confident. "Well, you've got fourteen new volunteers—those deserters will fight now."

He reacted dubiously. "With respect, sir, they've already run away once. This isn't even their country."

"Yes, but now they're far more scared of Chief Rork than the Spanish."

"Aye, aye, sir," he chuckled. "Request permission to ask a question the bluejackets've been asking me."

"Go ahead, Mr. Gavin."

"Thank you, sir. If the exile battalion is already inland with General Lacret, why loiter around here and get shot at?"

"Valid question. We're staying until mid-afternoon because the Cuban Liberation Army is planning to attack the Spanish rear then. If they can do that, and we can hold our line at Isabela, the Spanish will be defeated. Such a victory could prove to Madrid the uselessness of continuing in Cuba. We have a chance to shorten the war and save a lot of American lives in the future."

Gavin didn't look convinced of the wisdom of that. "Thank you, sir. I'll tell the men. When do you think the enemy will hit us again?"

"At dawn. They'll be stronger and smarter than they were today. Keep everyone alert."

"Aye, aye, sir," Gavin mouthed by rote, then trudged away to share the commodore's morale speech with his men.

It was twelve-fifteen a.m., and going to be a very long night.

56

The Main Performance

Isabela, Cuba
Saturday morning at dawn
30 April 1898

The attack began in the diffused light, thirty minutes before the sun appeared on the horizon. It unfolded quietly and methodically—completely unlike Arce's arrogant parade the previous day.

That told me that Arce, the despised thug who celebrated victories over defenseless civilians and hopelessly outnumbered rebels, but was humiliated by us the day before, wasn't in charge anymore. I wished he still was, for Arce would've petulantly had his men blindly charge our positions.

Somewhere out there a true professional soldier had arrived and was in command of the Spanish forces, making calculated probes to ascertain our weaknesses.

We had a three man observation post in the northeastern corner of the cane field. They fired a couple of rounds at some advancing enemy soldiers and, per orders, ran back to our line.

At their signal, I nodded to Gavin, who passed the word back to the machine gunners. They in turn, sent a runner to the ship, where Southby gave the order to fire two pre-aimed rounds.

It may be recalled how *Kestrel*'s main six-pounder guns, both fore and aft, were masked from firing by a cane warehouse to her starboard. Thus, they could not target areas of the battlefield to the right of the road leading out of town. The forward gun could, however, hit the left-most edge of the battlefield, which included the northeastern corner of the cane field.

In the previous day's battle, the enemy never reached that area *en masse* and therefore *Kestrel*'s gun was not used. I hadn't wanted to alert them to our ability to target there.

Today was different, for the enemy was no longer completely ignorant of our dispositions. I had to assume the Spanish at some point had figured out our Quaker mine ruse. I also presumed they would, in an effort to stay away from any more possible fougasse traps in the roadside ditch, try to overwhelmingly attack along the opposite side of the road, through the cane field area.

But that is not what I wanted them to do. I needed the enemy to make their assault straight down the road. Fifty yards before they would overrun our defense line, my plan required them to divert obliquely to their left—our right flank—where the seemingly abandoned flatbed railcar waited for them. *Kestrel*'s forward gun, the caltrops and *chevals de frise* in front of our lines, and the machine gun in the line, would stimulate that diversion.

Kestrel's two rounds exploding in the cane field would simulate actual mines going off right about when the Spanish skirmishers advanced through that area. This, I hoped, would renew enemy doubts as to whether all the mines they saw were real or fake, and thereby delay or deter them from using that route of attack. This ruse was not perfect, of course, for they could hear the report of the gun behind us on the ship, but it was the best I could do.

We saw them moving through the field. It was done well, dashing for three seconds before going to ground, then dashing again, zigzagging closer and closer toward the corner where our men had been. These men were experienced soldiers, staying low and varying the timing and course of their runs.

I turned to Gavin. "With five rounds, begin independent fire on the right flank."

Twenty sailors began peppering away at the enemy, with little effect at such a long range. It wasn't done to hit the Spanish soldiers—it was done to provide enough noise to cover the sound of *Kestrel*'s gun firing and for harassment.

The first round arrived just as one soldier leaped up and began his run. He disappeared in a fountain of sooty earth, emerging on his hands and knees before collapsing. Another soldier ran over to him and the second round impacted near where he had been. We could hear others telling each other to crawl out exactly the way they entered, the procedure for withdrawing from a mine field. The ruse worked. Gavin had his men cease fire.

It wasn't their only probe of our defenses. Over on the right side we couldn't see them, but did faintly hear the rustle of a scouting party along the edge of the mangroves, near the fougasse ditch.

A few minutes later, after their men withdrew from the cane field, the Spanish field gun captured from Barida fired four rounds into the fake mine field. It was an attempt to set off any other mines we had lurking there. I was further impressed with my adversary's abilities.

I remembered each caisson of Barida's guns carried twenty rounds. They had already fired five the day before, and four recently, meaning they had eleven rounds left. Unless they procured more artillery, or more ammunition for the British-built gun they had, then we could withstand a bombardment. It would be costly, but we could withstand it.

The Spanish commander began his barrage just as I completed the calculation of his remaining ammunition. The first shell impacted forty feet from me, sending a hail of hot metal shards in all directions, including mine. I was one of the few Americans standing, having walked over to the center of the line to see down the road better. A dozen red blooms spread across my faded blue cotton duck shirt and navy blue trousers, which I'd chosen in lieu of my eminently targetable tropical whites. Though small, the wounds hurt like hell and elicited curses that would've done Rork proud.

"Character cuts—you were lucky, Peter. Damned fine shooting!" muttered Woodgerd, while admiring several of his own lacerations.

In the next four minutes they fired six more, progressing from left over to our right, landing them exactly as the artillery manual taught, twenty feet behind our lines. Yelps, curses, groans, and screams erupted from the line as the men's backs and legs were gouged by the shrapnel.

Ten men were dragged away for a cursory examination by *Kestrel*'s cook in a shack a hundred feet to the rear. That unfortunate individual had been designated by Southby as the *ad hoc* hospital apprentice for the day. Several former deserters were among his patients, with Rork warning the others to stay in place, his revolver aimed their way.

"Cavalry coming, sir," reported Bosun Mack on the right flank, seconds after the field piece ceased fire. A troop of forty or fifty horsemen came around the curve of the road into view, quick-trotting in the seconds until they got to the cane field, then changing into a full gallop toward us.

The bombardment began again, shells randomly landing every forty-five seconds along the same transverse line as before, nailing more men with the shards. Rork glanced over at me and held up five fingers. I nodded back in acknowledgment. The Spanish were now out of captured artillery ammunition—I hoped.

Behind the cavalry were infantry at the quick-march but without music or drumbeats. Through my binoculars, I saw their regimental flag and knew we were in dire straits. It wasn't Arce's regiment's banner, a standard design common among most of the regiments. This one was much larger, the golden flag illuminated by the morning sun, accentuating the angry lion rampant of the ancient kingdom of Leon, topped by the crown of Spain.

We were facing some of Spain's best—the 38th Infantry, the famous Leon Regiment. There were a thousand men in the 38th and all were veterans.

Confined at the curve by the narrow lane of road and track between the mangroves on either side, they fanned out upon reaching the cane field, their light blue tunics contrasting with the dark green forest behind them. They were not in ranks or formation as Arce's men the day before, but in loose skirmish order, with every bayonet fixed and every rifle of the soldiers in front levelled at our line.

I'd forgotten how fast professional cavalry advanced at the gallop—my last experience facing them had been at Peru in 1881. Thirty seconds after first appearing, they had covered a quarter-mile and were now halfway between the cane field and our line. As I registered this, a bugle abruptly sounded and they transformed into race horses, every rider leaning forward in grave concentration, pistol hand outstretched and aiming, every mount stampeding toward us. There were no yells, no more commands or bugles. The only thing heard from them was the increasing thunder of the hooves.

They hit the scattered caltrops and several horses stumbled and fell. Their riders were trampled by the others, but the remaining cavalrymen kept coming.

Two horses went down at the tripwire across the road. The others spotted it and leaped clear, never slacking the pace, their masters never taking their eyes off us. They seemed inhuman man-beasts, which nothing could stop.

"Steady, men. Take aim and wait until the command . . ." I called out over the din, as much to myself as the sailors.

That devilishly omnipotent thunder filled our senses, vibrating the ground below me like an earthquake. It was impossible to focus on anything other than those dead-hearted behemoths, enveloped in a cloud of dust, coming to kill us.

The *chevals de frise*, obliquely angled in front of the left side of our line, fulfilled their deterrence duty, for the charging Spanish gravitated away from that side and headed for our center and right.

I fought the primordial need to flee from this scene of horror. Out of the corner of my eye, I briefly could tell others were nervously glancing around them to see if anyone was running. No one was.

I raised my shotgun and aimed at a Spaniard with chevrons. Next to him, a comrade was charging directly for me, the soldier's eyes fixed on me.

As they got to within a hundred yards, the sound of their charge became an overwhelming tumult, and I knew I would have to yell the next command as loud as I could to be heard. Gavin looked at me. Woodgerd came over and stood beside me, his Martini-Henri rock steady at the shoulder firing position. Rork's shotgun was trained at an onrushing Spanish officer whose saber was levelled right back at him.

At fifty yards range I shouted the order. "Entire line . . . by volley . . . *FIRE!*"

The roaring cavalry drowned out even the blast of the fifty-gun volley. For an instant, I wondered if my men even heard the order. The horses kept charging as if nothing had happened. A shot of panic bolted through me.

But my men *had* heard and fired, and had hit their marks. It was only the momentum of half a ton of each horse moving at twenty miles an hour, even after they and their riders had been hit, which gave the illusion. Incredibly, the momentum carried the war horses another hundred feet until they began to stumble and fall. Cavalrymen were thrown, but most recovered and emptied their revolvers at us while crouched behind their horses' twitching bodies.

Only a handful of the Spanish got close to our lines. I called out, "*Second volley . . . Fire!*"

With that, the last of the Spanish cavalry collapsed only a few feet in front of the sailors. The thunder ended. Scattered Spanish pistol shots still popped at us.

"Independent fire at the enemy still moving out there . . . *Fire!*"

The cavalrymen's shots ended. Even the wounded horses stopped screaming in pain, for the sailors had put them out of their misery. Silence descended like a suffocating invisible cloud. It had been very close, too damned close. I saw my right hand trembling. I had to grip my shotgun again to stop it.

"Cease fire! Mr. Gavin, report casualties and available ammunition as soon as you can."

"Well done, Peter," said Woodgerd, without his usual acerbic wit. "And now, the grand finale is about to start."

He pointed down the road, where the dust cloud was clearing. "Take a look out there."

The Spanish infantry had reached the cane field, stretched from the mangroves on the left across to the mangroves on the right. I climbed an orange crate and studied the enemy through my binoculars. They were endlessly arrayed, their flashing bayonets visible back up the road for as far as I could see. I descended from the depressing sight.

Gavin suddenly showed up. "Runner from *Kestrel* just arrived, sir. Enemy squadron is approaching from the sea."

57

The Grand Finale

Isabela, Cuba
Saturday morning
30 April 1898

I unfolded the note Gavin handed me, and wished I hadn't.

8:02 a.m., Saturday, 30 April 1898

Commodore Wake,

1—At 7:54 a.m., Maravillas observation post reported three small enemy ships approaching from ten miles to the west, close along the coast, in echelon-ahead formation. They appear to be torpedo or gun boats, possibly of the Ardilla*-type. Speed of approach is approx eight knots. Unless otherwise directed, we will engage them with* Harrier *and* Falcon *at the pass between Cayo Maravillas and Cayo de la Cruz if they try to enter the bay.* Kestrel *will get under way and engage if the enemy gets past* Harrier *and* Falcon *into the bay.*

2—Lt. Bilton has sounded the area around the entrance to the river and is trying to get Osprey *inshore on your left flank to provide indirect gunfire for you. If it works, he will be in position by 8:30 a.m. Please advise me on potential target area and I will relay to him by lamp.*

3—I will keep you advised on enemy ships, our dispositions to meet them, and Osprey*'s actions.*

*4—*Kestrel *is standing by to fire more rounds on the pre-aimed target area and awaiting your word to fire.*

Respectfully,

Captain James Southby, USN

So the naval engagement would be right around nine o'clock, two bells into the forenoon watch—probably right about the time of the next Spanish Army assault on Isabela.

I showed the message to Woodgerd. He was a reporter, but first and foremost he was a soldier. In his twenty years as a mercenary, he'd been with the underdogs quite often. I hoped he had some valuable advice, because I sorely needed some.

"Very interesting," he pondered aloud. "I wonder if they coordinated it? Damned impressive, if they did. My advice? Cut your losses and get the hell out of here, right now."

Valid and logical. Still, I refused to lose confidence. "Not yet. As long as they're only gunboats, our squadron can handle them, Michael. I'm not worried about the Spanish vessels. They're a major factor, but I'm more worried about what will happen ashore."

"Oh yeah, I agree about the boats. Those are nothing. Your *real* problem is here on land, and the commitment you made to the Cubans. It's time to decide priorities, Peter."

Woodgerd was a jaded soul, never committing anything to anybody without substantial money being involved. And even then, only on sure things. Woodgerd never gambled.

"We have to hold on for another five hours, until the Cuban attack at one o'clock, Michael. Then the Spanish will be caught in a vice."

"Five hours is an eternity, Peter. Your men can't hold out that long. Hell, we'll be doing pretty damn well to repel the next attack. After that, your squids'll be finished. They're not used to this sort of work."

The enemy fortified his comment right then by attacking early.

"Here come the Spaniardos, sir," announced Rork from the gun line.

Three hundred yards away, a solid wave of soldiers in light blue stood as one—a battalion, *en masse.* The entire line fired their rifles at us, then ran forward thirty yards and went to ground seconds before the rank behind them fired. Instantly, the front rank was up again and firing, then running forward. They went through precisely the same maneuver again and again, coming ever closer to our defenses. Their volleys were missing our sailors on the ground, but not by much.

I'd never seen anything like it. The attack was perfectly orchestrated. It was mesmerizing—actually magnificent—in some terribly lethal way. A slower motion version of the cavalry charge.

"Oh yeah, they're good. Very good," Woodgerd commented, then smiled evilly. "But they have a weakness. They're doing it by the numbers, and therefore are predictable. Timing is everything, Peter."

I was thinking the same thing and noted the duration of their next evolution of advance. It took thirty-five seconds. I timed the next few. All were exactly thirty-five seconds.

"Eyes front!" yelled Rork when several sailors glanced back at their commodore, fear etched into their faces, waiting for orders.

The leading ranks of the 38th Leon Infantry Regiment were only two hundred yards away, well within our rifle range, but I called out, "Steady men. I'll not give the order to fire until we see the whites of their eyes!"

Admittedly, it was a ridiculous homage to American patriotism, which I said without forethought, then thought sounded rather bland. Fortunately, some sailors laughed, breaking the tension.

Another Spanish volley zinged toward us, now much lower. They could see where we were. The next one would hit flesh. The first Spanish rank was running, about to go to ground. The second rank beginning to aim and fire, as soon as the front rank was out of the way.

This was the ten-second gap when they were vulnerable.

I shouted, *"Left* side of the line . . . by volley at the second enemy rank to your front . . . *Fire!"*

The front Spanish rank had just gone prone. We hit the left side of the rank behind them a split-second before they fired at us. A good third of the Spanish line was hit and faltered. Our sudden volley interrupted their officers' orders, which had been in a rhythmic monotone.

I exploited the enemy's momentary confusion. *"Right* side of the line . . . by volley at the enemy *left* side . . . *Fire!"*

More Spanish soldiers of the second rank were hit. The first rank stood up and I quickly shouted, *"Left* side of the line . . . by volley at the enemy to your front . . . *Fire!"*

Theirs went off simultaneously with ours, but ours was fired from low positions, the trajectory ascending into the Spanish as they stood unprotected. More enemy fell, but not enough.

Woodgerd observed quietly, "Here comes the charge."

This was when my annoying insistence on detailed preparations paid off, for the long period of our waiting had been used in readying our line, our men, and other weapons.

Every sailor lay protected behind a foot-high mounded ridge of sand which stretched along our entire front. This was then topped another foot higher with various debris. Firing ports were placed between the debris for each man, with thick notched sticks dug into the ridge for his barrel to rest upon, thereby improving accuracy and endurance. Range stakes, each distance displaying a different color, were placed out in the killing zone. This enabled our sailors to set their rifle sights without delay or uncertainty. Drills on reloading, clearing blockages, and fixing bayonets had been performed over and over, both day and night.

Spanish buglers sounded the charge. The first five ranks of seven hundred soldiers rose up and ran toward us. Their officers' sabers angled over, directing their men to shift the attack to their left, which was our right flank. That is a difficult movement to accomplish while under fire, but the Leon Regiment was one of the best. With parade ground efficiency, the Spanish on our left turned the axis of their attack diagonally, heading for our right side. The entire battalion headed for the same place.

They fired from the hip as they ran, but that sort of shooting had nowhere near the accuracy of their previous efforts from the point shoulder position. Still, the hundreds of buzzing Mauser rounds did add to the chaos, and the strain on our men. The Spanish Mauser's ability to load a magazine of five rounds quickly and then be reloaded while running, was vastly superior to the slower loading procedure of the U.S. Navy's Lee rifle.

"Left side!" I called out in the next ten-second gap. "By volley into the enemy . . . *Fire!*"

Several went down, but fewer than before.

"Sailors! Fix . . . *bayonets!*"

Sixty right hands reached behind and grabbed bayonets, bringing them forward and locking them onto the barrel lug. Rork told the deserters to do the same.

I waved for the cart-mounted Colt machine gun to come forward from its hiding place in an alleyway. The gunners pushed it forward along the road at a run, stopping at a strangler fig tree at the edge of town where I stood, forty feet behind the line of sailors. The tree offered partial concealment but the gun still had a broad field of fire. Rork's former deserters manning the center of the line vacated their positions and crawled on their bellies quickly to the right flank, getting them out of the Colt's line of fire.

A shout to Gavin on the left got his men firing independently at the Spanish to keep the pressure up on that side. Over on the far right side, Bosun Mack was in charge, crouched down behind an overturned handcart. He calmly kept his men under control, a monumental demonstration of discipline as the Spanish closed to within fifty yards, their rounds now hitting among the sailors.

Mack swiveled to look at me, his right hand holding a lanyard which led out beyond his defense line to the railcar. Spanish bullets thudded into the cart within inches of him. Several sailors cursed they'd been hit. Mack's arm slowly tensioned the lanyard, his eyes locked on me as the Spanish soldiers entered the blast zone.

I waited. A Mauser round zinged near me, then another. I heard the gunners behind me cock the bolt of the Colt machine gun.

A squad of Spaniards sought cover at the railcar, then ran toward Mack's side of the line. An enemy subaltern, seemingly a teenager, urged the men behind him not to falter, but to charge on and overrun the *yanquis*. They were only yards away from the sailors now. The main body of infantry was nearing the railcar, a major in the middle, other officers scattered among the soldiers.

Another fifteen feet to go.

"Steady, lads . . ." Rork ordered.

The enemy was massing all around the railcar. Their major trotted over to them, pointing toward our line. Five feet more and he would be right in front of the bomb. I felt my chest tightening as I faced Mack.

"NOW!"

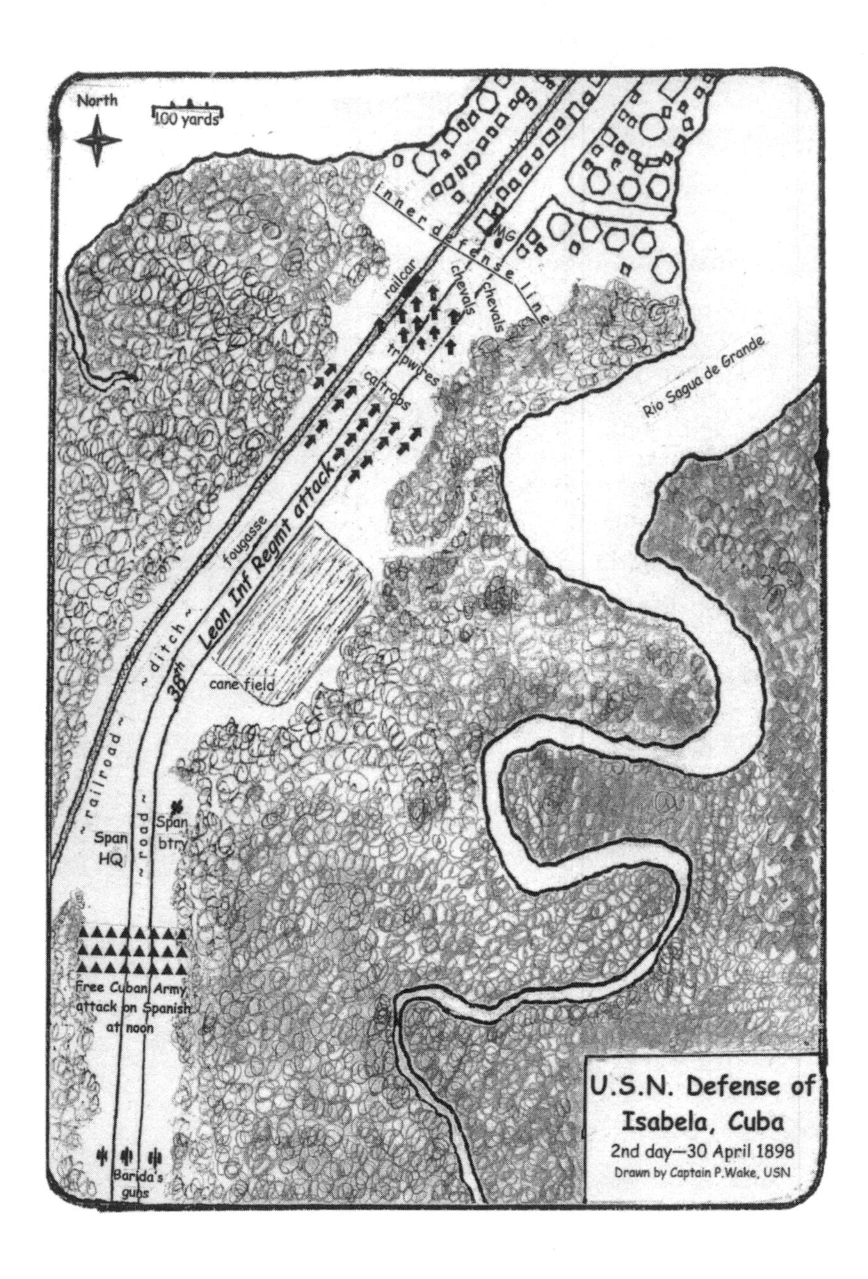
North
100 yards
inner defense line
MG
railcar
chevals
chevals
tripwires
caltraps
Rio Sagua de Grande
fougasse
38th Leon Inf Regmt attack
~ ditch ~
cane field
~ railroad ~
~ road ~
Span HQ
Span btry
Free Cuban Army attack on Spanish at noon
Barida's guns
U.S.N. Defense of Isabela, Cuba
2nd day—30 April 1898
Drawn by Captain P.Wake, USN

58

The Crescendo

Isabela, Cuba
Saturday morning
30 April 1898

The detonation was a blinding flash of light in front of the sailors. The shock and heat wave picked up everything in its path and flung it into the line of sailors.

Everything near the railcar instantaneously disappeared in a ball of orange fire. Some seconds later, I found myself twenty feet on the other side of the tree, dazed. I felt hands pulling me up. It was one of the Colt machine gunners.

"Forget me—start firing, man!" I yelled into his face. He staggered over to the machine gun, which his mates were setting back upright.

When building and placing the bomb, Yeats and his petty officers had estimated the amount of high explosive packed into the boiler would make the blast the equivalent of a battleship's 10-inch gun's anti-personnel round. They said it would be contained to the top and ends by the flatbed railcar and its trucks, and confined to the rear by some iron plates found in the town—projecting the blast and assorted shrapnel laterally across the road in front of our defenses. When I asked if they had ever seen a 10-inch gun round explode, or the effects of it afterward, none had. Neither had I. Few in the navy had. Our planning for the effects of the blast was merely guesswork. It was based on intuitive logic, but remained only a guess. It turned out we'd guessed wrong.

The Colt began firing short bursts through the haze of choking dust and smoke. From my left, Gavin shouted to cease firing and save ammunition. The Colt stopped. No one was moving in front of us. There were no targets.

I headed for the right side of the line to find Rork and the others nearest the blast. Rork was sitting on the ground, stretching his neck, a pained look on his face. His former deserters were arrayed in various stunned poses around him. Most held their ears, some bled out their noses. I knelt beside Rork and leaned close. I couldn't see any obvious wounds.

"Are you hit, Sean?"

He gave me that insane grin of his. "Me noggin's hurtin' somethin' fierce, an' me neck's strained, but that's it, sir. You?"

"No, I'm all right. Your men, what of them?"

The grin morphed into pride. "Banged an' bruised, but still here. The lads never ran, sir, never flinched. Nary a one o' `em."

So they could all hear, I said, "Well done, men. Well done. *¡Bien hecho!*"

The air cleared a bit, and I searched for the railcar, but it was gone. So was the railroad track, and even the track bed beneath it. The whole area was a wide crater, with mangled ends of track twisted up in odd shapes on either side.

There were no Spanish soldiers near the crater. Not even any bodies. Then I saw an arm. Other fire-blackened body parts were scattered everywhere in the sand.

I got to Mack and his men. The little mounded ridge, topped with various debris, had been swept away by the shock wave. The bosun had reformed the defense line about fifty feet to the rear. Behind them, by a blown-down shack, a dozen men lay holding their heads.

"Bosun, are you wounded?" I asked Mack, who was as dazed as everyone else. It took him a moment to answer, and when he did, he squinted at me.

"I think so, sir. Little hard to see. Some of our men are wounded. Concussions I think. But everybody looks alive. Haven't gotten to all of them yet. Most of the blast went over us."

"Where is the enemy?"

"Don't know, sir. The bomb was bigger than we thought it'd be. I guess it took them all."

Gavin ran over to us and knelt down, grabbing me by the shoulders. "Commodore, are you wounded, sir? Your ears are bleeding."

"It's just a concussion, like everybody else. How's the left side of our line?"

He kept hold of me. "No casualties among the sailors on the left, sir. We were far enough away from the blast. Are you sure you're not wounded, sir? You don't look good."

His concern was starting to aggravate me. "Mr. Gavin, I am not wounded and you can let go now. Thank you for your concern. The Spanish—where are they?"

He let go, but still eyed me closely. "Gone, sir. On this side of our line, the blast got them. On the left side, they ran back to the cane field. Your defense plan worked, sir. It stopped the attack."

Not entirely, I thought. *The Spanish will be back.*

A young sailor in an impossibly clean uniform walked hesitantly toward us from the road. I recognized him, a sixteen-year-old serving in his first ship. *Kestrel*'s youngest man. He stared horrified at the scene around us, and then at me.

In trembled voice, he asked, "Are you really Commodore Wake, sir?"

I waved away Gavin's impending reprimand for violating naval protocol. The boy had delivered messages to me many times on the ship, but his confusion was understandable. Besides the carnage around us, I didn't look like the commodore anymore, for my uniform, like everyone else's, was ragged, filthy, and bloody.

"Yes, son. I'm Commodore Wake. Are you delivering a message from the ship?"

He came to wide-eyed attention and handed me a folded note. "Ah, yes, sir. Message from Captain Southby, sir."

8:41 a.m., 30 April 1898

Commodore Wake,

1—Enemy gunboats now two miles west from Maravillas, steering for outer channel.

2—Light cruiser in sight ten miles to southeast, approx. one mile offshore, steering northwest at apprx eight knots—unknown nationality, but does not look American.

*3—*Osprey *in position in 3 fathoms, one mile to northeast of the left end of your line—at 80 degrees West, 22 degrees, 56 minutes North. Lt. Bilton requests target locations.*

4—Heard blast—request status on USN and enemy ashore.

Captain James Southby, USN

Lieutenant Bilton was taking chances—*Osprey* had maybe four feet of water under her keel, and the tide was ebbing. In a few hours, *Osprey* would be aground. Conjuring up in my mind the geography of the chart, I scrawled a quick reply on the back of the note.

8:52 a.m., 30 April 1898

Capt Southby,

1—Continue defense plan against gunboats if they try to enter past Maravillas.

2—If cruiser is Spanish and attacks thru channel—take squadron and try to escape among islands inside the bay. There will be no time for embarking us. Do not wait for shore party.

3—Target for Osprey *is area of cane field, road, and track—and for half-mile to the rear (SW) from that area. Fire five rounds immediately. We will correct from those.*

4—SitRep ashore: enemy repulsed and now in cane field and beyond. Main mass (most of regiment) probably at curve of road. Expecting another attack. USN casualties minimal and line still holding—moving it to edge of town now. Send food & water.
Commodore P. Wake, USN

The messenger ran off to the ship far faster than I saw him arrive. Rork and Woodgerd walked over and sat down. I motioned for Gavin to sit as well. Mack started to leave, but I had him stay.

When I had the attention of the circle, I turned to the lieutenant. "Mr. Gavin, I need several things as soon as possible: a casualty and ammunition report; a reconnaissance report on exactly where the enemy is, and their dispositions; the moving of our defense line back to the shacks at the edge of town; and some water and food from the ship distributed to the men. It should arrive soon. Questions or suggestions from anyone?"

The four replied "No, sir" in unison. I studied them for hesitation, but there was none.

"Very well, then. *Osprey* has worked inshore to a position where her guns can reach the enemy. I estimate she'll have another one to two hours before the ebb forces her out of range. They will be opening fire soon with five rounds. We will send corrections, relayed by *Kestrel*.

"The enemy gunboats which appeared earlier are nearing Maravillas. The squadron can handle them, but now a light cruiser has just appeared ten miles east along the coast. Nationality is unknown at present, but probably Spanish. If the cruiser enters the channel and attacks our ships, I have directed the squadron to try to escape through the small islands in the bay, if they can. That means we here will be on our own, because there won't be time to extract us before they have to flee."

My men solemnly acknowledged the bad news. Woodgerd said nothing.

"If forced by circumstances to be on our own, we will have a rear guard of volunteers under Rork's command continue firing at the enemy, while the main body wades across the shoals at the mouth of the river. Once across, they'll head upriver along the far bank. The rear guard will then run for it to the river and cross before the enemy realizes we've vacated the place.

"The Spanish won't expect this strategy. They will expect us to remain fighting while waiting for rescue. But we'll be gone from Isabela. Once we get up the river, we'll make contact with the Cuban Army, and arrange with them for our withdrawal from Cuba somewhere else."

I paused, again gauging their attitude. They looked dubious. I injected some levity. "Once we get to Key West, drinks are on me for all hands."

The last comment got an obligatory laugh from everyone. I couldn't blame their lack of humor. My escape strategy sounded improbable to me too.

59

The Idea

Isabela, Cuba
Saturday morning
30 April 1898

Twenty-six minutes later, at nine-eighteen a.m., *Osprey*'s rounds hit the area of the cane field and road. We could see the Spanish soldiers withdrawing from the open area and heading to their rear, about two hundred men in all. Shortly thereafter, the same young messenger arrived to take range and azimuth corrections back to *Kestrel* for signaling to *Osprey*.

There was no reason to bombard the area where only Spanish wounded were. A wounded man requires at least two healthy men to transport and care for him, so I wanted those wounded to survive and be a burden to their regiment. I also wanted *Osprey*'s precious rounds to impact the enemy concentration at the curve of the road. My message was to increase elevation and range another three hundred yards, and bring the azimuth arc out to twenty degrees. This would spread the impact area across the width of the open area where the enemy was massed. After five more rounds were fired, further corrections would be sent.

Southby's update on the enemy warships arrived with the messenger.

9:15 a.m., 30 April 1898

Commodore Wake,
1—Spanish gunboats loitering three miles offshore Maravillas
2—Cruiser is still unknown and heading this way
3—Understand order regarding actions if cruiser attacks—will remain at wharf until then
4—Food and water sent to you with this messenger
Captain James Southby, USN

I looked up and saw a line of sailors, each staring around them at the destruction, carrying small casks and boxes. Mack met them and began calling out men from the line to get their portions. It was the first sign of liveliness I'd seen in them since the blast.

Then Gavin walked up. "I have the casualty, ammunition, and reconnaissance reports, sir."

"Go ahead, Mr. Gavin."

"Aye, sir. Casualty count from the last attack is twenty-seven men with apparent concussions, five of them serious enough to be sent to *Norden*, sir. Of the remaining twenty-two, sixteen are in the shade until they get their wits back. The other six have returned to the defense line among the outer shacks of the town. None of our men were killed, sir."

"Remaining effectives?" I asked.

"Thirty-three completely unwounded men, accompanied by twenty-two recent ambulatory wounded, including the ten previously wounded, making a total of fifty-five officers and men able to shoot, which includes the deserters."

"*Former* deserters, Mr. Gavin. I think they've earned a change in description. They'll be referred to as volunteers from now on. Ammunition?"

"Yes, sir—*volunteers*. We've redistributed the ammunition and each man now has thirty-one rounds, sir. The Colt gun still has four hundred eighty."

"Reconnaissance report?"

"Chief Rork just returned from leading the scouting party, which included several of the deser. . . I mean volunteers . . . sir. He used them to interrogate the enemy wounded they found out in front of our line. The chief estimates approximately one hundred and fifty-one enemy dead. Seventy-three are wounded. All of them need immediate medical attention, but there's nothing we can do. By the way, sir, they include the lieutenant colonel of the Leon Regiment. He led the attack and was hit by the railcar blast. Has an iron shard sticking out of his thigh."

The wounded, with one them high ranking, was the opportunity I'd been hoping for.

"Really? Pass the word for Chief Rork, and continue the report."

Gavin called for Rork, then went on. "The main Spanish line seems to be beyond the cane field, concentrated back at the curve of the road, sir, right where you thought they were. Chief Rork made it up to the cane field, found no unwounded enemy in the field or fougasse ditch. He estimates approximately six to eight hundred enemy have formed up back at the curve. He thinks the Spanish are probably scattered back into the mangroves on either side also."

The report agreed with my rough estimates during the attack. So far, the 38th Leon Regiment had suffered a devastating number of casualties. They would concentrate on regrouping before coming at us again. With a rail line leading right to them, reinforcements were only hours away.

Rork trudged up and I bid Gavin to stay.

"You look like hell, Rork," I said, meaning it. "Sit down and take a load off your bones."

He lowered himself to the ground with a groan. "Thank ye, sir. Me ol' bones're needin' it."

"Me too, Sean. Listen, what's this Spanish lieutenant colonel like?"

He paused in concentration, then responded, "The ol' sod's me own age an' in pain, sir. Ooh, an' he's a ol' school grandee o' Spain, through an' through. Got a name a mile long, but the main part o' it is Rodrigo Azul Ortega. Maybe royal, by the looks o' `im."

An old school grandee officer suited me. Royal blood would be even better.

"What's his attitude on what happened?"

"The gent's stunned at our defense, sir. Said the Spaniardo commanders all thought we were just a small raidin' party o' *yanqui* sailors. Figured it to be a cake walk for regulars such as `em, even after what we did to Arce's crew yesterday. Now he thinks he fought the whole o' Uncle Sam's bloody Marine Corps an' this is a major friggin' invasion. Methought it best to leave the ol' boy with that impression, sir."

"Good thinking, Rork. That's exactly what we want them to believe."

I shifted to the lieutenant. "Mr. Gavin, I need a sheet of ship's stationery immediately."

After it arrived, I spent five minutes carefully scripting a message. I called Gavin, Rork, Mack, and Woodgerd to return.

"Mr. Gavin, right after *Osprey*'s next barrage hits, you will carry a flag of truce to the enemy lines. With you will be one of the volunteers, who will interpret for you. Present the enemy commander with this letter."

I passed it around for each to read.

9:45 a.m., 30 April 1898
Isabela, Republic of Cuba
To the Honorable Commanding Officer
38th Leon Regiment of Spain

Dear Colonel,

It is my military duty to inform you that approximately 73 of your soldiers lie wounded and in need of your immediate medical attention on the battleground. They include Lieutenant Colonel Rodrigo Azul Ortega. Regrettably, we have no prisoners from your regiment—for all the other Spanish soldiers on the battlefield are dead, a total of approximately 141 men and officers. Therefore, in the interest of common humanity, I propose the following:

1—That an immediate State of Truce be mutually declared by both of us upon receipt by you of this message and your word of honor to the messenger, Lt. Gavin, which will last until 11:30 a.m., this day.

2—That until 10:30 a.m., this day, my forces collect and deliver the Spanish wounded to the edge of the cane field nearest your lines, for repatriation to your regiment.

3—That once the wounded are delivered to the aforementioned location at 10:30 a.m., your forces come out and bring your wounded back to your regimental surgeons.

4—That at 10:30 a.m., you also deliver Captain Mario Cano, of the Free Cuban Army, who is known to be one of your prisoners, and any other Free Cuban Army prisoners in your possession, to the aforementioned location, for return to our forces.

5—That at 11:30 a.m., this day, the State of Truce will end and a State of War shall resume between our forces.

6—That this State of War shall only be avoided by the surrender of, or withdrawal by, all Spanish forces from the area of Isabela by 11:30 a.m., this day.

7—That once surrendered, all Spanish officers and men of the famed 38th Leon Regiment, and other accompanying Spanish units, shall be given military parole and treated with the highest esteem and honor by the Allied forces, with officers retaining their side arms and baggage, and regimental colors staying with the regimental commander. It will be our pleasure to arrange decent accommodations and cuisine, and repatriation to Spain in the near future.

These proposals are rendered by your most admiring adversary, with the utmost respect,

Commodore Peter Wake, United States Navy

Supreme Commanding Officer, All Allied Land and Naval Forces in Northern Cuba

Gavin shook his head in wonder. Woodgerd gave me an approving look. Mack stayed neutral.

Rork verbalized his opinion. "Commodore—you've got `em right where you want `em. Those grandees'll have to go for this to get their precious Ortega back. Aye, an' they'll be convinced we're stronger than we are. We'll get Mario back, an' a nice little delay `til the Free Cuban Army arrives to box the bastards in."

"Yes, if they buy it."

60

The Bluff

Isabela, Cuba
Saturday morning
30 April 1898

Southby's next message said the Spanish gunboats were continuing to loiter off Maravillas. Were they waiting for others in order to attack in greater strength or merely surveilling us. Or were they diversionary bait to lure us away from Isabela? The cruiser east of us had gone farther offshore and slowed down, exact identity yet unknown.

Osprey's five-round ranging barrage landed right where I wanted, a demonstration of our newly positioned firepower. Shortly afterward, Gavin set out on his mission, marching down the road under a waving bedsheet from my cabin in *Kestrel.* Both he and his assistants, a gunner's mate from *Harrier* and the newly reinstated Sergeant Julio Rivera, were cleaned up, shaved, and looking sharp in new uniforms. They were counseled to act refreshed and unconcerned, as if the outcome of the battle, and the war for Cuban independence, were foregone conclusions in our favor.

As Rork predicted, the Spanish commander, Colonel Tomás Diaz Fernandez de San Martín, accepted the offer of exchanging the wounded for Cano. He also declined to surrender, as expected, and made a very shrewd demand of his own, which I didn't expect.

Colonel Diaz wanted to meet me.

It was apparent he wanted to gauge me personally. I couldn't come up with a way to avoid it. I'd made the subtle bluff about our strength, and now I had to meet him or risk Diaz's seeing through the ruse and attacking us immediately.

We met at 10:30 a.m. in the cane field. On my way to the rendezvous, I accompanied the stretcher of Lieutenant Colonel Ortega, the iron shard still protruding but his pain deadened by a large dose of our limited morphine. He and I conversed about my visits to Spain in '74 and '95, mainly discussing the wonderful wines of Andalusia.

As his surgeons and soldiers took away their wounded, Diaz marched from his lines up the road to the field. A few paces behind him came Captain Mario Cano, walking with a pronounced limp.

The colonel embraced his friend Ortega, then turned to me. Since I was the senior officer, Diaz saluted me and presented his name, rank, and respects—in surprisingly fluent British English. I presented my name, rank, and compliments to him in return.

These pleasantries ended when Diaz's expression turned stony.

"So Commodore, I finally meet the American who married the beautiful Doña Maria Ana Maura of Spain, and even convinced her to renounce her faith and her country."

Many in Spain knew of our marriage. It was no secret. I desperately searched my memory to see if Maria had ever mentioned him, but nothing came to mind.

My subordinates had been standing behind me, and no doubt were wondering what was happening between their commander and the Spanish colonel. I was about to utter some sort of reply, but Diaz wasn't quite done. He beckoned an officer accompanying his surgeons to come over to us. The young man marched up, clicked his heels, and saluted. He turned toward me, his visage burning with hatred.

It was Juanito Maura.

Enjoying every second of my discomfort, Colonel Diaz smugly continued. "Commodore Wake, may I have the honor to present Captain Juan Maura, one of our fine reserve officers who has volunteered for active duty in order to defend Spain and her most faithful isle of Cuba. I must say we were quite fortunate to have him posted with our regiment. He is my aide de camp, and has proven to be an efficient one. I believe you two have already met, and so you probably have an idea of his zeal and abilities, and complete devotion to Spain."

I had to say something. "Thank you for the introduction, Colonel. I do, indeed, fully understand Captain Maura's remarkable intelligence and accomplishments. You have my congratulations on getting such an able staff officer."

Diaz waved a hand. "Oh, no, Commodore. You misunderstand. Captain Maura is not only a staff officer, he is a *combat* officer as well. In fact, Captain Maura is leading the final attack on your positions today, which will begin as soon as our short truce ends. I suppose I should reciprocate your kind and generous terms of surrender and offer them likewise to you but, alas, I cannot. Too many Spaniards have died by your atrocious barbarities, which defy all standards of morality among professional warriors."

Diaz made his next comment with deliberation. "No, after what you have done to stain the profession of arms, Commodore, Spanish honor demands a total victory, without quarter or mercy on the men who have perpetrated such crimes against decency."

Without waiting for a reply, Diaz and Maura executed an about-face and marched back down the road. I turned around far less martially, only to find three faces staring at me in disbelief over how the whole parley had transpired.

We returned to our lines in silence.

61

Inferno

Isabela, Cuba
Late Saturday morning
30 April 1898

Instead of what I anticipated, a full scale charge up the road, the first enemy gunshots came from the mangrove jungle on both our flanks. Each one of the half-dozen rounds on both sides had been aimed and ready when a bugle sounded at the Spanish camp. Instantly, each round struck a sailor. Somehow, during the truce, the Spanish had infiltrated up to our lines through the thick mangroves without our seeing or hearing them. There weren't many, perhaps a squad on either flank, but their initial success was enough to embolden their comrades.

Meanwhile, Lieutenant Bilton in *Osprey* followed orders and fired his guns at 11:35 a.m., striking the curve of the road where the main regiment was located. The regiment didn't stay there, however, for they were already quickly trotting out of the barrage zone toward Isabela, arranged by companies in line ahead. Arce's survivors must have been with them because it looked to be far more than six hundred soldiers heading our way.

Assessing our assets after returning from Colonel Diaz, I counted our rifles; the Colt machine gun; *Osprey*'s two six-pounders for the next twenty-one minutes, before the ebb tide got too low; and *Kestrel*'s bow six-pounder for the left side of the cane field. The main defense line consisted of a few dozen sailors and volunteers, half of whom were already wounded in some way. Everything we had wasn't enough to stop, or even slow, the Spanish. We would be overwhelmed within minutes—if we did what the enemy expected.

I had absolutely no intention of doing what Colonel Diaz expected.

First, I brought all hands up to date on the situation. Against Rork's opinion, I explained my relationship with Cano and Maura. I didn't want false rumors degrading our morale. Then I made sure everyone knew Colonel Diaz's declared fate for us. This revelation proved to be quite the rejuvenator for my exhausted men. Nothing motivates quite like fear.

Finally, I explained my new plan, and the fact they had only fifteen minutes to prepare for it. Deception was everything. The Spanish must believe they were winning, pushing us backward, and we were trapped in the town, but not being fully aware of our true strength ashore or afloat.

Our first deception consisted of the figures in navy uniforms standing by the doorways or windows of the shacks. They were straw men, with a board delicately balanced inside them which would keel over when a bullet hit. Thus, the Spanish sharpshooters in the mangroves would see every one of their first shots of the final assault knock down a despised *yanqui* sailor.

The straw men were reinforced by dead men—the enemy dead—in U.S. uniforms. These were also propped up as if defending a position, and also strewn about as if casualties of the Spanish assault.

Simultaneously, it was important the enemy lose some men to our defending fire, so our sharpshooters were in concealed positions scattered throughout the town. The sailors assigned to this duty had a clear route of escape to a ship's boat waiting to take them to the closest American vessel when it came time to run. Our snipers at the edge of town began firing at the Spanish sharpshooters in the mangroves, also sending rounds down the road toward the advancing regiment.

The Colt gun was kept on its cart and stationed near the burial ground of the Spanish sailors. It would fire down the road until the last moment, then be spiked. The crew would run to *Kestrel.*

The retreat phase of the plan was simple. Time would tell if the enemy would allow the second phase to be enacted.

Within five minutes the Spanish regiment was past the cane field, taking some casualties from our Colt gun and snipers, but not enough to slow the advance. The Spanish riflemen on the mangrove flanks weren't moving forward either, which told me they didn't know we'd evacuated our flanks.

A lull came in the firing. Spanish bugles rang out, echoing the call to charge.

The entire mass of light blue lifted up from the kneeling position and ran toward us. I could hear in their battle cries they wanted revenge. It was an unstoppable rage, the Spanish officers urging it on. Their furious momentum would take them deep into the town before wiser heads, which did not include Juan Maura, would question their good luck.

By the time the Spanish arrived at our former defense line, I had most of the sailors and volunteers aboard *Kestrel.* She was no longer moored to the pier, merely sitting alongside, with full steam up and ready to go astern and away from the various buildings which blocked her guns. On the other side of the town's peninsula, *Osprey* had backed away from the shoals and was in deep water well off Punta Barlovento, at the mouth of the river. That gave her a clear range of fire at the entire town. *Falcon* had steamed across the bay from Maravillas to a location just off Punta Sotavento, the extremity of the town's peninsula.

The three small yachts-turned-gunboats were now in position to systematically rake the town with point-blank gunfire from three sides. All we needed were the targets, and those would soon be supplied by the seemingly triumphant Spanish regiment.

Concurrently with the other evolutions, *Norden* and *Harrier* moved with minimum smoke toward the eastern side of the bay, near a winding narrow channel, Pasa Boca del Serón, between mangrove islands. *Harrier* would lead the squadron's escape out the channel when the time came.

In a gamble, I'd left no ships guarding the main channel entrance at Maravillas. Our route of escape was to the east, where the mystery cruiser lurked offshore. I was betting on surprise, and that the enemy would think we'd escape to the west, the side closest to Key West.

The Spanish Army was behaving as I hoped. But would the Spanish Navy?

62

Carpe Diem

Isabela, Cuba
High noon, Saturday
30 April 1898

The Spanish assault quickly passed our defense line from the day before, and drove deep into the town. *Kestrel* had just embarked our last men and even managed to retrieve the Colt gun, which was manhandled aboard.

As Diaz promised, I saw Captain Juan Maura leading the Spanish regiment, and the few men who were dropped along the way by our sharpshooters didn't dampen his élan. From my vantage point, I'd watched him coming, leading from out in front of his men, sensibly holding a revolver instead of a sword. He was doing well, watching his flanks, the unit behind, keeping his men moving and spread apart. Juanito kept leading his troops north through the town, but changed over to a parallel alley that ended at the side street by the wharf.

Of course, I shouldn't have been ashore. I should have been on *Kestrel*'s bridge with Southby. But I wasn't. I was right there at the end corner of the alleyway, with Rork and Woodgerd beside me. Cano wanted to come too, but I forbade it—his leg wound precluded the necessary agility.

Any military or naval officer reading this knows I violated every precept of command and every dictum of logic as I stood there. But I will admit that right then, I wasn't thinking like a professional. I was thinking of my Maria, and feared what the loss of her remaining son would do to her. I had to try, against all odds and sense, to prevent that.

I heard the sound of my stepson's approach. Fortunately, he was still in front of his men, issuing an order as he rounded the corner. I rammed the butt of my shotgun into his face, propelling his flailing body backward into the waiting arms of Rork, who had leaned out a doorway.

Rork slung him over a shoulder while I fired five double-ought buckshot shells in rapid order at the other soldiers in the alleyway, sending forty-five separate .33 caliber rounds into them. Most dropped. The rest took cover. Woodgerd covered the other direction, but the Spanish hadn't gotten there yet.

Then the three of us ran to the ship, which was already moving slowly astern, Southby being under strict orders not to wait if things went wrong. Sailors cheered us on as we leaped, including Rork and his burden, over the growing gap between wharf and ship. All of us miraculously made it, and fell onto the main deck. I raced up the ladder to the bridge, where Southby was directing gunfire into the Spanish charging up the wharf toward us.

The Colt machine gun had been reset upon its portside main deck pedestal mount just in time, and unleashed its mechanical hail of lead into the enemy. Within the next sixty seconds, four hundred rounds had swept the wharf of enemy soldiers. Now free from the blocking structures, the bow gun was already firing a dozen rounds of grapeshot into the town, the stern gun doing likewise into the shore line to starboard.

From the other side of the peninsula, *Osprey* fired high explosive into the main road at the edges of town, where I could see regimental banners flying. Colonel Diaz's headquarters staff was already entering Isabela, but much of the place was alight, ignited by the bombardment. The thatch homes burned in seconds, churning up thick black smoke, carried away inland on the growing sea breeze. Whereas Isabela was dismal when we first arrived, now the scene was chaos.

"What's the situation at Maravillas?" I breathlessly asked Southby.

"*Falcon* just signaled, sir. Those Spanish gunboats are entering the channel."

"Signal *Falcon* and *Harrier* to engage them. Let's get *Kestrel* around the town and heading east."

A signalman I recognized from our land defenses rushed to the portside bridge wing and began clicking out the message on the signal lamp.

Southby pointed inland. "I can't tell in all this noise, sir. Is that gunfire from down the road? Maybe the Cuban attack?"

I couldn't tell either. The time was twelve twenty-one. If it was the Cuban Liberation Army under General Lacret, they were attacking early. Who else could it be?

As *Kestrel* backed to starboard, the starboard Colt gun began sweeping the shacks to stop the enemy from firing at us. Then the six-pounders joined in, blasting the cane warehouse apart.

Rork arrived on the bridge and shouted in my ear he'd left Maura unconscious in a chair and manacled to the bulkhead in my cabin. Rork's medical evaluation was a broken nose, and maybe some cracked teeth, but the prognosis was my stepson would live.

I walked out onto the starboard bridge and pointed south. "Rork, is that the Cuban artillery I'm hearing down the road?"

Rork cocked his head to listen. "Aye, sir. That's one o' those beautiful Brit twelve-pounder field pieces. Barida an' his Limey guns are attackin' the Spaniardos' rear!"

"Well, I'll be damned. They actually did it,"declared Woodgerd, who'd just walked in.

"They did, indeed, Michael," I replied. "They probably captured the enemy's cache of supplies without much opposition.

Diaz had all his troops facing us. But now he's trapped and our job is done. Captain Southby, it's time to leave Cuba."

"Aye, aye, sir," Southby rejoined. "Helmsman, make your course zero-four-zero degrees, with revolutions for fifteen knots. Standby for rapid helm orders."

"Signal from *Falcon*, sir," interrupted the signalman from the port bridge wing. "Two enemy gunboats attacking. Am engaging enemy gunboat targets number one and two."

Every man on the bridge looked northeast toward *Falcon*. She had altered course to bring all her guns to fire. Out in the gap between Cayo de la Cruz and Cayo Maravillas, two vessels were steaming abreast with foaming white bow waves, heading right for us, their forward guns winking.

Why are only two of the three Spanish gunboats attacking? I asked myself, then got the answer when the signalman announced another message coming in.

"*Falcon* reports enemy gunboat number three entering bay to the northwest at Pasa Boca Ciega, west of Cayo de la Cruz. Moving at ten knots toward *Kestrel*."

It was a flank attack. Using my binoculars, I saw the third gunboat emerge from the shallow passage between behind Cayo de la Cruz. All three Spanish gunboats were converging on us at full speed.

"Captain Southby, signal all ships. *Kestrel* will engage enemy gunboat number three. *Falcon* and *Harrier* will engage gunboats number one and two. *Osprey* will continue bombardment of town."

The squadron acknowledged and each ship began firing on their designated targets. The Spanish gunboats near Maravillas concentrated their fire mainly on *Falcon*, which was surrounded by fountains of rapid-fired near misses. One of *Falcon*'s rounds hit the right hand gunboat, fragments and smoke blasting up from her small bridge

The signalman had another message. "*Harrier* reports unknown cruiser now over northern horizon."

"Time for the squadron to make a run for it, sir?" asked Southby.

"*Carpe diem*, James. Signal *Norden* to head out to sea at full steam and head northwest to Cay Sal Bank, thence to Key West. Signal all other ships to continue firing on enemy gunboats while following *Norden* out through the eastern passage."

"*Carpe diem* it is, sir," Southby replied in a jovial tone and gave orders for *Kestrel*'s new course as the signalman sent the message out.

Even though the enemy gunboats were firing at us, they were already astern and unable to catch up. The officers and men around me remained focused on them, but relief the cruiser had departed was plain to see on their faces.

For the first time since leaving Congo Town in the Bahamas, I felt hopeful. Soon, we'd be out of Cuba.

63

Skewered

Isabela, Cuba
Saturday
30 April 1898

The third enemy gunboat fared better than the first two. They were shot up by *Falcon*, *Kestrel*, and *Harrier* as they made their attack. Halfway across the bay, their battle damage slowed them down, black smoke flowing out of their hulls. The one on the right began listing heavily to port, then veered in a circle to the east and north, steam and smoke spewing out. Her companion followed suit as they both retired toward Maravillas. I ordered our ships to cease fire to conserve ammunition.

Rork left the bridge to check on Maura. Southby went out on the starboard bridge deck to survey the situation in Isabela and the enemy astern of us. I stayed inside the bridge, reexamining our escape route on the chart.

The third gunboat astern had a smart commander. Ducking his vessel behind Cayo Paloma in the middle of the bay, he thereby escaped our gunfire for most of their approach. By the time she emerged from behind the island, the gunboat was only a mile away. Her forty-two-millimeter bow gun fired continuously, precisely at the same time we had to stop our six-pounders from further firing due to overheated barrels. We were at least five knots faster than the gunboat and she had no hope of catching us, but for the next several minutes we were still within range of her main gun.

Our port side Colt machine gun started in on her, but not before she landed some rounds on our stern, causing some damage. Luckily, it was nothing crippling to our rudder, my main worry at that point. Then came the final Spanish shot fired at us. It turned out to be one of those quirks of chance.

Skidding along the boat deck aft of the bridge, it deflected upward off a ringbolt, and slammed into the outside of the bridge's after-bulkhead, right where I was standing. I'd left the chart table and was looking aft out the large porthole, estimating the rate of comparative speed between the gunboat and ourselves. The round hit six inches below the opening.

Since we were built like a yacht, not a proper warship, the bulkhead was mahogany, not steel. That meant a one foot-wide section of the bulkhead exploded into a hundred barbed splinters which fusilladed across the inside of the bridge. Four men were impaled.

Nine of the biggest damned splinters managed to skewer right into me.

The force of the blast spun me around and sent me into the helmsman, my body fortunately shielding him from injury, before doubling over and falling to the deck. I felt something huge speared into my left cheek. For a second it didn't hurt. Several inches long, the nasty devil went in just below my eye. There were others, from my knees to my chest, but that thing in my face dominated my attention. Then everything started to hurt, a searing pain so strong it took my breath. I clenched my guts to try and block it.

Southby got to me first. What with the blood and mess covering my face, his anguished question was understandable. "Are you alive?"

"Yes," I replied with effort. It's hard to talk with a hunk of wood sticking through your face. "Tend the ship and squadron, James."

He ignored my command and tried to lift me. "We'll get you below."

This perturbed me greatly, and I gasped, "Get back to work. Now!"

Rork, Mack, and Woodgerd were my next companions, followed shortly after by Cano. They all had a horrified look on their faces.

Southby ordered, "Get him to his cabin. Clean and dress those wounds right away."

This time it was Woodgerd who did the heavy lifting, and none too gently, I might add. At any rate, the entire entourage ended up in my cabin, a motley assembly if ever there was one.

Even with all the excruciating pain and mental confusion, I noted the peculiar group which providence had assembled in my cabin. There was my longest and dearest friend, my beloved son-in-law, one of the last Negro bosuns in the navy, my rather eccentric mercenary comrade-in-arms, and my step-son-turned-prisoner of war who despised me. Thankfully, he was still passed out. None of us was in the mood to deal with *him* right then.

Rork cut away my uniform and washed away some of the gore, poking around my face and torso. His own face was firmly set in a severe pose, which did nothing for my courage.

"Can you believe it, Rork? Nailed by a lucky shot, last one fired," I said, trying to remain calm.

"Ooh, boyo, `tis only to be expected, you know," he said softly. "You been around me so long you've the bloody black luck o' the Irish followin' you. Here, lad, we've found a wee somethin' in the medical chest to take your mind off your troubles, so take a whiff o' this an' dream o' love."

I felt *Kestrel*'s hull rise to an ocean swell, then fall and rise to another, and knew we were free of Cuba. Rork nodded in confirmation. "We're goin' home, Peter."

My last sensation was a strange smelling cloth being placed over my face.

64

Heaven and the Angel

Tampa, Florida
Wednesday
4 May 1898

It was a wonderful dream—the loveliest I've ever had—and it blissfully went on without end. Time had no measure. Anxiety, pain, and anger were sensations of the past. All I felt was peace and happiness.

The dream centered on an incredibly beautiful angel dressed in white. She and I floated effortlessly in the clouds of Heaven as she attended to my every need. Close by, harps were playing while other angels sang and laughed. My angel had long black hair, shiny and soft, and seductive eyes of indigo blue. Her mirth was lyrical and clear, like a soothing song. Her touch was tender and light. No hint of ill intent or duplicity marred the ambiance. Only the purest form of peace and love filled this Heaven, and every part of my being. I wanted to live there forever.

I was reposed in a grand bed, impossibly soft and covered with silky linens. Wisps of clouds waved in the wind around us. I lay back on fluffy pillows, the fluffiest I've ever known. Our surroundings had a diaphanous light, which shed a gentle tinge on everything. It was perfect. I was perfect, my failings and flaws far in the past. I was in pure harmony with the angel and Heaven. I knew then, with absolute certainty, Heaven was real.

"Happy fifth anniversary, darling," the angel murmured, kissing me. "I love you."

I've been in Heaven for five years? Something didn't make sense. She said it again, with another kiss, this one even more intimate. The passion of her kiss and specificity of those words—fifth anniversary?—concentrated my mind. The angel crystalized into sharper focus, like a ship at sea through a long glass. She smiled at me as I caressed her welcoming face, looking deep into those indigo eyes.

"It is a miracle, Peter," she said. "You came home to me alive, and you brought my Juanito."

Juanito? Oh, Juanito Maura. My bliss ended.

Reality intruded. The wondrous light grew garishly yellow, like the glow from an electric light bulb. The dream's clouds morphed into lace curtains, swayed by a faint breeze, hot and humid, through a window. The harp music disappeared, replaced by someone banging out a minstrel song on a banjo, some ridiculous thing about an old black man named Joe. A hammer clanged raucously on metal somewhere close by, followed by the shriek of a distant steam whistle. My pillow was soaked with sweat. So was I. Everything in my body hurt. I missed Heaven, but didn't know the way back.

"What is wrong?" Maria asked me, her face confused. "Peter, what happened? You look angry."

She was sitting on the edge of the bed, wearing a white dress with a red cross on the front. "Maria? You're the angel. Where are we?"

"Tampa Bay Hotel, Peter. Don't you remember? You got here this morning. Captain Bendel brought you here from Cuba. We gave you morphine. You have been sleeping."

"This room . . ." It looked familiar, a corner room with windows on two sides.

"This room is where you proposed to me five and a half years ago, Peter. Today is the fourth day of May. It is our fifth wedding anniversary, darling."

The fog in my brain vanished. "I love you, Maria."

Tears streamed down her face. "You are my hero, Peter. Thank you for coming home, and saving Juanito and Mario. I told my son what you did for him, and what the Spanish did to his brother. Juanito has changed his feelings about you."

That was difficult to believe. "Where's Rork?"

"At sea with the navy. But Mario, Useppa, Juanito, and Michael Woodgerd are all here in Tampa. One of your young officers, Grover Yeats, is recovering in the next room.

"And I have the very best news—you are going to be a grandfather! Useppa is four months pregnant. The baby will be born in early October. She just told Mario and he is thrilled. If it is a boy, his name will be Peter, and if a girl, she will be named Linda."

It was so much to take in. "A baby . . . Linda . . ."

Visions flooded my mind of Useppa's mother holding her as a baby. Seventeen years after Linda's death, I still missed her. The emotions were almost too much for me.

Misty-eyed, Maria embraced me. "Useppa told me she wants me to be a real grandmother, not a step-grandmother. That meant so very much to me."

"You will be a perfect grandmother."

"Won't it be nice to have a baby in the family, Peter? To know the innocence and pure love of a little child again. This is God's gift to us all, when we needed it the most."

I suddenly realized her dress was the uniform of a Red Cross nurse. "You're a nurse?"

She blushed. "I came here only to organize the hospital, but they asked me to help with the patients because we are so short of real nurses. But don't try to speak any more, darling. Let the drug work. You need to rest and heal. We can talk tomorrow."

One question filled my mind. *Why was Rork back at sea already?*

She caressed my face. "Go to sleep."

Then everything faded.

65

Family

Tampa, Florida
Friday morning
6 May 1898

At breakfast two days later, Maria sat beside me in bed, sharing stories of dealing with local ineptitude and army bureaucracy while setting up the Red Cross hospital in Tampa. She was getting to the part about the medicinal spirits when we were interrupted by a commotion out in the hallway. Two women were arguing over something, which I quickly realized was me.

A gentle black voice said, "The gentleman's resting, ma'am. Maybe you can come later."

The reply was an indignant command. "Stand aside this instant—I'm his *daughter!*"

Useppa rushed in the room and embraced me. *"Daddy! Oh Daddy* . . . I was so scared for you both! Thank you for saving my husband. Maria said she told you our splendid news."

"She did and I am thrilled, dear."

Her husband limped into the room. Mario grabbed and held my hand. "Peter, it is good to see you doing better. I have a lot to report to you."

"So I've heard. Congratulations on becoming a father, Mario."

"And to you on being a grandfather. Remember our conversation about that? You gave me an order, as I recall."

"I'm glad you followed the order! Now, tell me how is your leg healing? You'll need both sticks working to keep up with your new child."

"The wound is through and through, without infection. I should be dancing with Useppa in a month. Though I fear my military career is over for a while."

"Thank you, God!" blurted out Useppa as she hugged him.

I knew my son-in-law would have the answer to the question nagging my mind. I'd asked Maria again that morning, but her reply was vague and she quickly changed the subject.

"Mario, where exactly is Rork? He *did* make it back, didn't he?"

He hesitated, glancing at his wife and mother-in-law. "Yes, he did—undamaged. Sean's plan was to stay in the room Maria got him here at the hotel for a couple days while you recovered. Then he was going to take a week of leave and see his fiancé Minnie down at Patricio Island. You remember they were planning to be married this August.

"Well, when I went to the post office to get my mail, I saw that your mail and his mail had been sitting in general delivery, so I picked them up. Sean only had one letter, postmarked two months ago. Later, I wished I had not delivered it to him."

"Minnie, the fiancé . . ." I guessed the rest, and its effect on Rork.

"Yes, sir. Minnie explained the engagement was off. She met a man in Fort Myers back in February, and they were getting married in April. She wrote that the life of a common sailor's bride was not for her, when she had a better offer. It was cruel."

I'd had a feeling this would be the outcome. Rork was old and lonely, and desperately wanted what I had with Maria, but his intended wasn't the same as Maria.

"What did he do?" I asked.

"Evidently, right after he read her letter, Sean quietly left the hotel without a word to anyone, including us, and got on the Plant Line steamer to Key West, presumably to rejoin the fleet. We didn't even know he was gone, or what had happened, until he was missing from dinner. I went to his room and found her letter to him, along with this note for you."

I recognized Rork's large looping cursive. Though it was written in self-taught proper English, I could hear him saying the words in his distinctive Wexford brogue.

Tampa Bay Hotel, 4 May 1898

Dear Peter,

You made it home, old salt, so enjoy every minute with dear Maria and the family. Happy fifth anniversary, you lucky dog. No such fair wind and tide for me—Uncle Sam is calling. Times are tough, but it's good to know us ancient main deck tars are still wanted by somebody.

Don't dare forget, you owe me a decent drink for my surgery job, payable on my return. Used a sailmaker's broad seam stitch on that ugly mug of yours—not the prettiest stitch, but it can take the strain of a storm wind, just like you.

You did good work in Cuba, my dear friend. All our lads lived because of your decisions.

Always remember that.

Sean

Everyone watched my reaction, so I presented a positive one. "It's better Sean's back at sea, even if it is in a war. The worst thing is for him to brood alone at home."

I turned to Mario. "Now, please brief me about the squadron."

Mario reverted to his military role, presenting the facts concisely. "The squadron sank one of the attacking Spanish gunboats, badly damaged another. The one that got you escaped from us. All your ships got out of the bay through the narrow passage between the islands to the east. By the way, the cruiser that worried everyone turned out to be a neutral German, the *Gneisenau*. They've got four warships at Cuba now under Commodore Thiele, and they are openly pro-Spanish. They're watching the Americans closely and probably sharing the information to the Spanish, according to Captain Bendel."

"I know Thiele, a very competent naval officer. And what of your fellow prisoner, the notorious Colonel Zaldivar? What happened to him?"

"When I was exchanged, he was being taken to Havana as a prisoner. I could tell the Spanish loathed him as much as his own men did."

"Yes, well that's not surprising. Nobody likes a shyster, especially one who bolts when it gets tough. Exactly how did we end up here in Tampa? There's a naval hospital at Key West."

"Captain Southby took the squadron for more coal and then went on blockade duty. Captain Bendel brought you, Juan Maura, me, and two of the wounded sailors to Key West in *Norden.* When he went ashore and saw the naval hospital was run down and overcrowded, he said he was not putting us in such a place. On his own, he steamed directly here, for the new hospital recently set up in tents. That was where we saw Maria. She immediately got rooms for you, Yeats, and the two wounded sailors, right here at the hotel—much better than any hospital tent. Thank you, again, Maria"

Maria took that moment to ask our leave, explaining she was needed at the hospital. As Useppa walked her out, I asked my son-in-law about the outcome at Isabela.

"Not certain of the very end, sir, but Lacret's Cubans attacked the Spanish forces from the rear, using Barida's new guns to maximum effect. Combined with our bombardment, they were trapped. Last thing I saw was Spanish soldiers trying to get out, but Lacret's forces had reached the edge of town.

"It looked like a solid victory to me at the time. Once we got here, I sent a full report to my friend Horatio Rubens with the exile government in New York. He cabled me this morning that the Republic of Cuba greatly appreciates your sacrifice and victory. You are quite the hero to them, Peter. Oh, and I heard Lacret wants to thank you himself. He may be heading here on some other matters. Not sure yet."

He rubbed his chin. "Here comes the curious part of all this. I checked and found there has been no coverage of the battle in any newspaper, either in the United States or Cuba. None. I find that very odd, don't you?"

I didn't. But my reply was cut short by the arrival of Woodgerd, who marched into the room and plopped into a chair. His face was contorted with anger. Without preamble, he nodded to Mario and launched into a tirade.

"Ha! Those lily-livered bastards won't print it because your defense was *too* effective!" "My idiotic editor thought the fougasse and bomb blast would repulse readers as *un-gentlemanly*. Too nauseating—might make people sick at the breakfast table. As if war is supposed to be a pretty parade where nobody gets hurt? He said the Spanish papers won't print anything about it either, because they lost the battle. That puffed up poser said if any U.S. press does print it, the Spanish will accuse us of barbaric war crimes at Isabela. The fool actually wrote all that to me in a telegram this morning. Want to see it?"

I shook my head and he returned to his diatribe. "Can you believe this crap? We were outnumbered ten to one, and they want our defenses to be *fair*? That's it, boys. I'm through with this press silliness. Just sent a cable back that I quit and Hearst should get his own dainty ass out of the cocktail parties at Newport and down there in the gawdforsaken Cuban jungle to write the next story."

There was no stopping Woodgerd at this point, so I let him continue blowing off his considerable head of steam. "Fellas, the victory at Isabela will be unknown, because we mustn't offend the squeamish stomachs of the weak-kneed sonsabitches in the New

York press. Those slimy toads would much rather have a heroic American defeat fought in a *gentlemanly* manner."

"What about Washington?" asked Mario, not knowing Woodgerd's hatred for the place.

"The army and navy brass in Washington are no damn better! The official comment is there was a skirmish at Isabela, nothing more, even though they damn well know the real story. Those armchair slugs are the very same ones who eight years ago called Wounded Knee a noble victory after one of their own killed three hundred Lakota women and children. Hell, they promoted the officer in charge of that outrage to *general.* The two-faced bastards have no shame. Never did."

Temporarily out of breath, Woodgerd scowled out the window. I felt exhausted by the effort of merely listening. The room's sinking morale wasn't improved when Grover Yeats arrived right then, in a wheelchair pushed by a porter.

It was heartbreaking. He was in uniform, his head completely swathed in thick bandages, grotesquely appearing to be almost twice as big. There were holes for his eyes, ears, nostrils, and mouth. Mario and Woodgerd gave him subdued hellos. My sentiments at seeing him were so distraught, I couldn't speak.

"Morning, sir," came from mouth hole. "Looks like we both got hit in the same place."

The muffled words came out slow and slurred. His face wound far more destructive than mine, I realized. His morphine doses must have been much heavier. I thought of my own young son, Sean, in *Oregon* heading around the Horn for the war in Cuba. He and Yeats had been classmates at Annapolis.

"Yes, we did, Grover, but we'll make it. Your innovation saved the lives of a lot of our men that day. Thank you."

"Petty officers did the hard work, sir. I put that in my report and hope they get recognized for it."

"They will, Grover. How are you doing now?" I asked. "Is there anything we can get for you, son."

"No, sir, there's nothing anybody can do. I'm going home," Yeats answered. There was no tinge of anger or sarcasm in his tone, just a simple acceptance. "My naval career is over. Lost part of my lower left jaw and inner ear. The army doctor told me this morning it can't be fixed."

"Your family is in Iowa, right?" I inquired, trying to find something positive to say.

"Yes, sir. Ida Grove, Iowa. I'll head back there and try farming. The corn won't care what I look like. I've got to go now, sir. They have to change the bandage. It takes a while."

"Grover, promise me you'll let me know if I can help in any way. Understood?"

"Aye, aye, sir," he said, probably for the last time in his life, as he was wheeled out.

The three of us sat in silence for some time. After a while, Woodgerd walked over to my bed. "You made the right decisions in that battle, Peter. Second-guessing them later doesn't help."

"Yeah, you're right. But it's damned hard not to," I admitted to my friend.

Then they departed, leaving me alone with my thoughts.

66

For the Duration

Tampa, Florida
Saturday evening
4 June 1898

It'd been a month since I arrived at the Tampa Bay Hotel. The army doctors who attended my recovery expressed particular admiration for Maria's nursing skills.

My wife took the accolades in stride, saying my physical state would improve even more when we got back to our home up in Alexandria. She fully expected her hero husband to be granted a long leave at home, a "fifth anniversary honeymoon," as she called it. I knew better.

My mended physical condition was known to the naval leadership in Washington. Every experienced naval officer was needed for the growing fleet and impending actions. They wouldn't let me go home. And the truth of the matter was I wouldn't be content sitting at home while all this was going on. As much as I loved Maria, right then I needed to be with my navy.

The army didn't have many officers experienced in operating larger than brigade formations. That became apparent very early. The first regiments arrived in Tampa without plan or preparation. Chaos ruled every aspect of the military camps scattered around the city. It was getting progressively worse as more and more soldiers showed up, because no one had taken overall charge of the logistics—transport, supplies, provisions, munitions, communications, sanitation, medical support, etc.

There was, however, someone at Tampa officially in overall command.

General William Rufus Shafter, a 330-pound gentleman of sixty-three years, suffering from gout, heat rash, and headaches, was chosen to lead the army forces in the invasion of Cuba—the newly created Fifth Corps of the United States Army. Rumor had it he was chosen for this critical command for his complete lack of political ambition or intrigues, but the man's lethargy was not confined to politics. Shafter allowed events at Tampa to evolve on their own, so they evolved very badly. I became closely aware of this, for the general's headquarters were set up inside the Tampa Bay Hotel.

The army headquarters staff suffered from a complete dearth of knowledge about Tampa, Cuba, Spain, the U.S. Navy, ocean transport, and landing operations on foreign soil. Since I was the only officer there who had actually been to Cuba, I was frequently waylaid on the hotel verandah and pressed for pertinent information, opinions, and suggestions. As they shed their pride and came to increasingly rely more on me, this navy fellow, for answers, I had the disturbing feeling someone would try to make the relationship a more permanent one.

Fourteen days after the army staff officers first arrived at the hotel in mid-May, two telegrams arrived for me—one from the U.S. Navy and the other from the U.S. Army. It was a little after six o'clock on a Saturday evening. I was sitting alone on my end of the verandah, sipping a glass of very nice Bordeaux (Chateau Clerc Milon, 1892). The lovely gardens were highlighted by the lowering sun, the flowers' color bursting from the lush foliage. It was a relaxing scene, accompanied musically by a mockingbird's remarkably accurate impersonation of his feathered neighbors' songs.

This soothing entertainment allowed me to ignore the vaunted hero himself, General Shafter, at the other end of the verandah, where he pontificated truly inane comments to the equally naïve questions asked him by a herd of Hearst and Pulitzer reporters. I congratulated myself on my self-restraint—Woodgerd would've done something rash to stop the mindless noise.

I had just switched my focus to a proud little cardinal at the bird bowl when a steward delivered the Western Union envelopes. Taking another sip to calm my nerves, I naturally opened the navy's first.

XXX—TO CAPT P. WAKE—X—DOCTORS CONFIRM AND NAVY DEPARTMENT CONGRATULATES YOUR MEDICAL RECOVERY—X—AS PER SECNAV ORDER ALL HOME LEAVES FOR NAVAL PERSONNEL ARE CANCELLED FOR WAR DURATION—X—EFFECTIVE IMMEDIATELY YOU ARE PLACED ON TEMPORARY LIAISON DUTY WITH ARMY 5TH CORPS HQ AND UNDER DIRECT COMMAND OF GENERAL W. R. SHAFTER—X—THIS DUTY WILL BE UNTIL 30 JUNE 1898 OR UNTIL OTHERWISE DIRECTED BY THIS DEPARTMENT—X—EXPENSES AND SUPPORT WILL BE FURNISHED BY 5TH CORPS—X—BY C. ALLEN ASST SEC NAVY—XXX

Charles Allen was Roosevelt's replacement as assistant secretary of the navy, and a worthy man. These orders were highly unusual, though. I couldn't recall ever hearing of a navy man assigned to an army staff.

This would make Maria happy. If I couldn't go home with her, she'd think at least I would remain in Tampa. I wasn't so sure about that.

I'd heard the army corps would leave Tampa for the invasion of Cuba in mid-June. My liaison orders didn't specify any location, just the unit, and the unit was going to Cuba. The worst case scenario, which was entirely probable, would have me in the jungles of Cuba during the summer yellow fever season, tethered to Shafter's staff. It is precisely the wrong season to engage in large-scale operations in the tropics with unacclimated and untrained soldiers.

I looked over at my new commanding officer, who was struggling to get out of his rattan lounging chair, to the stifled amusement of the reporters. There was no way the man could survive in the jungle.

I opened the telegram from army headquarters in Washington.

XXX—TO CAPT. P. WAKE USN—X—NAVY DEPT ORDERS YOU TO LIAISON DUTY WITH 5TH CORPS—X—REPORT TO GEN. SHAFTER MONDAY 6 JUNE 1898—X—TRANSPORT FROM PRESENT LOCATION TO NEW DUTY STATION TO BE REIMBURSED BY USA HQ—X—BY COL. R. MILLER ACTG ASST ADJT TO SECWAR—XXX

Apparently, the army in Washington didn't know the location of the army in Tampa, yet another shining example of military efficiency. I had the whimsical idea of sending an expense voucher to Washington for transport from my end of the verandah to the other end, but thought better of it. The army has never understood dry navy humor; it's far too sophisticated.

Glancing down the verandah, I saw the reporters had disappeared inside to the bar, and General Shafter had finally loosened the chair's grip on him. He stood there, straightening his uniform, trying to regain his dignity. Other army officers on the verandah politely looked anywhere else.

I heartily wished Rork was nearby. His sense of humor was needed right then. With him alongside, I could endure the monumental insanity I knew was coming. But Rork had joined *Oregon* at Key West a week earlier, after she arrived from her epic voyage from San Francisco. He and my son Sean were already bound for the fleet off the coast of Cuba. They were where I should be.

So I sat there alone, thinking about this development while waiting for Maria to return in three hours from her shift at the hospital. The twilight was beginning to fade, and I heard the army officers speak of gathering for dinner. In a moment, one of them would walk over and invite me out of politeness, for they were a very sociable lot and thought me quaint.

Tonight I would join them, using the opportunity to subtly ascertain what would be expected of me at Fifth Corps.

67

For Honor and For Cuba

Tampa, Florida
Midnight, Saturday
4 June 1898

The clock slowly struck out the twelve chimes of midnight, startling me. I hadn't realized Maria and I were talking that long—ever since she'd come home from the hospital. It was a lovely night to stay up late in bed, sipping the last of our Matusalem rum. Outside our window, mystical rays of moonlight peeked through the live oaks, their moss waving in the warm night's land breeze. The Hillsborough River was a ribbon of silver, edged by golden lanterns along the shore. A night heron softly flapped by our window. Gardenias and jasmine lightly scented the humid air. It was enchanting.

In the midst of this romantic setting, just as my thoughts were turning amorous, Maria felt the need to discuss the war. She hated everything about it, she said. Her opinion was hardened by our sorrows and terrors of the previous five months, and by victims of the camp diseases she nursed in the hospital. She dreaded what she'd see when even more wounded began returning from Cuba.

But with a quiet display of courage, Maria also said she understood my sense of duty and that she knew I had to follow it. Especially now, when so many American and Cuban lives were at stake. She understood my hard-won knowledge of Cuba was much needed by the army leadership in Tampa to prevent those lives being wasted.

We spoke freely about the hospital, my joining the army staff in Tampa, the war dragging on inside Cuba, our hopes for the conflict's outcome. But there was one topic I did not share, for I didn't know how. It was what a staff colonel had revealed to me at dinner earlier in the evening.

The colonel had whispered, in pathetic drunken "confidentiality," that General Shafter wanted me to be the American liaison with Generals Gómez and García inside Cuba. The daunting mission was to get into Cuba quietly, find the Cuban generals, and convince the Cuban military to ensure an unopposed American invasion of the island, at a place yet undetermined.

My name had been suggested to General Shafter by two army officers, who were due to arrive soon at Tampa with their regiment. I knew both of them. Colonel Leonard Wood was commanding officer of the First Volunteer Cavalry. His new assistant regimental commander was none other than Lieutenant Colonel Theodore Roosevelt. They had insisted to Shafter that I was the only American officer, army or navy, who could accomplish that crucial mission.

Oh hell, Theodore has struck yet again, I reflected. *How will I tell Maria?*

The colonel had further informed me I would receive my orders upon reporting to General Shafter on Monday morning. My covert departure for Cuba would be soon afterward.

The inebriated staff colonel then gushed his congratulations and envy for my exciting assignment. He'd finished his sappy *sotto voce* speech to me with the ultimate in ignorant statements. "Yes, sir. We've got ourselves an honorable war to fight. Lot of folks're saying we'll get our very own empire out of it."

It had been all I could do not to gag at that point, for I'd felt sick deep inside.

As I sat there with Maria in bed and talked, I debated inwardly about how and when to tell her. I would have to tell her, but a moonlit boudoir wasn't the place. With yawns, we lay back on the pillows, two lovers intertwined. A nearby frog began his mating call, making us laugh. Our embrace tightened. The war seemed far away.

I was about to turn out the oil lamp when, suddenly, Maria propped herself up on an elbow. She wasn't smiling anymore.

"Promise me you will come home from Cuba, Peter."

"*What?* Who told you?" I stammered out, trying to deduce how she had gotten such restricted information. And if she knew, who else did?

She stopped me with a finger to my lips. "Peter, we both know you are eligible to retire right now. Though the navy pension will not be much, with my accounts we have enough money to live comfortably."

She paused, moving her delicate finger from my lips across my new scar and softly down my neck, then continued before I could say anything. "But I know you are not going to retire. Our friend Martí's dreams for the Cuban people finally have a chance to come true, and you have a need to be there to help. So you are heading back into the war. Please respect me enough not to try mollifying me with empty if's and when's and maybe's."

She was right about my belief in Martí's dreams for Cuba. My reasons for staying in the navy and going back to the war were morally deeper than fulfilling professional duty or pride. A surge of affection went through me for this remarkable woman. Her strength and compassion were awe inspiring.

I took her hand in mine. "Yes, you are right. I am going back to Cuba on a clandestine mission. And yes, Maria, you have my word—I *will* come home to you. We will love each other and grow old together while we enjoy our new grandchild."

Her serious scrutiny softened into a sweet smile. "Thank you, *mi amor*. You truly are my hero, Peter. I love you more than life itself. I think we will be extraordinary grandparents."

I turned out the lamp. Our hearts didn't need words anymore. We shared a long passionate kiss, then held each other close. Maria rested her head on my chest and soon slipped off to sleep. But no slumber came for me.

How could it be possible? I am here with what is usually only a wish or dream or thought, which keeps me sane throughout the worst of times. My Maria is by my side. I stroked her skin, breathed in her essence, and gingerly kissed her silky hair.

But now, only the reader of this could be more perplexed than I, knowing I was otherwise already back in Cuba.

Endnotes by Chapter

Chapter One—A Muffled Thud

—The Cuban fight for independence from Spain began on 10 October 1868, and went on for thirty years, until September 1898. During this time there were three hot wars (1868–1878, 1879–1880, 1895–1898) with periods of intense clandestine revolutionary activity in between. Cuba was occupied by the United States from September of 1898 until May of 1902, when she finally achieved full independence. Wake was part of this long struggle in the 1880s and 1890s.

Chapter Three—Eleven Months Earlier

The "Goat Locker" is the old sailors' term for the Chief Petty Officers berthing and mess area. The name comes from the days of sail, when livestock was kept in that area for fresh milk and meat, guarded over by the senior petty officers. The name can still be heard today on warships.

—The "Black Gang" refers to the men working down in the boiler, engine, and adjacent machinery spaces. The term isn't about their ethnicity, but about the coal dust and machinery grease in their working spaces becoming imbedded in the exposed areas of their skin, making them appear dark-skinned.

—The same call for sweepers is used in the U.S. Navy today. American warships are always cleaned every morning, one of many legacies carried on from the Royal Navy.

Chapter Four—The Last Mile

—The Brooklyn Navy Yard served the country well from 1806 until 1966, when Secretary of Defense McNamara closed it for budgetary reasons. At the time of its closing, the yard had 9,000 workers. It is now a commercial/industrial center.

—Whitney Island, where the Cob Dock was located at the south end, also had the Ordnance Dock at the north end. The island no longer exists, having been dredged away in the early 1900s and the fill being used to expand the shoreline naval docks, which do still exist.

—U.S.S. *Vermont* had a sad history. She was authorized by Congress in 1816, designed and laid down at Boston Navy Yard in 1818 as a 74-gun ship of the line, one of a very few in the U.S. Navy. Seven years later her construction was finally finished, but she stayed up on the ways until launched in 1848. Then she sat unused at dockside until commissioned into service in 1862. By that point she was far too antiquated to be good for anything other than a floating warehouse for stores and temporary barracks for sailors and Marines. For thirty-seven years, from 1864 until 1902, she sat at the Cob Dock of the Brooklyn Navy Yard, an ancient relic of a time long gone. Eighty-four years after her construction was begun, *Vermont* was sold by the Navy and towed away in April, 1902. Her final fate is unknown, but she was probably broken up for the wood, fastenings, and fittings.

Chapter Five—The Pleasure of Your Company

—"Colors" is sounded at 8 a.m., or eight bells in the morning watch, when a warship is in port. The national ensign (flag) is hoisted on the ship's stern staff. The traditional watch and bell system of the navy is simple. The ship's bell was struck every half-hour, the time it took for sand to run out of a half-hour sand glass. The bell was struck once for every half-hour of a four-hour watch that had gone by. Thus, one bell for the first half hour, two bells for the second half-hour, three bells for the third, and so on, until eight bells were struck when the watch reached four hours and was over. This went on all day, every day. From 4 p.m. to 8 p.m., the watch was divided into two equal "dog watches" (the "First" from 4 to 6 p.m., and the "Last" from 6 to 8 p.m.) so that the sailors' schedule would change each day. Why call it a "Dog Watch?" Maritime folklore says it was because the first star seen after sunset is frequently the "Dog Star"—Sirius. Bells are still heard in the U.S. Navy, though in many ships the watch system is different from the old days.

—U.S.S. *Newark* was one of the first steel-hulled cruisers in the U.S. Navy. She was commissioned in 1891, displaced 4,083 tons, was 311 feet long, armed with twelve 6-inch guns and ten secondary guns of various calibers, had a speed of 19 knots, and a compliment of 393 officers and men. She was decommissioned in March 1897 for an extensive overhaul and recommissioned in May 1898 to serve in the Spanish-American War. She also served in the 1899 Philippine-American War, and the 1900 Boxer Rebellion in China. After 1906, she served as an auxiliary vessel at the New York Naval Militia, Guantanamo Bay Naval Station, and Norfolk Naval Station. In World War One, she was a hospital ship at Newport Naval Station. *Newark* was sold in 1926 and broken up for scrap.

—Pierre Loti was the famous *nom de plume* of Julien Viaud (1850–1923), a French career naval officer and novelist. Loti and Wake became lifelong friends at the 1883 Battle of Hue, in Vietnam, when the French Navy attacked and defeated the forces of the emperor. Read about it in *The Honored Dead.*

—Useppa Wake Cano (born in 1865 at Useppa Island, Florida) lived at Tampa in 1897 with her Cuban attorney husband, Mario Cano. In addition to his legal career, Cano was in the Cuban Revolutionary Party and a confidant of the late José Martí (1853–1895), the famous Cuban writer and orator, and Wake's dear friend. For more about Cano, Martí, and Useppa, read *The Assassin's Honor.*

—Wake met Theodore Roosevelt (1858–1919) at a society dinner at New York in January 1886. He was not impressed with the brash young man, but over the ensuing years they became close friends. Wake is twenty-one years older than Roosevelt, and a mentor figure for him. For more about their meeting and friendship, read *The Darkest Shade of Honor.*

Chapter Six—Survival of the Fittest

—Theodore Roosevelt built his beautiful 22-room home, Sagamore Hill, in 1886, and lived there until his death in January 1919. The home is named for the Algonquin word for "Chieftain," and located at Cove Neck, near Oyster Bay on western Long Island. Wake was a frequent visitor in the 1890s and early 1900s. Roosevelt's presidential museum is on the grounds, and the entire site is a national park. For more details, go to: *http://www.nps.gov/sahi/index.htm*

—Wake's depiction of Roosevelt's speaking style tried to capture the intensity, both aural and visual, of the man, which never failed to impress an audience. To hear a recording of Theodore Roosevelt, go to the website of the fascinating G. Robert Vincent Voice Library of the University of Michigan.

—The man Parker to which Roosevelt refers is Andrew Parker, a fellow member of the New York City Police Commission, with whom Roosevelt had a long-standing and ever-worsening feud.

—Roosevelt wanted to be the actual Secretary of the Navy, but McKinley was averse to giving him that much power, fearful of his bellicose ideas and manners. After much political influence on Roosevelt's behalf over several months, McKinley yielded and made Roosevelt Assistant Secretary of the Navy. Roosevelt's political enemies in New York City were glad to be rid of him—little did they know he would return in two years as their state's governor, and president of the United States a year later!

—John Davis Long (1838–1915) was a respected lawyer, academic, supporter of women's rights, governor of Massachusetts, and civic leader who became Secretary of the

Navy despite his lack of knowledge or interest in naval affairs. Like Roosevelt and Wake, Long lost his first wife in the 1880s and later remarried. Long and Roosevelt had different political views and personal temperaments. Roosevelt liked the man, but didn't respect Long's continued ignorance about the important position he filled, or his apparent hypochondria.

Chapter Seven—L'Avenir Déjà Vu

—William McKinley (1843–1901) served as an officer in the 23rd Ohio Infantry Regiment and was in several horrific battles. He despised men who spoke casually of war.

Chapter Eight—The Island

—Patricio Island is northeast of Useppa Island, and west of Pine Island, in Pine Island Sound, on Florida's lower Gulf Coast. In 1908, President Theodore Roosevelt designated it, and several other islands in the area, as part of a national wildlife refuge. Today there are 38 islands in the refuge. The old settlers' rain-water cistern still remains on the shell ridge, among the gumbo limbo, sabal palm, and strangler fig trees. Landing on the island is restricted.

Chapter Nine—Back into the Fray

—The State, War, and Navy Building, built in the 1870s and 1880s, is now designated as the Eisenhower Executive Office Building (EEOB). The offices of the three Cabinet departments have long been taken over by the White House staff. In the 1980s, several of the important offices and public rooms in the building were renovated to their beautiful original style. The original Secretary of the Navy's office is now the ceremonial office of the Vice-President of the United States. Wake would recognize quite a lot in the building today.

—The story of Ida Saxton McKinley (1847–1907) is a sad one. She never recovered from the death of her children, and her epilepsy became more debilitating as the years went on, with seizures sometimes occurring in public. The treatment was laudanum and other sedatives, which further complicated her life. William McKinley was absolutely devoted to her, and even the cynics in Washington understood the depth of their mutual love. After her husband was assassinated in 1901, Ida's depression grew worse, and her younger sister had to take care of her. Ida visited her husband's grave every day until her death six years later.

Chapter Ten—Cuba's Pain

—General Máximo Gómez (1836–1905) was born in the Dominican Republic, served in the Spanish Army, and eventually joined the Cuban Revolution in 1868. Over the next thirty years, he rose in rank to supreme commander-in-chief of the Cuban Liberation Army. He was wounded twice, the first a bullet through the neck, which left an open hole he frequently covered with a bandana or plugged with cotton. Gómez was a soldier's soldier and disdained politics, turning down the presidency after the war. He is a national hero of the country.

Chapter Eleven—El Consorcio de Azúcar

—The *Cuerpo Militar de Orden Publico* was a uniformed Spanish police regiment centered in Havana, and well known to history. There is no record of Wake's perennial nemesis, Colonel Isidro Marrón, or his secret "Special Section" of the regiment. For more about Wake's previous encounters with Marrón, read *The Darkest Shade of Honor, Honor Bound,* and *Honorable Lies.*

Chapter Seventeen—Too Much Fun

—Wake first came in contact with the Jesuits in 1874 at Sevilla, Spain, when they saved his life. Ever since, it had been a mutually beneficial relationship. For more detail about Wake and the Jesuits, read *An Affair of Honor, A Different Kind of Honor, The Darkest Shade of Honor, The Honored Dead,* and *Honorable Lies.*

Chapter Eighteen—Blue Mold and Black Shank

—Blue mold and black shank are serious tobacco leaf diseases which can quickly spread and devastate a regional crop. They are tightly monitored today in North Carolina.

—Corojo leaf is primarily used as the wrapper for cigars.

Chapter Nineteen—A Little Complication

—The Olayita Massacre was in February, 1896. The perpetrators were never brought to justice.

Chapter Twenty-One—Searching for Goatsuckers

—For more about how Rork lost his left hand in Vietnam, read *The Honored Dead.*

—The folklore that the Cuban nightjar (AKA: Antillean goat-sucker) bird sucks milk from a goat has never been proven, but it still widely believed in the Caribbean.

Chapter Twenty-Two—City of Shadows

—Charles Sigsbee (1845–1923) was a well-respected officer in the U.S. Navy for forty-five years (1862–1907) and famous for his oceanographic work. The Sigsbee Deep, the lowest point (12,000 feet) in the Gulf of Mexico is named in his honor, as is Sigsbee Park Island, a naval housing area in Key West.

Chapter Twenty-Four—Love in a Linen Closet

—The Havana Yacht Club was founded in 1886. In the twentieth century, it was very active and hosted the renowned St. Petersburg to Havana sailing race for 25 years. After Castro came to power in 1959, it went defunct. This breakfast was one of the last social events ashore Sigsbee attended before his ship was destroyed.

—Fitzhugh Lee (1835–1905) and later-President William McKinley faced each other at many Civil War battles. During the Spanish-American War, he was one of three former Confederate generals who were made volunteer U.S. Army major generals (along with Joe Wheeler and Thomas Rosser). Lee did not see combat, but during the occupation afterward, he was military governor of Havana and the province of Pinar del Rio.

Chapter Twenty-Six—Numbers

—Though seemingly archaic and simplistic, the code system used by Roosevelt and Wake was standard espionage tradecraft in the 1890s. Within a decade, it got far more complex.

Chapter Twenty-Seven—The Invisible Functionary

—To this day, communication techs and clerical personnel are favorite targets for recruitment among international intelligence agencies. The most sophisticated cybersecurity system can always be betrayed by a disgruntled private, as recent headlines have shown.

—Castillo de Farnes still exists and is a nice little restaurant, one of my favorites in Old Havana.

—Matusalem is Wake's favorite sipping rum. It is still available. Visit: *www.matusalem.com*

Chapter Twenty-Eight—A Diplomatic Bombshell

—Don Enrique Dupuy de Lôme (1851–1904) was a successful career Spanish diplomat from Valencia. He served as Envoy Extraordinary and Minister Plenipotentiary to the United States from May 1895 until February 1898, when he resigned following the exposé of his letter.

—The two petty officers who tried to save Ensign Breckenridge, Gunner's Mate Third Class John Everett (1873–1956) and Ship's Cook First Class Daniel Atkins (1866–1923), both received the Medal of Honor. In those days, it was awarded for peacetime heroism also. By February of 1898, Atkins was the thirteenth African-American sailor to receive the Medal of Honor.

Chapter Thirty-One—Jupiter's Thunderbolt

—To me, the Fortaleza de San Carlos de la Cabaña, commonly known in English as Cabaña Fortress, is a disturbing place to visit. Its history of terror and extra-judicial or quasi-judicial executions extended from the 1860s into the 1960s. Most of the victims were political enemies of the regime in power at the time.

Chapter Thirty-Three—Just Lollygagging Around

—The "muffled thud" was an important clue. Several investigations over the past forty years have shown the cause of *Maine's* explosion was probably spontaneous combustion in the forward coal bunker—hence the muffled thud—which immediately set off the ammunition magazine next to it, making a catastrophic blast which killed 266 of the ship's 374 officers and men.

—The official explanation of the Communist regime in Cuba is that the U.S. government blew up its own ship to have an excuse to join the war against Spain, which the Cubans had been fighting for years and were already winning. In this way the U.S. could dominate Cuba's future.

Chapter Thirty-Five—Without Explanation or Dignity

—The Cuban crocodile (*Crocodylus rhombifer*) is regarded as the most aggressive crocodile in the Western Hemisphere and the most intelligent in the world. With males growing only to eleven feet, it is not as large as its cousins in Florida, but is far more dangerous. Once widespread in Cuba, its habitat is now only in the Zapata Swamp and the Isle of Youth of Cuba's southern coast. There is a small colony at Gatorland in central Florida, where pack hunting behavior has been observed.

Chapter Thirty-Six—Mightily Envied

—The U.S. Navy, desperate for ships to form the blockade and for other needs, took in 38 yachts in 1898, converting them into commissioned warships. Many stayed in the Navy after the Spanish-American War, and several became famous, serving for decades. I do a lecture on this fascinating subject entitled "*Yachts that Went to War.*"

Chapter Thirty-Eight—Outwitting the Parasites

—Irish-American inventor John Holland (1841–1914) tried to get the U.S. Navy to use his submarine designs several times in the 1880s and 1890s. In 1900, they finally commissioned U.S.S. *Holland*, the first true fully submersible American submarine. Holland's production company eventually became the well-known Electric Boat Company.

—Samuel Langley (1835–1906) was a brilliant engineer and pioneer of early aviation, but never got the U.S. government to use his inventions. Many of his colleagues used his work as a foundation of their own, and in 1911 one of them, Eugene Ely (1886–1911), was the first aviator to successfully fly off an American warship, U.S.S. *Pennsylvania*. The first U.S. aircraft carrier was named *Langley*, serving in that capacity from 1922–1936.

Chapter Thirty-Nine—The Squadron

—Wake's squadron wasn't the last to know Congo Town. The U.S. Navy has had a presence on the coast of Andros Island since the 1960s. There are several installations up and down the coast belonging to the Atlantic Undersea Test and Evaluation Center (AUTEC). They do classified work on the surface and in the depths of the Tongue of the Ocean.

Chapter Forty-One—Blossom Channel

—This channel, named for H.M.S. *Blossom*, is the deepest of the half-dozen which lead through the maze of reefs at the southern end of the Tongue of the Ocean. Never transit this dangerous area unless the weather and sun conditions are suitable for "eyeball navigation," and even then try to obtain some local knowledge.

Chapter Forty-Three—Briefing "The Liberators"

—There are no records anywhere of anyone named Ruben Ramon Armando Zaldivar de Aviles y Vega, or of a unit titled Batallón Nacional Orgullo de Cuba. I think Wake fictionalized the name and title.

Chapter Forty-Six—Assuming the Worst

—A Quaker mine is a version of the sailor's old ruse known as a Quaker gun, a wooden replica meant to represent a real cannon to deter an enemy. It cannot be used to hurt anyone, hence the name.

—*Fougasse* is a centuries old defensive technique using explosives or flammables. In World War I and World War II, fougasse was refined by the British military as a tactic to help defend Britain from invasion. Flame throwers evolved from that effort. The term fougasse is still used for such devices. Modern napalm is an aerial version of fougasse.

—Caltrops have been used against infantry and cavalry since Alexander the Great in Persia. The word comes from the Latin *calcitrapa,* "foot-trap." In ancient times, camels were the most susceptible, due to their soft feet, but even war elephants could be stopped by caltrops. In their spike strip form, they are widely used today by law enforcement to deflate the tires of recklessly driving criminals.

—*Cheval de Frise* means "Frisian horse" in French and comes from a coastal area of Holland that used the devices to strengthen their defensive works. Benjamin Franklin designed under water *chevals de frise* for the Delaware River defenses in the 1770s. It was used extensively from the 1500s until World War I, when barbed wire was proven more effective.

—*Trou de loup* is French for "wolf hole." Julius Caesar used them in 52 B.C. and they have been commonly used for defense ever since. The British Army in 19th century India used the local term "punji pits," for the type of stake along the sides which was inverted downward to hinder escape. In the Vietnam War, punji pits were used extensively against American troops.

Chapter Forty-Seven—They That Go Down to the Sea in Ships

—The 107th Psalm was written as a song of thanksgiving to God by King David around 970 B.C.

—The 38th Leon Regiment had a long and proud history. It began in 1694 as the Tercio Provincial Nuevo de León and was stationed in Pamplona, Barcelona, and León. In 1704, its title changed to the Regimiento Provincial de León, variations of which it retained. It received the numerical designation in1847. In 1895, two-thirds of the regiment, just under a thousand men, were sent to Cuba to fight the revolutionaries.

Chapter Forty-Eight—Time Dwindles

—The Navy Colt machine gun fired 400 six-millimeter rounds per minute and was used by sailors and Marines in many engagements. Onboard, it was mounted on a pedestal. Ashore, it used a tripod. The army still used the much heavier Gatling gun. The exception was Theodore Roosevelt's 1st Volunteer Cavalry, which bought two seven-millimeter Colt machine guns with their own money and used them at the Battle of San Juan Hill.

Chapter Fifty-One—Let the Games Begin

—Colonel Michael Woodgerd and Wake first met in 1874 at an Italian train station, after Woodgerd killed a man for abusing a stray dog. They remained friends ever since. Read *An Affair of Honor* to learn why Woodgerd left the army, and *Honor Bound* for how he saved Wake's life at Haiti in 1888.

Chapter Fifty-Three—The Confession

—The prefix "Don" would have been a powerful incentive to the laborers recruited into Zaldivar's battalion. It is still considered an honor in the Spanish-speaking world. The female counterpart to it is "Doña."

Chapter Fifty-Six—The Main Performance

—The Lee rifle used by the U.S. Navy in the Spanish-American War was an 1895 Model six-millimeter (.236-inch caliber), manufactured by the Winchester Repeating Arms Company. It had a muzzle velocity of 2,560 feet per second and fired semi-jacketed bullets from smokeless cartridges in a five-round en bloc clip. The maximum range was one mile, effective was 300 yards.

—Barida's British 12-pounder field pieces were breech-loading, 76.2-millimeter (3-inch), rifled guns with a muzzle velocity of 1,710 feet per second and a maximum range of two and a half miles. It was not a favorite with the British Army due to its weight and malfunctions and went out of service in 1895. Several were sold off to other militaries.

—The six-pounder quick-firing guns to which Wake refers are Driggs-Schroeder (named for the naval officers who designed them) guns, manufactured by the American Ordnance Company. They were almost identical to the Hotchkiss six-pounder. The breech-loading guns fired a 57-millimeter (2.24-inch) round at 1,818 feet per second and had a range of about two miles. A well-trained gun crew could fire twenty-five rounds a minute. Designed in the mid-1880s, it was the standard secondary gun for American battleships and cruisers until 1900, and versions of this gun were used in various large navies all the way up to 1945. To see one in detail, visit U.S.S. *Olympia*, the only Spanish-American War vessel still afloat, at Philadelphia.

—Veteran cavalry units of the 19th century could charge at twenty to thirty miles an hour, but because of equipment weight were limited to a mile at that speed, at most.

Chapter Sixty-Four—Heaven and the Angel

—The massive Tampa Bay Hotel still exists and has been restored to its original opulent condition. It is now part of the University of Tampa and much of it is open to the public. The building, museum, and grounds are very well worth the visit. During the Spanish-American War, the hotel was the center of military and social activity for the senior army officers.

Chapter Sixty-Five—Family

—After José Martí's death in combat in May of 1895, Tomás Estrada Palma (1835–1908) took over as leader of the Cuban government in exile, which was headquartered in New York City and commonly known as "the Cuban Junta." When Cuba became an independent nation after four years of U.S. occupation, Estrada served as the first president, from 1902 to 1906.

—Horatio Rubens was an American lawyer who fervently supported the cause of Cuban freedom and served as legal counsel to the Cuban Junta.

—U.S.S. *Oregon*, a 10,000-ton battleship with 13-inch guns, was commissioned in 1896. She made the 14,000-mile voyage from San Francisco to Florida (the Panama Canal wasn't completed until 1914) in a record setting sixty-six days, arriving on 24 May 1898. She fought at the Battle of Santiago on 3 July 1898.

Chapter Sixty-Six—For the Duration

—William Rufus Shafter (1835–1906) was a former teacher who joined the U.S. Army at the beginning of the Civil War as a second lieutenant in a Michigan regiment. He was awarded the Medal of Honor for bravery in combat and over the next four years rose to the rank of brevet brigadier general. After the Civil War, he stayed in the army, earning the nickname "Pecos Bill" during the Indian wars. His career lasted until 1901.

Prior to the Spanish-American War, Shafter commanded the Department of California as a regular brigadier general. He arrived in Tampa in mid-May, 1898. Shafter's decisions and leadership style during the Cuban campaign, which have been criticized ever since, were greatly influenced by his debilitated physical condition. In addition, he inherited an inefficient logistics system, had no experience in overseas military operations, and was under immense political pressure. The invasion of Cuba was nearly a disaster and was saved only by the incredible will power of the American soldiers themselves.

The next novel in the Honor Series, *Honoring the Enemy*, will cover that phase of the war.

Acknowledgments

The research for this novel began many years ago and, as always, entailed two major categories: academic research for the facts of history, and field investigation ("eyeball recon") to learn the flavor of history. Combined, they provide an in-depth view of events in Cuba, Spain, and the United States at the beginning of the Spanish-American War.

In addition to the research materials listed in the bibliography, I want to thank some special people who have helped me for years in gathering information about Cuba, Key West, Tampa, Washington, and New York: Randy Briggs (now retired) and his team of biblio-sleuths at the Pine Island Library; Tom Hambright and the legendary vault of the Monroe County Library in Key West; Ela Ugarte Lopez, Editor-in-Chief of the Centro Estudiantes Martíanos in Havana, Cuba, and foremost Martí scholar in the world; Chaz Mena, Martí scholar and actor/writer/director; Mario Cano, student of Spanish and Cuban history; Elizabeth McCoy and Carl St. Meyer of the Ybor City State Museum; Dave Parsons of the Hillsborough County Public Library in Tampa; and Vickie Jewett of the Port Tampa Library.

Some organizations get special mention for their difficult work in preserving historical materials which were of great help to me: the United States Naval Institute, the National Security Agency, the Theodore Roosevelt Association, the Office of Coast Survey, the Smathers Library of the University of Florida, the National Security Agency, the Vincent Voice Library of Michigan State University, and the *New York Times*.

Thanks go to a dear friend, Reverend Ann McLemore of the Episcopal Church, who was so kind as to give me the 1863 Danish New Testament Bible used in the novel. At the other end of that spectrum, thanks go to Mike Woodgerd, a man with an interesting past, for his professional acumen concerning brutally effective defensive tactics against overwhelming odds.

Arnold Gibbs, another friend with an interesting past, gets my appreciation for sharing tales from his childhood at Congo Town, on the island of Andros, in the Bahamas.

For in depth discussions on Cuban history and culture, I thank my father Robert Charles Macomber in Fort Myers, Uncle Raul Laffitte in Cape Coral, dear friend Roberto Giraudy and many others in Havana, Mario Cano and Chaz Mena in Miami, and the gentlemen of the Grand Masonic Lodge of Cuba.

With gratitude I recognize Rich Rolfe as my go-to man for German historical research and translations. He and Ron Kemper also helped me understand the fascinating world of cryptic communications.

On the subject of ship handling, thanks go to some real masters whom I've observed performing that difficult art, which can go dreadfully wrong in a heartbeat: Captain Paul Welling, U.S.C.G. (USCGC *Eagle*); Captain Chuck Nygaard, U.S.N. (USS *Spruance*, USS *Vicksburg*); Commodore Ronald Warwick, R.N.R. (RMS *Queen Mary 2*); and Captain Ullrich Nuber (MV *Hamburgo*), German Merchant Marine. They all made it look easy. It isn't.

Nancy Ann Glickman is the one who gets the biggest thank you. In addition to doing the ornithological and celestial research for my novels, she manages the business end of the operation. She is also the steady hand at the wheel of my personal life. Like Peter Wake and his Maria, I am nothing without Nancy.

And then there are the Wakians. Without these loyal supporters enthusiastically spreading the word, Peter Wake would have faded away years ago. Thank you all for being the best readers a writer could ever hope for. I am continually grateful.

Onward and upward, *toward those distant horizons…*

Robert N. Macomber
The Boat House,
St. James, Pine Island, Florida

Bibliography of Research Materials

About New York City:

The Epicurean, Charles Ranhofer (1894)

Repast, Dining Out at the Dawn of the New American Century 1900–1910, Michael Lesy and Lisa Stoffer (2013)

Ephemeral New York, Historical New York City articles (website & blog), The Word Press *http://ephemeralnewyork.wordpress.com/?s=1897*

New York Songlines—Historical Walking Tours of New York City (website), Jim Naureckas *www.nysonglines.com*

About Theodore Roosevelt:

The Rise of Theodore Roosevelt, Edmund Morris (1979)

Theodore Rex, Edmund Morris (2001)

Colonel Roosevelt, Edmund Morris (2010)

The Autobiography of Theodore Roosevelt, (1920 edition) Theodore Roosevelt (1913)

Theodore Roosevelt's Naval Diplomacy, Henry J. Hendrix (2009)

The Bully Pulpit, Theodore Roosevelt, William Howard Taft, and the Golden Age of Journalism, Doris Kearns Goodwin (2013)

New York Times 1897 and 1898 newspaper articles (website) *http://spiderbites.nytimes.com/free_1897/articles_1897_02_00001.html*

William McKinley: The American Presidents Series: The 25th President 1897–1901, Kevin Phillip and Arthur M. Schlesinger (2003)

Grover Cleveland, The American Presidents Series: The 24th President 1893–1897, Henry F. Graff (2002)

"*The Right of the People to Rule,*" 1912 Roosevelt campaign speech recording (recorded by Thomas Edison), Vincent Voice Library, Michigan State University

The Arena, Volume 95, Issue 2, Newsletter of the Theodore Roosevelt Association, March/April, 2015

About Washington D.C.:

Everyday Life in Washington, Charles M. Pepper (1900)

The Cosmos Club on Lafayette Square, Thomas M. Spaulding (1949)

Victorian America, Transformations in Everyday Life 1876–1915, Thomas J. Schlereth (1991)

About the U.S. Office of Naval Intelligence:

A Century of Naval Intelligence, Captain Wyman Packard U.S.N. (Ret) (1996)
The Office of Naval Intelligence, The Birth of America's First Intelligence Agency 1865–1918, Jeffry M. Dorwart (1979)
United States Cryptologic History, The Friedman Legacy: A Tribute to William and Elizebeth Freidman, National Security Agency (1992)
Masked Dispatches: Cryptograms and Cryptology in American History, 1775–1900, (Series I, Pre-World War I, Volume I) Ralph Weber, National Security Agency (1993)
The Archaeologist was a Spy, Sylvanius G. Morley and the Office of Naval Intelligence, Charles H. Harris III and Louis R. Sadler (2003)
The Spanish American War: Blockades and Coast Defense, Captain Severo Gómez Núñez (Spanish Army), compiled by the Office of Naval Intelligence (1899)
War Notes (1 to 8) from Abroad (German and Spanish reports), Spanish-American War, compiled by Office of Naval Intelligence (1900)
Characteristics of Principal Foreign Ships of War: Prepared for the Board on Fortifications, Etc., Office of Naval Intelligence (1885)
Coaling, Docking, and Repair Facilities of the Ports of the World, Office of Naval Intelligence (1909)
Bible used in Roosevelt-Wake fictional coded messages: *The New Testament* (translated from the original Greek into Danish and English), The American Bible Society, 1863

About the United States Navy in general in 1898:

Conway's All the World's Fighting Ships 1860–1905, Editorial Director Robert Gardiner (1979)
The American Steel Navy, CDR John D. Alden U.S.N. (Ret) (1972)
U.S. Cruisers 1883–1904, Lawrence Burr (2008)

The Naval Aristocracy, The Golden Age of Annapolis and the Emergence of Modern American Navalism, Peter Karsten (1972)
Navalism and the Emergence of American Sea Power 1882–1893, Mark Russell Shulman (1995)
Admirals and Empire, The United States Navy and the Caribbean 1898–1945, Donald A. Yerxa (1991)
With Sampson through the War, William A.M. Goode (1899)
The Fate of the Maine, John Edward Weems (1958)
John P. Holland (1841–1914) Inventor of the Modern Submarine, Richard Knowles Morris (1966)
Remembering the Maine *in Key West*, Robert E. Cray, *Naval History* Magazine, United States Naval Institute (February 2015)
Naval Customs, Traditions, and Usage, LCDR Leland P. Lovette U.S.N. (1939)
The Naval Officer's Guide, CDR Arthur A. Ageton U.S.N. (2nd edition, 1944)
The Naval Officer's Guide, VADM William P. Mack U.S.N. (Ret) and Captain Thomas D. Paulsen U.S.N. (9th Edition, 1983)
Watch Officer's Guide, ADM James Stavridis U.S.N. and Captain Robert Girrier U.S.N. (15th Edition, 2007)
Naval Shiphandling, Captain R.S. Crenshaw U.S.N. (Ret) (4th Edition, 1975)

About Cuba, her thirty-year struggle for independence, and the Spanish-American War:
Cuba, or the Pursuit of Freedom, Hugh Thomas (1971)
History of Cuba, the Challenge of the Yoke and the Star, Professor Jose Canton Navarro (2001)
Insurgent Cuba, Race, Nation, and Revolution, 1868–1898, Ada Ferrar (1999)
Commercial Cuba, William J. Clark (1898)
War Map and History of Cuba, Ebenezer Hannaford (1898)
Marching with Gomez, Grover Flint (1898)
Under Three Flags in Cuba, George Clarke Musgrave (1898)

A Message to Garcia, Elbert Hubbard (1899)

Kuba und der Krieg—Eine Darstellung de Spanish-Amerikanischen Kreiges Nach Eigener Anschaung des Verfassers (Cuba and the War—The Spanish-American War based on personal observations of the author), Joseph Herrings (1899)

In Darkest Cuba, Two Months Service under Gomez along the Trocha from the Caribbean to the Bahama Channel, N.G. Gonzalez (1927)

The Naval Annual of 1891, T.A. Brassey (1891)

Maps, Charts, and Sailing Guides:

Upper Caribbean Sea and Gulf of Mexico, American privately published chart with U.S., British, French, and Spanish survey data (1860)

Gulf Stream—Caribbean, Gulf of Mexico, Atlantic Ocean, Lt. Mathew Fontaine Maury, U.S.N., U.S. Office of Coast Survey (1852)

Hudson and East Rivers, New York, U.S. Office of Coast Survey #369(4) (1890)

Washington D.C., Sanborn Fire Insurance Map (1888)

Key West, Sanborn Fire Insurance Map (1892)

Key West Harbor and Approaches, U.S. Office of Coast Survey #469 (1896)

Map of Cuba and the Provinces, within *Commercial Cuba* (1898)

Map of Havana, within *Commercial Cuba* (1898)

Map of Santa Clara Province, within *Commercial Cuba* (1898)

Straits of Florida and Northern Cuba Coast, U.S. Office of Coast Survey (1895)

Approaches and Channel to Isabela Sagua, NGA chart# 27062 (1995)

Cuba, a Cruising Guide, Nigel Calder (1997)

A Cruising Guide to the Caribbean and the Bahamas, Jerrems C. Hart and William T. Stone (1976)

For more books from Pineapple Press, visit our website at *www.pineapplepress.com*. There you can find author pages, discover new and upcoming books, and search our list for books that might interest you. Look for our weekly posts and giveaways, and be sure to sign up for our mailing list.

The Honor Series of Naval Fiction (in order of publication)

At the Edge of Honor. Winner of the Florida Historical Society's 2003 Patrick Smith Award for Best Florida Fiction. This nationally acclaimed naval Civil War novel introduces U.S. Navy officer Peter Wake, who in 1863 battles the enemy in Florida and social taboos in Key West when he falls in love with the daughter of a Confederate zealot.

Point of Honor. Received the 2003 John Esten Cooke Best Work in Southern Fiction Literary Award. In 1864 Wake searches for army deserters in the Dry Tortugas and finds an old nemesis in Mexico.

Honorable Mention. In 1865 Wake chases a strange vessel off Cuba, liberates an escaping slave ship, and confronts the enemy's most powerful ocean warship in Havana's harbor.

A Dishonorable Few. In 1869 Wake heads to turbulent Central America to face a former American naval officer turned renegade mercenary.

An Affair of Honor. In 1873 Wake runs afoul of the Royal Navy in Antigua and becomes embroiled in a Spanish civil war.

A Different Kind of Honor. Received the American Library Association's 2008 W.Y. Boyd Excellence in Military Fiction Literary Award. On assignment in 1879, Wake witnesses history's first battle between ocean-going ironclads and runs for his life in the Catacombs of the Dead in Lima.

The Honored Dead. On what at first appears to be a simple mission in French Indochina in 1883, Wake encounters opium warlords, Chinese-Malay pirates, and French gangsters.

The Darkest Shade of Honor. It's 1886 and Wake meets rising politico Theodore Roosevelt, befriends José Martí, and is engulfed in the most catastrophic event in Key West history.

Honor Bound. In 1888 Wake travels deep into the jungles of Haiti to discover the hidden lair of an anarchist group planning to wreak havoc around the world—unless he stops it.

Honorable Lies. In September 1888, Peter Wake has five days to rescue his two captured operatives from a dungeon in Spanish-Colonial Havana.

Honors Rendered. Peter Wake is sent in 1889 to the South Pacific to avert a war with the Germans.

The Assassin's Honor. With command of a new warship in 1892 and the love of a fascinating lady, Wake is finally happy—that is, until he is ordered to prevent an assassination.

An Honorable War. Politics, love, and war swirl around Captain Peter Wake (USN) in Havana when the USS *Maine* explodes on a quiet evening in February, 1898.